Geoffrey lay a finger at the spot beneath her ear, then traced a line down the curve of her throat to her collar bone. 'Twas only in this instant that she saw what her caring had awakened in him. He would seduce her, finding in his masculine pleasure a release from his own pain. She should go. Immediately. Aye, this very instant. If his mere touch could make her feel so, she'd soon be as drunk with him as he said he was with wine.

"You must do that no more," she warned him as his hand moved over her shoulder to rest against her nape. The pace of her breath increased. Mary save her, but this was very dangerous. And marvelous. Oh, but if it was so wondrous now, what pleasure would their joining bring her? Her body urged her to discover it.

"Run, Elyssa," he begged softly. "My need to kiss you exceeds my sense."

"This is very wrong," she breathed.

" 'Tis," he agreed, taking her mouth with his.

Autumn's Flame

Denise Domning

A TOPAZ BOOK

TOPAZ
Published by the Penguin Group
Penguin Books USA Inc., 375 Hudson Street,
New York, New York 10014, U.S.A.
Penguin Books Ltd, 27 Wrights Lane,
London W8 5TZ, England
Penguin Books Australia Ltd, Ringwood,
Victoria, Australia
Penguin Books Canada Ltd, 10 Alcorn Avenue,
Toronto, Ontario, Canada M4V 3B2
Penguin Books (N.Z.) Ltd, 182–190 Wairau Road,
Auckland 10, New Zealand

Penguin Books Ltd, Registered Offices:
Harmondsworth, Middlesex, England

First published by Topaz, an imprint of Dutton Signet,
a division of Penguin Books USA Inc.

First Printing, November, 1995
10 9 8 7 6 5 4 3 2 1

REGISTERED TRADEMARK—MARCA REGISTRADA

Printed in the United States of America

To all the members of
Paradise Valley Toughlove.
Without your love, care,
and support, I could not have
continued past Adam's death.

And, to my newest nephew,
Geoffrey. May your life
never be touched by tragedy.

Prologue

Late September, 1194

"Come forth, you cocksucking spawn of Satan!"

'Twas a joyous shout. Reginald, younger brother to Freyne's lord, knew no greater pleasure than hunting boar when autumn's spice was in the air. Not only that, but bloodletting always made him forget the miserable life fate forced upon him.

The midday sun shot narrow beams through a tangle of branches, balding now that Michaelmas was upon them, to reveal the great humpbacked beast hunkered therein. Reginald urged his mount forward and jabbed his spear into the thicket. Barely old enough to be hunted, the wild black pig squealed and clashed its tusks, but held firm in its hidey-hole. Ah, well, he was a patient man; Reginald could wait for it to come to him.

Turning his horse, he rejoined the mounted men, taking his place between his brother, Aymer, Lord Freyne, and Aymer's eldest son, Theobald. 'Twas Theobald's upcoming betrothal that was the cause for this day's pleasure. Aymer's foster brother, Baldwin de Gradinton, and the girl's father, Henry, Lord Lavendon, had arrived early to spend a few days in private celebration before the crush of the event began.

Aye, Reginald enjoyed the hunt, but his reasons went beyond simply chasing beasts. Only in these few hours was he, a penniless knight, the equal of these landed peers. Every man here, even the dozen or so foot-bound Englishmen who accompanied their Norman masters, wore the same leather hauberks over thick woolen chausses or braies tucked into their boots. For this little while Reginald could forget that he was slipping into life's later years, having never been more than someone's hireling.

Aymer, his capuchin thrown back to reveal hair more gray than brown since passing his fiftieth year, lifted his hand. At this signal, the huntsmen shouted and the beaters banged on their drums. Yipping in excitement, the sleek greyhounds dove into the copse, only to be thwarted by the thorny branches. Yet held on their leads, the two massive alaunts paced and snapped as the scent of blood woke their vicious nature.

Hawk-faced Baldwin de Gradinton, his black hair and beard streaked with silver, snorted in mock disgust. "You call this entertainment, Aymer? This is some weak-balled piglet, not a boar. What honor will there be in having a bite of him?" Exhilaration gleamed in the big man's blue eyes, belying his complaint.

"Who cares what sort of balls he has?" laughed Henry, Lord Lavendon, plain and plump. "Drive him out, and we will cook him for the dogs."

"Come out, piglet," Baldwin called, softening his rough voice until he sounded like a mother crooning in her babe, "else we'll think you no boar, but some fat sow. Come now, sweet thing, let me spill your blood and end your humiliation."

Where Reginald laughed, enjoying the men's jests,

Aymer's arrogance found insult. His brother's pale skin reddened and shame drove him to recklessness. "Free the alaunts," Freyne's lord shouted as he swung down out of his saddle.

His spear yet caught in his fist, Reginald's portly brother strode for the tangled shrubbery. "Coward," he bellowed to the hiding animal, "come out, damn you, else I'll drag you out with my bare hands!"

"Have a care, Father," Theobald cried after him, his newly deepened voice cracking as he spoke. Barrel-chested and narrow-hipped like his father and uncle, the youth's brows lifted over his brown eyes. "Who knows when that youngling will discover his manhood."

"As you have discovered yours, boy?" Reginald shot his nephew a chiding look. Although Reginald was Freyne's steward, the passing years had turned him into panderer for both his married brother and his nephew. 'Twas the worst sort of irony, when Reginald wished to love and honor only one woman. But even if he could marry Clare, doing so would make her Aymer's servant, thus prey for his brother's enormous appetites. This thought made his voice sharp.

"Yestermorn has made you a sire, once more. That's a bastard for each of your last three visits to Freyne. This girl's father is none too happy over it, refusing the coins I offered and crying that you forced his daughter."

"What use are peasants save to do my will?" The insolent brat sent his uncle a glance that mingled both scorn and pity. Squiring Theobald with an earl only increased the arrogance he'd learned at his father's knee. By his attitude, this dirty-assed babe said he held his landless uncle in less regard than the common women he used.

Excess of practice made Reginald's humiliation too easy to swallow. He endured their sneers for love of Freyne. 'Twas the place of his birth and here he'd remain until it became the place of his death. Nonetheless, the boy's blow deserved a response.

"Brother, come back," he shouted to Aymer over the noise made by the beaters and the dogs. Freyne's lord turned, brows lifted in unspoken question. "Let Theobald prove his skill. Let your son be the one to drive the pig from its lair." With any luck, the boar would savage the boy. Reginald followed his evil thought with a quick prayer begging a forgiveness he did not crave.

"Aye," agreed Gradinton, unwittingly playing into this sly game, "let the lad show us his bravery."

The boar chose this instant to explode from the brambles. Reginald roared in excitement as all thought of vengeance evaporated. He turned his horse and lowered his barbed spear in the hope of a blow.

Short legs flying, its feet tearing up the soft earth, the creature raced away from Aymer and the mounted men. If it saw an easy escape through the footmen, it had not counted on the alaunts. Noble and commoner alike shouted in excitement as the newly freed dogs leapt upon the pig's humped back, their teeth tearing through the bristling hair and tough hide to draw blood. The smaller greyhounds circled around, darting in to nip whenever they could.

Suddenly, the alaunts were tossed aside as if they weighed nothing at all. One of the big dogs yelped and collapsed to the ground, belly cut. The swine squealed as it ripped its way through the greyhounds, turning back toward the brambles, rather than standing its ground as its breed should.

"Nay!" Aymer bellowed. "Craven beast! You'll not hide from us."

As if stung by this human's insult, the huge pig halted. Ignoring the tormenting hounds, its head swung toward the nobleman, tiny eyes red with rage and foam at its evil mouth. Tusks clashing, snout to the ground, it flattened its ears against a narrow skull.

"He comes for you, Aymer," Reginald cried, jabbing spurs into his mount's side as he urged his steed forward.

Even before his horse was into its stride, the boar charged. Aymer took his stance, bracing his spear to impale the beast. The remaining alaunt leapt at it, only to rebound off the pig and into Aymer. Reginald watched in horror as his brother fell and the boar was on him. Blood sprayed as the keen tusks tore through leather to the screaming man beneath it.

"Father!" Theobald shrieked.

Shouting in rage and fear, Reginald spurred his steed toward the savaging beast. It lifted its head from Aymer to fend off this new attack. He drove his spear deep into the boar's throat. From the other side came Baldwin's lance. Squealing in agony, the boar staggered away from the broken man to topple onto its side.

"Aymer!" Reginald threw himself from the saddle and fell to his knees at his brother's side. The leather hunting vest and wool tunic beneath it were naught but tatters. Aymer's torso lay opened from stomach to groin, steam rising from his bloody flesh. "Mother of God," Reginald breathed in horror as life's light died from his elder sibling's eyes.

Theobald, his eyes wide in shock and his face ashen, stumbled to his father's side. "Papa," he cried softly.

Without his usual sneer, he looked younger than his sixteen years.

Reginald grabbed his nephew's trembling arm. "Theobald, away. You need not see this."

The boy stared blankly at his uncle, his lower lip quivering until he caught it with his teeth. There was a moment's inner struggle, then his mouth steadied. "Nay, 'tis not meet that Freyne's new lord sob like a babe," he warned himself.

Reginald caught a sharp breath. *Jesu,* no longer was he his brother's hireling, but this brat's servant. The thought of taking commands from a snot-nosed babe cut like a knife. Ach, but what alternative did he have? He wanted to live in no place, save Freyne.

What if *he* were Freyne's lord? Reginald shoved away that thought as impossible. His brother had two sons, Theobald by his first wife and Jocelyn by his second. To own Freyne, both boys would need to die, and two deaths so near each other would burn like a beacon, shouting of murder.

As quickly as he rejected the idea, the solution offered itself. There was no need for two murders, only one. Aymer's second son was a weakling for whom each dawn's arrival was a miracle. With his elder brother gone, the frail Jocelyn would need to be squired. 'Twouldn't be long before knighthood's rigorous training ended Aymer of Freyne's line.

Theobald raised his head to look at his uncle, his brown eyes yet wide with shock. "Aye," he said, speaking more loudly now as he sought to wear a man's face against this tragedy, "I must take up my duties as Freyne's lord, and my first is to tell my stepmother that her husband is dead. I must ride like the wind."

For all the command in his tone, the lad came

slowly to his feet, then clutched his arms around his midsection. One of the huntsmen came forward to help the lad mount his horse. "My lord, should not one of us ride with you?" the man asked of his new master.

"Do I look like a child? I have no need of your help," Theobald snapped, finding his arrogance once more. He turned his horse's head, then kicked his heels into its sides. The steed cried out in complaint as the boy sent his horse hurtling into the woodland.

"May our Lord grant you peace, old friend." Baldwin de Gradinton reached out to close the dead man's eyes. A moment of silence followed as all those in the clearing paused to offer prayer for the man's soul, then blessed themselves.

Gradinton eased back onto his heels and wiped his bloody hands on his rough chausses. "Damn, but Theobald's underage. It galls me that the royal court will meddle with my friend's property."

Reginald glanced at the nobleman. 'Twasn't the court Baldwin resented, but that this shire's sheriff would become the warden of Freyne and its heir. Since the death of Gradinton's sons in December past, great animosity raged between Gradinton and his former son-by-marriage over custody of the sheriff's daughter. The girl was now Gradinton's only heir.

Lord Lavendon looked up, his broad face wearing a sudden wary expression. "There is no help for it. Amyer has no overlord, holding as he did of his king. Until the boy reaches one and twenty, the court rules Freyne."

"Ah, but there is something we can do." Baldwin's mouth lifted in a wicked half smile as he spoke. "We must celebrate a wedding, rather than a betrothal. Then, 'twill be you who has custody of Freyne."

Reginald rocked back on his heels. Lavendon's home keep lay only ten miles distant. By Gradinton's look, he knew the baron intended for Lavendon to fetch his daughter here immediately, leaving no time for Theobald to meet his end. While there was disappointment at this thought, Reginald's relief was by far the greater.

Lord Lavendon blinked. "My daughter is not yet eight," he said quietly, a touch of disgust in his voice. "Even if she were older, I have no desire to cheat court and king of what is their right."

"This arrangement could be more profitable to you than you think, Henry." In Gradinton's harsh face grew the determination to bend Lavendon to his will, but not before a witness. The wealthy peer shifted in his squat to look at Freyne's steward. "You should ride with Theobald, he's more shocked than he would have us know. Send a cart back for Aymer's body."

Reginald leapt to his feet as murderous thoughts roared with new life. "Jesu, my own shock numbs my brain. Of course, I must go after him. What if he falls from his saddle because of his grief?"

Within two breaths, he was atop his mount, urging the steed to its greatest speed. If he caught Theobald, Aymer's eldest son would follow his father into hell this very day.

Chapter 1

Lady Elyssa, widow to Aymer of Freyne, glanced behind her to see if anyone came, russet plaits swinging with her swift movement. 'Twas a paltry effort. The garden was no sanctuary, and Gradinton and Lavendon would soon be hunting for her. Or, rather, for Jocelyn. Gray clouds roiled behind Freyne's tall, wooden hall, promising rain and the end of this stretch of mild October weather. Soon, the sky would match Freyne's tiny keep that stood atop its ancient Saxon mound.

No one followed, not even Gradinton's morbid wife, Lady Sybil. Elyssa breathed a prayer of thanks for that. Not only did the noblewoman watch her on Gradinton's behalf, but Lady Sybil spent her hours moaning and raging over the recent deaths of all her children. While Elyssa understood her pain, enough was enough.

Elyssa threw open the garden's gate, and with her hand to her son's back, shoved him into the walled enclosure. Clare, her cousin and companion of ten years, followed them in, quickly shutting the gate behind the three of them.

Jocelyn turned, a frown creasing his broad brow. "Maman, do not push so. I almost fell. What if I'd broken something?"

Frail and achingly small for his twelve years, Jocelyn's fur-lined mantle was tightly pinned around him, disguising any sign of his red chausses and blue gown. With his hood drawn close over his sensitive ears, only a short fringe of his pale brown hair showed. His delicate hands, fit only for scribing, were warmly gloved.

"My pardon, love," Elyssa said, struggling to keep distress from her voice. "I shall be more careful in the future."

"I didn't want to eat our meal in the women's quarters, and I'll not spend a full hour here," Jocelyn went on, his tone aggrieved. 'Twas Elyssa's custom to spend an hour every day out of doors, believing fresh air a healthy necessity. Her son's lip lifted in scorn as he looked around him. "This garden isn't near as nice as our own at Nalder. None of Freyne is as fine as Nalder."

Elyssa could hardly disaggree with him. Her dower house in the city of Nalder, her home for the past ten years, was a small but pleasant abode in which to live. Freyne, on the other hand, was backward and graceless. Its garden was but one example.

Lawn, unbroken by a single decorative plant, stretched from her toes to the single, molting pear tree set smack in the square's center without a trace of artistic thought. From the tree to the back wall, the earth wore the drying remains of peas, beans, and herbs. Elyssa kicked at the hems of her yellow and green gowns, trying to free them of fallen leaves.

"You may not care for it, but here we must stay." Her tone was yet commonplace, revealing nothing of what raged in her. Jocelyn was susceptible to nervous stress, and his upset often brought on illness.

"When can we leave Freyne?" Jocelyn looked up

at her, brown eyes wide with pleading beneath peaked brows. "I am missing so many of my lessons."

Elyssa's heart broke at his question. "Soon," she lied. "Now, Tante Clare and I must talk privately."

Although his eyes narrowed in resentment, Jocelyn wandered to the pear tree. Elyssa watched, her heart still aching, as he began to methodically strip leaves from its lower branches. Mary save her, but life without Jocelyn would be unendurable.

Clare, who was no aunt but Jocelyn's third cousin, came to stand beside Elyssa. Extending from beneath a wimple as prim as her cousin's, Clare's gray-brown plaits lay atop the nubby surface of her mantle. When she crossed her arms, her cloak opened to reveal a sliver of Elyssa's cast-off blue gowns. A fourth daughter left without dowry or hope of marriage, forty years of impoverished and purposeless life had sapped Clare; she faded like an autumn leaf, drying into fragility, crumbling into dust.

"Do you truly believe you can hide him in here?" her cousin asked.

"Nay, but what else can I do? I must stall Lavendon," Elyssa said, keeping her voice low. "Mother of God, but I sent that petition three weeks ago. The Michaelmas court is closed now. How much longer can it take for the court to grant me custody of Jocelyn?"

She'd sent her plea winging to the court on the very day of Aymer's death. That document, as well as her own request to be spared a third forced marriage, had been delivered into the hands of the shire's new sheriff, one Geoffrey FitzHenry, called Lord Coudray. As the shire's representative, 'twas his duty to present her pleas to the court.

"Forever," Clare replied. " 'Lyssa, do not fool yourself. The court won't give you Jocelyn, not now that Theobald is gone."

Elyssa's eyes filled at this reminder of Theobald's death. Yesterday had seen Freyne's eldest son's final return, his head broken by the fall from his horse, his body eaten by exposure to the elements. In her imagination, Theobald's broken face became Jocelyn's. The thought of her precious child made cold and dead by what a warrior's world wanted of him wrenched within her.

"They must," Elyssa retorted frantically, struggling to convince herself as much as Clare. "Jocelyn is not like other lads. They need only look on him to see he'll not survive squiring."

As her voice rose to a pained cry, Jocelyn looked around, his concern for her written on his plain face. " 'Tis nothing, sweetling," she called to him, forcing her smile.

Then, closing eyes the same russet color as her hair, she fought to catch hold of her emotions. "Why, Clare? Why did I bring him back here?"

"You came because your husband ordered you to arrange Theobald's betrothal," Clare said with a wry twist of her mouth. "Now, don't go thinking that staying in Nalder would have changed things. Someone, whether Gradinton, Lavendon, or the sheriff, would have come to fetch Jocelyn."

"I should have refused," Elyssa said in a harsh whisper, ignoring Clare. "I meant to. But Aymer promised if I did this for him, he'd put Jocelyn into his monastery. More fool me for believing him."

Aymer had also vowed to touch her naught whilst she dwelt here; her husband had violated both vows. 'Twas but another example of how helpless she was against the men around her. Only her father, who'd died when she was but Jocelyn's age, had ever been trustworthy; but then, his love for a mere daughter made him unique among men.

Clare lay her thin hand on Elyssa's arm. " 'Lyssa, do not fret so over what you cannot change. You have no choice, but to release Jocelyn."

"Nay!" 'Twas a bitter whisper. She tore free of Clare's touch. "No one can ask me to sacrifice my child this way. He is all I have, Clare," she cried, her voice hoarse with pain.

"Nay, he is not." Protecting what Elyssa insisted remained hidden, Clare whispered, "You are with child. That life is equally as precious as Jocelyn's. Think, 'Lyssa, in seven months your aching arms will be filled by a new child."

"What sort of mother blithely gives away one child, thinking to replace him with another?" Elyssa said in scorn. "Nay, there'll never be another Jocelyn, and I can find no solace in such a promise. You know birthing comes not easily to me. Jocelyn nearly died in his advent and yet continues ever at death's door because of it. My sweet Katherine never recovered, her life stretching only six months."

Even at ten years' distance, Elyssa's heart still ached for her wee daughter. The very thought of losing another babe was unbearable. 'Twas in an effort to protect her heart that she fought loving what grew in her, the way she loved Jocelyn and still loved her Kate.

"You cannot be certain of loss," Clare insisted.

"Can I not?" Elyssa asked bitterly, catching her own dark mantle closer around her as the wind lifted and moaned. The scent of dampness hung heavy in its breath. "Am I not now one and thirty, the age when women shuck the title Maman for Grandmaman? 'Tis more likely what grows in me will kill me when it comes, then die after me." Aye, 'twould be easier if she died with its coming rather than to suffer its loss.

"Well then, why not tell Lavendon you are with child? You can tell him that taking Jocelyn from you threatens your new babe. It may well buy you a few more months with him."

Elyssa stared at Clare in shock. "Are you mad? If I do that, I make myself once more a man's prisoner."

Pregnant widows became the property of the sheriff. Not only would Geoffrey FitzHenry command her to the shire's seat, Crosswell, he'd be in her chamber to observe the birth of her child. The very thought of a man attending so intimate an event sent a shiver of disgust through her.

"Nay, we must find a way to stall until the court makes Jocelyn mine, then retreat to Nalder. There will I remain humble and cloistered until the babe is born." 'Twas an impossible wish, she knew it even as the words left her mouth.

"People will call the babe bastard and say you did not get him by your husband," Clare warned. "He'll have no right to his inheritance."

"You assume the child will live long enough to be concerned with those things, when I do not," Elyssa retorted. But, what if he did live? How could she condemn a child to bastardy when he was not?

The aching in her grew, and she caught her cousin's hands. "Damn Aymer for doing this to me. 'Tis as if he reaches out from the grave to smite me, once more. Clare, would that I were you."

"Me?" Clare retorted in surprise, her thin brows lifting. Then, denial made her mouth move into a scornful smile. "You rave as one fevered. What woman seeks a life of poverty and childlessness?"

" 'Tisn't what I see," Elyssa said quietly. "You own

the one thing I do not: your own being. No man tells you to walk at his heel, demands you lay in his bed, or steals your son from your arms because he is a man and you are not."

From her father's death onward, she'd ceased to be a person and become property instead. As the court's ward, she'd been sold to Ramshaw, her first husband. If he'd left her womb as lifeless as a virgin's, his beatings had wakened in her a fiery determination to never again tolerate a man's abuse.

Within the year of Ramshaw's death, her monarch made a gift of her to Freyne—a reward for faithful service. Aymer's abuse was more subtle. He used her emotions against her, speaking words of love and awakening her passionate nature, only to dishonor her desire for him by his perverse needs.

After little Kate's death, she could tolerate his misuse no longer. She begged to separate, and he, bored with her anyway, had let her retire to Nalder. Now tears, the bane of her existence, leapt to her eyes. So had it been since her earliest years, her eyes the fountain of her heart. Elyssa freed Clare's hands to wipe at them. "Clare, I cannot wait to be free of any man's control, as you are."

Clare shook her head. "You mistake emptiness for freedom. Know you, I would trade all you say I own for a chance to experience what you reject. What I would not give to have a child to cherish as you do Jocelyn and a husband at my side."

For a quiet moment, Elyssa studied her cousin. Here was the reason for Clare's persistent joy over this babe, where Elyssa saw only tragedy. Clare would make her cousin's child like unto her own. As for the husband ... the corners over Elyssa's mouth lifted.

"Would it be Sir Reginald you see in your mind's image of a husband?"

Her cousin blushed a deep pink. "Mayhap."

"I thought as much. You cannot keep your eyes from him." 'Twas a gentle tease.

"We have become great friends these past two months," Clare tried to equivocate, but her continuing blush said 'twas more than friendship she felt for this man. Then all pleasure drained from her. " 'Tis foolish of me to dream, when he's said no word of love to me. Even if he did, 'tis useless. We cannot consider a relationship, being too close in degree of kinship. You were married to his brother."

Elyssa found herself smiling at Clare's girlish pining for a knight. Never, in all the years they'd known each other, had Clare given a man even the slightest hint of interest. Indeed, her cousin was exceedingly proper, almost prim, toward those men foolish enough to direct their attentions her way.

"You are beyond the age for bearing children. I think such a relationship cannot concern the Church if no children will come of it."

" 'Lyssa, say no more. You taunt me with what is hopeless. He'll not ask, even if he loved me with all his heart. I've no dowry," Clare said sadly.

Elyssa lay her hand against her cousin's cheek. "Know that I think giving your heart to a man is asking for hurt. Now, however foolish I think you, if 'tis truly your heart's desire, I want it for you. Although it couldn't be much, I'd settle something on you."

Clare's eyes glowed with the love she bore her kinswoman. " 'Lyssa, you have ever honored me by this affection of yours. Where my own sisters see naught but an additional mouth to feed, you make me dear."

The garden's gate flew wide with a sharp creak. Both women started in surprise. Elyssa turned to see the same man who owned Clare's heart standing in its gateway. Her brother-by-marriage glanced at her, then let his gaze linger on Clare. She freed a harsh breath, recognizing all too well the signs of desire in his rugged features.

Sudden anger woke in her. If he used Clare or hurt her in any way, she'd see him beaten from Freyne's gates. Her concern for her cousin made her words hard. "What do you want?"

Reginald's brown eyes, so like Jocelyn's, narrowed in dislike when he looked back at her. "Lords Lavendon and Gradinton would like to know if you intend to join them for the meal, my lady, the hour being almost done."

"Why, thank them for their concern," she threw back, "but we ate earlier, not willing to wait for so late a meal."

His brows closed on each other. "Pardon. I shall rephrase. The noblemen demand your presence in the hall, my lady."

Elyssa girded her heart. So the battle had begun. She might be fated to lose, but what sort of mother let her son go to certain death without a fight?

"Come, Jocelyn," she called to her frail child, then swept from the garden, leaving Clare to walk with the one she adored.

Chapter 2

With Jocelyn's hand clamped firmly in hers, Elyssa swept into the hall, stopping before the raised hearthstone in the big room's center. Tables, their surfaces covered with white cloths and stained with remains of this day's fish stew, lay on three sides of her. The two at her right and left were empty, the servants having returned to their chores. Only a maid, her belly bulging beneath her homespun gown, remained to clear the used bread trenchers into the alms basket.

'Twas at the high table that her foes awaited her. Henry, Lord Lavendon, his round face making him seem harmless, wore a tunic of bright green beneath a brown mantle trimmed with squirrel. Beside him sat that arrogant ass, Baldwin de Gradinton, his dark features twisted with a disgust that equaled hers for him.

The big man wore his wealth in his long tunic of red velvet, its collar and cuffs trimmed in vair. A thick golden chain studded with medallions lay atop his dark mantle. Beside him, sat the wife he wished to shed, Lady Sybil. She was a wraith of a woman, overwhelmed by her bejeweled gowns of blue and red. Her white whimple framed a pretty face gone hard against her life's tragedies.

In the silence that marked Elyssa's arrival, the fire

upon the stone crackled, the torches sconced high above her on the walls hissed and popped. A chill draught entered to stir the painted linen panels that decorated the room. It rustled in the now-dried garlands of autumn blooms, forlorn traces of a celebration that had not happened.

Elyssa's gaze shifted to the door in the hall's back wall. 'Twas the entrance to Freyne's private chambers. If she could but dart past the nobles, she might be able to bar herself and Jocelyn into the bedchamber, buying just a little more time.

"My lady, we must speak of your son," Lavendon said, keeping his voice gentle. "He is now an orphan heir and, as such, needs protection from those who might misuse him. Gradinton and I both believe 'twould be in the lad's best interest to betrothe him to my daughter and make him my squire."

"Maman! Say you'll not let them do this to me. Tell them how squiring will surely kill me." Jacelyn tore his hand from her grasp and looked up at her, his thin face alive with dread. "I do not want to die, Maman. Save me."

Fear for him roared through her. Glancing behind her for Clare, she silently begged her cousin to stand beside her. Although Clare's face reflected only the uselessness of Elyssa's efforts, she did as requested.

As Clare joined her, Reginald strode past their tiny family and took his place near one end of the high table. Elyssa sent him a sour look. His action clearly said he supported the nobles against his brother's wife.

Elyssa drew a breath, stiffening her spine to conceal her fear. If there was but one thing she'd learned in her marriages 'twas that to show fear to one of these vicious brutes was to invite trouble. Her face a mask of confidence, she turned on these would-be murderers armed only with a poor dodge.

"My lord, how dare you suggest betrothal when my husband's will stipulates Jocelyn is to enter a holy house?"

"Freyne was a fool to commit those words to parchment," said Gradinton, his dark eyes narrowed at her bold retort. He leaned forward, bracing an elbow on the table before him. "I think me he was an even greater fool to let you keep that boy until you'd spoiled him.

"Henry," he continued without moving his gaze from Elyssa, "I say we lock this lady into a storeroom while we call for the priest and your daughter to come. And, do not waste his holy breath with betrothals; let him wed the babes. Once the words are spoken, Lady Freyne's caterwauling will not signify."

Elyssa loosed a scornful laugh. "Attempt it and I'll sue for annulment. Your manuever cannot withstand such a challenge." She set her hand to Jocelyn's back, easing her way, step by careful step, toward the high table's empty end. Once they were past that edge, they could bolt for the door.

"Come now, my lords, be you reasonable," she urged to distract them from what she did. She had no illusions over how reasonable this sort of man was. " 'Tis hardly in Freyne's best interest to squire a boy who is unfit for that role. Let my child have the religious life he craves and give this place to Reginald."

Reginald started at her suggestion, his brows leaping up in what seemed almost fear. His pale skin flushed. "My lords, she speaks without consulting me," he said in swift rebuttal. "I'm not the sort of man who would steal an inheritance from my brother's son. This discussion is better held after I've left the room. If you will excuse?" This, he asked of the noblemen, instead of his lady, whose right it was to dismiss him.

Anger rose at his show of disrespect, and Elyssa waved her hand before either man could respond. "Go, then," she said.

Reginald shot her a cold look as he started for the hall's door. While Gradinton and Lavendon watched him make his way out of the room, Elyssa silently prodded Jocelyn toward the table's end. Clare, who also watched Reginald, did not follow, and Elyssa dared not warn her.

They had barely rounded its far corner when Lavendon returned his attention to them. Elyssa froze, Jocelyn clutched tightly to her side, yet too far from the door to dash for it.

"My lady, you must understand. We have no more choice in this, than you," he said, his face soft with pleading. "Do you not see that 'tis our Lord who's made Jocelyn Freyne's heir by taking both father and older brother? You cannot defy God's will. Surrender Jocelyn, spending your efforts on his behalf in prayers against his survival."

"Nay," Elyssa breathed, refusing his explanation and rejecting his faith. "If you do not want my lord's brother, insisting instead on Aymer's seed, take one of his bastards. Mother of God, but there are enough of them from which to choose. There"—she pointed at the pregnant serving girl—"there is another one, ready to drop any day now. Take her babe and raise it as you will."

Gradinton's impatient voice overrode hers in harsh command. "Woman, cease your argument and do as you are told."

Elyssa's dislike of him leapt into full-blown rage, her temper flaming to match the coppery color of her hair. "How dare you attempt to bend me to your will in this way! I am a widow now, subject to no man save our king. I think 'tis time for you and your wife to depart Freyne. Be gone with you." Her brusque dismissal rang in the painted rafters high above her.

Gradinton paled, made speechless by her insult. Lavendon closed his eyes, his face a picture of frustration. Lady Sybil eased out of arm's reach from her husband.

In the momentary quiet, Elyssa heard sudden activity in the bailey, a story below this room. Grooms called and dogs barked, then Gradinton slammed his fists onto the tabletop. Stew splattered as the whole board tilted.

"God's blood, but you are a foul and brazen excuse for a woman! Now I understand why Freyne kept you prisoner on your dower these past ten years."

"No man imprisons me," she said, her tongue honed to its finest edge. "I left the stinking pig, wanting no more to do with that brainless and perverted worm."

"Hold your tongue, bitch!" Gradinton's demand was a whispered roar. "I'll not tolerate such disrespect toward a man who was my friend."

"So you would say, being no different than he," Elyssa snapped in careless scorn.

Gradinton tore upright, his abrupt movement startling a cry from his wife. His hand clawed at his belt for his missing sword. When he did not find his weapon, his fists clenched and he took a step toward Elyssa. Rage gleamed in his dark eyes, and his nostrils flared with blood lust. He came a step closer, lifting his hand in threat.

Elyssa's anger ebbed into surprise, flavored with a touch of fear. He wouldn't dare beat a woman who was no relative to him. She glanced to Lord Lavendon.

The nobleman's shoulders sagged, and his face was concealed in his hands. With Reginald gone, there was no man in this room to say Gradinton "nay."

"Cease this instant," she commanded in her strongest voice. Her guest grabbed for her.

Pivoting out of his reach, Elyssa propelled Jocelyn toward that doorway and escape. Usually incapable of physical exertion, her son sprinted for the door and clawed at the latch. Elyssa had nearly reached him, when the nobleman caught her by the upper arm and spun her toward him. "Leave go!" she yelled.

Jocelyn leapt between them. "You'll not hurt Maman."

The back of Gradinton's hand sent her boy sailing. He landed in a crumpled heap near the table.

"Jocelyn!" Elyssa threw herself away from Gradinton with all her might as she surged toward her precious child. The nobleman yanked her back to stand before him.

"Stop, stop!" Clare wailed as she hurried toward them, wringing her hands in distress. "You cannot strike Lady Freyne."

"Clare, hold your tongue!" Elyssa shouted, her heart exploding in a fear greater even than that of Jocelyn's safety. Clare would spill their secret to protect the babe. She nearly wrenched her arm from its socket in her desperation to win free. "Help me, Lord Lavendon!"

Lavendon leapt for Gradinton, fastening his hands on the big man's upper arms from behind him. "Enough, Baldwin. This is a matter for her priest, not you." His efforts had no more effect than a flea's bite.

Clare took a step closer and all hope died in Elyssa. "Mary save me," she called to heaven above, a futile plea for rescue.

"What goes forward here?" Reginald's confused question came from the hall door. Elyssa freed a grateful breath of thanks to the Virgin and glanced over Gradinton's shoulder.

Reginald crossed the hall, a tall knight at his side. This stranger was dressed all in mail with a travel-stained yellow surcoat atop it. His head was bare of helm and metal hood, revealing golden hair. Following him was yet another knight, smaller and still wearing his helmet. At their heels was a virtual army of soldiers, all dressed in leather hauberks with swords in hand.

" 'Tis time to take a lesson in manners, bitch," Gradinton hissed, too far gone in rage to heed what went on around him. Instead of an open handed slap, he drew back his arm as if to punch into her stomach.

"Nay, you must not strike her so!" Clare spread her thin fingers protectively atop her cousin's abdomen. "Lady Freyne is with child!"

"She is what?" Reginald's shriek rose to an ear-piercing falsetto. He froze, mid-step, near the high table's edge.

"She is what?" Gradinton cried in utter surprise, catching back his fist, while still holding her trapped before him.

"Nay, Clare," Elyssa sobbed, sagging against Gradinton's hold. "Hit me," she begged, knowing he would not now do so. "Mayhap your blow will loosen Freyne's foul seed and free me of this cursed babe."

The two strange knights were now behind her. "Rise, boy," one said to Jocelyn, his voice a mellifluous baritone. "Martin, take him."

"You!" Gradinton roared. He shoved Elyssa away from him as he again clawed at his side for the sword he did not wear. "God's blood, you leave that boy where he is. To arms!" he bellowed.

Elyssa stumbled a few steps before catching her footing. When she turned, her son thrashed against the smaller knight's hold. His nose dripped blood, and an angry red mark crossed his cheek. "Jocelyn!"

"Maman! Help me!" Jocelyn reached out for her, his thin face twisted in fright, as the knight bore him toward the line of common soldiers that now stretched across the hall. "Save me."

"Nay," Elyssa screamed, lifting her skirts to race after the thief. "Stop, you. Free my son!"

The helmed knight passed through the wall of armed men, half the force joining him as he continued to the door. When Elyssa tried to follow, those who remained turned their shoulders and shifted. She rebounded off them to collide with the golden-haired knight behind her. He grabbed her by the shoulders to prevent her from making another attempt.

"Jocelyn!" she screamed, fighting to free herself.

From the bailey below the hall, men bellowed and horses cried, then there was the thundering of hooves. Cursing and shouting, the few men alerted by Gradinton's call belatedly raced into the big room, swords in hand. They came to a sudden halt at the sight of the army waiting for them.

"Peace," her captor called out, no hint in his musical tones to indicate that her battle to free herself cost him anything. "I carry with me the king's own writ giving me custody of both Freyne and its heir. As lord high sheriff, I command you sheathe your weapons."

Elyssa froze in shock. This was Geoffrey FitzHenry? Then the pain of yet another man's betrayal flowed over her, goading her rage to new heights.

"Thief! If you have custody, 'tis because you substi-

tuted your petition for mine." She blindly wrenched
herself around in his hold, her hands curved into
claws.

He caught her wrists, easily holding her at arm's
length. "Cease, my lady," he said quietly. "You can
do no worse than has already been done."

She stared at him, then choked down her curses.
Jesu Christus, this man owned a perfection of feature
she'd thought given only to angels. That was, until
someone had ruined his face.

Beneath a wealth of golden hair, high cheekbones
lifted over a strong, shaven jawline. His lips were
finely drawn, full without being overly so; his nose was
straight and neither too wide nor too narrow. His left
eye showed a beautiful, deep blue color, but his right
eye hid under a leather patch. A vertical scar cut directly down from that covering to curl into the corner
of his mouth. Another scar started at the top left corner of his brow, crossed the bridge of his nose to trail
off down his cheek toward his ear.

'Twasn't his scars that set fear trembling in Elyssa,
they were scratches when compared to what her father's face had worn, rather his unnatural calm. Not
the slightest trace of emotion touched the sheriff's expression. 'Twas as if his soul were dead, and he but a
stone effigy.

Live or dead, he'd stolen Jocelyn from her. "Bitch's
son! Stealer of children!" she cried, trying to hurt him
the way she now ached. "I trusted you to deal fairly
with me when I sent you my petition. Instead, you
betray me and take not only my son, but my right to
hold him as my own."

There was no responding anger in him at her insults.
"I took nothing from you. The court refused your petition because your son is over the age when a mother

might retain a grip on her child's body. I was given custody in your place."

Tears filled Elyssa's eyes. 'Twasn't he who betrayed her, but those men on whom she'd depended to protect her child. "Of course they refused me," she cried. "How foolish of me to think any man might understand that Jocelyn must stay with me. Thieves, all of you."

New worries tumbled one atop the other, and she braced her trapped hands against his chest in pleading. "Where does he go? Who cares for him? How does he travel?" Her breath caught painfully, a broken sob. "Give him back, I pray you."

"That I will not," he said, his face yet without expression. He released her wrists and stepped back from her. "However, in two hours' time I'll be on the road to Crosswell. If you can ride the distance, you may travel with me. 'Tis your son's destination, as well." He dangled the information before her as if to tease her into compliance.

As Elyssa understood she and Jocelyn were to dwell together in the sheriff's custody, a new relief filled her. For that brief second she was almost grateful for the unborn babe, since it made him law-bound to keep her at Crosswell. She'd be close at hand when Jocelyn fell ill, which he most certainly would do. Wiping away her tears, she said, "I ride with you."

"Just so," he replied. There was nothing in his voice to indicate either triumph or pleasure at wringing this concession from her.

"Geoffrey FitzHenry, may you roast in hell for the murder of my daughter." Sybil de Gradinton's words echoed throughout the now-quiet room.

As the sheriff turned to face his accuser, Elyssa stared in surprise at Lady Gradinton. Gone was the meek, sad creature. This woman stood lance straight, eyes glowing with righteous hate.

"Be still." Lord Gradinton's warning to his wife was a low-voiced growl. "You've done damage enough."

"Nay, I'll not be muzzled any longer," Lady Sybil retorted, pointing to the sheriff's face. "Look all you upon Lord Coudray's visage and see in those scars how my daughter struggled to save herself from her husband's attack.

"Challenge him," Lady Gradinton demanded of her husband. "This is the devil's servant who used his own babes in profane rituals and tormented my Maud before he most foully murdered her. Now he uses Satan's spells to keep my granddaughter from my arms. Bid him die upon your sword, before he kills your friend's heir, as well."

Elyssa gasped. Mary save her, Lord Coudray already owned Jocelyn. She turned to look at Gradinton. Surely, if his wife's accusations were true, he would attack his former relative, seeking not only vengeance for his daughter, but to rid the world of such evil.

"Damn you!" Gradinton's blow sent his wife sprawling, blood on her lips. Stunned, Lady Sybil made no effort to rise, only moaned into the rushes. "You'll hold your tongue, or I vow I'll murder you." His voice held the higher tone of panic; horror had replaced his rage and bluster.

Elyssa's heart fell to her shoes. Gradinton's reaction made his wife's tale the truth. *Jesu*, the vicious nobleman trembled at the thought of challenging the sheriff. She stared up her new goaler, desperately seeking something, anything, to reassure herself. Lord Coudray watched her in return, his face showing no reaction to Lady Gradinton's charges, not shock, outrage, or even irritation.

"You must say she is wrong about you," Elyssa whispered, hoping to prompt him into denial.

Geoffrey FitzHenry slowly raised a perfect golden brow, not a spark of life residing in the blue eye beneath it. "What if she is not?" 'Twas a quiet question.

Her senses reeling, Elyssa bowed her head, all courage gone. Mary save her, his soul was not dead, but black as all sin. Within her rose a lifetime's worth of warnings against evil. She must run from him, putting as much distance from him as she could, or so their tales reminded her.

Too late! He had Jocelyn. Her heart quaked at the thought of how he could hurt her helpless child. Elyssa fought to raise her head, but terror wouldn't let her neck straighten. Dear God in heaven, if she couldn't bear the thought of going alone into Crosswell, how was she to protect Jocelyn?

Elyssa turned to find her cousin. Clare stood next to Reginald, her eyes great dark circles in her ashen face. The terror rooted in Elyssa tortured her meeker relative. When she realized what Elyssa wanted, she gave a tiny, horrified shake of her head, refusing.

"Come, Clare," Elyssa insisted, moving from unspoken language to a tongue less easily denied. "We must prepare to leave for Crosswell." 'Twas a command, not a request.

Her cousin's thin face crumpled, but she dared not protest. Without Elyssa's generosity, Clare would have starved. She came, swiftly crossing the hall, all the while keeping her head turned away from the sheriff.

Regret shot through Elyssa, and she lay her arm over Clare's trembling shoulders in a poor attempt at apology. Still, knowing she wasn't alone restored Elys-

sa's vanished spine. Schooling her face into its usual
controlled expression, she led Clare toward the back
wall, grateful to escape Lord Coudray's evil presence,
however temporarily.

Chapter 3

Geoffrey, Lord Coudray and sheriff of this stinking shire, watched his new ward cross the room. May God damn the law that made him a nursemaid to pregnant widows, especially when the woman was the widow of his enemy's closest ally. Although Lady Freyne and Gradinton did not seem to be on the dearest of terms just now; it galled him to have to take the widow behind his walls. Judging from her yet-slender waist and slim hips, he'd have her for nigh on the whole of her pregnancy.

"Lady Freyne?" he called to her as she reached the door that separated the private quarters from the hall.

She halted, stiff and straight, then turned to face him. Beneath a fine wimple, two plaits the color of deep burnished copper descended past her waist. Her head covering clung to the gentle roundness of her cheeks and emphasized a short jaw and the warm ivory of her skin. If her nose was almost sharp, the fullness of her lips softened the effect.

Her eyes were a pretty copper brown color, wide set, and round. The brows above them did not curve at all. Instead, they slanted upward to peak sharply near their ends. 'Twas this odd arrangement of eye and brow that turned a pretty woman into an exotic beauty. Desire stirred in Geoffrey startling in its inten-

sity, then died. Even if he wished to tease her into his
bed, what woman would lay with one she thought the
devil's own?

On the heels of desire's departure came a deeper
disappointment. The widow stared boldly back at him,
her gaze not flinching from his face. There was not an
ounce of fear for him in her. He needed her fear, far
more than he might desire her body. As long as she
quaked, she'd keep herself distant from him and his
family whilst at Crosswell.

"What is your will for me, my lord sheriff?" Her
words quivered ever so slightly.

Geoffrey almost smiled, his relief was so great. Beneath her outward presentation of calm, she was properly terrified. "Take Lady Gradinton with you into
your chambers," he told her. "She must pack, since
she is departing even more swiftly than we."

Something in his request startled her, for Lady
Freyne's brows jumped upward. She gazed at him a
moment, then her eyes narrowed and she gave a
brusque nod. "I am at your command."

Although the quiver was gone, Geoffrey was content. No matter her strength or ability to hide her
emotions, here was yet another female, fallen victim
to Sybil's lies. He watched as Lady Freyne stooped
to aid his former mother-by-marriage in rising, her
movements fluid and graceful. As the door closed behind the women, it cut off the sound of Maud's mother
and her keening.

A shred of pity for Sybil flickered to life and death
within Geoffrey. She was as much a victim in this farce
as he. Although her accusations had caused his home
and life to be explored by churchmen with more ques-
tions than he dared answer, Geoffrey was grateful for
her story. He used it, encouraging its spread. More

than walls of stone or writs of custody, 'twas this tale of his evil that protected his daughter from what harm the truth could do her.

He looked at his former father-by-marriage. Now that Freyne's heir was out of Baldwin's reach, Geoffrey could afford to enjoy this minor victory. Gradinton glared at him, hatred filling his eyes. Geoff only lifted a brow.

The big man turned on Lavendon. "You did this," he accused. "You betrayed Aymer's death to the court, then dwaddled on wedding that brat to your daughter as you awaited this bitch's son's coming. He pointed to Geoffrey. "I should have seen through your delays."

"Now, don't go looking for scapegoats," Geoffrey said, raising his voice before the plump nobleman need answer. " 'Twas the widow's impossible request for custody of her son's body that brought me rushing here. Baron and bishop alike wished to know why a woman might ask to hold tight to a boy halfway into manhood. But, if my motivation is beyond suspicion, let me say your presence here is not. Leave within the hour and I will pretend 'twas but a mistaken attempt on your part to protect a friend's orphan son." Geoff's goad did as planned and prodded Baldwin's rage onto him, thus sparing Lavendon.

"Beyond suspicion?" the big man spat out. "Who can believe a word a devious bastard like you speaks? You are worse than an eel, with your many ploys to keep my granddaughter from me. I'll not let the likes of you steal my friend's home, as well."

Geoffrey raised a brow at the insults. "Devious bastard, am I? Thief as well? How delighted Sybil will be to discover you've changed your mind and will now challenge me."

Pausing to strip off his gauntlet as if he meant to strike Gradinton with it, Geoffrey marveled at how the thought of his own death woke only peace in him. "How shall I let you send me from this earthly vale, Baldwin? On your sword? Or would you rather I swing at a rope's end as murderers do? Perhaps, to please Sybil, I should burn as befits the devil's servant. I am at your convenience."

His taunt made Gradinton's body tense. The big man's neck corded, and his lips drew into a snarl. For a moment, it appeared he might accept the challenge despite what Geoffrey's death would cost him. Then, greed triumphed, stronger even than Baldwin's great pride.

"Here now," Gradinton said, throwing his arms out before him in an unwilling gesture of peace, "I meant nothing by my words. 'Twas but the upset of the moment that caused a slip of my tongue. There is no need for violence between us."

"Of course not," Geoffrey returned, " 'Twouldn't do to kill me, not when my daughter is my only heir as well as yours. If I died, the court would take control of Cecilia, just as they now own Freyne. That would gall you right smartly, eh, Baldwin?"

"What right have you to hold her from me?" Gradinton said, rage making his voice rise.

"Why, right of custody," he said, his voice without inflection. "Do you not remember? 'Twas only a year ago that you ceded Cecilia to me in full. I believe you said I could keep the useless bitch. Those were your words, if memory serves."

Gradinton's face flamed, the dusky heat driven as much by Geoff's taunt as his own arrogance in giving up any claim on Maud's daughter. "How was I to know my sons would both die without heirs in the next month? Damn you, until I can free myself from this fruitless marriage, you must give Cecilia to me. 'Tis what custom dictates. Is that not true, Lavendon?"

Henry, Lord Lavendon, his arms crossed in stony silence and a pinched look on his broad face, glanced from Gradinton to Geoffrey. There was another moment of silence before he spoke. "I told you before, Gradinton, I've no wish to be drawn into this squabble of yours." His voice was carefully neutral as he strove to straddle a dangerous fence. Lavendon's seat lay cheek to jowl against one of Gradinton's biggest estates.

Baldwin freed a fiery breath of frustration as he turned back to Geoffrey. "Marry again," he almost pleaded. "You are but nine and twenty. Sire yourself new heirs and give me my granddaughter."

"You waste your breath when we've said all this before," Geoffrey replied. 'Twas better that he live the remainder of his life alone, being thought the devil's own, than to give up Cecilia. Baldwin would only finish the destruction Maud had started.

Geoff glanced over his shoulder at the men who yet stretched across Freyne's hall. At his look, they stepped forward in a show of force. He turned back to Gradinton. "Sand is slipping through the hourglass, grain by grain. Best prepare to go." 'Twas a soft adieu.

Gradinton's eyes were white-hot with rage. He glared at Freyne's steward. "I will wait in the gatehouse. See that my wife and belongings are brought to me there."

Geoffrey's men parted to let the nobleman pass as Baldwin stormed from the hall. The few men Gradinton had with him turned to follow their master. A moment later Baldwin's bellows could be heard from

the bailey as he vented his rage on those unfortunate souls.

"Hold a moment, steward," Geoffrey called to that
same man before he moved to answer Gradinton's
command. He glanced across the room and found the
only servant who remained within the hall was a very
pregnant maid. As she sensed his interest, she tried
unsuccessfully to disappear into the linen panels on
the walls. "You there."

"Aye, my lord?" The girl's voice was weak, and she
kept her face turned to the side, fearing her babe
would be deformed were she to look upon his scars.
Her crossed fingers, meant to protect her from his evil,
were only partially hidden in the folds of her skirt.

As often as it happened, as necessary as it was, this
reaction still left an aching in the pit of Geoffrey's
stomach. Until last year, he'd not known the depths
of his vanity. "Call the pantler and the cook to serve
my men."

"Aye, my lord," she replied, waddling as swiftly as
she could toward the hall door, her eyes averted.

Geoffrey signaled the steward to come closer.
"Bring your accounts. I'll review them before we
leave."

"Aye, my lord," the man replied, then hesitated.
"My lord sheriff, will you close the house or bring in
a castellan?"

"If I am pleased by your accounting, I see no reason
to bring in another to rule the house. Instead, you may
assume the role of castellan along with your duties as
steward. You will need to reduce the household, and
be warned, I will be watching your costs. If I feel you
misuse my generosity, you will be free to find another
position elsewhere."

The man's mouth lifted into a shallow smile, saying

two things. First, that his accounts would be true and, secondly, that the steward congratulated himself on choosing the correct side in this brief war. "You'll not be disappointed, my lord sheriff."

As the steward strode away, Lord Lavendon came to stand at his sheriff's elbow. Geoff glanced at the plain man who was foster brother to his two elder siblings and a family friend. Henry's arms were yet tightly crossed over his chest, his eyes narrowed as he looked up at the taller, younger nobleman.

"Geoff, you know that there is now but one heir, unless you count that surprise babe Aymer set in his wife." 'Twas a quiet remark.

"The steward said as much. It seems the older boy fell and died." Geoff retreated to the high table, seating himself on one of the benches.

"Aye. Strange, that," Henry replied, then his face cleared. "Ah well, 'tis no stranger than Gradinton losing all three children within two months. Not that the lads didn't deserve to die. Even more vicious than their sire, they were."

Gradinton's sons had argued at Christmas, purportedly over their sister's death at Geoffrey's hand, and slain each other in the process. A flicker of satisfaction woke in Geoff. 'Twas no less than Gradinton deserved after what the man had done to him.

"Henry, many thanks for your warning over Gradinton's plot. His attempts to have me dismissed by making me appear inept and corrupt grow bolder by the month. He liked it not when I bought the sheriff's position." Aye, once Geoff became sheriff, Baldwin ceased trying to forcibly reclaim his granddaughter Cecilia's properties, the majority of which lay in this shire. He feared, rightly so, Geoffrey would bring both shire law and Crosswell's forces down upon him.

" 'Twould be hard to make you seem corrupt, Geoff," Henry said with a quiet laugh. "He can but fail."

"I am counting on it." When Baldwin gave up subterfuge, there was but one option left to him: kidnapping. When that happened, he and Baldwin would meet on the battlefield. Even if he lost his own life, this farce would end with Cecilia free from threat.

"As for that note of mine ..." Lavendon smiled, the movement of his mouth almost sour, then came to sit next to him. "Don't be reading too much into it. Remember, no matter whether 'twas you or Gradinton who took the day, I still achieved my daughter's joining with Freyne's heir. My only reason for writing was that I disliked Gradinton's attempt to use my family for his own gain."

Then Henry lay his hand on Geoffrey's mail-clad arm. "Do not expect more from me. You know as well as I 'tis customary for the matriarchal family to take custody of female heirs, and property should follow the bloodline. Not that you would, but what if you chose to betroth Cecilia to Gradinton's enemy? His own lands could be used against him. At your age, Gradinton's well within his rights to ask you to remarry and begin a family anew so he can have your girl."

Geoffrey only sighed. "Two years ago, I would have agreed with you, insisting that the father give his daughter to her mother's relatives. But that was before 'twas my daughter I must give up and Gradinton the one to whom I must release her."

"Now, *that* I can understand," Henry laughed, "knowing Gradinton. Why not ask Rannulf—"

"Say no more," Geoffrey interrupted at the mention of his elder half brother's name. Rannulf had called him a fool for beggaring himself to buy the shrievalty, insisting it wouldn't solve the dispute between Gradinton and himself. To ask anything of Rannulf now would be an admission that his brother had been right, and Geoff wasn't ready to humble himself just now. "This is my issue, not his. There is no need for me to speak with him."

Henry lifted a scornful brow. "Arrogance, the plague of the FitzHenrys," he said quietly. "While I know not how it sits on the youngest of your brothers, I've seen how Rannulf suffers from it. But, I think me it affects you and Richard most deeply."

Geoffrey straightened in cold fury as Henry compared him to his father's bastard. "You trespass where you have no right in speaking that name before me. Richard is no kin of mine. He ceased to be when he threw off my father and the name our sire gave him."

"My, my, but the youth of today are a hotheaded bunch," Henry chided, borrowing on long acquaintanceship to lecture Geoffrey like a father. "Will you insult me to prove you need your brothers not at all?"

Geoffrey grimaced in regret. Between the stress of facing Baldwin and the sense of isolation that now lived within him, he had overreacted. "My pardon, Henry. 'Tis just that my half brothers are a sore issue with me. Say your piece and I will interrupt no more."

"I accept your apology." The older nobleman nodded slightly in approval. "I meant only to suggest that you find a great house in which to foster your darling girl, one friendly to both you and Gradinton. Once she's living with that family, you can release legal custody to Baldwin. He'll leave her be. 'Tis the right to control her properties he wants, not her body."

Geoff bowed his head. More than anything, he wished the solution were so simple, but almost a year's time had made no improvement in Cecilia. As much as he prayed for it, hope faded that his daughter would ever again own a normal life. " 'Tis a good thought, worthy of serious consideration," he finally replied.

"Do that then and end these hostilities. They threaten more than just the two of you," Henry said, then moved on to a subject far dearer to his heart. "I assume you took the right of marriage, along with custody of the boy?"

"Aye, and if you're asking whether I will approve your contract for joining your daughter to Freyne's heir, the answer is most likely 'aye.' "

"Most likely?" Henry's brows lifted in surprise. "I have my reasons for hesitating, but what are yours?"

Geoff's smile lay crooked along his mouth. "Call it a lesson well learned," he said. "The alliance is a good one, the properties being well matched, but I would see the two together before proceeding. Only if I feel they are suited to each other will we go forward with the betrothal." Never again, would Geoffrey view wedlock as the merging of properties, to be done without considering the needs of the two persons involved.

"Not all marriages are like yours was," Henry said in soft understanding, "but I appreciate your concern on my daughter's behalf. Rest you easy. Avice is a malleable thing, quick to adapt, much like her sire. She'll do well wherever I put her. 'Tis not she who worries me, but the boy. I'll not give her and her dowry to one who cannot protect them."

Geoff shot him a startled, sidelong look. "What do you mean?"

"Only that it now lies on your shoulders to make a knight from a would-be churchman. Here lies the greatest reason behind my note. I've two squires of my own and this boy would be far more of a burden than I'm willing to accept." Henry grinned his relief.

"Hold a moment," Geoffrey said, turning his head to better see the smaller nobleman. "He is not a squire already?" Even those noble sons intended for the Church received the same training at arms as their elder brothers. Aye, and if bishops weren't supposed to carry swords, thusly commanded by their Mother Church, mace and morningstar were no less lethal.

"Nay, and for that you may curse Freyne." Henry gave his head a sad shake. "The boy's been sickly from birth. Having no tolerance for weakness, Aymer gave his second son to his wife. Our fair Elyssa has indulged her boy in his frailty, seeking to shield him from life, instead of encouraging the development of strength."

Geoffrey stared at him, yet struggling to absorb the impossibility of what Henry was telling him. "You are saying that this boy's twelve and has had no training in arms?"

"Nay, I am saying more than that. Not only has the boy never held a sword, his dam refuses to sit him atop a horse, fearing he might fall and die." Henry glanced up at him, lips pursed in disapproval. Everyone knew that if a child hadn't ridden by the age of seven, mastery of the skill was impossible.

This revelation made Geoffrey stiffen in shock and disgust. Pretty as the widow was, a new dislike woke in him at how she'd misused her son. "What sort of mother ruins a lad this way, and what sort of sire permits it? Well, the boy's mine now, and his dam will have no more influence over him."

Henry freed a laugh, low and harsh. "Do not be so certain. She's a firebrand, that one. I saw nothing in her behavior to indicate she conceded control of her son to you. Mark my words, she'll do all she can to stand between you and the boy, thinking she is protecting him from your hurt."

"Stand between us?" Geoffrey almost laughed. 'Twas the only compensation for being thought evil; folk rarely challenged him. Indeed, this shire's inhabitants were surprisingly eager to offer him the tax sums they owed their king. " 'Tis not possible. She is a pregnant widow, to be confined to a cottage in Crosswell's bailey, while her son will be my squire, living with me in my family quarters."

Skepticism washed over Henry's round face, then he shrugged. "If you say so. Nonetheless, if I were you, I'd put a distance greater than a single floor between lad and dam. Think on it. If she's lioness enough to fight Gradinton, she'll eat you alive."

The corner of Geoff's mouth lifted in dismissal of Henry's concern. "You overestimate her abilities. Set your gaze onto your daughter becoming Freyne's lady in the future and leave me to worry over the widow and my ward. I'll not fail you, Henry, if for no other reason than to repay your aid, such as you say it was."

Lord Lavendon rose with a laugh, then rubbed a tired hand across his face. "Well then, I gratefully lay the whole of it into your capable hands. After these past weeks ropedancing with Gradinton, then Lady Freyne, I've a pounding in my brain that will not quit. I think I'll collect my belongings from the gatehouse, bid you good luck, and be on my way back to my own peaceful, well-behaved household. Send word when you wish to have the babes meet." He thrust out his hand.

Geoff took it. "That I will. Godspeed," he offered, "and take to heart my gratitude."

As he watched the portly nobleman stride across

the room for its exit, a small smile curled Geoffrey's lips. If Henry knew him too well to pay heed to Sybil's tale, or the reaction of others to those lies, Geoffrey trusted in the sort of fear he'd seen in the widow. There wasn't a woman in this world brave enough to face down the devil's spawn.

Chapter 4

Eyes narrowed and temper raging, Elyssa threw open the door and let Clare bear the weeping Lady Sybil into the solar on its opposite side. Not a stick of furniture sat within what should have been her own, private enclave, nor was there a rush upon the floor to soften a footstep. Elyssa left it so, preferring to remain in the women's quarters beyond it, thus limiting her contact with overbearing noblemen.

Once Clare and her burden passed her, she shut the door, then braced her back against the panel. Terror was gone, destroyed by the brief glimmer of satisfaction she'd seen in the sheriff's face. While she trembled, he gloated!

Within her grew the suspicion that Geoffrey Fitz-Henry was no devil worshiper, but another son of Adam seeking to control one of Eve's daughters. "Holy Mother," she breathed in vehement prayer, "I have been your servant for all these years. 'Tis time for you to repay devotion with action. Smite down that man for his foul attempt to use my own fear against me."

Pointless request. Did not God sit next to the poor Virgin, ready to refuse His holy wife, simply because 'twas she who asked? As the heat of her rage died, caution awoke. She'd not risk her son's life because

Lord Coudray behaved like any other man. Was not Satan masculine as well? The proof she craved lay within Lady Gradinton.

Elyssa leapt from the door to grab the weeping woman by the shoulders. "Proof," she spat out. "I would see what convinces you that the sheriff is the devil's spawn. More to the point, I would see why it convinces you when no other man accuses him. If someone had, the sheriff would have burned already."

Lady Sybil had no reaction to her words, yet trapped in her tears, but Clare did. Her cousin released the sobbing noblewoman to back away, her face colorless in terror. "Look you not upon evil," she muttered to Elyssa.

Elyssa ignored her to grab Sybil's chin and force Gradinton's lady to look at her. "Listen to me," she commanded. "What proof have you?"

"My daughter wrote to me, just before she was murdered." Sybil's pale and watery gaze flickered across Lady Freyne's face, then her attention turned inward once more as she returned to what ached in her.

Elyssa's grip on the woman's chin tightened. "Where is this missive? Come now, 'tis my son's life and my soul at stake here. Were you not begging for Coudray's death a moment ago? Convince me, and I'll see him burn to spare my Jocelyn."

" 'Tis useless," Sybil keened softly. "If no man heeds me, why should they listen to you?"

"Then, I say you lie for your own purposes," Elyssa snapped.

This goad brought the woman back, rage alive in her eyes. "Think you so? Come you into the bedchamber, and I will show you my proof. I keep my daughter's missive ever near me to remind me of what Coudray has cost me."

Wiping away her blood and tears, the noblewoman turned toward the leftward of the two doors at the solar's back wall. Gradinton had claimed the room by right of rank after his friend's death. Elyssa started after her, but Clare caught her arm.

"I beg you, 'Lyssa, do not look upon evil. Be you but humble and quiet, keeping your eyes turned from him, and in seven months you'll hold a babe in your arms." 'Twas a frantic effort by her cousin to protect the child she held dear.

"Clare, I must, as much for this new babe's sake as for Jocelyn. If Coudray is truly evil, will he not seek to steal my infant from me upon his birth to use in his unnatural rituals? Think on it, he'll be in my birthing chamber."

This had not occurred to Clare, and now it made her brow crease. "Then, you cannot go to Crosswell."

"What choice have I?" she retorted. "You have made him my warden by spilling what I would have kept to myself."

"What have I done?" Clare murmured, her hand pressed to her mouth. "He'll take the babe and your soul, as well."

"Do not fret over it so. All in all, I am grateful. You've guaranteed I will remain near Jocelyn." She pulled free of Clare's hold, but her cousin caught her back, once again.

"Nay, look you not upon evil, else that babe will be misformed."

Elyssa caught her hand. "Clare, I must. My living son is more important to me than the promise of a child that may or may not thrive. I cannot let Jocelyn become the ward of some monster. If there's any hint of truth in this missive, I'll petition for a new guardian."

"Go, then," Clare said, tearing free of Elyssa's hold. "Take yourself to Crosswell."

"You won't come with me?" Elyssa asked in astonishment.

"Why? To watch you destroy yourself and your children? Nay, I'll not aid you in that." Her cousin crossed her arms and lifted her chin. "Nor can you order me to attend you, contrary to what you seem to believe."

"My pardon," Elyssa said in true contrition, "that was wrong of me. You have never been my servant and I know that. But, my fear of him made my need for you all the deeper. However much I would like you to come, I'll not ask. Return you to Nalder, where you can keep my house against my return or my death."

Elyssa gasped as she spoke of her own death; the words had fallen unexpectedly from her lips. They sent fear rushing through her all over again. "Oh, Clare, I need you. What if this babe does take me? I pray you, do not abandon me to face death alone."

" 'Lyssa, that tongue of yours," her cousin said with an irritable sigh. "You should learn to say nothing when you are upset. Of course I will come. How could I not, after all the good you've done me?"

"I do not deserve your loyalty," Elyssa said with a small smile.

Clare's mouth lifted in response. "True, nonetheless you have it. I'll begin preparing for our departure, while you do what you think you must to protect Jocelyn. Be warned, I will hear nothing of what lies upon that parchment. Unlike you, I have no desire to confront evil."

"Done." 'Twas no less than a harsh breath of relief. "My thanks, Clare."

Clare turned toward the right door and the women's quarters. Elyssa followed Sybil into the bedchamber to find the woman tearing through a traveling basket, as she sought her proof. Stopping a few steps into this windowless room, Elyssa stared at the great bed in its center.

It had been her grandsire's bed and was now part of her dowry. Expensive and beautiful, its posts and frame were carved like twining ivy, the thick foliage studded, however improbably, with acorns and hazelnuts. Heavy blue-and-red damask curtains hung from its wooden ceiling, offering privacy and warmth within its draperies.

Elyssa's lips twisted into a tiny, bitter smile. Aye, 'twas part of her dowry, but it was not hers. For the past thirteen years, Freyne had owned it. Before that, it had belonged to her first husband, Ramshaw. The only time she'd ever used it was when she parted its curtains to do her wifely duty, the last time two months ago.

Anger rose again, this time aimed at herself. Upon her return to Freyne, Aymer had sweetly cajoled, pleading love and vowing changes, then reminded her of her marital debt to him. His touch had reawakened her body's needs, bringing into sharp recall all the pleasure that joining could bring. Seduced by her own desires, she had agreed. Then, after their third night, he'd suggested adding another woman.

Her stomach turned at how she'd once again trusted him, only to be used. The babe within her added its own protest, complaining against the day's stew. Elyssa crossed her arms over her midsection. Ten years of barrenness had made her forget how impossible 'twas to eat during her first months of pregnancy.

As she swallowed her meal for the second time this

day, she looked toward Sybil. Gradinton's wife now sat on the bed's end, a parchment in hand. The noblewoman smiled at her, but there was more of hatred than amusement in the expression.

"Why did I not understand this sooner," Sybil asked of herself. "Where men hear nothing, another mother will listen. You are heaven-sent, Lady Freyne, being brave beyond a woman's scope. Be you my sword, destroying the one who has destroyed all I held dear."

Elyssa shook her head as she held out her hand for the missive. "You'll not name me your champion; I am nothing to you, my lady. If I serve your need for revenge against the sheriff by what I do to protect my son, 'twill be but happenstance."

"What care I for why you do it?" Lady Sybil replied as she stuffed a smudged piece of sheep's skin into her hand. "I care only that 'tis done. Look upon these words and see the truth."

The handwriting that filled the page was small and cramped, but owned an intensity that nearly ate through the parchment's thickness. Both sides of this bit were filled to all its edges with tiny words. Elyssa squinted to read.

My dearest Maman,

You must aid me. For two years my terrible lord and husband has been in league with the devil. This I came to know after I bore him our second child. Where I saw a thriving babe come forth, he said the child was stillborn. When I argued, telling our servants he'd done murder to our child, he said to them I was mad with grief, then confined me to our chamber.

Whilst thus imprisoned, the devil's incubi came to torture me with their fingers like claws and their touch burning like hot pokers. When I showed our priest how I was clawed and burned, he did not heed me, saying I had done it to myself. I know now that all Coudray's servants, even our priest, are the devil's minions.

When I could bear the attacks no longer, I lied, pretending to believe the babe stillborn. The incubi immediately departed, proving they are under the control of my lord husband. To protect myself, I stole holy water from our chapel, anointing a knife, then setting both vial and knife in a hidden place against the incubi's return.

Last week, before I came to childbed with our third child, I hid my blessed instruments beneath my bolsters. 'Twas a fine and healthy boy who came forth. I begged a private moment during which I anointed my child with the holy liquid. Not but an instant later, my fearsome lord came saying he would take the boy to be baptized. Pretending I suspected nothing, I gaily set my child into his arms.

When he returned, my lord's eyes glowed with evil rage and I knew I had thwarted his terrible purpose. But the child in his arms was not my son. Instead, he gave to me a hideous creature, its face bearing a terrible red mark and its limbs, withered. 'Twas the devil's child. I know if I am to regain my true son, this being must die.

Maman, my lord husband uses his spells and incantations to listen to my thoughts and find out what I know. I tremble when he turns his gaze on me, for his eyes pierce my soul. Although I have anointed my bed curtains and keep my knife at my side, his dark minions fill my room, hiding behind the panels that drape my walls. I dare not

leave this bed, fearing they'll take me away to hell.
But, if I do not soon escape, my lord must kill
me . . .

There was no finish to the sentence as the words
trailed off the edge of the skin.

Elyssa swallowed, anger gone and certainty shaken.
There wasn't a priest or churchman in the world who
didn't speak out against just these sorts of things.
Their descriptions of hell's creatures and those who
served the devil were no different than what Maud
had laid upon this sheet.

She held the parchment away from her by thumb
and forefinger, fearing that the evil it described might
seep into her skin. Mary save her, Clare was right; she
should never have looked. Her free hand came to cup
protectively at her abdomen, as if her touch could
shield the child within her. But, even as heart and
soul quaked, her mind insisted there was something
amiss here.

"Is that proof enough for you, my lady?" Righteous
glee filled Sybil's question.

"Well, 'tis certain that what your daughter describes
is an abomination," Elyssa managed in a muted voice,
"but I must wonder why Lord Gradinton did nothing
when he saw this."

Sybil's face drooped. "What cares he that evil walks
the earth's face? His time is spent cursing Maud for
producing only a girl child and our sons for dying
without heirs, while he works to free himself from
our marriage."

"What of your priest? What did he say when you
showed him this?"

"That coward?" Sybil's voice broke with pain. "He
fears my lord more than the devil. He tries to blame

my Maud for this, saying she was always strange and
that she made this tale to hurt her husband. When he
did nothing, I dared send word of Lord Coudray's evil
to his superior. For months, there was no word, so I
wrote again. The clerk who wrote back said my
charges were no more than the babbling of a grief-
striken mother. I think they refuse to challenge Lord
Coudray because he is closely linked to Bishop William of Hereford. 'Tis this bishop, so highly placed in
court and Church, who shields a favorite.''

Elyssa's soul ceased to quake as she listened. Lady
Sybil was wrong. If the Church knew and did nothing,
'twas because there was no truth behind the charges.
There was no greater joy to a churchman than rooting
out devil worshipers. At this moment, she'd lay every
coin she owned to wager FitzHenry was not one in
the ranks of evil.

She paused in her thoughts. So, if Lord Coudray
weren't evil, what reason had he for allowing Lady
Gradinton's charges to stand unchallenged? None,
save he sought to excite fear in her.

What did he gain from her fright? 'Twas certain
that a pregnant woman would keep her distance from
the devil to protect her child. That left only one question. Why did he need her to keep her distance from
him? Whatever his reason, 'twas a strong enough one
that he preferred to be thought the devil's own rather
than to expose it.

A smile touched Elyssa's mouth. In his hidden reason she found the tool she could use to protect Jocelyn
from what the sheriff would demand of him. The
sooner she knew what Coudray's secret was, the more
swiftly she owned him.

"Say you will stand beside me to accuse him," Lady
Sybil said, her eyes taking light once more.

"Nay," Elyssa said with a brusque shake of her head, "as awful as this tale is, 'tis not enough, else others would have already accused him. You know that."

Sybil's mouth twisted in angry disappointment. "How can you refuse me after you've read these words?"

"Now, do not go screaming that I have done you wrong, when I promised you nothing," Elyssa retorted in irritation.

"Coward! You are no different than the rest, too afraid to take action." Sybil thrust out her hand for the parchment. When she held it once more, she pressed it to her breast and rocked slightly. Tears again filled her eyes. "They're dead, and no one will help me punish the one at fault."

There was a tap on the door. "Come," Elyssa called out.

The door opened only a little. "Are you finished?" Clare asked. "We are ready to pack Lady Gradinton's belongings."

"Aye, 'tis safe." As she said as much, Elyssa found herself grateful she'd seen the missive. 'Twas better to give her soul to Satan than to quake in groundless terror before a foul, but all-too-mortal man.

Once again, her gaze caught on her bed. She reached out to touch a post in longing. Three weeks ago, she'd planned to celebrate her widowhood by scrubbing away all trace of the men who had used both it and her. It galled her to leave it here for another man to use.

Her stomach chose that moment to twist again. This time 'twas purely the babe's protest over the recent meal. Elyssa clenched her teeth against the urge. Although the wave of sickness passed, it left her shaken and weak.

"Not again," Clare said, then laid her arm around her cousin's shoulders. She hurried her from the bedchamber to the now-empty women's quarters, then urged Elyssa down onto her cot and set a basin in her lap. "See the price you pay for the day's upset? I cannot believe you're serious about riding to Crosswell. Not only will bouncing atop a horse make you ill, 'tis dangerous for the babe. Moreover, you hate horses."

"Do not lecture, Clare. 'Tis for Jocelyn's sake that I must hurry and I'll not be stopped," Elyssa said, clutching her arms tight over her stomach. The wave of sickness began to rise, slowly building to an inevitable peak.

She glanced down at the cot and thought of the uncomfortable months to be spent in some corner of Crosswell's keep. "Clare, do you think I should take my bed with us?"

"Why not? Even if there's no room for you to use it, I'd not leave so fine a piece out of my control, were it mine. Surely, Crosswell has storage sheds."

"Aye, 'twas my thought as well." She carefully kept her eyes averted from the basin as she continued. "Do you suppose Sir Reginald might disassemble it and send it on to us at Crosswell? I know he'd not do it for me, but he might if you asked him." 'Twas a broad hint for Clare to go. Spilling her stomach before a witness was humiliating.

"So he might." Again, her cousin blushed, but made no move to leave. "Aye, I should see him with regard to our mounts as well."

Elyssa gritted her teeth against her stomach's demand. "Why is it babes cannot be hatched like chicks? Go, Clare. I'll not have you watch me."

Her cousin freed a sound of irritation. "As if I'd not seen it every day for the past two weeks. Aye then, if you're certain?"

"Go. Please?"

"Only if you promise to rest until 'tis time to depart. You'll need all your strength for our journey."

"I vow," Elyssa breathed. Clare turned and nigh on raced from the room. As the door closed after her cousin, Elyssa gave herself over to her babe's control.

Chapter 5

Gone was the morn's mildness. The wind now howled across a weeping sky, turning spattering starts of drizzle into stinging needles of rain. It battered at Reginald as he stepped from the tower's upper chamber onto the wooden landing that topped the stairs.

Shutting the door behind him, he turned the bulky key in its slot. Iron scraped as the door's heavy latch shifted, letting the thick bar drop into place. Once retracted, the key rattled along the iron circle that was its ring.

'Twas this lock and Freyne's long years of peace that turned a last refuge into a treasury. The upper chamber's corner now housed the two chests containing what little wealth in cloth and coin Aymer had owned, along with copies of all the contracts ever signed and sealed by Freyne's lords. 'Twas in one of those chests that Reginald stored his book.

Over the years, this leather-bound collection of parchments had become more than a place in which to note expenditures and income. It now contained the yields produced by different types of seeds and the cycle of field rotations. There were even notes to himself on his many attempts to strengthen the left gate tower, which seemed to be sinking.

This precious volume tucked securely beneath his

arm and cloak, Reginald turned to make his descent. As always, the view of his beloved home stopped him, trapping him in appreciation. Although many found it drab and uninviting, Freyne was well protected for a manor house.

When his Norman progenitor captured this place, over a century ago, he made use of an ancient mound for his defense. Flattening the hill's top, he raised a tiny keep tower in its center, then ringed the crest with a wooden palisade. To make assault more difficult, he'd dug a trench around its foot, creating a dry moat, and built a drawbridge to make for easy crossing.

Within the next generation or two, his ancestors descended from the cramped and uncomfortable hilltop to claim a much greater area. Around the new, spacious bailey, his grandsire raised another wall, this one stone and as thick as two men were tall. He too trenched the second wall's foot with dry moat, guarding the opening in the stone with an impressive gatehouse and drawbridge.

Reginald let his gaze move from the hall, barns, and gardens of the bailey to survey what he could have ruled, save for Aymer's need to futter everything in skirts.

Freyne's holdings stretched along a small plain, the fertile expanse trapped between rolling hills and the tangled wildness of the king's forest. The land here had long worn the regular outlines of fields and orchards, tofts and crofts, civilization's growth turning it into nothing less than a giant chessboard. Hundreds of thatch-capped, whitewashed cottages were pawns to a bishop, as represented by the large, stone church, complete with its own squat tower.

If farming yet remained the community's mainstay,

occasional placards now hung over cottage doors, offering shoemaking and tailoring, dying and fulling. This change was a source of great pride to Reginald, for it had happened at his hand. Unlike his sire, he recognized that a bushel of barley was always the same, but a one-penny fee could be raised into two.

Despair woke in him as, in that moment, he recognized Aymer's unborn heir as God's retribution. In daring to dream of owning his home, he'd made the desire to achieve this goal no less than his need to breathe. This torment would be his penance for aiding in one nephew's death in order to guarantee the other's demise.

His eyes narrowed in refusal. Why should he be denied wife and home? He'd worked like a peasant to make Freyne what it was. If Lady Elyssa and her babe must die to make way for him, then die they would.

Deep within his mind came a tiny, snaking voice, hinting that murder was not necessary. His brother's wife had begged for a miscarriage. If she wished to be rid of Aymer's babe, he had the means. The village midwife kept his brother's whores supplied with a concoction that could cleanse a mother's womb. Although it wasn't always successful, it worked more often than not. Now all he needed was the means to get the potion to his sister-by-marriage.

Caught in this evil thought, he descended the stairs and started along the downward path toward the bailey. As he reached the drawbridge crossing the inner ditch, a woman appeared from around the hall's corner. She hurried toward the stables. Her cloak flew wide in the wind, revealing blue skirts. Clare.

His spirits ebbed to an even deeper low. 'Twasn't enough to hold Freyne; he wanted this woman, his own lady, at his side. Another hopeless dream. This was the day his love departed Freyne, no doubt never to return.

The need to touch her at least once more before he saw her nevermore spurred him. Reginald raced heedlessly across the drawbridge and into the bailey. "Lady Clare!"

She turned, then came toward him, her every step grace in motion. Beneath the shadow of her cloak's hood, her face was delicate and fine. Pleasure woke in him at the gleam of her vibrant smile.

"Why, Sir Reginald, you are just the man I needed to find," she said. Her voice was sweet, her tones all femininity, unlike her cousin's abrupt, almost masculine manner.

"Me?" Within him, his heart sang, daring to hope that she'd sought him out for love's sake. "What is it that you would have from me, my lady?"

She took another step toward him. Reginald half reached out with his free hand, ready to pull her into his embrace. His heart leapt in his chest.

" 'Tis in preparation for our departure. Lady Elyssa insists on riding with the sheriff. We'll be needing two gentle palfreys. Also she would take her bed with her into Crosswell. Could you send it after us as it best suits you? You'll probably wish to use the cart that brought us here from Nalder."

His hopes crashed to earth as his empty hand fell to his side. He was nothing but a casual acquaintance to her. "That I can do, my lady," he said with a brusque nod. He waited for her to turn and leave him. Instead, she held her place, her gaze yet clinging to his face.

"My thanks." 'Twas but a fairy breath as she watched him, brown eyes bright. Her cheeks, already

pink from the chill, grew to a deeper rose. At her
continuing stare, a new warmth filled him, flowing
across his skin.

"Is there aught else I might do for you, my lady?"
His question was husky against his growing need.

She blinked as if startled by his words, and her smile
died. "Nay," she said, all life gone from her voice as
she turned as if to return to the hall.

Reginald caught back a cry of pain. She was going,
and he'd never see her again. Before he could stop
himself, he reached out and took hold of her elbow
to draw her back to him. "Stay a moment," he
begged quietly.

Although she made no attempt to break free of his
grasp, when she raised her face there was a bitter cast
to her mouth. "To what purpose?" The ache in her
words spoke of the same longing he knew within
himself.

Reginald sighed in pleasure mixed with pain. He
risked both pride and heart on his next words. "Because I wish to look upon you. Your beauty ever
leaves me breathless."

The color grew in her cheeks, but she did not chide
him for his forward response. Instead, she lay her
hand on his forearm. "I am an old woman," she whispered, "beyond my fortieth year. There is no beauty
left in this worn face."

A smile crept across Reginald's lips. "You are not
old to a man reaching for his fiftieth year. And, even
in my dotage, I know beauty when I see it."

"I will call you blind, old man," she teased gently.

Reginald's smile deepened. "Will you linger to
speak with me?"

Her blush was fierce, lending her a girlish glow. "I
would like that very much."

Her reaction answered the boyish pounding of his own heart. "Then, come you out of the wind, Lady Clare."

He led her around the corner of a shed, then threw open the door. 'Twas filled with odds and ends, unfinished wheels, casks of tar, pieces of wood for creating new sheds and such. Although the interior was no warmer than the air outside, the thin walls protected them from the wind's biting edge. Clare hesitated at the door.

"We shouldn't be alone," she said with a sudden quiver in her voice. In her eyes lived a virgin's fright.

The thought that she might yet be pure, untouched by any other man, made Reginald's pulse leap. "You have no reason to fear me or my motives, not when you own my heart. What I want from you can only be had after we've spoken vows before a priest." He stepped into the shed, setting his book upon a barrel top and leaving the door ajar.

Her eyes widened in surprise, then joy shone in her face, her smile wild with happiness. "You would ask me to wed? In all my life, I never expected to hear these words." Buoyed by his revelation, trust washed across her fine features. She stepped boldly into the small building's darkened interior.

When he came to stand before Clare, he took her hands in his. Like everything else about her, her fingers were fine and delicate, but cold as ice. He enclosed them in his grasp, hoping to warm them a bit.

"My thanks," she said, her teeth rattling. "It has grown fearsome cold this day. I cannot say I look forward to riding in it."

"Your departure will leave my life cold and dead." He sighed against his future pain.

A glorious smile curved her lips. "This affection of

yours for me is no less than a miracle. For all the times we conversed about the weather, the betrothal, and other such nonsense, there showed no clue to this on your face. Here I was chiding myself for a fool to let my heart fix on you, when 'twas more likely you disapproved of me as did my sisters' husbands. I am but an extra mouth to feed.''

Reginald frowned at her lack of self-worth. "Never say that." 'Twas a ferocious whisper. " 'Tis your cousin who tells you lies such as this. Would that I could protect you from her. She treats you as her servant when you are her equal. Look how she makes you carry her messages.''

"You are wrong," she whispered shyly. "She cares for me, treating me far better than my own kin did. Do you know she has offered to settle some small worth on me, so I will not come to you a pauper." Longing for him again woke in her expression, and she freed her hands to brace them against his chest. "Would that we could wed on the morrow, then there'd be no need for us to part," she cried softly.

Joy exploded from Reginald in a deep laugh. He caught her face in his hands and touched his mouth to hers. Her lips softened beneath his. Although he warned himself to be gentle, the passion he carried for her would not be denied. His mouth took hers with all the heat he knew for her. Clare flattened herself against him, winding her arms around his neck as she answered his emotion with her own.

Need grew in him until he was giddy with it. He caught her at the waist, lifting her slightly to place her woman's softness against the part of him that would be one with her. She gasped at this, her breath of protest startling him back to his senses. Shaken, he stepped back from her, catching her hands in his as he moved.

"You wake a fire in me that I fear I cannot control." His voice broke under the weight of his need.

Fear tangled with pleasure in her expression, then tears gleamed in her eyes. "Never have I felt like this. Over the years, men have pursued me seeking to steal with flattery and paltry gifts the one thing I hold most dear. I rejected them all, sometimes needing to drive them away with my screams when they refused to heed my 'nays.' But here you are, retreating instead of pursuing me." She shook her head against the wonder of this.

" 'Tis a precious thing you offer me," Reginald said, his voice yet trembling against the power of the emotions she stirred in him. "I fear I have nothing of equal value to give you. Wed with me, and you doom yourself to a lifestyle far less comfortable than the one you now claim. We will be but servants to Freyne's lord."

"What care I for that when 'tis you I want," she replied with a smile. Then her happiness dimmed. "Do you truly think the Church will let us wed? We are within four degrees of kinship. 'Lyssa says they'll not be concerned, as I am past the age of bearing children."

He shook his head, a bit surprised that she had discussed so much with her cousin. "My life has been spent doing what is in the best interest of others. Now that the chance has come for me to take what I want, I'll not let a churchman stop me. I will draft a petition. But, be you warned, if the Church refuses me, I will beg you to accept me with nothing more than a hand-fast between us."

Again, her smile burst forth, glorious in her affection. "If there are to be no children for us, what does it matter if we speak vows before a church or only before God himself? I will accept you. I cannot tell you how your love supports me. 'Tis like a shield, protecting me from Crosswell's evil." She shuddered and fell silent.

"Clare, love, do not take to heart what Lady Gradinton has spewed." Reginald drew her close, wrapping a protective arm around her. "I think me, 'tis but another attempt on Gradinton's part to destroy a man he hates."

"Would that I could believe you." She buried her head against his shoulder, tucking her face into the curve of his throat. "Oh, Reginald, I do not wish to go to Crosswell."

"Then, stay with me," he offered.

"I cannot," Clare replied, a wishful tone to her voice. " 'Lyssa needs me. After her many kindnesses, I cannot abandon her to go alone to that horrid place."

Reginald caught his breath at the opportunity in her words. If Clare's cousin were not with child, there'd be no need to go to Crosswell. He opened his mouth to offer the potion, then caught back his words. It had been Clare who'd intervened between Gradinton and Lady Freyne, seeking to protect the babe. 'Twas better to go slowly, probing for the right path rather than leaping blindly only to destroy what he most desired.

"Lay your blame for this trip upon my brother's head, for he is the one who once more set his seed into his wife," he said, his heart pounding in his throat as he sought again to murder his brother's get. Although the guilt stabbed at him, 'twasn't as deep as when he'd first begun to contemplate killing children.

"True enough, but 'tis too late for that now. Ah well, I must find my strength in your assurances, for go to Crosswell I will." She freed a short, sweet laugh, her breath warm against his neck. " 'Twill be my job to see my pigheaded cousin doesn't goad the sheriff into abusing her as she did to Gradinton."

"So, how long must you reside at Crosswell?" For the potion to work, Lady Freyne must not be past her third month.

"In seven months time, that is, if she manages to carry the poor, wee thing through her coming heart-break." Clare eased back from him a step and shook her head in worry. "My 'Lyssa loves too deeply. When she finally admits she's lost Jocelyn, I must be at her side to see she doesn't lose this babe as well. Already, I worry that the seed hasn't set as firmly as it should. She is very ill."

If her words made it clear she longed for Lady Freyne's babe, Reginald's spirits took flight át her worry. The potion worked best when the babe was not well settled within the womb. But how could he make certain Lady Freyne drank the brew?

He drew Clare close once more, then stared into the shed's darkest corner. If she believed what she did was for her cousin's good, she would give it to her. The words he needed to win her compliance clung to his tongue's tip. 'Twas wrong to use her this way; such trickery did not honor her love for him.

Aye, but if he became Freyne's lord, Clare would be its lady instead of a mere servant. Surely, this justi-fied his intervention here. After all, 'twas hardly mur-der if the babe might have been miscarried anyway. Suddenly, he was grateful she couldn't see his face.

"Over these last years, I have gained great respect for Freyne's midwife. She has many ways of strength-ening a failing seed. If you'd like, I could see to it you have one of her concoctions, even before you leave here this day."

Clare pressed her lips to his jaw. "You are so kind. Thank you, I would like that very much."

Her words were bolts of guilt through his heart. "Then, you shall have it before you depart," he said. "Now, I must meet with the sheriff. Say me a fare-thee-well, holding in your heart my love and my belief that we will soon stand before a priest."

Even by the murky light in the shed, he could see the joyous glow in Clare's eyes. "Fare thee well, my love." She took a single step toward the door.

"And, thee, as well, my love," he replied, his arms aching to hold her once more.

She paused, then threw herself at him. Her arms caught him around the neck, and she showered kisses on his face. "I cannot go without speaking of my love for you, just once more. My heart is yours, my love, adoring as I do your kindness and care for me and mine." 'Twas a heated whisper against his lips, then she turned and ran from the shed.

Reginald watched her go. He was right in what he did. Clare, and her love for him, was too fine to degrade by making her Freyne's servant. To offer her Freyne as a wedding gift was worth the risk of any sin.

Chapter 6

"My lord, what would you have me say to her?"

The question, expressed by Crosswell's master-at-arms, was no less icy than the last frigid blast of wind. Before Geoffrey could answer, his big gray steed reacted to the nearness of the soldier's mount. The war-horse sidled and snorted, lifting his forelegs in threat.

"Cease, Passavant," Geoff suggested, knowing that to demand compliance from the strong-minded brute only ever led to war between them. 'Twas a calm and steady hand that kept Passavant on task.

Geoffrey turned his head to consider the gaunt knight who had served the sheriffs of Crosswell for the past ten years. Broad of face with a nose so beaked it nigh on bent his helmet's nasal, Sir Osbert's mouth was caught in a dour downturn and his pale eyes glittered with dislike. Whether 'twas a distaste for his new sheriff or his present role as messenger, shuttling between nobleman and noblewomen, Geoffrey did not know. Nor did he care. The men who filled Crosswell's garrison were either mercenaries, like Osbert, or soldiers drawn from local lords for the forty days of required military service landholders gave their king; they owed their sheriff neither love nor personal loyalty. No matter. All Geoffrey wanted from them was their obedience.

The newest sheriff of Crosswell gave his head a brief shake against the widow's request. "She cannot crave a stop so soon. We have hardly been in our saddles an hour yet." 'Twas a flat remark.

"Her lady cousin says she is very ill." Osbert's cold tones were as emotionless as his master's.

Geoff looked away from the man in frustration, the feeling persisting longer than most emotions did in him. Traveling with a breeding woman was utter idiocy, and yesterday's ride had proved it. Although they'd started out well after midday, he'd expected to do better than five miles before nightfall. Pressed for time, he couldn't return fast enough to Crosswell, but the widow begged a halt every hour, claiming exhaustion and illness.

There was no one to blame for this, save himself, who'd purchased the position. He'd done so, knowing that the past six years had seen three sheriffs come and go, each inflicting his own version of chaos on Crosswell. Now the Archbishop of Canterbury was demanding all his sheriffs bring their tax collections and backlogged legal actions up to date. In little less than a month, the itinerant justiciars would be at Crosswell to open courts, and he wasn't ready. That pressure, coupled with an invalid widow, set a sudden aching in his neck.

As he looked up to ease the pinch, another ferocious blast of wind hit the rolling line of treeless hills ahead of him. The sky's raging breath tore at the short grasses clinging to their crests. Pity woke in him for those tiny blades; he knew just how they felt. After surviving so many months in hell, this woman was the final thing, the one detail that would destroy him.

"My lord, what would you have me say to her?" 'Twas an almost impatient prompt.

Irritation followed frustration, creating inner warmth where before there'd been nothing. "Say?" he snapped. "Say to her that if she were half as delicate as she claims, she'd be dead by now and I'd be free of her torment."

So unexpected an outburst sent Osbert's wan brows flying upward as his mouth moved oddly. "God's truth, my lord? You would have me tell her that?"

Geoffrey grimaced, surprised at the depth of his dislike for the lady, when he truly knew her not at all. "Nay, best you not, however much I chaff at her pretense of feminine frailty." He opened his mouth, meaning to tell Osbert they would not stop, when an entirely different set of words exploded from him in a heated breath. "By our Lord's cock, I pray this is no harbinger of the months to come, else I'll not survive her stay."

The man riding beside him coughed several times at his most recent master's wholly unusual behavior, then gave vent to a low rumbling chuckle. "If you will permit, I shall add my prayers to yours, my lord."

That his reaction to the woman could tease so friendly a comment from a man given to naught but harsh and icy glances set a wry twist to Geoffrey's mouth. A momentary sense of camaraderie woke in him. "My thanks for the offer, but what reason has God to listen to your prayers? Are you a holy man, Osbert?"

"As the pope, himself, my lord sheriff," his master-at-arms replied with a cocksure lift of his brows.

Without warning, a laugh broke from Geoff. The sound brought with it a wondrous reminder of earlier times when a smile and a jest had come as naturally to him as breathing. "I fear these next months will find me relying heavily on your holiness."

Osbert's expression thawed until the man grinned. In the six months Geoffrey had been sheriff, 'twas the first time he'd seen the knight's teeth; despite his middling years, Osbert yet held tight to every one of them. As the coldness departed the man's face, it left behind only the general sort of blandness adopted by a hireling when dealing with their employer. "So, what shall I tell the lady?"

"Naught. I'll not ask you to do what should be mine and 'tis my chore to tell the widow what I expect from her. I think me, I must discover for myself how fragile this woman truly is."

He raised a hand to signal the troop to halt. As men called his command back along the line, protesting leather sighed into quiet, followed by the stamp and blow of resting horses. Geoffrey turned Passavant and started down the roadbed.

Those who made up Crosswell's present contingent barely glanced at him as he rode past. If only four of them openly blessed themselves, most of the others gazed skyward or at the road's rocky surface. The pleasure he'd felt at Osbert's sudden friendliness was lost against their reaction to him.

Bearing the fear and hatred of others was not a task for the faint of heart. Because he'd lived the majority of his life content with only himself for company, Geoff hadn't expected this shunning to so affect him.

When he reached the center of the line, he drew his mount to a halt and frowned. This was where he'd commanded the women to stay, surrounded by Crosswell's men for their own protection. There was no sign of them.

"Where are the noblewomen?" he asked one of the braver souls who dared to meet his gaze.

"At your call to stop, the two of them took for yon

hillock," the commoner replied in heavily accented French.

Geoffrey glanced over his shoulder. A small mound, half hidden by barren trees, stood not ten yards from the roadbed. The two weak-livered palfreys the women rode stood at its edge, heads down, manes and tails streaming in the wind. He turned his attention back onto the soldier.

"You let them go without an escort?" 'Twas more snarl than question.

There was a brief instant of startled silence within the commoners' ranks at his unexpected vehemence. Then, saddles groaned as men shifted, craning their necks to watch what went forward from over their comrades' shoulders. The recipient of the rebuke tried to shrug.

"Nay, my lord. We tried to follow, but they warned us away, saying they needed a moment's privacy. They are noblewomen, my lord. What could we do?" The man's voice took on an aggrieved tone as a hedge against blame.

Geoffrey's spine straightened at the meaning behind the commoner's words. The widow had openly flaunted his command, putting herself in danger. May God damn that fool of a woman a thousand times over.

He drew a sharp breath. Fool or sly vixen? Were he to allow her disobedience to stand unchallenged, 'twould erode his control over Crosswell and its troops. Her husband had been Baldwin's friend. Could it be a coincidence that in less than a full day of wardenship, Lady Freyne sought to make him appear incompetent?

Geoffrey's shoulders relaxed. What did it matter whether 'twas Baldwin who'd set the widow on this path? He did not tolerate such behavior in his own keep, nor would he now. Lady Freyne's defiance would end right this moment.

"Dismount you and hold this beast of mine to keep him calm. I've got me a widow to fry." The vicious tone of his voice set nervous laughter rippling among those within hearing distance.

Geoffrey threw himself from Passavant's saddle and stalked toward the mound. His mail jangled with each step, harsh music to feed his irritation. At the hillock's opposite side, Lady Clare leapt up and whirled on him, her cloak spread wide to shield her cousin from the intruder's view. She gasped when she saw that 'twas he who came, rather than Osbert or one of the common soldiers. Geoffrey stopped within arm's reach of her.

"Tell your lady cousin that I will not tolerate her disregard of my commands. When I say she is to remain with my men, then remain she must. Disobey me again, and you'll both taste the same lash that chastises anyone within my vale fool enough to defy me."

"You wouldn't dare," the lady in question gasped from behind her relative's woolen shield.

"Wouldn't I?" he retorted, his glare fixing on the more timid of the two.

Lady Clare squeaked, her gaze darting away from his. She shot a frantic look over her shoulder at the woman behind her. " 'Lyssa, enough," she hissed. "I pray you, say no more."

" 'Tis an empty threat," Lady Freyne replied, her voice weak. "The court does not allow those under its protection to be abused."

"My lady, you mistake discipline for abuse." Geoffrey raised his voice to be certain the widow heard every word. "As for the court's control of you, until that babe is come, you belong to me as if you were my own family. Thus are you subject to the same rules that I apply to those directly connected to me. And no one, not even you, challenges my rightful discipline."

"My lord, we meant no harm and will be more cautious in the future," Lady Clare said, her voice trembling as she attempted to soothe him. It might have been more effective had her gaze not been fixed at some spot in the distance. " 'Twas just that Lady Freyne was very ill and wished to relieve herself in private."

"Aye, and here is another issue we must address," he said. "I can no longer tolerate the delays Lady Freyne costs me. If she is ill, let her return to the manor house where we spent last even'. I'll send a cart for her once I've reached Crosswell, allowing her to travel at her leisure."

" 'Tis a kind offer, my lord—" Lady Clare started.

"Nay! You cannot leave me behind. We do not accept," Lady Freyne cried out, her voice choked and hoarse. Then she gagged.

Her cousin turned to crouch beside the widow, glancing once over her shoulder to make certain her charge was yet shielded from his view. "How can you empty your stomach, when you've put nothing in it since midday yesterday?" she asked in gentle commisseration.

"I am not emptying it, I'm only thinking about it," Lady Freyne managed, her voice thready. There was a moment's quiet, then the widow sighed. "Ah, it eases. Clare, I think me 'tis that potion of yours. The babe dislikes it as much as I do. God be praised, he doesn't demand I expell that latest dose."

"It cannot be the tonic. That is to strengthen you,"

Clare soothed. The loose surface of the hill shifted beneath her feet, and she slipped backward to sit on the gently sloping ground. Her movement exposed Lady Freyne to Geoffrey's veiw, and he caught his breath in surprise.

His ward had not only thrown back her cloak hood in preparation for her sickness, but removed her wimple as well. Thick russet hair tumbled out of what had once been a tight roll, spilling softly over the slender line of her shoulders. The wind toyed with the pretty stuff, making it dance around her. Her head lay on her cousin's shoulder, exposing her profile to his view. Aye, and all of her throat's slender line along with it.

"I care not what its purpose is," Lady Freyne sighed, her eyes closed. "Neither of us can tolerate another drop of that foul brew. Pour it out for the moles to drink."

Her head shifted on her cousin's shoulder until she faced Geoffrey, her eyes still closed. Although propriety demanded Geoffrey turn his back, he stood rooted to this spot, his gaze refusing to shift from her visage.

Shadows clung to the hollows beneath her eyes and cheeks, proving that the child within her rode her hard, indeed. So, if she was truly sick, why did she insist on traveling with him? His brow smoothed in understanding. 'Twasn't Baldwin whose puppet she was; she belonged to the boy at the other end of this journey. Where her unborn babe begged her to go slower, her worry over her elder child goaded her onward.

Dear God, but she was lovely. The shifting air sent soft tendrils across her fine, wide cheekbones. He watched as a single strand caught on the fullness of her upper lip. Desire woke in him, sharp and strong, and touching her mouth with his suddenly became the item of greatest importance in his life.

She sighed once more, then opened her eyes. Her gaze caught on his face, once again without flinching away from his scars as other women's did. This only fed his need. He'd run his fingers down the soft curve of her cheek, then see if she reacted when he touched her nape. He watched her hand rise to brush away the hair clinging to her face, vowing his fingers could feel the softness of her skin.

With a sharp cry, her eyes widened, and she struggled free of her cousin's embrace to sit upright. Instantly, she jerked her cloak hood up over her head, concealing her face in modest shadow. It was with great reluctance that Geoffrey gave up his desire.

"For shame, my lord sheriff." Her chide started as a throaty breath, but grew in steel and strength as bright color flared in her cheeks, a testimony to the depth of her embarrassment. "Why did you not turn away as you should have?"

Within him rose a sudden urge to smile at her distress over such an innocent moment. "Your state of dress was unexpected. Given the circumstances, I can hardly complain you behaved lewdly. I vow, I will say nothing of what happened," he offered in reassurance.

Her eyes widened, and she freed an angry gasp. "*You* will say nothing of *my* behavior? 'Tis not I who did wrong here, but you who violated my privacy. Fie on you."

A swift, harsh breath escaped him. There was not an iota of fear for him residing in her. *Christus,* why was the only woman who paid no heed to Sybil's tales also the only woman placed in a position to do the most harm to his daughter?

She wasn't finished. "Aye, then you continue and

wrong me again when you threaten to abandon me at some nameless place along the road. 'Tis your duty to escort me the full distance to Crosswell. Shirk it and I shall complain to the court."

Anger at her commanding manner exploded in him with a single, brilliant flash, shattering his emptiness. In the fiery rebirth of his inner emotions, he could see every miserable day of the next months stretching ahead of him with aching clarity. Unless he could stop her, she would ever be at his heels, nagging and harassing on each slight she imagined he did her. Of all the threats facing him just now, this was the most horrible, worse even than the possibility that she sought to ruin him at Baldwin's behest.

"Do you wish to ride with me, my lady?" 'Twas not a polite question. "You are welcome so long as you understand that from this instant onward I will pause only to rest and feed the horses. If you cannot keep pace, you will be left behind."

She scrambled to her feet, leaving her cousin to sit meekly at her feet, head bowed. Lady Freyne set her hands on her hips, while her eyes narrowed in anger and defiance. "Nay, that I will not allow."

"*You* will not allow?" he shouted, his fists closing. "Do you think me a servant to be told to go faster or slower at your will? Since you are so powerful, tell me how is it you intend to stop me from riding on while you dawdle?"

The widow drew a furious breath, but could only glare at him in silence. After a moment, she crossed her arms before her, then lifted her chin. Even though she had no answer for him, she would admit neither defeat nor his right to command her as he saw fit.

Geoffrey's teeth clenched so tightly they hurt. No wonder Gradinton had been ready to beat her. She persisted where even a man would have bowed and acknowledged another's greater power. Such was the natural order of things. How could she think to defy nature?

Damn her, but she could not. She must submit. Did she not realize that her defiance left him to choose between beating her into submission or appearing as her fool? The very thought of what needed doing made his stomach turn; there had to be some other way to bring her to her knees before him.

As Geoffrey recognized what it was, his hands opened and his shoulders relaxed. "I suggest you have done with these useless commands and threats of yours. They neither become you, nor do they serve your son. You can hardly expect me to think fondly on him when his dam seeks to abuse me in this way. Or, have you forgotten which one of us now controls him?" He raised a scornful brow.

"*Mon Dieu,* what have I done?" she gasped, her hands coming to catch at her throat. Pain twisted her mouth, and sudden tears glistened in her eyes. Her knees more buckled than bent as she knelt, head bowed. "Nay, my lord sheriff, do not hurt him. I will take your beating, for 'twas I who has wronged you with my rudeness. Do not hurt him, I pray you ..." A quiet sob trailed from her last word.

Geoffrey groaned within himself. Her care for her son was no more than an echo of what he felt for Cecilia. Where he had the wealth and connections to protect his daughter from Baldwin's rightful control, the widow had naught but herself to set between him and her son. With regret, his need to touch her returned, this time seeking to ease the pain he'd caused her.

"*Jesu Christus,*" he breathed in shock and dismay

at himself. "Enough, my lady. Come in the next moment or stay behind."

Geoffrey whirled on his heel and started back around the hillock, striding as swiftly as he could back to the waiting soldiers. 'Twas Osbert who now held Passavant. The knight watched him, his face scrupulously blank. Geoffrey grabbed his reins and swung himself back into the big gray's saddle.

"What is your command, my lord?" There was an odd tone to Osbert's voice, as if he laughed deep within himself.

Geoffrey stared at him, but there was no sign of amusement in the man's pale eyes. "If the women have not remounted in the next few moments, you'll stay with twenty men to escort them back to the manor we left this morn. If they decide to ride with us, there will be no more delays ... and keep them as far from me as you can." He urged Passavant into a trot.

"Our Father," Osbert said, just loudly enough to be heard. There was a sudden clearing of throats among the ranks.

Geoffrey ignored him. Every bit of his energy was focused on destroying the terrible softness the widow woke in him. He concentrated on her strident, commanding manner until anger's fire blazed through him once more. Although trading emptiness for rage might not be a positive change, 'twas far better than vulnerability.

"Surly bitch," he muttered to himself; the fire grew, eating his heart as it went.

"Cruel and unfeeling bastard," Elyssa muttered, her throat ragged, burned raw by unshead tears. "Cold-hearted son of a sow. I vow, he'll pay for his threat against my son.''

These words were the only barrier standing between her and hysteria. Promises of vengeance had become like the prayers she intoned as her beads slipped through her fingers. 'Twas also the only thing keeping her upright in her saddle. Just now, she would happily drop to the ground and move never more.

Having never been a great rider, Elyssa had completely foregone travel by horseback after a fall early in her first marriage. Now her legs and back ached beyond enduring. Even at a walk, the motion of this horrible beast kept her stomach aggravated.

She glanced ahead of her. The road crested over yet another hill, while behind her the descending sun shot knife-edged rays of light through a thick sea of clouds. Orange and red, the sun's lifeblood poured through these rents to stain an already dead and barren earth. Metal gleamed dully at the forefront of the long line of men. 'Twas the sheriff, his big steed lifting willing hooves to trot up the final distance to the hilltop.

Elyssa's eyes narrowed. "And, if you dare to hurt Jocelyn—" Then what?

Helplessness deflated her. The sheriff cared nothing for what she felt nor would her emotions stay his hand if he wished to abuse Jocelyn. Her head drooped, bowing now when her neck had refused to bend this morn.

"Fool, fool, fool," she wept softly to herself in guilt. "All he asked was that you acknowledge his right to command you to his will. Why could you not give it to him? Look how your pride has put your child in harm's way. What sort of mother are you?"

This was all Freyne's fault. Ramshaw had been willing to beat her into submission, but their marriage had lasted a bare two years. Aymer had stayed his hand, even letting her leave him to pursue her own life. Had he not done so, she might have learned, as other women did, to hide her disrespect and defiance behind submissive female behavior.

Her palfrey started up the steepest bit of the road, its muscles straining beneath her. Her fear of falling made Elyssa grab for the saddle's edge as her body slid; the reins dangled uselessly between her fingers. Given this sudden freedom, the horrid creature erupted into a swift trot up the remainder of the incline. The change in gait nearly jostled her from the saddle.

"My lady, slow your mount," one of the men riding alongside warned, spurring his own horse to stay abreast of her.

Elyssa gasped against her fear, but managed to release her hold on the saddle and yank on the reins. Why did they worry so over how fast she went? Even if the beast wished to run, surely her keen-eyed escorts could easily overtake it.

As the horse slowed back to its hoof-dragging pace, she looked out over a rippling plain. Here, the land was torn asunder, the grassy flesh laid open with gaping holes and trenches, far into a treeless distance. Not a quarter mile distant and caught in the bend of a swiftly flowing river, a great square keep dominated the earth, rising out of the flatness like a hard fist.

Built of yellowish stone, its corners were trimmed in white blocks, adding an artistic touch to what was truly nothing more than a garrison and gaol. Two walls surrounded it. While the inner one clung close to the tower, the outer one flew wide to embrace a generous expanse of bailey, its opening guarded by a gatehouse that was almost a fortress in itself.

Beyond these defenses was a third wall, this one belonging to the city that lived alongside the king's fortress. Only a small portion of the houses crammed within the city's wall were visible. Rude dwellings with walls of mud and manure stood alongside the more refined half-timber buildings, their upper stories all white walls framed by dark beams.

The sight of the better abodes made Elyssa home-sick for her house at Nalder, for it was of that same sort. In her memory, she wandered from her home's cellar and storeroom to the first-floor hall, where her few male servants slept and the household took its meal. But 'twas the second floor that was most precious to her, being her own private domain.

Spacious and airy, that room had wide windows with shutters to be thrown back so summer might stream in and a fine brick hearth to chase winter back outside the walls. In that room did her two women spin, weave, and sew, as per her contract with Freyne, and she and Clare embroidered, their work donated to Nalder's monastery.

She drew a shaking breath, thinking of all the happy hours she'd spent listening to the dialogues between Jocelyn and his tutors. No more. The very thought of returning to Nalder without her son made tears sting in her eyes.

As they drew nearer to the keep, Elyssa wrinkled her nose. The setting sun's breath brought with it the acrid smell of burning pit coal, torn from yon gaping trenches. If wealth could be judged by stink alone, then this was a rich place, indeed. With the stench came the echoes of smiths at their work, a steady clanging of metal against metal.

"Is this Crosswell?" From her position behind Elyssa, Clare asked this question of one of their escorts.

"Aye, my lady," a man replied.

"Thank the Lord." Even though Clare was much more comfortable atop a horse, there was the same tone of exhausted relief in her voice that Elyssa knew at his answer. "Might I ride beside Lady Freyne for the remainder of our journey? 'Tis but a short distance."

The man must have agreed, for Clare was suddenly beside her. Her cousin gave a sharp cry. " 'Lyssa, you look as if you will drop at any moment! Why did you persist when what you do threatens your babe?"

"What care I for whether the babe stays or goes?" Elyssa replied, her answer made harsh by the regrets now nipping at her. "I warn you, if you plan to carp and chide every moment over this babe, you may as well leave for Nalder on the morrow. Begone with you."

"Nay," Clare replied. Although she kept her voice low to share as little as possible with their escort, there was enough strength in her denial to startle Elyssa into glancing at her. Her cousin's eyes were narrowed with surprising determination.

"You need me. I will be the one to treat your bruises when your warden gives way to rage and beats you for your misbehavior. I only pray he does not murder you as he did his poor wife. If you care so deeply for Jocelyn, how could you goad the sheriff as you did?"

"No more, Clare," ELyssa begged with a catch in her voice. "Do you think I've not been asking myself that same question over these past hours?"

"I suppose you have," Clare offered in soft apology. "Why did you do it?"

"I do not know," Elyssa sighed, fighting her desire to weep until she could cry no more. "I suppose 'tis because he made me angry by saying he'd abandon us the road, when my need to reach Crosswell is desperate."

"Whatever shall I do with you," Clare said tightly. "I think me you'll not live to childbirth if you don't learn to hold your tongue."

"I will try," Elyssa offered, "for your sake if not for this babe's. I know how precious he is to you."

He? Elyssa frowned. When had she started assigning gender to this seed growing in her? She barely heard her cousin's relieved thanks. Nay, she would not start to think of what grew in her as a being.

There was no helping it. As she searched her heart, she found this babe already locked within it, belonging to her as much as Jocelyn did.

Elyssa relaxed in acceptance. How foolish of her to imagine she could love what grew in her any less than she did his elder brother. In that moment, her palfrey stumbled slightly and the creature's lurching motion sent her stomach into a sudden sickening dance.

A tiny smile touched her lips. As if she had any choice in this. More so than the other two babes she'd borne, this child owned a strength of will that surpassed even her own. She could only hope he had more sense.

Chapter 7

As always, Crosswell's oppressive atmosphere reached out to envelop Geoffrey, dragging his soul down with its dreariness. He glanced up at the two massive gate-house towers. Thick and ugly, they framed an entrance that was more tunnel than gateway. Each time he entered, he thought of a hell's mouth, the gaping maw waiting to consume a grievous sinner.

'Twas for certain that serving as Crosswell's sheriff was akin to being in hell. The illusion was aided by the city, which shared with the fortress the reek of its ever-burning forge fires, the creaking of the water-driven machines working the raw iron ore, along with the constant clamoring of hammers. But, if Crosswell was dirty and harsh, it also represented a strength that Coudray lacked. Here could Cecilia find shelter from a world that had already wounded her near to death and waited to finish the task, if given the chance.

Passavant crossed the wide, outer bailey at a walk. 'Twas a crowded place, this keep, hosting endless rounds of travelers, messengers, and complainants. Only the nights were quiet as day's end sent soldiers retreating to hall or garrison, while a goodly number of those who served the keep's daily needs departed Crosswell for family in town.

Geoffrey glanced ahead of him, his gaze catching

on three tiny whitewashed cottages set near the inner gateway. Although standard housing for the impoverished sort of noble widow who came seeking a sheriff's protection, these houses were a poor substitute for a home, not wholly unlike Crosswell's hall. But, no matter how tiny and inconvenient, within their walls the women would find a privacy not available to them in any other part of Crosswell.

No smoke rose from any of their rooftops. Geoffrey frowned at this. He'd sent a man ahead with the order to make one ready for the widow. Someone would rue this day if his message had been ignored. He'd not have the widow and her noble cousin sleeping in the hall, only to cry rape the next morn. He let his thoughts shift from Lady Freyne to her son.

The chaotic moment of their meeting left Geoffrey with an image of a pasty-faced lad who was too thin for his gown. From what he remembered of Aymer of Freyne, the man had been a great bull with too-loud laughter and a cock standing ever ready to find a sheathe, however perverse. How could such a man have gotten so whey-blooded a son from the bold bitch who was his wife?

Suddenly, an image of that fiery vixen, unclothed save for her glorious hair, flashed before his inner eye. Geoffrey caught his breath as the picture brought his body to instant aching. He stifled a groan. Why her, when not even the prettiest of whores stirred his blood?

Passavant gave a startled snort, waking Geoff from his own perversity. One of the keep's corps of children was sprinting toward them, dashing from the narrow inner courtyard toward the gate that separated court-yard from bailey. For a moment Geoff's heart took flight, dreaming it might be his daughter come to greet him.

They entered the brief dimness of the gateway at the same time from opposite ends. The child raced on past him. By the time Geoff guided Passavant onto the cobbled apron at the keep's base, he was nigh on drowning in his false hope.

"My lord!" The cry came from above him. Geoffrey looked up, his lopsided vision framed by the arch of his helmet's nasal into its brow. His undersheriff, Martin de la Bois, flew from the keep's door and down the stairs to ground level. On the young knight's heels came the servants and soldiers who'd been in the hall. "Freyne's heir escapes!"

"Hie, all you men and after him!" Geoffrey shouted as he spurred Passavant into a turn and came face-to-face with a crowd of mounted men.

Stirred to violence by the cries and the surge of men and horses around him, the big gray raised himself to strike. Cursing quietly, Geoffrey worked with hand and knee to convince Passavant this was no battle. Men tried desperately to wrench their mounts out of the way. A massive iron-shod hoof caught a smaller palfrey on the shoulder, sending the poor creature stumbling and shrieking, while its rider fought free of the saddle.

Only partially reassured, the big gray circled once more, then settled, head toward the keep's door. Geoffrey stared at the portal in surprise. Standing on the landing in full view of the courtyard was a tiny figure. Although what little light escaped the hall left her face in shadow, he knew her.

Cecilia.

His daughter clung to the stair rail, the lift of her chin indicating she peered toward the inner gateway.

Geoffrey let his vision fill with her. Her dark hair was wild, meaning she yet resisted her caretaker's comb. The dress she refused to relinquish was rent and worn in places and now too short. In the next moment, her head lowered and she scanned the inner courtyard where he sat on his mount.

Geoffrey froze, incapable of breath as he awaited her reaction to his presence. Her gaze barely touched on him before she was gone, vanished as if she were spirit rather than flesh. His heart died, just as it had all the other times she rejected him.

Once, eons ago, she had loved him. Although it had been almost a year since he'd last held her, Geoffrey could still recall the sweet smell of her as she lay her soft cheek against his neck. There had been joy in feeling her small hands locked in perfect trust around his neck.

His jaw tight against the pain of losing her, Geoffrey dismounted. Why did hope persist? He thrust Passavant's reins at the gray's regular groom, then yanked off his helmet. He needed to accept that the daughter who had loved him was gone, destroyed by the same madness that had consumed her mother. All he had left of his Cecilia was an empty shell, speechless and fey.

He turned, only to discover that Crosswell's men were still in the courtyard and still mounted. "Damn you all," he shouted, and the pressure in his heart eased. "Do not sit there with your fingers in your ears. Dismount and help Sir Martin fetch back that boy."

As men scrambled from their saddles, Osbert's voice echoed off the tall inner walls. "My lord, we have him. He but wished to greet his lady mother."

"God be praised that there are a few men in this keep with wits in their heads," Geoffrey snarled, then turned on those in the courtyard. "Get you all within your barracks and out of my sight. Brainless asses, every one of you." He strode for the gateway.

"Welcome home, my lord sheriff," one of the guards called to him. "We didn't recognize the boy, else we'd have stopped him."

Geoffrey grunted in surprise at the greeting. Generally, his passage to and from the keep was completed in silence on both sides. He glanced ahead of him and saw a ring of men, some mounted and some on foot, surrounding the woman and her child. At his quiet word, the men turned away as grooms came from the stables to take the horses. Within a moment, 'twas only himself, Sir Martin, and Lady Clare who remained to watch this meeting between mother and son.

Lady Freyne sat where she'd dropped after dismounting, her hands now cupped against the boy's beardless cheeks. Tears glistened in the widow's eyes. The chin piece of her oh-so-proper wimple was already damp with the fruit of her heart.

Irritation woke in Geoffrey. Lord, but the woman was worse than a monk's water clock. Drip, drip, drip. He glanced at Lady Clare. The second noblewoman stood well back from her cousin, her stance saying she felt she had no place in this meeting.

Lady Freyne drew a shaking breath as a smile trembled on her pretty lips. "God be praised. Jocelyn, my dearest boy. How I feared for you."

The woman's voice was filled with the love she bore her child. Envy, sharp and painful, rose in Geoffrey as the lad hugged his mother. She could speak with her child, touch him, and be touched in return, while his daughter refused him because of what her mother had laid upon his face.

"Aye, and so you should have, for 'twas terrible," the boy said with a deep and tragic sigh. "Maman, you must save me from these cruel men. That one"— he pointed a quivering finger toward Martin—"made me sit before him on his horse, even when I told him I must never ride. And, when I warned him I could not bear the wind in my ears, he but laughed and said it would not kill me."

Geoffrey's brows rose in admiration at the boy's cleverness. In the same breath, Jocelyn of Freyne fed his mother's worries for him, while he worked a subtle attack against the man he viewed as his kidnapper. And the boy received a swift and satisfying reward for his efforts. While Lady Freyne cried out in dismay, Crosswell's undersheriff pounced on the insult the same way a hawk took a lure.

"What sort of nonsense is this?" Sir Martin snarled. Dark of hair and beard, the young knight's brows drew sharply down over eyes equally as black. Anger made dusky color creep over his bold features, staining his olive skin. "You complain when you are none the worse for your journey, save for the pinch hunger puts in your belly. And that is your own fault, since you refuse to eat with us."

Geoffrey glanced askance at the man. Martin de la Bois was cursed with an overwhelming good nature. That one so eager to inflict happiness on others could be goaded by a boy into such a show of impatience did not speak well of his new ward.

Jocelyn of Freyne turned on Martin, a scowl on his small face. "I told you I was ailing, but you only laughed at me," he retorted.

Not only was there a touch of vindictive triumph in the lad's voice, but an utter disregard for the respect due a man who was both ten years his senior and knighted. This show of spirit, however ill meant, made Geoffrey eye Freyne's heir a little more closely. Henry was wrong; the boy was not the weakling the world believed.

"Why, you nasty brat," Martin cried. The young knight advanced on Jocelyn, his hand raised to deliver the correction the lad so richly deserved. Geoffrey stepped forward and caught his undersheriff's arm to stop him. A slight shake of his head was enough to remind Martin that such chastisement was not his to give.

Left unchallenged in his misbehavior, the boy's mouth quirked upward in brief triumph, then drooped into a sad expression. Jocelyn turned on his mother and coughed weakly. "Maman, I ache. The air catches in my lungs, and my skin warms with fever."

Instead of scolding him for his disrespect, Lady Freyne laid her hand on her son's high forehead. "Aye, you are a bit warm," she agreed, then leaned her head against his chest to listen. A tiny frown appeared between her brows. "Your breathing is clear enough, but I think me we must have a care with you over these next days." 'Twas a gentle remark.

She looked up at Geoffrey, a new humility touching her face. "My lord, Jocelyn will need to remain within doors for the next week, else he'll be taken by a cough. 'Tis a terrible thing, this cough of his. It wracks him for weeks, leaving him gasping for every breath."

Geoffrey stared at her. Her meek manner was but a shield, behind which she hid this iron command. Why in God's name was he drawn to her? She was like her son, offering not the slightest shred of the respect due him.

"My lady, Jocelyn is no longer your concern, but mine." 'Twas a blunt statement.

Her shoulders bent in what seemed acceptance, but 'twas only momentary. In the next instant, her spine stiffened and her jaw squared. "So he is, but if he's to become Freyne's lord, you will need to heed my warnings as to his health."

Jocelyn shot her an astonished glance. "Maman, you know full well I'm to be a monk, not Freyne's lord. Tell him so." The boy looked up at his new warden, his chin thrust out in defiance.

"A monk!" Martin retorted, his words sharp. "Not even the Church would want you. At least, not until you've had some manners beaten into you. 'Tis something I would happily offer to do."

Lady Freyne gasped in shock at the young knight's threat. "Nay, do not speak so to him, for it only sends him into melancholy." She grabbed her son to her, a hand stroking his back in an effort to soothe.

From above his dam's head, the boy shot a triumphant glance toward Geoffrey's undersheriff. Then Jocelyn stepped back and turned a commanding look onto his mother. "Maman, I hate this place. On the morrow we must leave for Nalder."

Geoffrey choked back his rising dislike of the lad. Save for the fact that 'twas he who was stuck with the spoiled and overbearing brat, this whole encounter might have been hilarious. He slipped off his steel-sewn gauntlets and tucked them into his sword belt.

"Jocelyn of Freyne, I have heard enough of your rudeness. Know you that from this moment on, so unruly a tongue will bring you only the sting of my discipline." Geoffrey held up a bared hand to indicate exactly what would sting the lad. "Take you my first command and hie yourself back into my hall."

Lady Freyne gasped, but the boy only turned his back on his new lord. Taking his mother by the shoulders, he shook her. "Maman, you must get me away from this place," he said, as if she were his servant and not the one who'd given him life. "I am growing ill, I can feel it."

Geoffrey's hand flashed from his side, catching the boy across his face. 'Twas a blow calculated to startle more than bruise. Jocelyn stared at him for a brief instant of shock, then dropped, sobbing, to the ground.

"Jocelyn!" His mother scooped him into her arms. When she looked up to their warden, her coppery eyes were wide with fear for her child and still glistening with moisture. "Oh, my lord, I pray you do not abuse him so. Did I not beg your pardon?"

"You name rightful correction abuse?" Geoffrey stepped back, shocked by her open insult. Damn the bitch, but Henry was right. She meant to stand between him and the boy at every turn.

On irritation's heels came regret. 'Twas his own fault, for making it seem he might hurt her child because of what she'd done. He drew a breath and attempted an explanation. "My lady, 'tis not on your doorstep that blame for this incident lies. Jocelyn has behaved rudely, and 'tis only this I seek to correct. Now that he has earned his just reward for his behavior, the matter is quit between us."

"Striking out is your manner of correction?" she protested. "Please, my lord, look upon him and see how small he is, so frail and thin. You'll break him with your blows."

Geoffrey shook his head both to refuse her words and acknowledge the impossibility of being warden to both the woman and her son. "My lady, I find myself suspecting the only frailties and weaknesses he owns are the ones you've taught him to use."

He reached down and took the child by one of his thin arms. "Rise, boy, and come with me. The morrow will ask much of you. 'Tis time we both retired."

"Maman, stop him this instant!" Jocelyn screamed, clinging like a limpet to his dam. "How can you let him take me when you can see how I will be abused?"

"I cannot stop him," Lady Freyne said helplessly, her arms yet holding her child. Written on her face was her struggle between head and heart. Where one said she had no choice but to release her son, the other demanded she hold him tight.

Geoffrey lifted the child from her embrace. The boy thrashed against his hold with astonishing vigor for one so close to death's door. Jocelyn's face twisted into a mean expression as Geoffrey set him on his feet. "Maman, I think you love me no more, wanting me dead so you may love that new babe of yours," he shrieked, attempting to hurt her in his spoiled determination to have his way.

"Boy," Geoffrey roared, truly shocked at the way the child wounded the one who cared so for him. "Hold your tongue or feel my wrath."

Lady Freyne's control crumbled under her son's assault. "Nay, Jocelyn, 'tis not true. I will always love you. My lord, do not take him from me while he thinks I love him no more."

"What is wrong with you, woman?" Geoffrey scolded, not certain who angered him more: the willful and disobedient child or the widow who had pampered her son until he'd lost his natural respect for a parent. "You refuse to bow before me, a man who is your guardian, yet you turn yourself into a quintain for this lad while he uses his words like a lance to send you spinning."

The pain her son had caused her was so great, she

hadn't heard a word he'd said. "Mary save me, you cannot have him. Leave Jocelyn to me, taking this new babe of mine in his stead, raising him as you will."

As Martin gasped against the depth of the insult the widow did Crosswell's master, Geoffrey stiffened in outrage. His hand drew back in instinctual reaction to her slur. "Mind your tongue," he snarled.

"You'll not hit my mother," Jocelyn of Freyne warned quietly from Geoffrey's side, fighting to position himself between lord and lady.

Not only did the boy's protective movement distract Geoffrey from his rage, it set a grain of hope in him. So there yet lived the nubbin of a decent lad beneath what was rotten. As Geoff glanced back at the boy's mother, his rage ebbed. Lady Freyne's words had spilled from her heart, not her head.

"Never again say such a thing to me," he told her. "When you ask me to take your unborn babe in this boy's place, you infer that you think me a thief, willing to steal from one child to give to another. Were you a man, I would have the right to seek your death on the field for speaking such words."

As the widow buried her face in her hands, Geoffrey turned, dragging the boy around with him, and started across the bailey and inner courtyard. Jocelyn lagged behind, seeking to make himself as much of a burden as he could without overtly resisting.

"Walk or know the consequences for your behavior," Geoffrey snapped.

Although Jocelyn began immediately to bear his own weight, Geoffrey was startled by his harsh reaction to what was a child's normal trick. He sighed at himself, deciding he was overwrought. Aye, and not just by this day, but the whole year. They climbed the stairs, the boy careful to keep pace, then Geoffrey paused on the landing before the door.

Here had Cecilia stood. For the first time since Maud's attack against them, his daughter had reached beyond her quiet world to seek out someone. Why not him, who loved her so?

The ache returned to his heart. What right had he to scorn the widow for her fears over her son, when he tortured himself over his daughter? Geoffrey glanced down at Jocelyn.

The boy watched him in return, resentment and dislike written openly on his face. What ached in Geoffrey deepened at yet another rejection. Why should he expect otherwise, when even his own daughter would have nothing to do with him?

Then Jocelyn's eyes narrowed, glimmers of rebellion clinging in his gaze. Geoffrey could not bear it. The pathway to this boy's heart would quickly be littered with traps and snares against his warden if the widow continued to interfere. And, of course, she would. From what he'd seen, he doubted she could stop herself.

So it would have to be another man who coaxed this boy out from behind his shield of weakness and into the life he must live. But where would he find a man with the patience and time to train a backward boy? It would have to be someone impervious to resentment.

Geoffrey smiled slightly as he identified just the one he needed. The morrow would see a messenger flying south along the road to Ashby manor. With a strong horse, 'twas certain he could have his response the day after.

"Come, boy," he said with a new gentleness in his tone, "you'll need to get what rest you can tonight.

The morrow won't be an easy one for you." He led his now-temporary burden across Crosswell's undecorated hall, up the spiraling stairs at the room's back and into his second-story living quarters.

Chapter 8

Elyssa woke with a start, then tensed, awaiting the wave of sickness that usually came at this instant. Nothing. With a prayer that the babe in her would leave her in peace today, she welcomed hunger's dull grind.

Where was she? Her breath coalesced before her in a chilly cloud. The only thing shielding her from the cold air was the rough, woolen blanket. Beneath her lay another coarse blanket, prickly and harsh.

With another start, Elyssa realized she was alone. She glanced around the darkened room, relief rising as she recognized the darkened outline of her cloak on the clothes pole. It hung there on its own, its hem brushing the top of their traveling basket but without a trace of their riding gowns. She sighed. Clare must have been here, and taken their garments to the laundress.

As panic departed, she groaned at the stiffness in her back and legs and fell back against this mattress, such as it was. Her eyes felt gritty and swollen from last night. Once her sobs had started, the moment the sheriff wrenched Jocelyn from her arms, they'd refused to cease. Numbed by her body's exhaustion, she barely remembered Clare leading her to this place, wherever 'twas.

Yesterday's events returned with alertness in all their painful details. There was no hope that Lord Coudray would listen to her. Last night, he had despised her fears for Jocelyn, inferring that she imagined her son had nearly died a dozen times. Jocelyn *was* going to die, and there was nothing she could do to stop it.

The hopelessness of her situation made her eyes fill. Elyssa wiped away her tears, cursing this weakness of hers, even as she sought protection from the memory of Lord Coudray striking Jocelyn. How dare he make good on his petty threat of retaliation by hurting her son?

Not true, her conscience chided quietly. Jocelyn had been unspeakably rude. Had she not been so overwrought with concern for his well-being, she might have scolded him herself. But not abused him.

Elyssa frowned at herself. What did it matter whether the sheriff was in the right or wrong in correcting Jocelyn? He was still the same man who refused to understand that her son could not be trained in the ways of knighthood. The memory of Maud's letter flickered through her thoughts. Somewhere in that tale lay the tool she needed to force Geoffrey FitzHenry to heed her. If she was to protect her son, she would have to be swift in finding what she needed.

With her mind set on a goal, she rolled onto her back, suddenly aware of a cacophony of sounds. There was the dull, continuous clanging of smiths' hammers against metal. A chicken clucked from just outside her wall. From nearby came the steady thud of hooves against beaten earth followed by the tug and groan of a cart, moving to the tune of the beast's steps. A man called out, asking name and business.

She peered up through the room's dimness at the

ceiling. Above her a crisscrossed framework of sticks was topped by a layer of thatching. It rustled with more life than could be accounted to the wind. Grimacing at the nasty sorts of creatures that might drop on her from the bundled reeds, she sat up, braced on her arms.

There was a merry fire dancing on the hearth, a slab of stone about ten feet from her toes. Where the smoke should have been drawn upward through a hole in the thatching, most of it seemed to remain within the chamber. A sliver of sunlight crept beneath the door to reveal a hard earthen floor. The light was just bright enough to show that time and dampness had stripped big patches of whitewash from the walls.

Beside the heap of straw that served as her bed, the room held only two stools near the door, and a tiny table against the far wall. Atop the table lay Elyssa's green-and-yellow everyday wear, taken from her traveling basket, her stockings and shoes sitting beneath it. God bless Clare.

The blanket rustled beneath Elyssa. A rat! She yelped and flew to the table side. She shuddered in revulsion and looked around the dirty hovel for signs of the rodent.

"He takes my son and then subjects me to this? Mother of God, but the peasants at Freyne lived in better style than I will at Crosswell," she said, anger coming on panic's heels. Her determination to repay the sheriff in kind grew. She would find his secret and bend him to her knee.

The cold seeped into her bones and she dressed swiftly, tugging on gowns and cinching her belt around her waist. She dug in her purse for her comb, then dug deeper still. Beyond her prayer beads, she had only four silver pennies. Elyssa freed a disgusted breath. Why hadn't she thought to bring more coins with her?

As soon as she could, she'd collect coins from Nalder's treasury and her mills, the dower from her marriage with Ramshaw as well. Aye, she need all the wealth she could gather to soften the atrocities her foul warden meant for her.

Fingers flying, she plaited her hair, then donned her wimple. Once she was properly attired, she turned to the table. Clare had done more than set out her clothing. Beside a basin of water lay a cloth, a small loaf of thick bread, a sizable wedge of cheese, and a cup of watered wine. There was also a bowl of pottage. The babe and she found the bread and cheese tolerable, but not breakfast soup.

After she'd washed her hands and face, she made it her day's goal to find Crosswell's bathhouse and truly soak the dirt from her body. She pinned on her mantle, then grabbed up the water basin. Throwing open the door, she made as if to dispose of the water, only to grab back her motion so abruptly the water sloshed over her arm.

An old woman dressed in red was passing within arm's reach of Elyssa's door. The grandmother, her face as soft and wrinkled as a dried apple, limped along, a heavy sack over her bowed shoulders.

A soldier in a boiled leather vest over a dark tunic and chausses pushed his elder aside. "Out of my way, old woman."

Striding past Elyssa's doorway, he exited Crosswell's inner gate and bumped shoulders with another oncomer, a man whose gray hood was pulled so low Elyssa couldn't see his face. 'Twas his ink-stained fingers, laced before him as if in prayer, that suggested he was a clerk.

Mary save her, this hovel was so close to the gate that every passing foot and hoof would send dirt and noise scattering into its interior. She closed the door behind her, then walked around the cottage's corner. Chickens pecked and scratched at the wall, suggesting 'twas a treasure trove for them.

Impulsively emptying the basin onto the unsuspecting fowl, which scattered in a flurry of squawks and feathers, she left the broad dish on its side to dry, then scanned Crosswell's bailey. Fortress or not, geese grazed alongside horses on the grassy open area, just as they might at any other place. Doves ascended and descended over one end of the field, suggesting that there was a cote beyond her field of vision.

Directly across the rutted pathway from the cottage, stood a blank length of raised stone. The wall lacked the thickness given to defenses and was barely taller than most men. Extending from the inner wall into the bailey a short distance, it took a sharp turn. A garden?

Elyssa crossed the path, then followed the abutting wall to where it was breached by a small gate. When she pushed open the wooden door, she smiled. Who would have believed it of such a rough-hewn place as Crosswell? Not just a garden, but a beautiful garden.

Protected from the wind, the enclosure was a bit warmer than the outside world. Two gravel pathways quartered the interior. The back left quadrant was hidden from her view by a tall hedge, its entrance a square cut from the greenery. The back right quarter was a kitchen garden, filled with neat lines of pot herbs and winter vegetables.

The two front areas were yet carpeted by grass, retaining color despite the season. Beds, empty now for their winter's rest, swirled across the sod in sweet flights of fancy. Roses, dormant as well, were set be-

tween the espaliered fruit trees and grapevines that
lined the inner walls. Some of the trees yet held tight
to their dying foliage, making for bright splashes of
color against dull stone.

She retreated, closing the gate, then wandered to
the garden's opposite corner and peered around it.
Two long buildings stood here, one of them using the
garden's wall as its own back support. Stables. Even
with the stink of burning coal heavy in the air, her
nose still told her this.

A paddock stood behind the second building, extending slightly forward so she could see one end of it.
Instead of hurdles—the usual fencing made of uprights
woven with branches—this enclosure was hemmed in
by slats bound by leather thongs to thick posts. There
was enough space between the slats for Elyssa to see
that the ground inside the enclosure was torn and broken, churned by many a hoof.

"Left hand!" a man shouted from behind the stable
wall. "Come now. Cease this nonsense and do it."

A trotting pony appeared in the paddock heading
straight for the fence line. In its saddle sat . . . Jocelyn.
Her son wobbled, then his feet flew free of the stir-
rups. He slipped to the side and dropped to the
ground.

"Mother of God," Elyssa breathed in panic as she
raced for her son. Her boy lay, stunned and helpless,
beneath the creature's hooves. "Jocelyn!"

She tried to thrust herself through the slats of the
fence, but her skirts tangled around her legs. A hand
caught her by the upper arm and yanked her backward. She cried out in surprise and not a little fear;
soldiers were no respecters of women, regardless of
rank. Elyssa freed a breath of relief when she saw
'twas the sheriff.

Today, Lord Coudray had left off his mail and wore a short tunic of a deep blue color under a gray mantle. His legs were clad in brown chausses with boots of the same color. With his hood thrown back, the sun gleamed golden off his hair.

"This is no place for you," her warden said sharply as he dragged her away from the paddock. With her arm yet captive in his grip, she had no choice but to follow him.

"My son! He's hurt," Elyssa cried out in protest, trying to dig her heels into the hard earth and hold her place.

"There are others to tend him now," her captor said in frigid reply.

When she continued to resist, he caught her around the waist. Pinned to his side, she had to keep her feet apace with his. His grip was almost painful. Elyssa looked up at him, ready to complain, then thought better of it. He was staring straight ahead, the tense line of his jaw suggesting deep rage.

As much as she despised herself for it, her old fear returned. Here at Crosswell there was no one to save her from the sheriff should he choose to beat her. 'Twas time to consider a retreat.

"My lord, I only wished to aid my son."

He said nothing, his fine profile so hard, it could have been carved from marble. Fear rose to a higher pitch as he forced her past the garden wall and toward the cottage she'd just left. He meant to abuse her in private where he need not worry over interference.

They crossed the rutted pathway and stopped before the hovel's door. Lifting his booted foot, Lord Coudray pushed open the thick door. Dry and hard, the leather hinges cried as the wooden panel swung wide. He shoved her into the small chamber.

Elyssa stumbled across the room, righting herself as she caught the edge of the table. Behind her, the door slammed shut and the bar dropped. She snatched up the bowl of pottage and turned, ready to launch it at him.

He stood directly in front of her. With a flick of his hand, the bowl flew from her fingers. It shattered on the hearth, the contents sizzling in the fire.

The urge to bend her shoulders, to protect herself from the coming blows, rode her hard. Elyssa's back stiffened in protest. Never again. She was no man's wife now.

She launched herself over what had been her bed, but her feet slipped in the loose straw. Instead of reaching the doorway, she fell into the heaped mattress. Lord Coudray caught her by the waist and lifted her with ease. In the next moment, she found herself trapped against him, her back to his chest.

With a short and desperate cry, Elyssa strained against the arm around her waist. Her fist in her hand, she thrust her elbow toward his stomach. He caught her arm, preventing the blow. She lifted a foot.

"Do it and you'll rue this day for years to come." 'Twas a low growl.

"Leave go," she shouted to hide the fact that his threat had set her foot back upon the ground. With her free hand, she tore at his arm around her.

"Cease, madam." His arm tightened until she could feel his belt's knot cut through her gowns. "I am no more impressed with your bad manners than with your son's. How do you dare step between me and that boy after I commanded you away last night?"

"Damn you to hell, but you will free me," she said, her voice softening as defeat washed over her. 'Twas time to accept she could do nothing for her son. Mary save her, she couldn't even protect herself.

Nay, she wouldn't give way to him. Her heart pounding in her throat, she arched away from him. "I do not recognize your right to command me away, not when my son is injured and needs me."

"Injured?" The man behind her freed a harsh laugh. With his mouth so near her ear, she felt the warmth of his breath on her cheek. "That boy is not hurt, which is all the more astonishing since he throws himself from the saddle. This riding lesson had become a siege. I find myself wondering how bruised he'll allow himself to become before he decides 'tis less painful to ride than to fall."

"Throws himself from the saddle?" Elyssa said in disbelief. "That cannot be. No one wants to fall from a horse."

His arm around her eased slightly, as did his hold on her elbow. A moment of silence passed. Then another. His breathing calmed from that of rage to a more normal pace.

Elyssa leaned to the side so that she could look over her shoulder at him. Firelight gleamed golden in his hair and marked the strong lift of his cheekbones. The dimness hid his scars and turned the patch over his eye into naught but black velvet.

His anger was gone, but so, too, was the emptiness that had so chilled her two days ago. Instead, amusement sparked blue lights in his eye. Mary save her, if she'd thought him beautiful when his soul seemed dead, he was more so now.

"You fell from a horse." It was a quiet comment, accompanied by a quick, upward quirk of his brows.

Elyssa lifted her shoulders in tremulous acknowledgment. "Aye, and then it stepped on me." She shuddered against the horror of being trod upon by a horse, of hearing her own leg snap beneath its weight. " 'Tis a terrible thing," she finished in a whisper.

He watched her for another quiet beat, then he smiled. Elyssa caught her breath in surprise. His teeth were even and white. Amusement caused a tiny dip in one lean cheek and set strong lines to rising from either side of his chin. His smile was a beguiling thing, tempting her to return it with one of her own. It made her forget he now owned her child and that he'd given her this hovel as a home ... then it set her nerves on edge.

'Twasn't right that they should stand here this way, her back to his front and his arms around her. They were so close she could feel the pounding of his heart. Or was that her own heart's pounding?

She tried to turn in his arms. After a brief hesitation, he allowed her movement. Setting her hands on his chest, she pushed free of his now-loose embrace. Although he let her step back, he kept one hand on her hip. His touch seemed to burn through her gowns to sear her skin. She took another step from him, and his arm dropped to his side, his smile yet lingering on his lips.

Elyssa sought safety by returning to the matter at hand. "Horses are dangerous beasts. That one broke my leg, and I lay abed for months while it healed. I could just as well have died." 'Twas an earnest plea as she begged for his understanding.

Geoffrey FitzHenry nodded, then tilted his head to one side to better consider her. "Therefore do you seek to protect your son from what you fear will hurt him. And, so many are your fears for him, you've made him into the whining babe he is."

Elyssa huffed in outrage at his accusation. "My fears

are justified. Jocelyn nearly died in his coming and only just survived his first year. Since then, he's been plagued with illness. My lord, you must heed me. Jocelyn is not like other children. Although he owns strength of intellect, his body fails him."

"You have misjudged him, my lady." Amusement continued to tease at his mouth, keeping the corners lifted. "I see a strong and healthy boy hiding beneath the weakling he's convinced he is."

Elyssa crossed her arms against a vicious spike of temper. "In one day's time you know him better than I, who has had him twelve years at my side? Why do I waste my breath trying to make a man understand anything? Your sort hears only what they wish to hear. I tell you now, my lord, heed me or willfully blind yourself to the dangers that lay ready to destroy my son."

The amusement died from his face, taking with it all the life, until his features were stone once more. "My lady, I am but half blind and then not willfully so." Although his voice was harsh, pain flowed from him until she swore it filled the tiny room. He turned on his heel and started toward the door.

Elyssa freed a soft cry of dismay, having forgotten the patch that covered his ruined eye. Now he would return to Jocelyn and wreak vengeance for what had been unintentional on her part. She leapt forward and caught him by the arm. "Forgive my wayward tongue, my lord. Truly, I forgot your blindness."

Lord Coudray turned so swiftly, it startled her into a sudden backward step. "Did you?"

He stood before her, studying her face as if he could divine the answer to his question by his gaze alone. Unsettled by his intensity, Elyssa took another hesitant step away from him. At her movement, his face relaxed, warming from stone to flesh once more. How could a mere look seem like a touch against her skin and set her pulse to racing?

In that moment, she recognized his interest was no longer that of warden to ward, but man to woman. Oh, but there was danger for her here. Color rose in her cheeks.

"My lord, I think we should open the door. 'Tis not meet, you here with me alone." She meant this to be a strong suggestion, but it came forth as a wavering sigh.

For some reason, this made him smile, but there was more of curiosity than amusement to the curve of his lips. Although he did not move, of a sudden he seemed closer to her. Elyssa tried to step back, but the wall blocked her path.

Mary save her, but he was tall. Her crown reached barely above his jawline. Both of Elyssa's husbands had been short men, her father as well, and she found his height intimidating.

He raised his hand to lay his fingertips to her face. She stiffened. When his fingers brushed softly down the curve of her cheek, there woke a wondrous tingling in her skin. Her breath caught in her, both in fear and longing.

"My lord, you must not touch me so." Her attempt at strident complaint failed completely.

His thumb moved across the roundness of her chin, then stroked her jawline. Even clothed in her wimple, there was a responding warmth where he touched. He must be stopped. Grabbing his wrist, she forced his hand back to his side. When she released his arm, she gave a silent prayer of thanks that he didn't reach for her again.

Still, he watched her. His gaze touched her lips, then lowered past her throat to the thrust of her breasts.

Elyssa drew a shaking breath. With a simple look, he made her feel as if she were disrobed before him. Her whole being filled with a sharp awareness of the man before her.

Lord Coudray was lean of form, almost too much so, but his shoulders were broad, his tunic sleeves clinging to the hard curve of his upper arms. Where her husbands had been old and well girdled with fat, Geoffrey FitzHenry's belly yet held the trimness of active youth. His legs were long and well-formed. Elyssa's gaze drifted back to his shoulders. If he were to draw her near, she could rest her head against his shoulder with ease.

She gasped at the thought. Lean her head against him? This had gone too far already. Elyssa looked to the room's far corner. "My lord, 'tis most improper, you being here. You must go now." 'Twas a hopeless, husky plea.

Cringing once more against showing him her vulnerability, she glanced at him, praying he hadn't noticed. He had. His gaze returned to meet hers, pleasure and amusement mingled in his face. Anger replaced distress, shielding her in its fiery embrace.

"Go now." Much better. Hard and commanding.

He reacted by stepping back from her, the pleasure ever so slowly receding from his expression. "Not until you've heard and understood what I expect of you while you reside at Crosswell."

"Speak, then. I am listening," she said, her words chipped from stone. Aye, anger made it much easier to deal with him, especially since his presence still fed the twisted longing he'd wakened in her. At her harsh response, the remaining gentleness departed his features. Elyssa breathed a sigh of relief.

"This have I already told your cousin," he said. "Go

you no farther into the bailey than the garden gate, that place being set aside for your use. Nor do you enter Crosswelltown without my permission. Where right of law allows you to take your morning and mid-day meals in the hall and attend services in my chapel, do not trespass into what are the private areas of the keep."

Elyssa stared at him in disbelief, every sensation he'd made in her destroyed. After ten years without a man to tell her to sit and stay, it galled her to have to submit to these rules, especially since he was no relation to her. "My lord, what you ask makes me beholden to you for my every step. Would it not be simpler to fix a chain to my leg and set me in the rooms with your other prisoners?" 'Twas a scathing remark.

For some reason, her words made him smile again. "So it would. 'Tis a shame it isn't an option." He continued over her outraged gasp. "This is not a family keep, but a garrison filled with men whose charac-ter I do not know. Moreover, the coming weeks will see keep and town fill with folk from every walk of life wishing to receive the king's justice. What I ask of you is for your own protection. Disobey me and I will confine you to this room with a guard at your door."

"In here? I would die, eaten alive by the vermin that infest this place." 'Twas an angry, if futile, jab at him.

He glanced around him, then turned in more careful survey. "God's blood, this hovel isn't fit for swine." His voice was raised in angry surprise.

She set a fist on one hip. "If that is supposed to convince me you didn't know what this place was like when you set me here, you have failed most miserably."

Her goad struck home for answering fury flared in the sheriff's expression. "Do you think me so petty I would punish you in this way?"

Elyssa looked away from him and hedged. "I think we are two people who do not care much for each other."

"Truer words there could not be," he snapped. "However, I'll not subject you to such a dwelling."

"Kind of you," she murmured without much gratitude as he went to the door and lifted the bar. When he opened it, he was bathed in a sudden burst of sunlight. "My lord?"

At her call, he stopped and turned to look at her. His hair glowed like gold, his gown turned to sapphire. "What is it?" 'Twas an impatient question.

"In your rules for me, you forgot to mention my son. When am I allowed to see him?" Hope welled in her as she willed him not to refuse her.

He drew an irritated breath, then his expression smoothed into what seemed almost compassion. "Madam, you make this harder for yourself than it need be. Let him go. Set your thoughts instead upon the child growing within you. Jocelyn must now leave you behind, cleaving unto his foster father."

She trembled against the wound his words did her. "I cannot let him go, he is my child," she breathed. "How can you be so cruel? I tell you what you want from my son will be his death, and you not only ignore me, you say I must let him go with a smile upon my face. My lord, my heart is breaking. You cannot know how it hurts to have your child stolen from you as you are taking mine."

"You are wrong." Pain turned his words into a

hoarse and aching whisper. The sudden sadness in his face shot through her, deeper than her own misery. He stepped outside and shut the door behind him.

Stunned by the depth of his soul's agony, Elyssa stared at the door. True, he'd lost his sons, one to stillbirth and another after his birth, but he still had his daughter. Once again, the ranting phrases of his dead wife's letter rose in her. There rose in Elyssa a terrible fear that what Lord Coudray sought to conceal was better left hidden.

Chapter 9

From his seat midpoint along Crosswell's high table, Geoffrey glanced out at the crowded hall. The midday meal filled the big room with all those in Crosswell's employ, along with travelers and those folk who owned the right to eat at the king's expense. Two long lines of tables, concealed by white linens that reached the wooden floor, stretched from either end of his own table to the hall door. The flat ceiling above him kept the noise of so many folk, all slurping and chewing at the same time, trapped within these walls. 'Twas an awesome noise.

Suddenly, his heart longed for Coudray. Not only did that hall's high-flung rafters absorb some of the sound inherent in this close-quartered lifestyle, his home had grace and style, making life comfortable. Here, instead of plastered and painted walls, blank yellowish stones stared back at him. Without linen panels to block it, the rubble-filled walls oozed a damp mustiness into the atmosphere. This keep's only concession to the niceties of life was its chapel, and that was only because some previous sheriff sought to buy his passage to heaven.

Had this fortress been favored by the old king, it might have been better fitted. However, early in his reign Henry had sold his forest rights to feed the city's forges. In turn, Crosswelltown kept the kingdom supplied with iron products. But, without a forest, Henry came here no more. As for Richard, Henry's son and England's present king, well, he stayed in his realm not at all, disliking both the country and his subjects.

Geoffrey considered spending his own coin to prepare the place against the arrival of the justiciars, then discarded the notion. The swift coming and going of his predecessors suggested he might well bear the expense only to soften someone else's life. He turned his gaze back to the bread trencher before him.

Behind his right shoulder, Jocelyn coughed quietly. Usually, a squire offered his master portions from the day's dishes and filled his lord's cup. 'Twas an important lesson in the value of service and obedience. In Jocelyn's case, Geoffrey did not demand he serve, since the boy was not fated to be his squire. Nonetheless, 'twas a good lesson for the lad to stand at his better's shoulder for the duration of the meal.

There was another cough, slightly louder this time. Irritation washed over Geoff. Their riding lesson yesterday had ended in defeat for Jocelyn. However, once the lad had begun to pull the reins, he had also begun to cough. Geoffrey suspected it was a secondary form of protest.

At the high table's right end, just beyond the chaplain, there was a sudden scraping as a bench moved. Lady Elyssa rose from her place beside her cousin. Her dark red braids bounding at her hips, she walked swiftly for the hall's end and the door. So had she done the day before, leaving the hall before the meal ended at the sound of Jocelyn's cough. How she could possibly hear her child over the din was a mystery that Geoffrey could only attribute to a mother's native instinct.

Geoff watched as she paused at the screen guarding the room from its open door. She sent a worried look at Jocelyn, then her gaze slipped to him. If resentment and accusation, even dislike, touched her pretty features, there was no revulsion.

Wonder rose in him. She truly didn't see his scars when she looked at him. What was it that made her forget? As soon as she realized he watched her in return, she moved around the screen and was gone.

He looked back at his trencher as the corner of his mouth lifted in strange amusement. 'Twasn't his scars or Sybil's tales or even brute force that frightened that woman. Yesterday, she'd nearly leapt from her skin at the brush of his hand against her face. That a woman twice married could be so fearful of a touch was a riddle, begging for solution.

The boy behind him coughed again, distracting Geoffrey from his impossible thoughts for the lad's mother. Appetite died and he pushed back from the table. Martin, seated at his master's left, glanced angrily over his shoulder at the boy.

"My lord, stay and eat, while I take him. Just a day," he offered, a snarl on his lips. Geoffrey hid his grin as he heard Jocelyn sidle a little farther to his master's blind side, away from the undersheriff.

The porter called out from the door. "My lord sheriff, a messenger comes for you."

Geoffrey looked toward the door. A man, dressed in leather sewn with metal rings, his leggings and cloak hem mud-soaked, strode past the hearth stone at the hall's center. He paused there, waiting for a sign from the sheriff that he could approach. The flickering firelight showed Geoff 'twas the man he'd sent to Ashby.

He glanced to his undersheriff. "Martin, you may

stay and finish or come with me, but my meal is at an end."

"I'll come with you, my lord."

Geoff turned on his bench until he could see his ward. "Sit you and eat."

Jocelyn moved toward the bench, then halted and stared at the messenger. An instant later, his eyes narrowed and his arms rose to cross tightly over his scrawny chest. "I have to pray first."

"The chaplain said our prayer before the meal started," Geoffrey replied evenly with a negative shake of his head.

" 'Twas not the sort of prayer I am accustomed to saying," the boy retorted. "I would kneel in the chapel and give greater thanks."

"If yesterday's prayer was good enough for you, so is today's. Sit and eat." 'Twas a quiet command.

"My lord"—the chaplain leaned forward from his place next to Robert the Smith, the townsman who owned the greatest number of forges—"you shouldn't discourage such devotion in your squire. 'Tis a fine thing in a man."

Geoffrey glanced at the long-faced priest who served the keep. Although Father Raymond gave him communion and heard his confessions, the priest was still half convinced of his lord's unholy nature. Geoff's jaw tightened as he understood this battle of Jocelyn's could have repercussions beyond just the two of them. 'Twasn't worth fighting, not if yon messenger brought salvation from this wholly reluctant squire.

"He may do so, but if he's not returned to the table in a few moments, you'll have to fetch him and see that he eats."

The priest gave a brief nod. "That I shall do, my lord."

Geoffrey rose from his bench to look down on the lad. "Go, then."

His ward's eyes widened in insolent triumph. Without a word of thanks, since he limited the number of words he doled out to his warden, he turned and ran toward the chapel door. There was a sudden movement under the table near the townsman's feet.

As Geoff glanced in surprise at the rustling tablecloth, the wealthy commoner eased back on his bench to look. A dog's nose appeared from beneath the cloth. 'Twas the cur that Cecilia favored, the creature being as wild and masterless as his daughter. It pushed free of the linen, then trotted from one table to the next in search of scraps.

A wave of Geoff's hand commanded the messenger to follow him upstairs, into the privacy of the sheriff's office. Martin came abreast of Geoffrey as he started toward the spiraling stairs at the corner of the room.

"My old nurse always said the only thing worse than spoiled meat is a spoiled child," his undersheriff offered in a low voice. "If you stay your hand because of the widow, not wishing to endure her anger, I would happily beat the boy and take her rancor for it."

A subtle pounding woke in Geoff's head. Was there a situation for which Martin's old nurse did not have a saying? "I pray that won't be necessary," he replied with a quick glance at the young knight, then stepped into the stairwell.

The tightly turning steps were illuminated by north-facing arrow loops, cut through the thickness of the keep's wall. 'Twas a murky light to match a drear day. The enclosing stair wall opened on the second floor as the steps continued to circle beyond it to the third-floor storerooms.

Although the keep's second floor was the same size as the hall below it, it had been partitioned into chambers. A narrow corridor was created by an interior wall which ran along side the outer stone wall. Doors were cut into this innerwall leading into the private rooms.

The nearest chamber was his work room, the place where the more intimate details of his office were conducted. Well past the midpoint of the corridor lay the entrance into the royal bedchamber, his to use when there was no one of greater status in residence. The final door opened onto the tiny chamber where Cecilia and her keeper resided.

Geoffrey tried not to glance down the hallway toward that distant door. Despite his will, he looked. He always did. There was no sign of his daughter.

Entering the first door, Geoff strode within the room's dim and icy confines. Chests, containing the copies of contracts and agreements the sheriff kept for shire residents, hulked along its walls. Two tall desks, complete with stools for his clerks, sat close to a brazier. The glowing embers in the thing's brass pan were meant to keep scribling fingers nimble, not heat the room.

Near the far wall sat a chair, tall of back and thickly armed. 'Twas a smaller version of the one in the hall, the massive piece used by the justiciar when court was in session. Geoffrey sat in his chair, while Martin came to stand beside its arm. The messenger stepped forward, dropped to one knee, his head bowed.

"Have you a reply for me?" Geoff asked.

The man looked up, his face without expression. "My lord sheriff, Lord Ashby agrees to foster your ward only on the condition you bring the boy to Graistan keep and attend Lord Ashby's wedding to be held the day after All Saints."

"Not fair, my mother's youngest son," Geoffrey muttered. He'd already told Gilliam he couldn't attend his brother's hastily arranged joining with the heiress of Ashby. Graistan, Geoffrey's family home, lay outside this shire, miles to the south.

Martin howled with surprise and delight. "Gilliam? You would make your brother that brat's foster father?" The young knight rocked back on his heels, grinning widely at the thought of his dearest friend saddled with Jocelyn of Freyne. "Were it me who did it to him, I'd say it'd serve him rightly for all the pranks he's pulled on me, but whatever has Gilliam done that causes you to hate him so?"

" 'Tis a good opportunity for both of them." Geoffrey scowled irritably at his undersheriff.

Martin, well aware that his propensity to laughter wore on his employer, caught back his grin. Geoff's gaze shifted to the toes of his boots as he sought to hide his irritation from the young knight. If his need for Martin weren't so great, he might have dismissed the man on the spot. But, the de la Bois had been centered in this shire since the Conquest; locked in this knight's somewhat silly brain was a wealth of knowledge about the shire and its foremost families that an outsider like himself dare not disparage.

At last, Geoffrey freed a harsh breath at what his brother asked of him. "Damn Gilliam, but I don't have time to waste going to Graistan."

Martin cleared his throat. "Well, my lord, All Saints is yet two weeks away. With forethought, we might make more of your journey than just a ride."

Geoff looked up at him. "How so?"

"Four of the properties that need viewing lie not a

mile in any direction off the south road. Aye, and there's that complaint against Whiteknave manor. The widow asks we remove the tenant her stepson placed in what is her dower. The court sanctions his removal. Only three miles off the road. And if you circle to the west on your return, you can escort the appraiser, Ralph la Porcher, onto the manors of Dyster and Stouthyrde. He complains the bailiffs at those places resist him in the task set to him by the royal escheators. There could be others. In the meantime, I will send the summoners against the justiciars' arrival. Those who wish escort to Crosswell can meet you along the road and take protection in your presence.''

Geoffrey stared at the young man in astonishment. Where Geoffrey would have ridden, hell-bent for Graistan, then returned at the same gut-wrenching pace, fretting all the while over the upcoming courts, Martin made use of his steps. Such ingenuity deserved recognition. Aye, and an apology as well. 'Twas wrong of him to dislike a man simply because he was good-humored.

''Well-done, Martin. The idea would never have occurred to me. And, my thanks. You tolerate your surly employer well.''

Taken aback by the unexpected compliment, color flushed over Martin's face, even touching the arched bridge of his nose. ''I—I seek only to serve you well, my lord sheriff, being grateful for your trust in me. Nor do I find you surly, only liking of your solitude. Since I know I tend to the exuberant, I try to keep a tight rein in respect for your nature,'' he finished with a suddenly shy smile.

Geoffrey gave a brusque nod, his mouth held in a tight line. Jesu, if this was Martin's idea of reined exuberance, he'd never survive the unrestrained man.

"Well then," he said to the messenger, "if you have no more for me, go you and eat your fill. Martin, call the clerks and that boy who will be Gilliam's and let us be on to plotting my course."

As Elyssa left the hall door, she nearly collided with a muddy messenger on the exterior landing. Too worried and angry to notice, she flew down the steps. Is this what the sheriff called care? While Jocelyn coughed in coming illness, Lord Coudray made her son stand behind him and watch while he ate. The cruelty of it bit deeply into her heart.

When she reached the cobbled floor of the inner courtyard, she glanced beyond the gateway to her cottage. True to his word, her warden had commanded the place be refurbished. Workmen were now laying new thatch on its roof.

Not wishing to be alone in their presence, Elyssa hesitated. Gentle rain settled on her mantle shoulders. 'Twas too wet to use the garden. There was no place for her to go but back into the hall. With an angry huff, she returned to the doorway.

When she reentered, the porter had his back to her, having moved into the room with the messenger. She glanced around the edge of the screen and into the hall. Jocelyn saw her, and his brows lifted in hope. The pain in her grew. There was nothing she could do for him. Save pray.

She glanced to the southeast corner of the room. Here lay Crosswell's chapel. Slipping out from behind the screen, she made her way to that holy chamber, careful to keep near the wall and out of reach from the lowest servants.

The area set aside for worship surely reflected the depth of need in Crosswell's residents, for the room

was larger than her hovel and richly decorated. Walls
wore a thick coat of plaster on which had been painted
scenes representing the twelve stations of the cross.
So, too, had the floor been painted, red and gray-blue
squares to look like tile. A marble altar stood on a low
dais, covered by a cloth embroidered in silver thread.

As in the hall, thick arches of stone held the chapel's roof aloft. Here, their capitals were decorated with
a crosshatched design. Although there were spaces set
aside for either candle or lamp, no light burned. Instead, the confines were bathed in what moist gray
light flowed through the two, east-facing slits behind
the altar. Near the final slit, in the room's corner, was
the entrance to the wall chamber where the priest
lived.

In a habit borne over her lifetime, Elyssa dropped
to her knees before the altar step. Digging her beads
from her purse, she started into the familiar routine
of prayer, only to pause. Her gaze moved to the bits
of colored stone. The cross at its end slipped through
her fingers.

What good would prayer do? Mary save her, she
wasn't even allowed to spend a quiet moment with
her son. Elyssa drew a quick breath. Women, mothers,
should protect one another. Yet God's holy mother
had abandoned her.

"Damn you," she hissed to the Virgin, then threw
the prayer strand from her.

"Maman!" Jocelyn cried out as he flew into the
chapel.

Elyssa gasped in surprise, slipping down to sit on
the floor, then sent swift words begging forgiveness
and offering apologies heavenward. She threw open
her arms in invitation. Instead, her son grabbed one
of her hands, trying to lift her to her feet.

"Maman, come now. He is gone from the hall. If we are swift, we can leave without his noticing."

His words brought with them a wild flash of hope, but it swiftly died. Elyssa sadly shook her head. "Jocelyn, 'twould be a useless endeavor. You are mine no longer now that your sire and brother have died. Should we try such an escape, the sheriff would only hunt us down and return us to this place."

"What are you saying?" Jocelyn cried in outrage, resisting as she tried to tug him down beside her. "Do you want me dead? Maman, you saw me fall when they forced me to sit atop a horse. You must do something to save me."

Tears trembled in Elyssa's eyes. "What would you have me do, Jocelyn?"

His brows rose high in his forehead, while his brown eyes were liquid with hurt. "Maman, 'tis truly horrible for me. I am missing so many lessons. If I do not die soon, my mind will surely falter. 'Ere long, I will be but the same as my father, a dull-witted brute."

Elyssa gasped as she heard her own words fall from her child's lips. "Jocelyn!"

Her son ignored her as his complaints continued. "Not only that, but this place is perverse. There is a girl who comes into Lord Coudray's bedchamber at night. When I wake to say my prayers at Matins, she stares at me. Last night, she tried to crawl under my blanket with me. *Me!*" he cried in angry astonishment. "You must tell the lord sheriff that I am to be a monk, not a knight! Monks have naught to do with tarts like that girl."

In Elyssa's mind rose a picture of a sultry whore, the sort that a man as handsome as Lord Coudray could win to his bed. Educated by Freyne's tastes, a tawdry mélange of images flashed through her mind.

Oh, but numerous were the ways Geoffrey FitzHenry might ease his base nature. The thought of that same whore laying hands on her innocent child made rage well in her.

Elyssa came to her knees, her heart afire. "This I will not tolerate. 'Tis one thing for the court to take you, but quite another for Lord Coudray to debase you."

"Go away!" Jocelyn's voice rose in a high-pitched wail as something small darted into the chapel. "There she is again! Now she follows me everywhere. Maman, I have had enough of her. Tell her to leave me be!"

Elyssa caught the impression of a wee figure dashing around the altar. She rose, then came to squat at the altar's edge. Crouched at the wall, between the chamber entrance and arrow slit, was a tiny girl surely no more than five.

"This is your tormentor?" she asked, sending her son a laughing glance.

The child's hair was so dark a brown 'twas nearly black. Matted, it hung around her small, round face in ragged strands. Her dress had once been a pretty shade of rose. Now 'twas faded, stained, and torn in spots, the hemline ripped halfway 'round the garment. Yet, despite the dirt on her gown and her snarls, the girl's face was clean. Her hands, as well, with the nails neatly pared.

Elyssa looked past the shield of hair and caught her breath in admiration. The lass was a striking thing, with well-defined features, flawless skin, and fine, dark lines as brows. Her eyes dominated her face, fringed in thick black lashes with irises so gray, they were nearly clear.

Jocelyn's shadow watched her in return, lower lip caught in her tiny teeth. Elyssa shifted in her stance, moving just a little farther around the corner. The child stiffened, her wispy brows drawing down just a little, as if contemplating escape. In the end, she scuttled just a bit farther to the side, keeping herself out of reach.

Jocelyn stepped onto the altar dais and looked over the slab at the girl. "My maman says you must stop following me. I am to be a monk and will have naught to do with women."

The girl gazed at Jocelyn. Where there had been fear in her face when she looked upon Elyssa, there was only curiosity for the boy.

"Maman, you must say something," Jocelyn insisted, turning to look at his dam.

The wee child's gaze darted back to Elyssa, her lips mouthing the word "maman" and her brows raised as if in question.

Wholly fascinated, Elyssa lay a hand against her breast. "I am his maman," she said in soft explanation, pointing to Jocelyn.

The girl's eyes widened, and her brows raised in surprise. She glanced from the woman to the boy. When her gaze returned to Elyssa, she frowned in wary disbelief, as if such a thing couldn't possibly be true.

"I am indeed his maman," Elyssa said again. "Who might you be?"

Jocelyn gasped. "Maman, do not speak with her, heed me! I am falling ill." He coughed, loud and long.

Elyssa shot a glance at her son, then looked again. His eyes were narrowed, and his mouth was naught but a thin line. 'Twas the same look her husband had bent on her when he intended that she do as he said, will she, nill she. A new and different anger woke in Elyssa as she came to her feet.

"What is this?" she asked, her voice hard. In her ears rang the sheriff's words, saying she made herself a quintain for her son to use. "Do you speak so to your maman?"

"My pardon," Jocelyn said with but a modicum of regret, "but you were not heeding me."

There was a step at the door. Elyssa turned to see Crosswell's priest enter. Father Raymond nodded to her. "Pardon me, my lady, but 'tis time for the lad to take his meal."

"Maman, I do not wish to go from you." Her son threw his arms around her.

Elyssa sighed and freed herself from his embrace, then knelt before him. She brushed the strands of his fine brown hair from his brow. "You are not leaving me. Do I not reside at Crosswell with you? Now, love, go and eat. You must keep up your strength." She enclosed him in her arms.

For an instant he stood stiff and sullen, then he melted. "I do not want to die, Maman," he begged softly. "You must save me."

"Am I not here to tend you, should you fall ill?" she murmured in return.

Jocelyn pushed back from her, his face dark with hurt. " 'Tis not good enough. I want to go home. I hate it here." He turned and ran from the chapel. Elyssa came to her feet, her heart yet on the floor where it had fallen at her son's words.

"Did you come here seeking me, my lady?" the priest asked.

Elyssa stared at him a moment, longing to spill on him her worries over Jocelyn. Ah, but all she'd get for her trouble would be tongue-lashing for daring to complain over what God had set upon her son. "Nay, Father," she sighed in defeat.

The priest shrugged, then moved into the room, kneeling and bowing before the altar. There was a scrabbling sound from behind that holy table, then the little girl came racing around it. The lass skirted the inattentive priest and flew to the door.

"Who is that child?" Elyssa asked, staring after the girl. "It seems she's taken a fancy to my son."

The priest shook his head. "Pardon, my lady, I didn't see her. Even if I had, I'm not sure I'd know. We're plagued by children here, all of them by-blows. Our cook has a soft spot for them and sees them fed. Makes them swarm worse than rats, it does. Most likely, she's one of their ranks."

"No doubt," Elyssa replied dryly. "Thank you, Father."

When she left the chapel, Clare was waiting for her near the door screen. Glancing to the top of the room, Elyssa's gaze fixed on Jocelyn. 'Twas doubly hard to lose him, when he thought she'd abandoned him. If only he could understand how powerless she was.

She joined Clare, and her cousin offered her a weak smile, then lay her arm around Elyssa's shoulder in an attempt at comfort. As they walked from keep to cottage, Elyssa's thoughts drifted to the lass who found her son so fascinating. 'Twas a shame the child was the lowest of the low, without hope of any advancement. Not only was she a pretty thing, but there had been a quick intelligence in the girl's eyes. That thought brought Elyssa to so sudden a halt, Clare nearly stumbled.

"What is it, 'Lyssa?" her cousin asked in quiet concern.

"We were speaking French, not the Englishers' language," she said to her uncomprehending relative.

"That child is not some soldier's by-blow, not when she understands the Norman tongue."

As Clare continued to look blankly at her, Elyssa fell silent in the swift realization that Lord Coudray's daughter would speak French. Jocelyn said the girl came into the sheriff's bedchamber at night.

" 'Lyssa?"

Elyssa opened her mouth to tell her cousin about the child, then shut it again. Now, why would the sheriff's daughter be wearing rags?

Chapter 10

There was a quiet knock on the door, just loud enough to startle Elyssa from her sleep. Bracing herself on an elbow, she glanced around the room. With the fire covered, there was naught but heavy darkness within these walls. Who could be tapping in the middle of the night?

Beside her, Clare snored softly, yet deep in slumber. Elyssa yawned and decided she'd misheard. Rolling onto her side, she tried to find a more comfortable lump on the pallet that had replaced their pile of straw. Would that her bed might soon arrive. Ah well, at least this mattress was clean, the dried-grass filling yet retaining the sweet scents of summer.

There was another tap. "Maman?" His quiet call was accompanied by the hard pounding of a man's fist.

With a gasp, Elyssa leapt up. Lacking a bed robe until the remainder of her belongings arrived, she snatched her mantle from the clothing pole on the wall and threw it over her shoulders to shield her nakedness. Her unbound hair tumbled around her as she lifted the bar from its braces, then dropped it. It thudded dully against the hard floor. Oiled leather hinges, newly replaced, whispered a welcome to her son as the door swung inward.

Framed in the portal by the predawn grayness of the

sky was not only her son, but Lord Coudray. Standing behind them was a troop of horsemen, their mounts stamping and snorting. Over the rattling of harnesses, men coughed and swore softly against the cold morn air.

Elyssa stared at Jocelyn. Beneath his cloak her son wore a heavy brown tunic with fur cross-gartered to his legs. Gloves covered his hands. He was in traveling attire. A terrible notion occurred to her. She bit her lip and looked at the sheriff.

If Geoffrey FitzHenry's head was bare even against this icy morn, he wore his mail with a thick cloak over his shoulders. His gaze leapt from her face to her loosened hair and downward, then he blinked.

"Close your cloak, my lady," he breathed.

With a soft cry, Elyssa stepped back into the darkened room, clutching her mantle tightly shut. Lord Coudray followed her, his mail jangling quietly with each step. Jocelyn came, too, for his cloak was trapped in the nobleman's hand.

"Feed the fire so you can see," her warden told her as he closed the door, "but know you we haven't long."

Elyssa knelt by the hearth, her fear growing greater with each passing instant. Setting the cover to one side, she offered the glowing coals twists of straw and sticks until flames appeared. When she could delay no longer, she rose and faced her visitors.

"Why have you come here so early?" Although her voice was flat, her words broke against what trembled within her.

The tall knight released his hold on Jocelyn's cloak. "Bid your lady mother adieu," he told her son.

Jocelyn launched himself at her, his arms clutching frantically around her waist. "Maman, he is taking me away from you." There was more outrage than fear in his cry.

" 'Lyssa, what is it?" Clare asked sleepily, rising on her elbows to see.

" 'Tis the lord sheriff and Jocelyn." Elyssa's voice was strained as she fought for calm. "Stay where you are," she warned her cousin while she freed a hand from her mantle to hold Jocelyn more tightly to her. Her gaze returned to Lord Coudray. "Where do you take my son?"

"To his new foster father, Lord Ashby." The gentleness in his voice only made the hurt he did her worse.

She stared at him in bleak understanding. Her need to retain some control over her child had driven the sheriff to this decision. " 'Tis me, 'tis my fault you take him from Crosswell. My lord, if I vow to remain at a distance, will you reconsider?"

Lord Coudray shook his head, then raised a gloved hand to rub at his brow. "Lady Elyssa, in all truth, 'tis that our temperaments, your son's and mine, do not suit. He will be better served if Lord Ashby takes him. Now, kiss his cheek and bid him to be brave and thrive."

Although his words made it clear the path was set and would not be altered, his voice conveyed compassion for what this leave-taking cost her. Would that he scolded or shouted, then she might rage at him for once more stealing her child. Instead, she did as he said and dropped to her knees before Jocelyn. When she'd pressed her lips to her son's smooth cheek, she sighed, "Go with God, my precious child."

"Maman, do not let this happen!" Jocelyn's voice was sharp with disbelief at being forced where he didn't wish to go. "You must save me."

"Boy, did I not warn you to keep a civil tongue?"

Lord Coudray caught his hand in Jocelyn's cloak and pulled her son from her arms. Turning, he opened the door. "Osbert, come take the lad and see him mounted on his pony."

As Jocelyn departed, Elyssa sagged, her arms aching to hold him still. Her son would die, and she would die when this new babe came. Never again would she hold her own child in her arms. Tears flowed as she sat back on her heels, her sobs soundless.

Lord Coudray turned back toward her. "Have you any items you'd like to send with your son?"

She swallowed. "There's naught—" Her voice caught, then words spewed from her. "My lord, is this Lord Ashby who takes my son a good man?"

The sheriff drew a harsh breath at her question, then freed a short, sharp laugh and shook his head. He came to squat before her. Elyssa stared helplessly at him, her hand caught to her mouth to still its trembling.

With the first hint of a new day lightening the room, she could see the golden gleam of his hair and the bitter amusement that marked his handsome face. He watched her for a brief instant, then the scarred corner of his mouth lifted. This bit of a smile awoke the warmth in his blue gaze.

"Elyssa of Freyne, 'tis a miracle you've survived two husbands with that tongue of yours yet intact." His voice was low, as if he meant to keep his words private from Clare.

"What did I say that was amiss?" Her question was barely more than a breath.

"You imply that I would send your son to one who abuses children." He lifted his brows in a gentle chide.

Elyssa bowed her head. "My pardon," she managed, although that had been the exact implication of her question. There was cold comfort in his response. Although Lord Coudray didn't believe Jocelyn's new keeper would abuse him, there were so many ways her son could be hurt, and she'd not be there to see that he survived it.

Metal rings rasped, one against another, as her warden brought his arm forward to crook his finger beneath her chin and lift her face. "You must take heart," he said in quiet command. "It can do that babe within you no good for you to be so despondent." 'Twas as if he truly worried over her unborn child.

"I cannot help myself." Her voice was but a broken sigh. "He is my son, and I love him."

He nodded slightly in understanding. A tear reached her chin, and he brushed it away with his thumb. "If you are willing to bear the cost of a clerk, you are free to send missives to Ashby. Give your messages to Sir Martin, and he will see they reach the boy."

'Twas a sop, nonetheless Elyssa snatched for it. "Many thanks, my lord."

"You are welcome." Again, his mouth quirked upward, then he released her chin and rose.

She listened to the door shut behind him. Outside the cottage, men called and horses lifted their hooves into a trot. In another moment, there was nothing but the crowing of cocks, what with the forges silent at this hour.

"I have lost my son," Elyssa keened. "How can he survive without me to keep him safe? He will die, Clare."

"He is stronger than you believe," Clare said from their pallet. "'Lyssa so too must you be strong. For the babe's sake."

"I am tired of being strong," Elyssa said. "Despite

how I have worked and fought for him, Jocelyn is still torn from my arms. I need my child, else I live but half a life."

"You have a child, waiting to be born," Clare replied.

"This babe?" Elyssa pressed her hands against her still flat womb. "Why should I care for him, when his coming will most likely mean my death?" Aye, death would be easier to face than losing yet another child.

Then desperation surged through her. Yesterday, had she not chided the heavenly mother for deserting her, only to have Jocelyn appear in the next moment? Ignoring logic's scream against such fancy, Elyssa threw herself up from her knees. Tossing aside her mantle, she snatched her gowns from the clothes pole.

" 'Lyssa, what are you about?" her cousin asked warily.

"The chapel," she cried, her head trapped within the folds of her undergown.

"Ah, to offer your prayers for Jocelyn's well-being," Clare replied in approval.

Elyssa yanked on her overgown, then shoved bare feet into her shoes. Leaving her laces undone, she cinched her belt at her waist, then tied a thong around the mass of her uncombed hair. Once her mantle was pinned on, she stuffed her hair into her hood to hide her uncovered femininity. She turned for the door and saw Clare rising as if to join her.

"Nay," Elyssa whispered. She needed time to rant to the Virgin on her own.

Throwing open the door, she raced for the inner gate. The guard watched her come toward him. With dawn's light creeping into the sky, there'd been no sense in closing the gate after the master's departure.

It would only need to be opened again, to admit the flood of day workers.

"Wait," Clare called after her, leaning from the doorway in her undergown.

Elyssa ignored her as she crossed the short court-yard and took the stairs at a run. Newborn light streamed across the inner walls, bringing a warm golden glow to cold bricks. The keep would quickly come to life, the chapel filling with those who came to take mass. She pounded on the keep's closed door. "Open, damn you," she shouted.

The porter opened his peephole. "There's yet a quarter hour before I need do so." He yawned, sending the scent of yesterday's roasted garlic wafting into the air.

" 'Tis Lady Freyne. You'll open or I'll see word of this reaches Sir Martin. I have need of the priest," she lied.

At her threat, he grumbled beneath his breath, but the bar moved and the door creaked open just wide enough to allow her to enter.

The hall was smoky and dim, the air within fetid with the scent of so many bodies in so close an area. She picked her way over sleepers, then entered the chapel. Kneeling, Elyssa pulled open her purse and sought her beads. There was nothing in the leather pouch, save her four pence.

She gave a weak cry and pulled her purse free of her belt, then emptied it onto her palm. The silver coins rattled as they fell into her hand. Her beads were missing. Ah, but she'd left them here yesterday. She glanced frantically toward the wall where she'd thrown them. Nothing. Coming to her feet, she peered around the altar. Nothing there, either.

Tears filled her throat. 'Twouldn't be the same, but

she had to try. She knelt before the altar and demanded that God's Mother return her son to her. Moments passed. Jocelyn did not appear.

Elyssa sank back to sit on the floor. This had been a stupid thought from the first. Both God and his lady wife had closed their ears to her pleas, abandoning her as had every other soul from whom she'd sought protection.

Dawn's light, gone rosy, shot through the slitted windows to touch the altar. Stripped of its rich covering for the night, the marble table glowed as if bloodstained. Elyssa raised her face into the pink light.

"Know you, Mother of God, when your Lord Husband set Freyne upon Jocelyn's shoulders, He killed me. My son will die without his maman to keep him safe. Now, what reason have you and He left me for living?"

There was a soft touch on her shoulder. Elyssa gasped in surprise and turned, only to have her surprise deepen. 'Twas Jocelyn's wee shadow. The girl blinked, then reached out a finger to touch the tears on Elyssa's cheek. Her wispy brows rose in question.

"I am sad because Joceyln is gone," Elyssa told her, her voice trembling.

The lass's mouth formed an 'o' of understanding. Then, pushing off Elyssa's hood, she eyed the thick mass of russet hair that tumbled free. Extending her hand, the child combed her fingers through a loose strand.

There was great comfort in this babe's caress. Elyssa wanted nothing more than to gather the lass into her arms. Even holding someone else's child would ease her pain. She extended her arms, then caught back her embrace, remembering the girl's fear.

"My heart breaks for my son," she whispered to the child. "Might I hold you, *ma petite*?"

The girl's eyes flew wide at the endearment. Confusion and hope woke in her face as her mouth again moved. *Maman?* she asked, but there was no sound to it. Her unnatural silence only added to Elyssa's sadness.

"I am no one's maman now," she told the child.

Hope grew stronger in the child's expression, then died into what might have been disbelief. Her beautiful eyes narrowed, and the lass raised her gaze toward the door. With nothing more than a jerk of her chin, she asked in perfect silence after Jocelyn.

"He's gone." Tears choked Elyssa, and she bowed her head against her pain.

Suddenly, there were arms around her neck. The lass held herself still for a long moment, as if testing for her own reaction to this bold move. Elyssa raised her head. Fear and longing filled the child's face.

"Oh, but you need me," Elyssa breathed in hope.

The poor babe's teeth worried her lower lip as a frown creased her smooth brow. *Maman?* she asked again in her silent voice. 'Twas a terrible, lonely plea.

"Aye, come to me, poppet," Elyssa said in a whisper. "Ease what is tearing me in two. Let me be your maman."

The lass breathed a long sigh of relief, then leaned her head against Elyssa's brow. Her mouth moved, *Maman*.

Elyssa carefully closed her arms around the child. There was no resistance as she pulled the silent babe into her lap. Instead, the girl tucked her head into Elyssa's shoulder and closed her eyes. Rocking against her own loneliness, Elyssa bowed her head into the lass's shoulder and wept.

*   *   *

Reginald looked at the leather-wrapped package the
merchant had just handed to him, then glanced at the
commoner. "From Crosswell? You are a messenger
for the sheriff?" If he was, then Reginald would have
to feed him dinner and let him sleep the night in
Freyne's hall.

Heavyset with ruddy hair and skin, the Englishman
looked all the bigger wearing so many layers of clothing against these harsh mid-December days. He
grinned, revealing a missing front tooth. "Who, me?
Nay, I am but a traveler who passes through Crosswell
on my journeys, my lord."

Reginald fought a pleased grin at being addressed as
Freyne's lord. During the past two months of owning
Freyne, he'd slept in the lord's bedchamber and took
his meals in the lord's chair at the high table's center.
Each passing day, his desire to make Freyne his alone
had grown.

" 'Twas upon my last visit to that strong keep that
I didst meet a noblewoman, who resides there under
the sheriff's protection. She heard I came by this road
and asked that I bring you the packet. Aye, a sweet
lady she was," the merchant continued, "and most
concerned with your well-being. The Lady Clare fears
your days of Christmas will be lonely ones." There
was just the slightest bit of a leer in his tone.

Reginald straightened as joy poured through him,
then his brows drew down at the insult the merchant
inferred on his sweet love. "Do you have a care with
your tongue, man," he said, his voice low and
menacing.

Startled, the merchant stepped back, his mouth gaping in surprise as he saw a night's comfort and a warm
meal slipping out of his grasp. "My lord, I meant no

insult," he said in hasty apology. "A thousand pardons if I have done harm. Look you upon this packet and see that I have meant only good in bringing it to you."

Reginald relaxed. True enough. "Aye, and for that am I grateful," he replied. "Will you bide the night with us, partaking of our hospitality?"

"Why, my lord, your offer is kind, indeed. I would be honored." The big merchant bowed his head in acceptance.

Formalities addressed, Reginald snapped his fingers at the pantler. "Alexander, see that this man and his servants are fed and have a place by the fire this night. I am retiring." He turned, trying not to run toward the wall and bedchamber beyond it.

With his brother's chamber door shut on the outside world, Reginald knelt beside the hearth and peeled back the leather. White cloth. He tugged on the fabric and smiled at the shirt, his fingers rubbing appreciatively against the fine linen. She had made this for him as a wife might clothe her husband.

Setting the garment upon the cot he used, he tore off his tunic and shirt, then put on Clare's instead. His smile grew. She had done well in estimating his proportions.

Dressed only in her shirt, his chausses and boots, he returned to her packet. A fold of parchment remained within its confines. He opened it. The words filling the sheet were fine, with just a hint of flourish to their form. Had it been she or a clerk who'd penned this missive?

To my dearest love, Sir Reginald of Freyne,
    I pray this finds you in abundant health and strength of heart, yet missing me as I ache for you. There has been much ado at Crosswell whilst

*the justiciars held their court. What with the keep
and bailey so crowded with foreigners and uncouth
commoners, Lady Freyne and I were trapped in
our cottage. In our need to add variety beyond
embroidery to pass this heavy time, we turned to
sewing. Thus, do I pray you will indulge me in
this gift, given in the spirit of the upcoming holy
days. 'Tis my fondest wish that you might find
some little pleasure in what my fingers have
wrought.*

*Your last missive brought such disheartening
news. It seems impossible that the bishop would
object less to our degree of kinship, than to the
fact that you marry a barren woman. Know that I
will love you still if you find yourself unwilling to
flaunt convention.*

Reginald sighed and stared at her generous offer to
free him from his promise to wed her through the
more casual joining of a handfast. Such a thing would
have been acceptable if he were to remain Freyne's
steward, but he now meant to become Freyne's lord.
In that case, lack of a priest's blessing made Clare his
concubine and he, a laughingstock for taking a woman
who could provide him neither property nor heirs. A
touch of anger woke in him. Let them laugh. What
right had any man to tell him he couldn't own the
woman he wanted? He turned his eyes back to the
parchment.

*I would thank you again for your concern over
Lady Freyne and her child. Although my lady
cousin was incapable of swallowing the tonic, she
strengthened on her own. The babe seems finally
to have settled within her, no longer plaguing her*

with sickness. However, she waits daily for news of Jocelyn's death, now that he's been squired away from Crosswell. 'Tis her depression over this issue that concerns me. Although her health is good, my lady cousin now believes her child's delivery will take her own life. Thus, would I once more beg your aid.

When I related to Lady Freyne in what regard you hold Freyne's midwife, she remembered the woman and found comfort in what was familiar. 'Tis now our desire, hers and mine, that the woman might attend my lady cousin when she begins her laying in. Although I know the village would be loathe to relinquish her to us for a month's time, we hope she might have an apprentice to take her place while she serves her lord's widow by delivering yet another heir.

'Tis with enduring love and care for you in my heart that I end this missive. Signed this the sixteenth day of December, year of our Lord 1194. Clare, daughter of William de Romeneye.

Reginald freed a long, slow sigh as he refolded the parchment. He came to his feet and seated himself on the corner of his cot. The sheepskin crackled as he turned it over and over in his lap. 'Twas as he expected; Lady Freyne waited to hear of her son's death, Aymer's son being too weak to survive.

As for that babe who persisted in the widow's womb, once again, his own sweet Clare offered him the opportunity to do murder. Aye, but if he took advantage of her and was exposed, 'twould surely destroy the love she gave him. Ah, but if he didn't take the advantage, there'd be no chance to own Freyne. He wanted both, not one or the other.

The fire leapt and danced on its stone, the crack and snap of flame loud in the quiet room as he battled with himself. From outside came the low moan of the wind, soughing around the corner of the hall. In its eerie tones, he swore he heard his brother's voice, begging that he not give way to murder.

Reginald stiffened against that sound. Aymer should have held his ghostly tongue. A lifetime of doing naught but what was right and good for others, only to be repaid with crumbs and disrespect, burned in his gut. The decision coalesced more than was made.

There must be a way to finish the babe that would leave all concerned believing the birth had gone awry. Brows lifting in consideration, Reginald thought through the scenario. 'Twas doubtful Lord Coudray had ever seen a birth and, although Clare might have, it had been at least ten years since she'd done so. As for the midwife, she'd already killed those of Aymer's bastards not wanted by their mothers. For the right number of coins, she'd not flinch at another death.

He lay back upon the cot, his hand closing around the parchment. Clare's shirt lay on him like her body would. In only months, Romeneye's daughter would be warm in his arms forever.

Chapter 11

Yesterday, on the eve of Christmas, Geoffrey had returned to Crosswell for the first time in a month. Hope tortured him as he rode through the gate, his heart praying Lady Freyne's magic had worked. Today, he drowned in disappointment. True, Cecilia now ate in the hall, slept in a bed, and played as a child should play, but she yet hated her sire. The moment she caught a glimpse of him, she was gone.

Thank God for Martin; he'd known Lady Freyne took Cecilia into the garden each day at the same hour. Desperate to see something of his child, Geoffrey concealed himself in the hedged quadrant of the garden, wagering the area was too small and dark to attract the women. Seated on the wooden bench that stood against the garden's back wall, Geoffrey pulled his cloak tightly to him against the day's bitter chill and glanced around him.

Until today, he'd considered this spot wasted space. 'Twas barely wide enough for him to stretch out his legs before him and 'twas only a bit longer than he was tall. Although barren, the tangled network of fine twigs around him remained thick enough to prevent anyone from noticing him, as long as he stayed still. Ah, but with a narrow gap broken in the wee branches, he could see his daughter.

He watched as Cecilia spun past his opening. She was turning wide circles, her little boot steps crunching through a thin skin of snow. Her cloak hood fell back and neat dark plaits flew wide, bright with the ribbons braided into them. Pale skin, a mirror of his own fair coloring, was burnished red against the cold day, but her face was alive with happiness. Then she was gone.

Geoffrey's heart tore between pain and pleasure as he recognized what she wore. The dark green gown and the gray mantle lined in fox fur were his Christmas gifts to her. He'd sent them to Lady Freyne's cottage, where his daughter now resided. With them went a note, asking the lady to make his daughter understand they were from him. Despite that he had touched them, Cecilia chose to wear his gifts.

In that moment, love joined his hatred of the widow. It had been upon his return journey from Graistan, almost two months past, that Martin's message reached him. All that saved Elyssa of Freyne from death at Geoff's hand for stealing his daughter was that itinerary he and Martin had so carefully planned. Trapped by the shire's needs, Geoffrey hadn't breached Crosswell's gates until mid-November.

Yet, in those short weeks, Cecilia had shed her ragged gown and let her hair be combed. Still, worry plagued him. What lay trapped behind Cecilia's silence could ruin her life, but his need for Cecilia's healing was the stronger. Praying what had begun would continue, he didn't interfere, burying himself in his duties, instead.

It had been easy to do. The justiciars arrived barely a day after his return from Graistan, and the remainder of November was eaten by the needs of court.

December took him on the road, aiding the royal appraisers along with his normal duties.

Now, with Christmas come, the whole of England retreated behind their doors and settled before their hearths to celebrate. Even Crosswell's forges stilled, allowing the wind to carry away the reek of their fires. Geoffrey had had no choice but to return to Crosswell. Here, he'd be trapped until the twelfth day.

This time when Cecilia raced past his opening, her dark locks reminded him of Gradinton. In the past months Baldwin had concentrated his energies away from Cecilia. Through those justiciars who'd sat in Crosswell's court, William of Hereford, both friend and bishop, sent word that Gradinton had an envoy in Rome petitioning the pope for an annulment. Hope spiked within Geoffrey again. If Gradinton succeeded in remarrying and Lady Freyne healed Cecilia, he might truly regain the family Maud had stolen from him.

When his lass appeared again, flying out at the end of her outstretched arm was a wooden figure. Like her new clothing and her comb, the widow had aided his daughter in reclaiming this precious plaything, something she'd rejected since her dam's death. Hidden beyond the hedge, Lady Clare and Lady Freyne both laughed and clapped when his daughter dropped dizzily to the ground.

He shifted right and found he could still see Cecilia. Her pretty smile worth his every possession. Lady Freyne appeared within his narrow view. A gust of wind opened her cloak to show him the gentle curve of her expanding abdomen. 'Twasn't much, but having seen most all of her on the morn her son departed Crosswell, this was proof of her fecund state.

Love for his daughter glowed in the lady's coppery

eyes. Jealousy snapped at Geoffrey as the child who had once loved him went easily into this stranger's embrace. When his Cecilia threw her arms around Lady Freyne's neck, he turned his head aside, incapable of watching.

"Come, poppet," she said to his daughter as she bore the child to the garden gate. " 'Tis terrible cold out here. You've romped long enough, and there's a great feast to be had this night."

There was a pause. "Aye, there will be dancing and music. Now, what a shame it would be if you were to miss that because you'd played so hard you dropped to sleep."

Another pause. 'Twas strange, this one-sided conversation. "I know you are excited. Who will dance with you? Why, Tante Clare, of course. Tante Clare is quite the dancer."

"Oh, 'Lyssa," her cousin laughed as the garden gate opened. "You know very well I can but stumble to a tune." The garden gate closed, and their voices faded into silence.

Geoffrey held his place on the bench, trying to breathe against the tangle of hurt and hope in him. His daughter was excited about participating in a noisy, crowded event. Aye, but if Cecilia was to enjoy the feast, he'd need to keep himself from it. Where he was, his daughter could not bear to be.

He could remain in his bedchamber for the whole evening. Memories of Christmas's long past raced through him, bittersweet when compared to his present isolation. 'Twould be impossible to stay alone and listen to the revelers laughing and singing one floor below him.

The loneliness in him grew too great to bear. Just as had happened to his daughter, within Geoffrey grew the need to share this time with other folk. Ach, even if he wished to do so, he could not. Was he not the devil's spawn? 'Twould hardly do to be seen keeping Christmas.

He leaned his head against the wall behind him. 'Twas cold and solid, and no differnt than what now trapped him. The corner of Geoff's mouth lifted against the irony of what he did to himself.

The sky above him was clearing, the morn's thick clouds torn to shreds by a high wind. Nightfall and the bitter chill would bring crystal clarity to the heavens. From the garden, he'd not be able to hear the music and laughter in the hall. Aye, the moon and stars would be his companions—high, cold, and out of reach. It suited him.

Well then, if he was to spend his evening out of doors, he'd be needing a fire for sure. A blanket and a thick cloak would help as well. Geoffrey came slowly to his feet. Still, his loneliness nagged at him, refusing to be assuaged by simple stars. A skin of wine would help as well. Nay, two would do the trick. Perhaps, if he drank until he dropped, he would win an hour free of what ached in him.

Elyssa straightened the skirt of Cecilia's new green gown. 'Twas a handsome garment, well made and decorated by a band of embroidery done in bright threads. The cloak to cover it was even more expensive. A touch of irritation woke in her.

There had been such loneliness in Cecilia's face when she learned these gifts had come from her sire. The wee poppet had run her hands over the gown as if she wished 'twere her father she touched. Was it because of Cecilia's voicelessness that Geoffrey Fitz-Henry ignored her?

Elyssa freed a harsh breath. Nay, 'twas that Cecilia was no son. Geoffrey FitzHenry was but a normal man, who set little value on his female child. A gift once a year and his duty was done.

"There you are, poppet, ready for your evening." She smiled at Cecilia.

The daughter of her heart wrinkled her nose and smiled in return. Elyssa sighed. How beautiful she was, with her dark hair and pale eyes. Would that she could speak.

There was a feathery movement as the babe growing in her shifted. Instead of waking in her the promise of coming life, this only reminded her of what was to come. Her dread of dying during his birth not only set a longing in her to hear Cecilia's voice, but fed her ever-present sadness over Jocelyn. She'd hold her own child nevermore.

Cecilia lifted her brows, sensing more than seeing the pain in her borrowed maman. Eloquent in her quiet, she lay her hands on Elyssa's face in an attempt to soothe.

"Do not hurt for me, poppet," Elyssa said gently, pressing her lips to Cecilia's cheek. "Now, go with Tante Clare and dance until you can dance no more."

" 'Lyssa, you should come," Clare said for at least the hundredth time since Elyssa announced she wanted naught to do with this night's celebration. " 'Tis wrong that you should be alone."

Elyssa came slowly to her feet. "How can I feast and sing when my son sits in some forlorn place, keeping Christmas with strangers who are no blood to him?"

No doubt he ailed as well. December and January were the most dangerous months for Jocelyn. Twice, once when he was four and again when he was six, these winter months had nearly taken him.

" 'Lyssa, why do you think like that? You know nothing of how Jocelyn lives." There was a trace of impatience in Clare's voice.

She turned on her cousin. "You have never been without your family, but I have. Let me tell you of my first holiday away from home. I was but ten and four, a young bride taking the place of a woman who had ruled Ramshaw for twenty years. My stepson was ten years my senior and resented me, commanding the servants to ignore me. Ramshaw had bruised my face the day before because I had spoken boldly to him. They did not keep Christmas in the manner I knew. For them, 'twas but a regular meal, without games, dance, or gift giving. I wept the whole day through, so cold and lonely I thought I should die if I did not hear one kind word."

"But you did not die," Clare insisted. "You were strong and survived, as will Jocelyn. If there was aught amiss, you'd have heard, and you've had no message since that first one."

Ah, but 'twas this lack of communication that was the backbone of Elyssa's misery. Although she wrote on a weekly basis, the only missive she had from her son dated from November's beginning. In it, he wrote that he was feverish and coughing, but his new lord forced him out nevertheless, tromping through fields like a peasant. So too, had he said Ashby's lady was a vicious murderess who threatened to finish her husband and would as soon kill him as speak to him. His final words had been another plea for rescue before illness or his new mistress took him.

Hopelessness washed over Elyssa. She wanted her son. The thought of celebrating while he hurt made her eyes fill. "Clare, I cannot, I just cannot. Go, both of you. Dance for me where my heavy heart will not allow my feet to lift."

"As you will," Clare replied shortly, holding her hand out for Cecilia. "Come, poppet. Make merry with me, then."

Cecilia looked at Elyssa in a last request that she come. Elyssa only shook her head. With that, they were gone.

Setting the bar in the door, she seated herself on the stool before the hearth. Here, where the light was the greatest, stood her embroidery frame, the piece within it half worked. Clare's frame sat next to hers and between them was their basket of threads, brightly colored silks spilling from it.

Her gaze shifted to her bed. It crowded them, leaving no space for a table, but Elyssa didn't care. 'Twas hers. She'd scrubbed away all trace of the men who had owned her, burning the old mattress and refashioning the draperies into wall hangings. With her profits from the mills, she'd purchased a new mattress and then, holding her breath against the expense, bought new material for draperies. 'Twas a wondrous deep scarlet that she closed around herself, Clare, and Cecilia each night.

She picked her needle from the linen. This would be a piece for the abbot of Nalder's monastery, meant to repay him for his years of interest in Jocelyn. As she worked, turning creamy linen into the brown-and-green attire of huntsmen, her thoughts ebbed and flowed over Jocelyn. After an hour of torturing herself, the desire to crawl into bed, pull the covers over her head, and weep filled her.

Setting her needle back into the fabric, she unwound her wimple and loosened her hair in preparation for retiring. There was a quiet tap on the door. Thinking 'twas Clare and Cecilia returning early, Elyssa opened the panel without a challenge. A strange man stood in the doorway, his face chapped by travel and his clothing stained with mud.

"Lady Freyne, dam to Jocelyn of Freyne?"

"Aye," she murmured in surprise.

"I come to you this night from Ashby manor," he said with a tentative smile.

Elyssa gasped. Jocelyn was dead. The thought went through her like a spear, and she crossed her arms to hold herself together. "From the hall or from Jocelyn of Freyne?" she asked sharply.

The man's smile faltered at her fearful tone. "Why, both, my lady. Your son sends you this," he handed her a thin leather pouch. "I'm to return to Ashby on the morrow with your reply."

Elyssa took the weightless packet, her soul steadying in her. If it came from Jocelyn, then he could not be dead. Yet. Mary save her, she prayed 'twasn't news that he ailed.

"Might I visit the hall?" the man prodded.

Startled, she looked up, having forgotten him. "Aye, of course. Make merry with the residents of Crosswell's hall. Good Christmas to you."

"And, to you, my lady," he said, backing away and still eyeing her as if he thought her strange.

Elyssa closed the door, then sat on her stool. Her fingers trembled as she pulled the strings that tied the packet shut. Inside the leather cover lay a single scrap of parchment. She lifted it out, then eased closer to the firelight to read.

My dearest Maman, her son had scrawled. What had happened to the neatness she'd taught him to use?

Greetings from Ashby and good Christmas.

'Tis a fine place, Ashby, and I have many new friends. Maman, I have learned I am not sickly at all, but healthy and strong. Lord Gilliam is proud of my many accomplishments, especially that of throwing the pig's bladder. You were wrong, 'tis not only a sport of commoners as Lord Gilliam takes great enjoyment in it. I have but once beaten my lord in a race with his destrier. I can do no better until I have a stronger steed. When I skate on the millpond, I rarely fall anymore.

Lady Nicola and I ask that you seek out Lord Coudray, reminding him he must send us six kennet pups for Lord Gilliam. We fear he has forgotten, as they have not yet arrived. Maman, they must come before the twelfth night, as they are my lord's final gift. Your loving son, Jocelyn, heir to Freyne.

Elyssa stared at the sheet. He was hale and strong, not ailing at all. He was playing at sports and games, just as his father had. He signed his missive as Freyne's heir. Gone was his desire for the safety of the Church. Then anger roared through her. Two months she had eaten her heart in worry, and he was enjoying himself?

The need to scream out her frustration and hurt grew so strong she choked on it. Not here. With the hall filled with outsiders, the guard remained at the gate. If she made noise, the men would come running. She needed privacy for her rage.

Leaping to her feet, the parchment still caught in her hand, she threw her mantle over her shoulders. Shutting the door behind her, Elyssa raced for the garden. Within this private enclave, she needed no such caution. She slammed the gate with all her might. 'Twas a miracle the thing did not fall to pieces.

"He skates on the millpond? He throws a pig's bladder and races horses? How can he be so callous as to leave me suffering in worry over him, while he enjoys himself?" she shouted.

She stared up at the moon. 'Twas a cold disc, silver against icy blackness. The stars thrust their sharp edges into the darkness, much like the tears cutting at her eyes.

"Mother of God, here I am, so fearful for him that I cannot celebrate Christmas, while he is enjoying himself! He is loving it at Ashby. Do you hear me, Lady Mary?"

Chapter 12

"I cannot comment on behalf of the Virgin, but I can hear you, Lady Freyne."

Elyssa gasped in surprise. 'Twas the sheriff. There was no mistaking his smooth voice; it always made his words sound like music. His call had come from the garden's back quadrant, the area surrounded by the hedge.

Anger came tumbling in again on the heels of her surprise. This garden was set aside for the use of Crosswell's female guests, not its male residents. She stalked to the hedged enclosure.

Lord Coudray sat on the bench, his feet resting near a small blaze. His head leaned back against the wall, the angle of his jaw suggesting he studied the sky above him. With his hood pulled close around his face, Elyssa could barely see his profile. Near the small stack of wood he was using to feed the fire, there was a skin, flattened. Beside it, a cup rested on its side, the lees of what had been in the skin spilling out onto the crusted snow.

"What are you doing in here?" she demanded.

"Why, whatever else but keeping Christmas," he said to the moon. "I am positively drunk on all my cheer. Now, I will ask the same of you. Why are you not in the hall?"

"Because—" her word died half spoken. Because, she'd wanted time to grieve over her poor, lonely, abused son, who was none of these things.

"Oh, but I am a fool," she told herself, anger spiking again. Her words tumbled heedlessly past her lips. "How could he go from me screaming for rescue, then change? I've cried myself to sleep for two months, certain he ached for me in the same way." She extended the parchment scrap before her and slapped it with her free hand. "Then, he has the gall to send me this."

Lord Coudray freed a soft laugh. "How now, madam? Disappointed that your son has not died as you predicted?"

Elyssa caught her breath. "Mary save me, but that is what I'm doing. I'm angry because he thrives in his new life when I believed him incapable." Anger ebbed, but hurt remained. "Oh but, he has forgotten me."

"I doubt that." Her warden shot her a sidelong glance, then patted the bench beside him. "Come, warm yourself before the night makes ice of your tears."

She hesitated. Beneath her hood, her hair was uncovered and undone. They would be without a chaperon. She all too well remembered the last time they were alone. Then, he had watched her as if he meant to eat her alive.

When she didn't move, he turned his head and studied her. Firelight touched his face, laying shadows along his high cheekbones and the well-defined turn of his lips. His nose was fine and straight, his golden brows arched with the same perfect curve as his daughter's. She let her gaze move to the dark patch that shielded his right eye, then along his scars.

As they continued to ripen, they died back into flat white lines. Maud must have used the tip of a knife to wreak her vengeance on him. In another year, they would be nigh on unobtrusive. There was a sudden softening in his face.

"Bear me company this night, Elyssa of Freyne."

Need lay so heavy in his voice, she gasped against it. His loneliness reached out to her, almost frightening in its intensity. Try as she might, Elyssa couldn't turn her back on him.

"As you will, Geoffrey of Coudray," she replied with a brief smile. "Best you take heed. You know well enough I have a cutting tongue and that I speak my mind. I'll hold no truck with you being insulted by me, when 'twas you who asked me to stay."

"I stand forewarned." The smile flowed over his face, setting strong lines in his cheeks while it brought life and warmth to his features. She paused, surprised by her reaction to his amusement. 'Twas a dangerous thing, his smile.

She strode within the enclosure, pausing to lay Jocelyn's betraying missive onto the fire. It took light, sending the smell of burning skin into the still, fresh air. When it was consumed, she moved to his right, seating herself at the end of the bench.

This left her too far from the fire to garner much warmth. She drew her knees up, setting her shoes on the seat, then pulled her mantle around all of her. With her arms locked around her legs, she set her chin atop her knees and stared at the leaping flames.

After a quiet moment, the sheriff said, " 'Tis more likely your son is distracted by the hurried activity of his new life than that he has forgotten you. Much to my surprise, that backward boy of yours progresses at great speed. Lord Ashby is right pleased with him."

"You've had news of Jocelyn?" Elyssa scowled in irritation. "Why did you say nothing to me?"

As she sat on his blind side, Lord Coudray had to turn his head to look at her. He lifted a golden brow. "Would you have believed me?"

Elyssa made a wry face, the emotion aimed at herself. "Nay, I suppose not. By the by, my son wishes me to remind you of six kennet pups you were to send to Ashby. His messenger awaits your reply, planning a morning departure. I sent him to the hall so he might keep Christmas with the others."

"They are on their way," he murmured in acknowledgment of her words, his gaze returning to the sky above them.

Silence fell between them, but 'twas a comfortable quiet. In its embrace, she let her thoughts wander over the events of Jocelyn's life. She'd been so certain he couldn't tolerate becoming a squire. Why? There was no immediate answer to this question.

As the moments slipped by, the cold worked its way through Elyssa's cloak and gowns. 'Twas truly bone chilling, this night. After a quarter hour or so, she could no longer bear the discomfort. To keep her mind from it, she spoke her thoughts aloud.

"I cannot believe he writes to me of dogs. Until this moment, I would have told everyone I met that my son disliked the beasts. When he was but two he met nose to nose with one of his sire's hounds, an alaunt I think. It snarled and snapped at him, sending him screaming."

She drew a breath, meaning to say that since that day she'd made certain he met with no more vile curs. Instead, understanding flashed through her. Jocelyn had been struck in the mouth by a ball, so she'd banned the playthings from their home. Jocelyn slipped on ice, thus no skating. Her own mishap with a horse had made riding impossible for her son. 'Twas as Geoffrey had told her: she'd laid her own fears for her son onto his thin shoulders until they both believed him weak and incapable.

Realization set a sense of failure into her heart. Elyssa shook her head against it. Nay, all that she had done, she'd done for love's sake, wanting only to keep her son safe. Her teeth chattered gently.

Lord Coudray shifted, waking her from her depressing thoughts. "I find I do not like you sitting where I cannot see you," he said, turning his head once again to look at her. "Sit here," he touched the small stretch of seat to his left, "and I will share my cloak with you." He turned back the garment's edge to reveal a lining of otter fur.

Elyssa hesitated. To do as he wished was but a plea for trouble when she ought to go back to the cottage. Ah, but it would be empty and silent in that room for hours to come. Well then, she should join Clare and Cecilia in the hall.

She couldn't. The thought of the crowded clamor set her teeth on edge. She needed time to accept how her son had changed and understand why she'd felt it necessary to protect him so. At last, she simply sighed and did as he asked.

He opened his cloak for her, then, when she sat beside him, put his arm over her shoulders to draw her nearer. Although 'twas a big garment, there wasn't enough to cover them both; it gapped over his chest and legs. He reached beneath the bench and brought forth a folded blanket. Even with that spread over them, there was an area of him left open to the cold. Elyssa shifted nearer to him, pressing herself against his side as she lifted the edge of her own mantle over his chest. A thick strand of hair came with it, streaming across his breast.

"What is this," he chided softly, laughter touching his voice. He caught the strand in his fingers. "How incredibly improper of you, Lady Freyne. You have departed your door with your hair loose."

"I had assumed I'd be private," she replied stiffly.

He only smiled, then turned his gaze back to the stars. But, he kept her hair, his fingers toying with the strand. There was something soothing in his play.

"What do you seek?" she asked him, looking above her as she tried to see what so fascinated him.

"Everything, nothing. Mostly, I am remembering things."

"I hope your memories are more pleasant than mine," she said, lowering her gaze to the barren hedge across from the bench. The fire's light made the mass of intertwined twigs look like she felt, tangled and confused.

"What troubles you?" He turned his gaze onto her, letting her hair fall from his fingers.

They were so close, she could see the day's growth of beard along his clean-shaven jaw. The stubble caught the light, gleaming in a color just a little darker than his hair. Oddly, their nearness didn't unsettle her. There was a calmness to him that spoke of safety. 'Twas this that teased her into leaning her head against the bulk of his shoulder. Her mouth lifted into a bitter smile.

"I have just learned I am a selfish woman. I wanted so badly to protect my son, I denied him many pleasures. As a child, did I not skate and throw a ball?" She looked up at him without moving her head.

The corner of his mouth lifted, and his gaze darkened into a blue so deep 'twas almost violet. "Did you? I would have guessed you the sort of lass devoted to stitching, always crying in complaint of a lad's tease."

Elyssa's smile softened into one of true amusement. "I did that, too. All in all, 'twas more fun to run with my brother." Then, she sighed as regret washed over her. "I cheated my son. What sort of mother does this make me?"

"One whose heart cannot bear to see a child hurt," he said softly. "There is much good in that."

Relief and gratitude warmed her. "You are kind to so easily forgive me."

He shook his head. "I am the devil's spawn, not kind."

Elyssa freed a breath of a laugh. "A vicious lie," she murmured.

"What makes you so certain 'tis a lie, when no one else sees it so?" he asked with a lift of his brows.

"You," she replied with a hint of smugness. "When I showed you my fear over Lady Sybil's charges, you gloated."

His brows rose higher still. "I did no such thing."

"You did so," she insisted. "I saw satisfaction in your face. Aye, 'twas brief, but it was there. You meant for me to be frightened of you. If there's one thing I cannot abide, 'tis a man who seeks to force me to my knees. It matters naught to me whether he uses his fists or tries to use my own emotions against me, I'd rather break than bend."

His face relaxed, and a smile played along his mouth. "So I've noticed."

She stared up at him, fascinated by his beauty. Not even Maud's scars could tarnish it. Her gaze moved appreciatively over his features. Aye, she liked his visage well indeed.

He watched her study him in what was almost wonder. "You look at me and see none of the horror others find."

"What horror is there to see? You are a handsome man."

Elyssa cringed inwardly at what she'd said. In telling him she found him attractive, she offered him the advantage over her. Praying he hadn't noticed or, if he had, wouldn't attempt to use what she'd revealed against her, she hurried on.

"Then again, I suppose others might not see you with my eyes, conditioned as I am by my sire. Before my birth, my father had taken a blow across the face. It left him with a ridge from brow to jaw." She traced a line across his face to show him the path.

He caught her hand in his, his thumb moving in a soft caress in her palm. "Thus do you see beyond my scars. You loved your sire." It was more statement than question.

"Aye and he, me. He died when I was but twelve." She loosed a sad sigh. Had he lived, her father would never have given her to one such as Ramshaw, as her warden had done.

Her thoughts led by a twisted path from her father's love for her, through her husbands to this man, her current owner, and how he ignored his own child. "Cecilia needs more of you than you give her," she said suddenly. "She longs for you. I saw it this morn, when she looked upon your gifts."

He gave a small shake of his head, his fingers intertwining with hers. Where his skin touched hers, there awoke a tingling. It made her breath catch.

"She wants what I no longer am. Unlike you, she cannot see 'tis me behind the scars. What lies upon my face stands between us like a wall."

His words shocked her out of the pleasant haze of sensation he was making in her. "Nay, I cannot believe that." She straightened so she could look him full in the face. "A child as loving as Cecilia wouldn't do so."

Once again, he shook his head. "You have had her as your own for two months now. Have you not noted that when she spies me, she runs?" There was soft sorrow in his voice. He released her hand, then turned his gaze back to the sky above them.

Elyssa frowned, remembering how Cecilia had clung to her yesterday as she had not done for a month. Yesterday, Geoffrey had returned. Disbelief lingered. There was more to Cecilia's rejection than simply scars; there had to be.

Silence again lapped around them. She relaxed, settling her cheek against his shoulder once more. Before her, the flames danced, the constant shift and play of light lulling her into a sort of contentment she'd not felt in years.

How strange it was to feel comfortable next to a man. Pleasant, as well. Neither of her husbands would ever have managed such stillness. His quiet was soothing, while his arm comforted rather than trapped.

Between the quiet and his warmth, her eyes closed. She sighed, wrapping an arm around him as she sought a place of comfort for her head against his chest. His hand moved against her sleeve in a soothing caress. The crackle and hiss of the fire seemed to say that this man was a rare one, indeed. Aye, she'd not felt so, not since her father's death. She drifted into a pleasant, timeless place, letting the moments slide by uncounted.

"Do you know that I hate you?"

'Twas a flat, emotionless statement. Elyssa straightened, all enjoyment gone. Yet, when she tried to win free of his embrace, his arm tightened. He turned his gaze on her again. She frowned in confusion. There was nothing to read in his face, save the same contentment she'd been feeling.

"If you do, then why ask me to stay?"

"Why, indeed," he replied, then drew a slow breath. The intensity she remembered from that October day returned and, once again, his look became like a touch, brushing against her face. It set her nerves on edge, but not with fear. Oh, but she was suddenly, instantly, aware of the man against whom she leaned. 'Twas time she returned to her cottage and barred the door.

"Do you not wish to know why I hate you?" 'Twas a husky breath. His fingers on her arm set her pulse to leaping.

Elyssa bit her lip as she studied him, then shrugged. "Is it because of the trouble I have caused you, what with Jocelyn and my defiance?" She tried to free her arm from his hold, but he wouldn't allow it.

"Those are reasons for dislike, anger, irritation, not hatred."

How could he smile at her and talk of hate? "Why, then?"

He reached up with his free hand and once again caught a strand of her hair. When he let it slide between his fingers, she trembled at the caress. This sort of play was but a precursor to the games played behind bed curtains."

His smile died. "Because Cecilia loves you."

The hurt he carried in him stabbed past all concern she harbored against being lured into his bed and pierced her heart. He cherished his child, the way her father had loved her, and grieved for what he'd lost. Her eyes filled against what ached in him.

"She touches you," he murmured. He rested his palm against her cheek. His skin was warm against hers, his palm, hard and strong. "She kisses you." His thumb moved gently across the fullness of her lips as if to reclaim what his daughter had set on them.

The desolation in his voice released the moisture from her eyes. Her arms ached to hold him, to cradle him against her shoulder until he hurt no more. 'Twas her pain for him that seared a hot, wet line down her cheek.

"Always a tear, Elyssa," he said with a quiet laugh, wiping away her heart's ache with his thumb. "For whom do you now cry?"

"You," she replied softly. "I cannot bear your hurt."

He drew a deep breath, his hand returning to his side, then grew still. 'Twas as if her words rendered him incapable of movement. After a moment, he said, "Best you leave me now. 'Tis no longer safe for you to be here."

"Safe?" she cried, shaking her head against his warning. "Have I not been here almost an hour already? You have done me no harm. Besides, I cannot abandon you when you hurt so."

She lay her hand against his breast. His tunic was velvet, the thick fabric soft against her fingers. Beneath her hand she could feel the pounding of his heart. How could what was broken beat so strongly? "I fear what will become of you, should I leave."

This time when he raised his hand, it was to draw his fingertips down the curve of her cheek. " 'Tis your care for me that demands you go. I am very drunk and drink can tease me into doing things I later have reason to regret."

Elyssa stared at him, too startled by his words to pay heed to the sensations his touch woke in her. True enough, she'd seen the wine, but he was so lucid and calm. Ramshaw had been a raging bear with too much drink in him, while Aymer had giggled and grabbed.

When she neither spoke nor moved, he lay a finger at the spot beneath her ear, then traced a line down the curve of her throat to her collarbone. His touch set fire to her skin and made a terrible pressure build beneath her heart. Her breath caught against what she felt.

'Twas only in this instant that she saw what her caring had awakened in him. He would seduce her, finding in his masculine pleasure a release from his own pain. She should go. Immediately. Aye, this very instant. If his mere touch could make her feel so, she'd soon be as drunk with him as he said he was with wine.

"You must do that no more," she warned him as his hand moved over her shoulder to rest against her nape. The pace of her breath increased. Mary save her, but this was very dangerous. And marvelous. Oh, but if it was so wondrous now, what pleasure would their joining bring her? Her body urged her to discover it.

"Run, Elyssa," he begged softly, his arm across her back tightening.

He pulled her nearer, until she half lay across his chest. Her hood fell back with her movement, and her hair tumbled free to drape him. He drew a swift breath. "My need to kiss you exceeds my sense."

Hers as well. Her whole body was alive with what he awakened in her. When he tilted her head toward

his, there was no strength in her to resist. He held his
mouth but a breath from hers. Elyssa's eyes closed in
the prayer that he wouldn't soon regain his sense.

His lips touched hers, just the briefest brush of flesh
to flesh. She gasped at this soft caress. Again his
mouth pressed to hers, moving ever so lightly across
her lips.

"This is very wrong," she breathed.

" 'Tis," he agreed, touching his lips to the corner of
her mouth.

Then he took her mouth with his. The depth of his
need for her was headier than the finest of wines. Her
pulse lifted into a searing beat. Beneath her hands,
his heartbeat roared into her palms, matching her own
hurried pulse. She wound her arms around him to
hold him close. He made a quiet sound of pleasure at
her embrace and freed her mouth to kiss the line of
her jaw until he nuzzled her ear.

"I ache for you, Elyssa," he murmured. "Where no
woman has moved me in a year, you haunt my
dreams."

"I do?" she asked in quiet surprise. 'Twas flattering
to think a man such as he might be taken with her
when she was twice wed and two years his senior.

"Aye, you. I see you as I did on the road to Crosswell, the wind sending your tresses floating in the air.
You, in yon cottage, telling me horses are dangerous
beasts. You"—his voice grew deeper and as soft as
the fabric he wore—"on the day of your son's departure, your mantle gaping." His hand left her nape,
moving down along her neck. He let it descend until
he cupped her breast in his palm, his thumb moving
across its sensitive peak.

Even through the layers of her gowns, his caress set

fire to her. "Stop," she begged, even while her body cried out he should do no such thing.

"I think I cannot," he replied softly. "If I cease, you'll surely refuse me as you should."

Aye, she must refuse him, else she'd but debase herself. Oh, but look how vulnerable she'd made herself to him already. This was mad, especially when she was five months gone with child.

'Twas the reminder of the babe within her that restored her. Although her body sobbed in disappointment, she eased back from him. Catching his hand in hers, she moved it from her breast to place it against her own heart.

"Geoffrey, you are right, and I must leave you." Her voice trembled against the wanting he made in her. "If I give way to what you ask, I'll make myself naught but a whore."

"Marry me, then," he breathed.

Elyssa stared at him in shock, then struggled not to smile. He was drunk, indeed, to suggest such a thing. Not only was she his senior, her dowry, even with the profits she would collect on her dower properties until her death, was far less than his worth. His ridiculous offer, obviously meant to sweep her from her feet, did much to chase away the seduction of his touch.

" 'Tis fortunate you've told me you are in your cups, else I might be hurt when the morrow finds you rescinding your offer." She laughed. He made no attempt to hold her when she came to her feet. "I am going now. 'Tis time for you to return to the hall, else you'll freeze."

He looked up at her, longing still marking his fine features. "I cannot, being trapped here until Cecilia has retired. I'll not mar her Christmas."

"Then, come you and stay in my cottage until she

retires." The words were out before she thought about what she'd said.

Geoffrey's face warmed in pure, masculine pleasure. "Have you changed your mind, then?" He reached for her, catching her around the waist as if he meant to draw her near, once more.

Now, here was a man the way he was supposed to behave. Elyssa smiled and lifted his hands from her hips. "Nay, you twit. You will go to my cottage, while I go into the hall. When your daughter is ready to retire, I'll send a man to fetch you."

Her commonplace tone chased the remains of desire from his expression. He came slowly to his feet, then paused, swaying slightly. "If we but move like snails, I vow I'll not fall on you," he said. "Come, Lady Freyne, lead me to your bower."

Elyssa sighed. So, she was no longer Elyssa to him, but Lady Freyne once more. The morrow would surely find him with an aching head and the wish that he'd never allowed himself this intimacy. Then, 'twas for the best that she'd held tight to reputation and honor, reining in her carnal nature. But, if that were true, why was she choking on regrets?

Chapter 13

Geoffrey thanked God that the woman walking at his side had sense enough for both of them. He'd no idea what had happened to his. If not for her, morn's light would have seen her crying rape. Or, their marriage.

Marriage. Jesus, Mary, and Joseph, what had caused him to ask her to wed him? God be praised she'd taken his words as nothing more than a sot's mumbling. A drunken, lustful sot.

Geoffrey savored the depth of his desire for Elyssa of Freyne. Just now, he wanted her more than he'd ever wanted any other woman in all his life. Why? Was she not the harridan whose every other sentence was an insult?

By God, she was worse than that, she pried into his life. What right had she to chide him because she didn't think he saw enough of Cecilia. Never mind that he saw nothing at all of his daughter.

His foot caught in the rutted path, and he lurched against her. Elyssa put her arm around him to steady him, and Geoffrey could feel the soft roundness of her breast against his side. He drew a sharp breath, both against his lust and in understanding. He'd offered to wed her so she'd have no choice but to bed him, thus proving she cared for him as her tears claimed.

A chill shot through him, one not generated by the

night's bitter air. Remarriage would give Gradinton the legal right to sue for Cecilia. This thought shook Geoff to the core and banked the embers of his lust. Gradinton would not wait a moment; taking custody of his granddaughter would be far less expensive than an annulment.

Elyssa opened the door to her cottage, and Geoffrey followed her within, only to stop and stare. Much had changed in the few months the widow had dwelt in this tiny room. At the wall behind the hearth there were now shelves containing a variety of foodstuffs, dried fruits, nuts, and such like. This meant she and her cousin were no longer beholden to Crosswell's kitchen for every crumb. There was even a jug of wine. His stomach turned at that thought. *Jesu,* but he was going to pay dearly for overindulging on the morrow.

Thick straw mats lay on the earthen floor, keeping the chill from rising through it, while two oil lamps hung from the ceiling beam. Even the yellowish light given off by burning fat couldn't dim the glow of the blue-and-red patterned material covering the walls. He reached out and touched the nearest piece. It had the feel of a bed curtain. Nonetheless, it served to keep winter at bay; the room was tolerably warm.

'Twas the huge bed that caught his deepest interest. He crossed the room to lay a hand against one carved bedpost, then fingered the rich scarlet curtain. Here was a woman who understood there was more to life than just existing.

"Now, this is a piece of work," he said of the bed as he moved to sit upon the mattress's edge. "No wonder Cecilia chooses to sleep with you."

He watched in mild disappointment as Elyssa pulled her hair free of her mantle, drawing it over her shoul-

der to swiftly plait it. Her hair was an incredible shade
of red-brown, shot through with coppers and golds.
As she fastened the thong around its end, she said,
" 'Tis mine now, my reward for outlasting my husbands." There was such satisfaction in her face that
he could only laugh.

"I take it you weren't fond of your mates."

"Who is?" Elyssa gave a skeptical lift of her brows,
then caught up her wimple. With practiced ease, she
wrapped the thing around her head and fastened it
into place with its pins. "Will you sleep? If so, I'll
take your cloak and remove your boots for you."

"If you don't mind, I'll leave my boots on." He
shrugged out of his cloak and handed it to her. "Once
I've left this vale to sleep, I'll not be waking for hours
and then 'twill be to face my splitting head. You'll
need to have me carried out of here."

"You know this for a fact?" There was faint amusement in her voice. She hung his outer garment over
the clothes pole.

"I've had the experience a time or two, aye. My
sire and dam were."

"Were what?" she asked, looking at him from over
her shoulder.

"Fond of each other. You asked who was fond of
their mates."

Bitter regret twisted in him as he fell silent. Why
had he wed with Maud, instead of finding someone he
could have adored the way his father had loved his
mother? The answer formed within him as if he'd
known it all along and only just now looked in its
direction. 'Twas because he'd feared needing anyone
the way his sire had needed his dam. His mother's
death had cost his father his soul. Geoffrey released
a breath of dismay at what he'd done to himself for

fear's sake. He'd wed for property, only to lose son, daughter, and his soul, without even the memory of love to console him.

"Are they still fond of each other?" Elyssa asked, kneeling to clean what muck she could from his boots. "There. You may set them on the bed. As long as you keep them atop the bedclothes, we'll not begrudge you a little dirt."

"Nay, they're both dead now. My dam died when I was but seven, and my father followed her three years after." He turned until he could stretch his legs out on the bed.

"Then, you were the property of a warden, as I was," she said, her hand on the curtain as if to close it.

"Would that I had been," he said with a short and bitter laugh. "Instead, I have an older half brother, who to this day persists on behaving as if he were my father. He, along with my father's bastard, saw fit to make my life miserable. Two fathers, not one. Don't close the curtain. I prefer the light." The effects of drink washed over him, making his head spin. "Big bed," he added, striving for a steady world.

"I understand my grandsire was a big man," she replied softly. "Sleep well, Geoffrey of Coudray." She lay her hand against his shoulder in a friendly salute.

"So I shall. Till we meet again, Elyssa of Freyne," he replied. He heard the door close and drifted into slumber.

'Twas with a lilt in her step that Elyssa walked beside Clare as they left the hall. Although the hour of Matins was almost upon them, the celebration continued. The music had been rich, made so by an especially talented troupe, and the dancing energetic enough to leave Cecilia limp in happy exhaustion against Clare's shoulder. Even by starlight Elyssa could see her borrowed daughter's face was flushed a pretty pink. Hair floated around the child's head, torn from her braids by her efforts.

"Look, Clare, her hair still dances," Elyssa laughed. Amusement was followed by a sudden, sharp ache. "Whatever shall I do when 'tis time to leave my poppet behind? My heart is breaking already as I think on it."

Clare laughed aloud at this. "Oh, 'Lyssa, why must you always worry over the future? Your fears cheat you of ever enjoying the here and now. Let it go. Listen to me this time as you did not over Jocelyn." The woman lifted chiding brows as she stopped at their doorway and waited for Elyssa to open it.

"I am never going to hear the end of this," Clare's cousin replied, but without rancor. "You have my permission to engrave 'I told you so' onto my tomb."

Elyssa stepped inside, then held the door wide for Clare. Her cousin was right. Jocelyn was secure and happy; Cecilia was not hers. She should take what happiness she could against the possibility that the babe in her would be her death.

The room was cloaked in deep shadows, what with the fire having died to embers. One of the lamps had guttered, leaving the scent of burning wick heavy in the air. She shut the door, then leaned down to fetch the thick length of wood that was their lock. Clare went on to their bedside to deposit Cecilia upon the mattress.

"There is a man in our bed!" 'Twas a high-pitched shriek.

"Oh, sweet Mary," Elyssa said, dropping the bar into the corner and coming to look at Geoffrey. I forgot him."

Her cousin clutched Cecilia tightly as the lass, eyes wide in startled fright, was fighting to free herself. "You put a man in our bed, then forgot him?" Clare's shock echoed in the small room.

"Well, 'tis only the sheriff, so gone with drink I feared he would freeze 'ere the night finished," Elyssa said, claiming Cecilia from Clare, then set the squirming lass on the ground. "Run and fetch the guard before they close the gate, else we'll have to sleep around him."

"The sheriff was as drunk as that, and you put him in our bed? I think I will not ask the particulars of this tale," Clare said with a sharp look, disapproval thick in her voice.

"There is nothing to ask after," Elyssa retorted. "Hie, or I'll make you sleep with him, then tell the world you laid with Crosswell's sheriff."

Shaking her head, Clare went to call the guard, leaving the door ajar behind her. 'Twas clearly a reprimand. Unlike Elyssa, who had certainly lost her mind, Clare did not wish the world to think them lewd women.

Lost her mind? Elyssa shook her head. It had been a close thing between losing her mind and much more than that.

Cecilia stood at arm's length from the bed, staring at the back of the man who lay within it. Elyssa pursed her lips against the opportunity this presented. She leaned down beside the lass. "Who is that?" she asked softly, pointing to Geoffrey's back.

Cecilia fixed her tired gaze on her temporary mother, then blinked and shrugged.

" 'Tis your papa," Elyssa said, keeping her voice low and quiet.

The girl's eyes widened, but not with fear. 'Twas

excitement that touched her face. She leapt toward
the bedside, but Elyssa caught her by the hand and
drew her back.

"Why do we not look upon him together?" she
asked.

Confusion flowed over Cecilia's face, but she nodded her agreement. Elyssa lifted the child and carried
her to the bed.

Geoffrey lay with the scarred side of his face toward
the mattress. His hair tumbled over his brow, hiding
the beginnings of the longest mark. As Elyssa brushed
the thick strands from his face, she spoke to Cecilia.
"Do you remember what happened to your papa,
ma petite?"

The girl only frowned at her as if to say nothing
had happened to her father.

"Aye, something has." She took Cecilia's hand, then
pointed the lass's finger. "Touch here," she said gently, laying the child's finger against her father's temple.
"Do you feel that?"

Cecilia nodded, her brow yet drawn in confusion.

" 'Tis but a scar. Where there was a wound, the
flesh has healed. There is no hurt in it." She drew
Cecilia's finger along the raised line of flesh until it
reached the bridge of her sire's nose. "Do you understand me? It does not hurt your father to wear the
lines on his face." This had been the question Elyssa
had asked of her own sire, time and again.

There was worry in Cecilia's eyes as she looked at
Elyssa, but she gave a faint nod. When Elyssa released
the child's hand, Cecilia snatched her fingers away
from her papa's face to clutch her adopted mother
around the neck. The door opened behind them.

"Clare, tell them to wait a moment," Elyssa called
over her shoulder.

As her cousin did so, then came to join them at the
bed's side, Cecilia leaned back to look into Elyssa'
face. The child chewed her lower lip, then brought a
hand to her eye, the same eye her father no longer
owned. Her brows raised in question.

"Your papa can no longer see from that eye. For
him is it like this." Elyssa lay a hand against Cecilia's
face, shielding her eye. She felt the brush of the child's
eyelashes against her palm as Cecilia struggled with
the concept of an eye that no longer worked. Then,
the lass pulled Elyssa's hand away and blinked in dem-
onstration that once the obstruction was gone, sight
returned.

Elyssa smiled a little and shook her head. "Even if
he removes what he wears, he can no longer see. He
covers his eye because he is a very vain man. I think
he cannot bear for the world to view what became of
his face."

There were sudden tears in Cecilia's eyes. 'Twas the
first time Elyssa had seen the child release her heart's
moisture. Her wee poppet struggled to turn in her
embrace so she could again look at her sire.

"What is this, 'Lyssa?" Clare asked as Elyssa set
her on the ground.

"Cecilia is settling her fears over her sire," she replied in a whisper as the child clambered onto the bed.

Slowly and carefully, Cecilia worked her way
around her father. When she knelt at Geoffrey's head,
she again lay her finger against the scar that crossed
his brow. She followed the line, until she reached the
bridge of his nose.

Geoffrey murmured in his sleep, sighing and shifting
onto his back. Cecilia scooted away from him as she
came face-to-face with the patch she so disliked.

"Touch it, my little love," Elyssa urged softly. "You cannot hurt him."

Her eyes but a gleam in the darkness of the ceilinged bed, Cecilia looked to her father, then she stared at Elyssa.

"My lady, might we enter? 'Tis terrible cold out here," one of the men called out.

Elyssa didn't dare turn away from the bed, fearing Cecilia would think she abandoned her to what so terrified her. "Clare, can you let them in, keeping them at the room's end and bidding them to silence?"

"Aye, 'Lyssa." The woman turned reluctantly away.

"Do it, Cecilia," she urged. "Touch your sire and see that 'tis the same papa you once knew hiding beneath what's happened to his face."

There was a flash of white in the darkness as the child lifted her hand. Elyssa strained to see. Cecilia lay her hand against the patch shielding Geoffrey's ruined eye.

"Who is that, Cecilia?" Elyssa prodded. "Who lies there beside you?"

The daughter of her heart stroked her hand down her father's cheek, then put her fingers into his hair. She leaned down and buried her nose against his neck. With a sigh, Cecilia lay her head against his shoulder, rubbing her cheek against his soft tunic.

Yet deep in his slumber, Geoffrey reacted instinctively to the caress, his hand coming to rest atop Cecilia's head. Cecilia gave a yelp and flew back into the corner of the bed. Elyssa gasped at the hoarse and tiny sound.

" 'Lyssa," Clare breathed, "did you hear?"

"Aye." Hope soared in Elyssa. "Who is that, Cecilia?" she prodded again. "Can you tell me who 'tis beside you?"

Cecilia shook her head in the negative. 'Twas more the movement of the bed curtains that said she did so. The corner was so dark, there was no seeing the lass.

"Do you wish more time to see your papa?" Once again the bed curtains shook in denial. "Then, 'tis time for him to leave. Come you men, and fetch your master," Elyssa called behind her without taking her gaze from Cecilia's corner. "Clare, lay his cloak over him."

When Clare had done so and the two men stood at the bedside, she glanced at him. "Lord Coudray suggested you would need to carry him out, saying he would not awaken."

"Aye, my lady," one said as he indicated to his mate that he'd take the sheriff's feet. Between the two of them, they hoisted their lord's deadweight off the bed. Carrying him like a sack of grain, they struggled to the door. "Hits some like that, my lady. Good Christmas to you," he called as they carried him through the doorway.

"To you as well," Clare called after them as she went to close and bar the door.

Cecilia's foot caught Elyssa mid-back with a jarring impact. Trapped in a dream, the child thrashed and fought, fists flying. Elyssa struggled to her side, narrowly avoiding being struck.

Clare was not so fortunate. The sound of flesh striking flesh with bruising impact was unmistakable. With a yelp, Elyssa's cousin came upright in the bed.

"Cecilia, come now, 'tis only a dream," Elyssa said softly. She tried to catch the girl by her shoulders, but 'twas too dark within the closed curtains to find her. Elyssa threw open the draperies.

"'Lyssa, she's weeping!" Clare cried.

Elyssa turned in astonishment. The child's chest

heaved as she sobbed in utter silence. She caught the babe's face to hold her still. "Cecilia, poppet, you must wake." Cecilia fought on, twisting and turning. "Help me, Clare. Together, we must hold her, else she'll injure herself."

Together they grabbed the flinging arms and legs, then Elyssa held down her chest while Clare settled upon her legs. When Cecilia could fight no longer, a sound broke from her. 'Twas a high-pitched squeal, long and terrified.

"Poppet," Elyssa crooned into the child's ear. "Awaken now, poppet." She kissed her cheek, murmuring and crooning.

"Papa." 'Twas the tiniest of cries, the voice speaking it rusty with disuse. "Papa."

There was a long, indraw of breath, then Cecilia cried. Her sobs broke from her in great gusts. And, echoed in the tiny room, filled with all the heartbreak of which a wee lass of five was capable. As her voice came to life once more, Cecilia relaxed against the mattress. Elyssa gathered the girl into her arms, cradling her close and rocking her as Cecilia emptied the pain she carried in her.

Chapter 14

"Come now, poppet, bid your Papa good journey. He must take himself off to Easter court, and you'll not be seeing him again for weeks. Please? 'Twill be after April's start when he next comes home. Just a word?"

Geoffrey stood in the doorway of Elyssa's cottage, trapped in helpless hurt as his daughter turned her face to the side in refusal. The door was open behind him, showing the dawn of March's first day. As the sun lifted over the top of Crosswell's wall, he could feel its warmth spread along his mail. Warmth also stirred the air, the mild breeze toying with the hems of his surcoat. Shifting his helmet from beneath one arm to the other, he watched Elyssa crouch beside his sweet lass.

She lay her arm over his child's shoulders, then looked up at him. "Come closer, my lord."

Even knowing that his nearness frightened his daughter didn't stop hope from goading Geoffrey into taking one small step. Cecilia looked up at him, her brows raised in concern. He took another. His daughter began to tremble and tears touched her eyes.

"Please, poppet?" Elyssa begged gently. " 'Twould mean so much to him." Cecilia gave a wild shake of her head, then leapt into the bed. She scrambled across the broad mattress and cowered in the far corner.

"Leave it alone, madam," Geoffrey said as his heart shattered all over again. "I am content that she no longer runs when she spies me and now chooses to eat at the hall table with me. I'll not have you hurt her to prove how much you've accomplished."

"I have no intention of hurting her, my lord," Elyssa said, sounding irritated.

He offered his hand to aid her in rising. She hesitated for the briefest of seconds, then lay her fingers into his gloved palm. As she came to her feet, her expression eased into an aloof blankness. So it was now between them, ever since Christmas. She'd treated him with a courtly formality, and he did all he could to avoid her.

Her fingers still in his hand, he looked down at her. She had expanded with her babe, her belly now well rounded. 'Twas a new gown she wore, fitted to this additional girth. The fabric's golden tones suited her, making her eyes a soft brown and her ivory skin glow.

Geoffrey's gaze caught on the fullness of her lips. In that instant the memory of their passion roared through him. He wanted nothing more than to bring her near and feel her tremble at his touch. She had wanted him that night as much as he had wanted her.

As if she sensed his reaction to her, her lips parted and she sighed. She still wanted him. His head lowered, and he eased closer to her. Then her belly touched his. 'Twas a dash of icy water, bringing him back to his senses. He dropped her hand and stepped swiftly back from her.

Jesu, even this far gone with child, she set his blood on fire. Geoffrey was suddenly grateful for the concealment of his mail. "Well then, I bid you a good

Easter, and see you once April is upon us," he said, abruptly turning toward the door.

She caught him by the arm. "My lord, please, I wished to see you about more than simply bidding Cecilia adieu." 'Twas a brusque statement, almost as if she were angry with him. "Clare, would you take Cecilia outside?"

As Elyssa's cousin gathered his daughter from the bed's corner, Geoffrey shrugged. "Best make it very short. My men and the wains and my witnesses all await me at the outer gate. We move slow enough as it is."

Not only did he cart the barrels of pennies he'd collected in taxes from Crosswell to fill the king's treasury, he also escorted an assortment of shire dwellers to the Easter court. Drawn from all walks of life, these folk served as his witnesses, testifying to the barons of the Exchequer against the honesty of his accounting. Some of them rode, but a number walked or used a cart. His party moved like a snail on the road.

"We'll be in the garden," Clare said, then added, "good journey, my lord." With Cecilia's head tucked in her shoulder, she dodged behind him and exited. There was enough haste in the woman's movements to suggest she knew what 'twas the widow wished to say and wanted no part of it.

Geoffrey tensed, having long since learned that Clare's reactions predicted Elyssa's behavior. His ward meant to pry, once more. "Come then, spew it and be done so I can leave."

Irritation flashed across her face, but she smoothed it from her expression and said softly, " 'Tis about your wife's death."

Geoffrey's breath left him in a cold rush. "Cecilia speaks of this?" 'Twas a pained whisper.

She shook her head a little, her brow creased in worry. "Nay, my lord, and that is just the problem. She called me Maman, refusing to use my name. She refers to the babe in me as her brother, when he is not."

Relief washed over him. What Cecilia knew would ruin her life. Under no circumstances could she be allowed to utter the tale of Maud's death. "How is this a problem?"

"Do you not see how this can hurt her?" Elyssa asked him, sounding truly fearful. "I will eventually leave Crosswell. As long as she believes I am her mother, do we not risk Cecilia once more receding into silence at this second loss when I am gone?"

" 'Tis possible," he agreed slowly. 'Twould be terrible to watch Cecilia retreat again, when she'd come so far. "So what is your solution to this problem? I do not see how we can force her to believe you are not her mother."

"But we can, my lord. I would have you tell me the tale of Maud's death. When I know it, I can ease it from Cecilia, bit by bit. She will eventually come to accept that her mother is dead, and I am but 'Lyssa, the one who now cares for her."

Her words slaughtered any softness he'd ever known for her. Geoffrey froze, so cold he was beyond breathing. 'Twas better to give Cecilia to Gradinton, who'd lost his bid for annulment, than let this meddling, interfering woman ruin his daughter's life. "Nay."

"My lord?" his ward asked in surprise.

"Nay. This I command you. You will say not a single word to Cecilia over her mother's death." His voice was as cruel and threatening as he could make it.

Elyssa's eyes widened in shock. "Mayhap, you do not understand. I believe the memory of her mother's death festers in her. Until she spills it, she'll not be fully recovered from her silence.''

"I understand you very well, but you do not understand me," he retorted, his words honed to a cutting edge. "I have given you a direct command regarding my daughter. Disobey and I will take her from you." He whirled on his heel and started out the door.

Elyssa caught him by the arm with both hands, then yanked him back, heedless of the damage his knitted steel sleeve did to her palms. Her eyes were afire with anger. "Why you arrogant bitch's son! You would rather see her hurt than speak of what makes *you* uncomfortable."

Only by the barest margin did Geoff restrain his urge to draw his sword. He threw her hand from his arm. "I care nothing for what you think of me. Obey me in this or pay the price." Without another word, he stalked from her cottage. Mounting Passavant, he rode to the outer gate, his working eye as blind as the one Maud had carved out.

"Here. Right here is a foot," Elyssa said, leaning back on her stool to set Cecilia's hand against the hard curve of her belly. The babe within her obligingly moved his heel so the child in the outer world could feel it. Cecilia smiled, her small hand following the movement of an even tinier heel. Her fingers drew a line across the taut dark yellow fabric covering the mound where Elyssa's child lived.

The mid-April sun shed its warm light onto Cecilia's dark brown braids and glowed on the child's fair skin. Spring had crept swiftly upon them, bringing with it a wonderful freshness that even Crosswell's ever-present stink could not destroy. The grass greened and trees burst with new leaves, spring blossoms dotted the garden's expanse in magnificient clutches of color. Here, within these walls, the mating birds sang with such wild exuberance, they drowned out the constant clamor of hammers on forges.

Yesterday had seen the end of a long stretch of rain. Today, she and Clare gratefully escaped their confining quarters to spend the day out of doors. While they occupied themselves with their handiwork, Geoffrey's daughter had her own wooden poppet to keep boredom at bay.

Cecilia lifted her hand from Elyssa's belly. "My brother's foot," she said with all the firmness her yet breathy and tentative voice could manage.

Elyssa felt rage creep in behind the smile she offered her poppet. How dare that arrogant donkey's ass command her to say nothing?

"When can I see my brother?" Cecilia asked, rubbing her hands against Elyssa's swollen abdomen.

"May's end." Elyssa caught Cecilia's hand. "Poppet, this is not your brother."

Cecilia ignored her by closing her eyes and leaning her head against Elyssa's belly to concentrate on the babe's movements. So it had been from the moment the wee lass recognized Elyssa's expanding girth as that of a developing child.

"This is incredibly wrong," Elyssa said to Clare in frustration. "By commanding me to silence, he makes a liar of me."

Her cousin, seated only a short distance from her, lifted helpless shoulders. " 'Tis what she wishes it to be," Clare offered. "What harm can it do?"

Elyssa only shook her head and stroked Cecilia's hair. When she turned her gaze back to what remained of her lap, 'twas to look upon the gown she created for her babe's christening. She toyed with the garment's tiny sleeve.

A hiccough of fear shot through her, followed by the certainty of her own demise. No longer did the thought of sharing her babe's coming with Geoffrey disgust her. As angry as she was at him, she yet carried tight within her the memory of his deep calm on Christmas night. It had become her bulwark against what frightened her.

With her thoughts came understanding over Cecilia. "You are wrong, Clare. There could be great harm for my poppet if she confuses me for her own maman. What if I am no more after this?" she touched her belly, not wanting to speak openly of her death before Cecilia.

" 'Lyssa, do not think that way," Clare chided, her brown brows drawing together in her thin forehead. "Did not Reginald send the midwife as we asked?"

Elyssa made a face at that. "I have decided that between Freyne's midwife and me, one of us has changed. I think 'tis me, for I am no longer susceptible to the commands of others."

"What do you mean?" Clare asked.

"I mean, if I want to drink the red raspberry tea that I thought every pregnant woman uses to build strength, I'll do so. She can command me otherwise till she's blue in the face."

Clare only shook her head. " 'Lyssa, you are so contrary. Come now, Reginald thinks highly of her, and he cannot but wish the best for his brother's child. Has she not promised a painless delivery? It has gone a long way toward settling your fears, and that can but be healthy for both you and your babe." Her cousin turned her gaze to the basket to search for a new color. "Where is our red?"

"Hiding near the bottom. Someone"—Elyssa sent Cecilia a narrow-eyed look—"keeps taking it."

"I like red," Cecilia said, lifting her head from Elyssa's belly. Her gaze caught on a bird darting into a budding pear tree. "I am going to give it to the birds for their nests. They like it, too. Just one thread." She held up a tiny finger to indicate how small her need was.

Clare raised a brow, but snipped her a short length of red thread. "Do Tante Clare a boon, poppet, and like blue for now."

"Next week," Cecilia replied.

Elyssa watched as her poppet took the bit toward the tree, her heart growing heavier as the distance between them increased. Maud's death had nigh on driven the lass into madness. A second loss would surely destroy her. The need to protect Cecilia from hurt gripped her.

"Nay, he'll not force this on me. He has no right, even if this is his daughter." Elyssa reached over and lay her hand on Clare's knee. "Think on it, Clare. Should I die, however unlikely you think this might be, my poor poppet will have lost her maman twice."

Clare set her needle into her cloth as she understood what Elyssa intended. "Nay, 'Lyssa, you shouldn't interfere here. Cecilia is happy, and you will survive. When we are gone, 'twill be Lord Coudray's problem, not yours, to worry over."

" 'Tis my problem," Elyssa snapped back. "He gives me the right to interfere by allowing me to keep his daughter as long as he has. Now I cannot stand idly by and watch him destroy all the good I've done simply because he refuses to discuss the past."

"Aye, but—" Clare paused, then gave a lift of her shoulders. "Ah 'Lyssa, do as you see best. We are too

different, you and I. Where I am content to let life's
currents take me where they will, you plow through
them, charting your own course."

Anger ebbed at that, and Elyssa laughed. "So I do."

She set her sewing atop their basket and came pon-
derously to her feet, hands braced at the small of her
back. How glad she would be once this child was outside of her rather than constantly knocking from
within. She went to join Cecilia before the pear tree.
Her poppet had her hand aloft, offering her string to
any willing taker.

"Cecilia, we must talk, you and I." She caught the
child gently by the shoulders and turned her. Cecilia's
hand lowered as her wispy brows rose in question.
"Who am I, poppet?"

"You are my maman," the child responded with
a smile.

"The truth, Cecilia. Who am I?"

"My maman," Cecilia said swiftly. Too swiftly. Elyssa
heard in her voice the effort such a pretense took.

"Nay, you know I am not. Your maman is dead.
Nor is the child I bear your brother. Think back. Do
you not remember that your brother died just after
he was born?" There. 'Twas out, spoken aloud for the
first time.

Cecilia clutched herself tightly and blinked as tears
leapt to her eyes. "Maman shouldn't have done that."
'Twas a bare whisper.

Then, the child's eyes flew wide in horror. She tore
free from Elyssa's hold and raced for the grassy corner
where she'd dropped her wooden companion.
Snatching the doll into her arms, Cecilia looked frantically around the enclosure as if she feared being
chased. She backed farther into the corner, then
hunched against the wall.

Elyssa drew a shaken breath as Cecilia's reaction brought the words of Maud's letter again ringing in her memory. This time, the madness in them shone clear. Geoffrey's wife had believed the devil's mark lay on the child she'd borne. A new and frightening thought came to mind. Was it possible Maud had done murder while her daughter looked on? The very concept made Elyssa's stomach turn, but the idea fit too well with Cecilia's reaction to be discarded. Her heart sank against it.

"Mother of God, you must aid me now. This burden is too great for one so small as Cecilia to bear. Tell me what to say," Elyssa prayed. Then moving slowly, more to ease the child than to accomodate herself, she crossed to her poppet's corner. As she passed by Clare, she caught up her stool, then set the seat before Cecilia and lowered herself onto it.

Cecilia stared blankly ahead of her. Her fear was so great, Elyssa could see her gown move in the rhythm of the child's pounding heart. Her tiny hands were white as they clutched her plaything.

Elyssa drew a slow breath. "Poppet, did you love your maman?"

"I love my maman," Cecilia repeated, her voice only a whisper. Her face was ashen and without expression.

Fear woke in Elyssa. If she couldn't prevent it, her poppet might well disappear into silence once more. "But she frightened you," she prodded quietly.

"She shouldn't have done that," Cecilia whispered to herself. "Maman was bad. She shouldn't have done that." She looked down at the doll in her hands.

"She hurt your brother." Elyssa kept her voice flat and relaxed.

Still staring at her toy, Cecilia nodded, tears welling in her eyes. She drew a ragged breath, sparkling bits of moisture clinging to her dark lashes. She stared at Elyssa, horror and hurt tangling in her expression. "She shouldn't have done that."

Elyssa's own tears burned, clamoring for release, but she fought them. If she gave way, she'd not have the clarity of thought to say what Cecilia needed to hear. "You are right, my heart. Your maman shouldn't have hurt your brother." 'Twas terrible hard to keep the quiver from her voice.

Cecilia only stared at her. Elyssa prayed she was understanding. "Mamans are supposed to love their poppets the way I love you. She shouldn't have frightened you or hurt you."

There was a subtle release of tension in the child's shoulders. "Maman is gone now?"

"Aye, my heart," Elyssa agreed quietly. "She cannot hurt you anymore. She will never come back again."

"She is dead? Like my brother?" There was just a trace of normal curiosity in her voice.

"Aye," Elyssa told her.

"I do not like it, that she died," Cecilia's eyes shed some of the moisture caught in them. "I want my maman to come back."

"I know," Elyssa sighed, "but she cannot. Come, my little love. Come to 'Lyssa. I will hold you close and keep you safe from what hurts you."

Cecilia came to lean against Elyssa's side, burying herself as best she could into her temporary mother's embrace. As Elyssa rocked gently to ease the child's horror and pain, her own grew. The need to sob rose again. This time, she fought it back with anger. Just what did Geoffrey FitzHenry think he was doing, leaving his child alone with such a burden on her heart? Aye, 'twas past time she gave him a piece of her mind.

Chapter 15

Seated in his workroom, Geoffrey stared at the parchment in his hand, Martin reading over his shoulder. The other pages lay strewn across his lap. 'Twas unbelievable. The only thing Crosswell's miners had not requested in their latest contract was God's throne. A soldier came to stand before him. Geoff finished reading a line before he looked up at the man.

"What is it?" he asked, a little sharply at this interruption.

The man extended a fold of parchment toward him. "My lord, Lady Freyne asked me to bring you this,"

Geoffrey took the letter and flipped it open. Elyssa's hand was even and strong, flowing with well-formed characters across the bit of skin.

Lord Coudray, we must speak about Cecilia. Do not ignore me. Please recall that within weeks you will sit at my side, trapped with me while I give birth. 'Twould be better if you heard me out in private, else I'll be forced to spill what needs saying before the midwife and my cousin.

He stared at her words, stunned at the threat behind her commanding tone. With sudden certainty, he knew

Cecilia had spoken to Elyssa about Maud's death. Horror and desperation tore through him.

Should this tale spread, his daughter would be shunned, a pariah because of her mother's madness. Fear for Cecilia's future boiled over into deadly rage. Lady Freyne would die before she told what she now knew.

He lifted his gaze to the soldier as he came to his feet. Parchments slid to the floor, forgotten. "Where is she?" 'Twas a quiet, flat question.

The soldier's eyes went wide, and his face paled. "In the garden, my lord," he said, then moved swiftly for the door.

"My lord, can it not wait an hour?" Martin stepped back, one leaf yet hanging from his hand.

Geoffrey swung his gaze onto his undersheriff. "I think not."

Martin's brows lifted, then his eyes narrowed. "You'll be needing a chaperon for the lady." There was a steel edge to his voice, his usually smiling mouth caught in a grim line.

His well-honed words and their undercurrent of warning sliced through Geoffrey's rage. 'Twasn't Lady Freyne's honor the young knight sought to protect; Martin was warning him that he'd not allow murder to be done. With great effort, Geoffrey fought his emotions back into control. The tension eased from his muscles, and he released a steaming breath. Martin relaxed apace.

"My thanks," Geoffrey managed. In uttering these two words, the need to see blood shed moved into a milder sort of rage.

"You are welcome," Martin replied without a trace of humor. "Is there aught that I can do to aid you?"

Geoffrey shook his head. " 'Tis a private matter between us, but I thank you for your concern."

By the time he reached the garden gate, his reasons for thanking Martin had once again grown. As blood lust departed, sense returned. Had not Lady Freyne done all she could to protect her son? Such a woman would never allow harm to come to his daughter.

Still, anger remained at the tone of Elyssa's note. 'Twas the widow's absolutely impossible manner that ever drove him past sensible thought. He stepped into the garden.

Dressed in that golden gown of hers, with a sleeveless ivory overgown atop it, Lady Elyssa sat upon a stool near the hedge. From beneath her wimple, her plaits gleamed like burnished copper in the afternoon sun, while the day's warmth had set color into her face. Or, was it the babe in her that did it? Where pregnancy had eaten Maud, making her sallow and thin, Elyssa glowed with life and health. What he'd seen as exotic beauty in October was even more striking now.

Her eyes were narrowed, and her jaw was tight. Was she angry with him? Outrage grew, and he crossed his arms over the breast of his blue gown. 'Twas he who had cause for resentment, not she. She had no right to pry into his life.

When he held his place, she lifted her chin. "Either enter and shut the gate, or leave." The harsh tone of her voice sent his anger spiraling again.

Where he'd intended to leave the gate open for decency's sake, Geoffrey now reached behind him. The gate slammed into its frame. Again, her chin lifted, as if to say she was unimpressed by his display of pique.

"Goddamn your vicious tongue!" he said, his words like steel. "Just who do you think you are, commanding me to meet you or else? You threaten me at your own peril."

"Threaten?" she retorted boldly. "I made no threats, only promises. How do you dare face me with anger when you abandoned your daughter to carry what she did all by herself?"

Geoffrey felt his skin heat at her words. "I did no such thing. Had Cecilia given me half a chance, I'd have let her spill what she held onto me. Instead, she chose you, damned harridan that you are. Only God alone knows why." He leaned toward her, his finger pointed. "Now, 'tis time you marked your own words, madam. *My* daughter. Not yours."

She slapped his hand away. "Not mine by birth, mayhap, but surely mine by rebirth."

"No longer," Geoffrey snarled. "Cecilia needs you no more. So I command."

"You command," she retorted, her eyes widening in wild anger. She struggled to her feet, then grasped a handful of his tunic front. "You commanded me to silence, and fool that I am, I heeded you. Well, I will heed you no longer."

Geoffrey caught her wrist and yanked her hand free of his tunic. The violence of his motion forced her to step back from him. "You'll heed me or feel my wrath."

Elyssa tugged on her trapped wrist. "You left her alone with her mother." What started as a raging shout descended into a hoarse and quiet cry. "She watched her brother die at Maud's hand."

Too far gone in his own rage to heed his inner plea for caution, he let the remainder of the tale pour from him for the first time in a fiery breath. "She saw more than that. She watched her mother set these on me"—he raised his free hand to indicate his face—"after I tore Cecilia from Maud's hands to keep her from killing my daughter as well as my son. Then, Cecilia watched her mother die as I threw her from me to end her attack."

"Mother of God," Elyssa gasped, then a sob tore from her. To Geoffrey's astonishment, the widow wrapped her free arm around him and buried her head against his shoulder. "Oh, Geoffrey, I am so sorry."

Trapped in the stillness of utter confusion, Geoffrey let this impossible woman weep against his shoulder. After a moment and, mostly because he couldn't think of anything else to do, he released his hold on her wrist and embraced her. "Elyssa, cease your tears," he said.

"I cannot." 'Twas a muffled moan. " 'Tis a terrible thing that happened to you and Cecilia. If I, who did not witness it cannot bear it, how do you?"

Wonder rose in him. She cried for him, once again trying to share what was his hurt. Then sorrow washed over him, but instead of drowning him and shutting out his other emotions as it had in the past, the woman in his arms kept it from consuming him. He leaned his head against hers. "Sometimes, I cannot."

So they stood for a long moment. In their silence, the memory of Maud's death ebbed, some of its horror blunted. 'Twas with a sigh that he stepped back from Elyssa, his hands resting on her upper arms.

"You are right, we must speak over this issue. What Cecilia and I have told you can go no farther than you. To reveal the truth of that day is to condemn Cecilia to a life of unhappiness."

Elyssa wiped away her tears, then drew a shaking breath. "How so?"

" 'Tis a strange world we live in, Elyssa," Geoffrey said softly. "While my supposed cruel and evil nature will stop no man from offering his son to wed my daughter, her mother's madness dooms Cecilia to the life I see your cousin living."

Her forehead creased as she contemplated what he said. A single tear yet clung to the soft curve of her cheek. Geoffrey raised a finger to brush it away. Astonishment lingered. She cried for him.

Once again, her caring reached into him, seductive and taunting. And unbelievably precious. He found himself wishing she'd given way to him that night. Had she forced their marriage, there'd be no need to face her departure. Geoffrey caught his breath against this thought. Dear God in heaven, but he'd allowed Elyssa of Freyne to push her way into his life until his need for her made it impossible to let her go.

"Ah, so this is why you let Sybil's story of your evil nature stand unchallenged." She nodded to herself in understanding.

"Aye, 'tis far better for her to have a devil for a father than a madwoman for a mother. And now you know why I commanded you against speaking to Cecilia over her mother's death. What she knows, she must conceal."

"Geoffrey, she cannot keep it in her," Elyssa said, a note of pleading in her voice. "Until the whole of this memory's poison drains from her, she cannot be the daughter you remember. She must speak of it over and over, until she is at peace with it."

The softness he'd been feeling toward her died with her words. Geoffrey let his hands fall from her arms and took a step back from her. "This I cannot allow. The risk is too great. Others will overhear, and the tale will spread." Aye, 'twould fly even more swiftly than the rumor of his own viscious nature had spread.

Elyssa shook her head against his command. "This

is but wishful thinking on your part. I think it likely that many already know the truth, or at least suspect it."

Geoffrey tensed. She had to be wrong. "How, when few, outside of Coudray, know the tale? Those who do have vowed not to speak of it."

"Geoffrey," Elyssa said to him, her voice urging him to heed her, "Sybil showed me a missive she received from Maud, no doubt written only a day after your son's birth. Were it not for your attempt at frightening me, I might immediately have seen proof of Maud's madness."

He rejected this possibility. "That missive accuses me of being the devil's pawn, nothing more."

She only shook her head. "I tell you, her mind's illness nigh on radiated from that leaf. If I, who am but a woman saw what lay behind Maud's words, others will as well. That missive went to the bishopric. You know as well as I that churchmen are terrible gossips."

That made Geoffrey smile. "I appreciate your concern, but 'tis wasted in this instance. As he is content that neither I nor Maud were evil, the bishop has vowed to say nothing of this matter."

"Aye, but his clerks did not. Geoffrey, think," she insisted. "How many men handled that missive before it reached their lord's office? How many more will see it before Sybil ceases in her pursuit of vengeance? Yet, while they all know and spread the truth, you demand silence from Cecilia, even when I tell you that what you want will destroy her."

"You are not listening to me." Geoff raised a hand to his brow, frustrated by her refusal to understand. Baldwin had remained passive too long, while Geoffrey's need to own Cecilia had only grown. If the future demanded he give his life to protect his daughter, Geoff had to know his going would give his sweet lass a future worth holding.

Elyssa stepped closer and lay her hand against his scarred cheek, as if to soothe what ached in him. "I am listening, but what you say makes no sense. Do not make my mistake, Geoffrey of Coudray," she said softly, her fingers gentle against his skin. "I thought to save Jocelyn by shielding him from the hurt life could do him. Instead, I doomed him to a joyless existence. This will be Cecilia's fate if you seek to shield her from this."

Her words set war to raging in his soul, and Geoff jerked his head to the side to free him from her touch. A part of him, a very selfish part, wanted the world to know what Gradinton had done by saddling him with Maud. He wanted to scream against the terrible things Maud had done until he could scream no more, knowing that peace would follow in rage's wake. All this he buried, praying it would die beneath his greater need to protect Cecilia.

"You are wrong in this and 'tis not at all the same," he said harshly, taking yet another step away from her. "Your son's weaknesses belonged only to him. Once he proved himself capable, he could be judged on his own merit. How is Cecilia supposed to prove herself against what her mother was? *Jesu,* but she's been wild and silent for a year. If word spreads, her every mood will be watched. A single misstep and everyone will whisper behind their hands, 'There goes Mad Maud's daughter.' "

Elyssa remained calm beneath his onslaught. "This is true only if she behaves like a madwoman and Cecilia does not."

Geoffrey's eyes narrowed. She was going to refuse

him, damn her. "I say the risk is too great, and I'll not allow you to speak of this to Cecilia."

"Oh, I see it clearly now." Elyssa set a fist on her hip. "What's good for the goose is not so good for the gander, eh? You chide me for seeking to protect my son because what I did to him caused harm, yet refuse to listen when I turn your own lesson back on you?"

Cold rage rose in Geoff. She had to acknowledge his right to command her. "You will do as I say or I vow I will truly make a murderer out of myself."

"And thus deprive your daughter of two mamans?" Her voice rose as her rage matched his. "If this is how you love your child, I spit on your love."

Her words set fire to the fury in him, and he drew back his hand in threat. He'd wring her compliance, no matter the cost. "Bend or bear the consequences!" he roared.

She laughed, the sound hard. "Do you think you can frighten me now, after what has passed between us? 'Tis useless, Geoffrey. I know this sort of violence all too well, and you are not the sort of man who can do it. Try then, try and force me to my knees, but be you warned. When you fail, you'll have no choice left but to listen to me. I am right in this, and you know it."

"Damn you!" 'Twas a bellow of pain, not rage. He leapt forward and grabbed up her stool. It splintered against the wall. "I cannot condemn her to the life you would give her."

The garden gate opened. Ready to fry the intruder with all the anger he couldn't spend on Elyssa, Geoffrey whirled. Martin strode briskly into the enclosure.

"I told you this was a private issue," he roared.

"So you did, my lord. Pardon my intrusion," his

undersheriff said without the slightest bit of regret in his voice. "This has just come from Ashby, the messenger saying it demands your immediate attention." He thrust a parchment toward his employer. "Lady Freyne, are you well?"

"Martin," Geoffrey snapped, disliking the inference in his undersheriff's question. He tore the strings off the piece, his hands yet shaking with the force of his emotion. The words jumbled in senseless confusion as he stared at them, too hot to find the pattern in the letters.

"I am well enough, thank you for inquiring," Elyssa said calmly, "save for the deafening my pigheaded fool of a warden is bent on giving me." Martin had the gall to laugh.

Geoffrey drew a deep breath and stared at what his brother had commanded a clerk to scribe. As the meaning behind the words came clear, all anger died. *"Jesu Christus,"* he breathed and read again.

"What is it?" Elyssa asked, her voice moving to a higher pitch in sudden worry. She came to his side and reached for the parchment.

"Nay." He kept it from her. "Martin, leave us."

Martin stared at him, concern for his friend Gilliam of Ashby in his face. Geoffrey shook his head, letting his motion communicate that 'twas not over his brother that there was reason for privacy. His undersheriff's face relaxed in understanding and glanced toward Elyssa, then turned for the gate.

As the young knight left them, Elyssa loosed a tiny cry. "Geoffrey, you are frightening me. Has something happened to my son?"

After his rage of the previous moment, Geoffrey couldn't comprehend how compassion woke in him. Still, it was there and the need to soften his news was strong. He caught her by the arm, then drew her into his embrace. "There has been a battle at Ashby."

"Jocelyn!" she cried, pushing against him as she tried to break free. When he would not let her go, she leaned back against his arms, staring up at him. Her face was ashen, but, oddly, there were no tears in her eyes.

Geoffrey sighed as he realized her fear went too deep for tears. "I will not lie to you, he's been injured. My brother says the wounds he took are grave, but if he survives the night, he is expected to live."

"You have killed my son," she whispered, then whitened even further. At last, she gave way to the shock and slipped from the conscious world. He caught her against him.

"God will have to forgive me if he dies, Elyssa," he said to her as he lifted her inert body in his arms, "for I think that you will not."

Chapter 16

Although the hour of Vespers had passed and the sky was streaked pewter and mauve, Elyssa wasn't prepared to leave the garden. The need to pace was strong, as if doing so might help her escape her desire to weep yet again. She rose from her stool, the replacement for what had been destroyed, still clutching the missive sent by Geoffrey from Ashby.

Four days past, at May's start, Crosswell's sheriff left to escort a company of masons to that stinking manor. He'd gone more to ease her mind over Jocelyn than because there was a threat against the workmen. As if there could be any threat left near Ashby. The sarcastic thought seared through her mind. Had her son not nearly given his life to rid that foul place of threat?

"What does it say, 'Lyssa?" Clare asked.

"Lord Coudray writes that Jocelyn does not lay abed at all, but is up, even playing, although his arm is in a sling. So too, does he claim my son begs I not attempt to remove him from Ashby's care. Lord Coudray is convinced Jocelyn wishes to remain there."

"Good news, then," Clare said with a relieved sigh. "Now can you set your mind at ease."

Relief also tried to rise in Elyssa. She forced it

away, fomenting her grief to keep it at bay. What sort
of mother let her child remain in a dangerous place?

"Hah! Do you believe this? Jocelyn nearly lost his
life, he cannot want to remain. I say 'tis but a lie to
assuage guilt on Lord Coudray's part. Damn him,
Clare, but he returns on the morrow, not planning on
bringing Jocelyn here to heal as we discussed." 'Twas
an aching statement, reflecting the pain that had settled into the curve of her lower back.

'Twas no more than she'd expected. Geoffrey had
been oh so very kind these past three weeks, pretending he cared. A lie. Proof of that lay in his refusal
to bring Jocelyn to her.

Elyssa gave way to her urge to walk. Unseeing, she
strode, nay waddled, past clumps of violets and sprout-
ing pinks, unaffected by the perfume of blooming pear
and apple trees. If Geoffrey wouldn't do as he should,
she could force his hand in this.

At long last her aim of last autumn was fulfilled; she
now owned the means by which to control Crosswell's
sheriff. All she need do was threaten to spread Maud's
tale, along with the story of Cecilia's silence. Taken
together, 'twould be proof that Maud's madness in-
fected his daughter. In return for her vow of silence,
Geoffrey would do whatever she asked of him.

Cecilia's wee hand curled into hers. " 'Lyssa, I love
you," her poppet whispered as she sought to comfort
her borrowed maman.

The child's words were a sword's blow to Elyssa's
heart. How could she even imagine hurting Cecilia this
way? Yet how could she leave Jocelyn where he had
already been hurt? A terrible pain seared her core,
and she swore she was breaking in two, torn between
the children she loved. After a moment the pain
ebbed, and Elyssa wiped away her tears. She glanced

toward her poppet and tried to smile. "I know you do, my heart."

Gray eyes wide, Cecilia offered her support. "I do not like that Jocelyn was hurt. That shouldn't have happened."

"Nay, it shouldn't have happened," Elyssa replied, her tears threatening to start afresh. Must she destroy one to save the other?

"Why isn't Papa bringing him home?" While Cecilia awaited her answer, her teeth worried her lower lip. Over these past three weeks, especially since Geoffrey left for Ashby to see Jocelyn, Cecilia had begun speaking openly of her father.

A quiver touched Elyssa's lips once again. Geoffrey didn't bring Jocelyn because she couldn't use this sweet child against him. Mary save her, no matter where she looked, there was no way free of her heart's trap.

Clare came to stand behind Cecilia, her hands on the child's shoulders. "Come now, poppet, why not give 'Lyssa a moment alone?"

Cecilia's brow creased, and she stroked Elyssa's belly, then cradled her wooden plaything close. "My poppet doesn't like that Jocelyn was hurt, either."

Elyssa lay a hand atop Cecilia's head. "Whatever should I do without you to love me?" she asked. She couldn't, she wouldn't, hurt this babe, even to save Jocelyn. Mother of God, but what sort of parent betrayed the son of her blood for a temporary daughter only of the heart?

The terrible aching returned, but this time it passed from her soul's core to center in her womb. Elyssa bit her lip against the shock of it, incapable of drawing a breath. It ebbed slowly. She sighed as a strange relief flowed over her. Aye, death would be easier to face than this dilemma.

"Clare, the babe comes."

Night was almost fully upon his small troop as Geoffrey led them toward Crosswell's gatehouse. For the first time since becoming sheriff, the massive structure seemed welcoming. 'Twasn't that he'd developed any liking for Crosswell's defenses, rather, it was the woman who dwelt within these walls. She, and her caring for him, made this hellhole easier to bear.

How he could feel so after her weeks of tears and pleas over bringing Jocelyn here remained a mystery to Geoffrey. Especially so, since the journey she'd begged him to take had turned out to be a wasted trip, unless he counted his amusement at watching his brother Gilliam and his new wife. Jocelyn was hale and well, despite his injuries, and a far more enjoyable child than he'd been in autumn past.

He freed a tolerant breath. Not that Elyssa would believe him when he said so. Until she saw her son for herself, she'd worry, while Jocelyn refused to come, fearing his mother would lock him away in a monastery against his will.

"So, what will you be telling the lady, my lord?" Osbert asked in friendly inquiry. A year's acquaintanceship had thawed this knight, making for an amiable companion. "I think she'll not believe us when we describe the boy we saw."

Geoffrey glanced at the mercenary. "That, Osbert, is an unfortunate truth. I can hear her already. I'll utter no more than two words, before she'll yammer over me, denying what I've just said. When I tell her her child refused to return, the tears will fall like rain. By God, Osbert, but she's an impossible woman. Here her son displays great courage and military abilities far beyond his years, yet, instead of pride, she moans and complains as if he were an infant."

Osbert laughed as they halted before the outer gate, waiting for the portcullis to rise. Geoffrey shook his head over the coming confrontation. Why couldn't Elyssa see what harm she did her son by trying to protect him from life's normal flow?

His thoughts swung around like a morning star in motion to strike him with its backlash. Elyssa's fears for her son were no different than his worries over Cecilia and he, no more justified in his than she in hers. Like Jocelyn, who'd found a lion's heart in Gilliam's love for him, Cecilia would find what she needed wrapped in Elyssa's support and care.

"Oh, so 'tis irritation you find in Freyne's widow, is it?" There was deep amusement hiding in Osbert's tone, and the knight shot him a sidelong glance as they rode together into the bailey. "Do you know, my lord, I've long since ceased to pray for you? Say, since Christmastide." 'Twas a sly aside.

The corner of Geoff's mouth lifted in a wry smile, and he looked at the man. "Am I so obvious as that?"

"Mayhap to none of them," Osbert jerked his head toward the soldiers who followed them, the latest contingent of outsiders to man Crosswell's garrison, "but I have known you a year now."

"And familiarity has destroyed my reputation, eh?" A sudden gratitude rose in Geoffrey. If Cecilia stood on her own, he could release the cloak of his reputed evil in which he'd attempted to shield her. To be feared and shunned no longer would be a wondrous thing.

"Nay, my lord, 'twasn't you, but Lady Freyne who revealed you. You should've beaten her that day on

the road to Crosswell. The devil and his minions are
not known for their patience or mercy. With Lady
Freyne to do the pushing, it all rolled downhill from
there." Osbert stared at the inner gateway, mouth
tight against a smile.

Geoffrey shook his head in amusement, then
glanced toward the widow's cottage. 'Twas caught in
deep shadow, pierced only by what little light escaped
between Elyssa's door and frame. That soft illumina-
tion called to him, whispering of its owner's caring
nature. So too, did it hint at the passion they'd created
between them. Aye, irritation was the least of the
emotions she raised in him.

The need to see her this very moment struck. He'd
go, not only to relate Jocelyn's tale to her, but to
speak of Cecilia's future. As Henry of Lavendon suggested, his daughter could be fostered once Cecilia
was strong enough to bear separation from Elyssa.

And, in giving Cecilia her future, Geoffrey re-
claimed his own. Now that Cecilia was healed, there
was no need for him to die. The desire to live rushed
through him, stunning in its intensity. But he would
not be alone. In his imagining 'twas Elyssa who shared
his life with him, just as she shared his pain. He turned
Passavant's head toward the stables.

"My lord?" Osbert asked.

He glanced at the man. "Since you've found me
out, I see no reason not to do as I please," he replied
with a quirk of his brows. "Just now, I've a need to
speak with the widow that cannot wait."

The mercenary laughed, then called behind him his
lord's intent. The soldiers groaned loudly against this,
several freeing potent curses. Aye, Crosswell was indeed feeling much more like home.

"You'll not die for a few steps," Geoffrey told them

as he dismounted before the stable door. He handed Passavant's reins to his groom, then removed helmet, gloves, and sword for Osbert to bear into the hall. Not wishing to make a public announcement of his intentions toward the lady until she'd agrede, Geoff waited for the commoners to precede him into the inner gateway. When they were gone, he strode along the garden wall.

Where Coudray fell gratefully into night's soft embrace, finding rest and comfort in its depths, Crosswell warded off the darkness with torches and lamps. 'Twas as if both town and keep feared day's ending. The slight breeze yet retained the foul stench of burning coal. It also brought with it disjointed snatches of music from some nearby inn. At Crosswell's outer gate a whore called out to a passerby. When she was refused, she let fly a string of insults against the unfortunate's manhood. Somewhere in the bailey, men shouted and cursed in argument over a dice game gone bad.

Geoffrey paused before Elyssa's door, his hand lifted to knock, then lowered his fist. What if she refused him? After all, her petition to the court stated she wished to never wed again. Christmas night and the passion of their kiss woke in him once more. She'd melted against him, echoing his desire with her own. Nay, he'd not allow her to refuse him. His knuckles rebounded off the thick door.

'Twas a long moment before the panel swung open. Martin stood in the portal. Jealousy roared through Geoffrey. He reached for his sword, meaning to end his undersheriff's life for this trespass, only to discover there was no weapon at his side.

"Thank God, you've returned," Martin said in a low

voice, oblivious to his lord's sudden desire to murder him. "She's been calling for you."

Geoffrey stared, the man's words making no sense. "Calling for me?"

" 'Tis no good, I think me," Martin replied with a sad shake of his head. "My lord, I'd rather battle my worst enemy with my bare hands than contemplate giving birth."

Jealousy ebbed into embarrassment, then shock at how strong his claim on Elyssa was. Finally, the whole of what his undersheriff said penetrated. "She dies?" he breathed. Fear drove deeply into him. She couldn't, not now.

"Aye, she and the babe slip away," Grief already touched Martin's dark eyes.

"Nay," Geoff hissed, pushing past his man to enter the tiny room.

Although May's warmth made a fire unnecessary, flames leapt on the stone to shed its precious light around the room. A woman, the midwife no doubt, crouched near the hearth heating something in a cup. Cecilia lay in the other corner, curled beneath a blanket and already deep in slumber. The bed was framed by its curtains, the scarlet material caught tightly to the posts. Clare stood at its head.

Geoffrey started toward Elyssa's cousin. At the jangling of his mail, she turned to look at him. Her usually shy reaction was buried beneath her tears for her relative.

"God be praised, 'tis you, my lord. Mayhap you can wake some fight in her. I vow she is willing herself into death." Her frantic tone shot through him.

Geoff stared into the bed. Elyssa lay on her side, facing him, her plaits falling over the bed's edge. She wore a simple, white shift, clothed for modesty's sake against in this witnessed birthing. Her eyes were closed, while deep lines of exhaustion marked her face. So still did she lie, it seemed death already held her. He damned himself to hell and back. Why had he left her with the babe's coming so near?

Her hand lay open, palm down, upon the mattress. Geoff crossed the room and lay his own over the back of hers, intertwining their fingers. Raising her arm, he sought a pulse at her wrist. Weak, but still there.

The movement of her arm made her draw a deep breath. Then, as if the effort were almost beyond her, she opened her eyes. Without moving her head, she looked at him.

"You came." 'Twas a bare breath. A soft sort of peace flowed over her features, and Geoffrey liked it naught at all. He'd never seen her like this; she wasn't fighting to live.

"Aye," he replied, trying to smile, "and here will I stay until your babe is come."

"Jocelyn?"

"Thrives. Elyssa, he is safe and content, this I vow on my own life. He refused to come to Crosswell, fearing you will set him in a monastery." 'Twas hard to tell if she was placated, as she only closed her eyes once more.

"My lord," Clare said quietly from behind him, "the midwife has something for her."

Geoffrey moved back, setting his hand on the post. The knot in the tie that held the bed curtain aside was uncomfortable against his palm. He glanced at it as he shifted his hand, then looked again.

When Maud labored so long with their stillborn child, the midwife set the servants to removing every knot in the room, saying this would make the labor easier. Belts had been opened, the laces in their shoes untied, even Maud's hair had been loosened. Elyssa's hair was yet tightly bound in plaits.

Geoffrey stared at their coppery lengths as the sense that something was amiss here rose in him. The midwife set the cup to Elyssa's lips, forcing the liquid into her patient. "What is that you give her?" he asked.

The surprise in the midwife's face quickly became professional disdain. "My lord sheriff, this is a female matter. The law says you must watch, but I'll not have you interfering." To Elyssa, she said, "Aye, my lady, drink you all of it."

"I think it cannot be interfering to ask what sort of potion you give her." Geoffrey's voice rose in command.

" 'Tis something to soothe her," the woman deigned to reply. Her patient swallowed slowly, as if even this simple act was too difficult for her. "Now, if you'll take yon stool, you may watch what goes forward. Send that other man from here. One of you is all I will bear."

Geoffrey caught the woman's arm, preventing her from pouring the final dregs into Elyssa. The midwife turned on him, her dark eyes hard with the insult he did her by his questioning. He studied her, but there was no expression save professional pique to see in her broad English face.

"You came from Freyne?"

Insult ebbed as confusion woke in her face. "Aye, my lord. The lady requested that I come. 'Twas I who brought her first two children into the world."

"I think me Freyne is a backward place," he said, "else you'd have known to loosen these knots." He tugged on one end of the string holding the bed curtain aside.

The midwide started against his comment, the surprise on her face not against the necessity of opening knots, but that he'd known she should have done so. After surprise came wild fear. Her eyes shifted as if she sought some avenue of escape.

Beside him, Clare gasped aloud as she, too, saw the sudden guilt. What in God's name was afoot here? Rage flared in Geoffrey. "I think I'll have me a taste of this brew."

He reached to take the cup from her hands, but she twisted it, trying to spill what remained within it. The contents splattered against Elyssa's shift, dark against white linen. Geoffrey wrenched it from her. Although there was naught even a sip left in it, the wooden container retained the flavor of the last draft. At the unmistakable bitterness of wormwood, he threw the cup. It rebounded off the wall, then rattled along the floor mats.

"You idiot," he roared, "she's already half dead. This stuff will send her the rest of the way to heaven. I pray for your sake you're but an incompetent, else your life will be the forfeit."

"I've done no wrong, my lord," the midwife moaned, backing away from the bed while she wrung her hands. "What works one way for a man works another during a woman's travail. How can you be expected to understand what is a female trade?"

"Then, I'll ask another of your ilk to verify your claim." 'Twas a threat, cold and deadly.

The woman bolted for the door, but Martin was there to block her path. She whirled, new desperation filling her face. "My lord, you mistake my purpose in giving her a sleeping draft. She can go no further without rest." Her words ended in a yelp as Martin caught her by the back of her gown. "My lord, I beg you, I've done no wrong here."

"If that were so, then you should have been forth-coming when Lord Coudray first asked," the young knight snarled into her ear. " 'Tis a dismaying lack of honesty you own, bitch. My lord," Martin said to him, regret now coloring his features, "I have seen her give draft after draft to Lady Freyne and never thought to ask after them. Pray God, 'tisn't too late."

"No harm's been done," the woman cried, trying to kneel as her face flooded with tears. Martin wouldn't let her knees reach the floor. "Bring any midlife you wish, and she'll say the same. The lady but rests against the next stage of her delivery."

Geoffrey subdued his urge toward simple murder. "We shall soon see. If she dies, I vow you'll die for murder." The woman moaned, hanging limp from Martin's grasp as she sobbed. "Let her spend her night with the rest of my prisoners," he told his undersher-iff. "Send the porter to Robert the Smith begging that he send to his lord sheriff the town's best midwife. There can be no delay in her coming. If she's here within the quarter hour, I'll pay four times her fee."

"Aye, my lord." Martin exited, dragging the weep-ing woman with him as the midwife sobbed out yet another plea against her innocence.

The door closed, and Geoffrey turned to Clare. Elyssa's cousin cried softly, her face buried in her hands. "Lady Clare, you must take heart. Your cousin will be needing both of us if she's to survive."

Clare caught back her sobs, then looked up at him. Her face twisted in a hurt that went deeper than grief for her relative. In the woman's soft features, Geoff saw the breaking of her heart.

"My lord, 'tis my fault for this. I am the one who wrote to Sir Reginald, requesting he send us Freyne's midwife. I never understood—" her voice broke and she bent beneath her grief. "Oh, but I am such an idiot, foolishly believing what I waited a lifetime to hear, when I should have stoppered my ears."

Although confused by her words, there was no mistaking that she blamed herself for what happened to her cousin. Geoffrey caught her by the shoulders. "You meant only good with what you did, and there's no wrong in that. Come now and help me disarm. Between us, we'll see she stays in this world awhile longer."

"Aye, but if she goes, I vow I'll go with her," Clare muttered to herself as she reached for the tails of his mail shirt.

Chapter 17

Elyssa drifted in a timeless place, dark and blessedly safe from the unending pains. Dying had turned out to be a far more difficult and lengthy ordeal than she'd expected. Then, from deep within her rose a flicker of relief. There was no longer a need to die. Geoffrey had vowed on his own life that Jocelyn was content and safe. Even as one corner of her depression lifted, the fear of producing naught but a dead babe at the end of this travail dragged her down, once again. 'Twas too much to face.

Someone threw back the bedclothes, then forced her to lie upon her back. Her shift was lifted. She managed a cry against an intrusive hand, but it took more energy than she owned to open her eyes. After a moment the inspection was finished, and her shift was pulled down around her knees once more.

Words flowed around her, the tone brusque and efficient. She listened, not certain if she dreamed them or if there truly was someone new in the room.

" 'Tis not as hopeless as you might think, my lord. There's none of the discharge that says the babe suffers, but, if she's labored more than a day, as her lady cousin says, we'll need to be swift in wresting the infant from her." 'Twas a husky voice, defying identification as either male or female.

"Was this done apurpose?" At Geoffrey's fluid tones, Elyssa sighed in the memory of his calm strength. He would keep her safe from what hurt her.

"Apurpose?" The other voice freed a bark of laugh. "If stupidity is intentional, then 'twas, my lord. I swear rural folk have the strangest practices. Even when I can show them a better way, they cling to things as they've always done them. No respect for learning or progress, my lord. Here, make her drink this."

Elyssa was lifted into an upright position. She let her head fall back against a shoulder. A strong arm came to brace her into this position as a cup was set to her lips. Thirst plagued her, but this stuff was foul, worse even than the other. She tried to turn her head aside. 'Twas caught and would not move.

"Come now, drink it. All of it." Geoffrey lay his words softly into her ear, his lips nigh on brushing her cheek.

She relaxed and tried to swallow. The stuff hit her stomach and made it lift in complaint. "Nay, no more," she protested, barely able to force her mouth to make words.

"Good," the other voice said, "now, she'll spew what's in her."

As if it had been listening, her stomach twisted in protest, threatening to do just that. Elyssa groaned. Where pain and fear couldn't rouse her from her lethargy, her dislike of spilling her gullet before witnesses did. She gathered her energy and forced her eyes open.

Geoffrey sat beside her, wearing only a shirt and a rough pair of chausses. He smiled at her. Damn, but she'd not empty what was in her stomach before him.

"Not while you look on." This simple sentence cost her dearly. She had to close her eyes and rest when it was out. He gave vent to an irritated breath, but called to Clare.

Although the jostling made her stomach's ache worse, Elyssa sighed in relief as Clare took Geoffrey's place on the bed. A basin was set in her lap. This was followed by the scrape of closing bed curtains. She leaned her head against Clare's shoulder.

Her cousin trembled, then freed a muffled sob. Elyssa opened her eyes. Even in the darkness of the bed's cloaked interior, she could see Clare's tears.

"Do not cry for me," she breathed, "only vow that if this babe lives, and I do not, you'll love him as I have loved Jocelyn."

"With all my heart I so vow," Clare managed to reply, her voice breaking. "But know you make a blind idiot your child's caretaker."

The need to spill her stomach made it impossible to ask after Clare's meaning. Once purged, Elyssa gratefully let her cousin wash her face and hand her a cup of watered wine. Long moments passed as she sipped the tart liquid. Slowly, her thoughts began to steady, and her mind began to focus. Clare set about opening her plaits as another cup was thrust through the curtains.

Elyssa caught it in her yet-trembling hands. This potion was sweeter than either of the others, and she drank it easily. She sighed and leaned back into Clare's embrace.

It came on her, like darkness's creep at sunset, until her whole body was tight against the ache. Only then, did she make sense of all she'd heard. This midwife was going to force the babe to come swiftly. Elyssa groaned against what hurt in her, clutching at Clare until it passed.

"Ah," the husky-voiced midwife said, "I think me

this babe is eager to leave his mama. Bring her out of the bed, my lady. Your noble cousin must walk."

The bed curtains were thrown open. Geoffrey leaned into the interior and aided Clare in easing Elyssa toward the mattress's edge. He took hold of her waist, meaning to help her to rise.

"Come now, Elyssa of Freyne, 'tis time you released your hold on my ward. Walk with me so I can take him." He smiled at her.

Irritation woke at his jest. She was dying here, already exhausted beyond belief. Be damned if she was going to leave her bed. If she hadn't the strength to escape Geoffrey's grasp, she resisted as best she could his efforts to pull her from the mattress. "Leave me."

The new midwife came to stand beside him. Hair gleaming silver over a wrinkled face, the woman's eyes were like unto bright amber beads. "Berta's my name, my lady. If you want that babe, you'll walk."

"I didn't walk with my first two," Elyssa argued, confounded by this Berta's unnatural request. "I but lay still and waited on them to come."

"You've had two before?" Berta said in pleased surprise. "Then, this one should come all the easier. Heed me now, my lady. The potion I just gave you is meant to make your pains come closer and harder. You can writhe and scream against them, or rise and walk to ease them. If you walk, your babe will come all the sooner, putting an end to all your aches."

"You don't know what you've done," Elyssa protested, even more loudly. "I nearly died with my first two, and they came slowly. What you want will tear me in two." She caught at Geoffrey's sleeve. "Tell her she cannot do this. Help me, she's trying to kill me." Another pain welled up in her, and she tensed against it, clutching at Geoffrey's arm as it overtook her.

"What a coward you are," Berta scoffed, then turned on Crosswell's sheriff. "Pay her no heed, my lord. Birthing women are all the same, needing to be driven into doing what's in their own good. She's been lazy long enough. Make her walk."

Geoffrey laughed at that. "Prepare yourself, good-wife, this woman's difficult even when she doesn't labor. She'll fight us every step of the way. Lady Clare, push your cousin off the bed and into my arms."

There wasn't enough strength in Elyssa to stop them. When her feet met the floor, Geoffrey caught her in his embrace, then turned her. "Walk, Elyssa, walk for your babe."

She moaned, but he forced her across the short room. Yet another pain came over her. Elyssa arched against it as it settled in her back. Geoffrey held her close to his side, his hand massaging at what hurt her.

"Try not to battle the pains so, my lady," Berta suggested as she came to support Elyssa on her other side. "Relax rather than tensing."

"And just how am I supposed to do that?" she cried, then anger roared through her. "Damn you both. If you want me dead, leave me in my bed to die in comfort." Another pain hit her, and she sagged between them to moan. " 'Twas never like this before. I want Freyne's midwife back. She understands I cannot bear the pain."

Berta made a scornful sound. "Aye, so understanding that she gives you sleeping drafts. 'Tis a miracle you didn't lose your first two babes." Crosswell's midwife fixed her with a superior look.

Elyssa straightened and stared at the woman. "I did lose my daughter," she whispered. "And my son nearly died."

"Well, you'll not lose this one." Berta offered a grin

so gap-toothed, it suggested she'd birthed herself a goodly number of children. "What will it be, a daughter or a son?"

"Son," Elyssa replied without hesitation.

"If you want him, you'll work for your son, my lady. Walk her, my lord," the midwife said to Geoffrey.

"Come, 'Lyssa," he said, dragging her once more across the room. "Give me my new ward."

"I cannot walk," Elyssa hissed, fighting to free herself from Geoffrey's embrace. "I hurt, do you not understand? Now, touch me no more. I was wrong to wish for your presence. You are a cruel man."

"You idiot, just do what she says and you'll have both life and son," he snapped at her. "Just this once, do not fight me."

"I hate you," she cried, trying to grasp at the bed post to keep him from moving her any farther.

"She doesn't mean it, my lord. 'Tis the babe and her pains talking." There was a cautious, worried tone in Berta's voice, saying she feared the nobleman's reaction to the lady's spiteful pronouncement. It startled Elyssa to realize how confident she was that Geoffrey would never abuse her.

He didn't disappoint her. With a laugh, Geoffrey caught her close once more and forced her back across the room. "Hatred, is it now? What a shame, since I've decided I love you. Come now, my love, short steps or long ones?"

"Once more and push," the midwife commanded. "Tuck your chin, my lady. My lord, force her to do so, else she'll hurt herself."

Good God, but birthing was no coward's job. Seated behind Elyssa to brace her into a semi-sitting position, Geoffrey put a hand to her nape and bent her head as the midwife commanded him. 'Twas the deepest portion of the night, dawn yet hours away. Clare, having watched over her cousin for longer than a full day's time, had dropped in her exhaustion and joined Cecilia in her corner. Elyssa, who had taken her rest in drugged slumber, now struggled against her own exhaustion, brought on by her continuing labor.

"Come now, 'Lyssa, give him to me." His voice had grown hoarse over the past hours, but Elyssa vowed his words calmed and soothed her. He tensed for her as she strained to force the babe from her body.

"Rest," the midwife commanded.

Elyssa freed her breath in a great gust, and Geoff released his hold on her neck. Instantly, she threw back her head, letting it rest against his shoulder as she cried out in wordless complaint. He leaned his cheek against hers, rocking her slightly in his embrace.

"Not much longer, my love," he breathed into her ear. She murmured in reply as Geoff worked at the stiff muscles in her back.

"Again," the midwife commanded.

"I'm done for," Elyssa moaned.

"You cannot quit now. Release Aymer's heir for me," Geoff urged her. "Do you not want to see your son, my love?"

"I am not your love," Elyssa muttered, but breathed deeply in preparation.

Geoff only laughed, tucking her head for her once more. Over this night's span, speaking this endearment aloud had made it the truth. Now, as his love for her grew steadily in him, so did the disappointment that Elyssa saw his words only as a goad.

"I have his head," the midwife called in triumph. "Another push and we'll have the rest of him."

Elyssa cried out in sudden excitement, finding

strength in some hidden reserve as tears filled her eyes. "Help me, Geoff," she demanded, remembering to tuck her head on her own this time.

"I've got him," the midwife crowed. "You were right, my lady. 'Tis a son you've got here. Big one with a tuft of red hair lighter than your own. Breathe for me, lad," the woman commanded of the child. A moment passed without a sound.

"Nay," Elyssa gasped, grasping behind her for a handful of Geoffrey's shirt. "He cannot die," she begged of him. "Geoff, I want my son." She tucked her head into his shoulder, sobbing against her fear.

Geoff caught her close, his grief matching hers. Somehow, participating in this babe's coming had made the child dear to him. He stroked her arm as a still-weeping Elyssa straightened to watch the midwife work on her babe. "Do not look, love," he urged.

"Cecilia," Elyssa gasped. "Geoff, fetch her away. I'll not have her see another child die."

Geoffrey came upright with a start. The midwife had shifted in her efforts. Behind her stood Cecilia, dress rumpled and hair wild with sleep. His daughter was watching in fascination as the woman turned the babe upside down, seeking to expell what blocked his lungs. Love grew. Dear God, but this woman was precious, her fear for his daughter equal to her fear for her own babe. But how was he supposed to fetch his daughter when she ran from him?

He arose from the bed, letting Elyssa lean back against the headboard. "Cecilia, lass, come to me," he said quietly, fearing her rejection as deeply as he feared 'Lyssa's babe wouldn't breathe.

"Aye, Papa," his daughter replied, crossing the room to his side. "Hold me," she demanded sleepily.

Geoffrey rocked against her request, but reached

for his child. Cecilia caught him around the neck, wrapping her legs around his waist as he lifted her. She turned her face until she could lean a cheek against his shoulder.

'Twas too sweet to bear. His arms around his daughter tightened against his heart's pressure as his knees trembled. He braced himself against the wall and gloried in the feel of Cecilia. She had grown, lengthening substantially in the time span between Maud's death and this day.

"Come, lad, you're a big, strong boy. Show me those lungs work," the midwife crooned. There was a tiny gagging sound, then the infant gave way to her command and freed an irate cry.

"Geoffrey!" Elyssa cried out with a sob, "he lives."

Her son lived; his daughter was his once more. The joy was too great to hold as his own. Geoff laughed, the sound ringing with his heart's new life. This only fed the babe's angry squall.

"Listen to him. He's as contentious as his dam." His voice trembled.

In the bed, Elyssa thrust out her arms. "Give him to me," she demanded of the midwife. The woman set the babe into her arms.

Geoffrey sat upon the mattress beside her, still holding Cecilia close to him. 'Twas, indeed, a brawny lad who filled Elyssa's arms, with a coppery swatch atop his head and a healthy set of lungs. His squalling and squirming ceased as his maman crooned to him, making soothing sounds.

"Elyssa of Freyne, may you take as great a pride in this son as you do in his older brother," Geoffrey said quietly, incapable of banishing his smile. "What will you name him?"

Elyssa looked up at him, her joy making her eyes shine. "Simon. I'll call him for my sire."

Then, as Geoffrey watched, he saw her love for her new son tangle with her need to hold every child she claimed as hers alone, defying all others to wrench them from her. Deeper still lurked the knowledge that she would someday have to let this son go, just as she'd freed Jocelyn.

"I see your thoughts in your eyes, my love," Geoffrey said, smiling at this strange need of hers. He leaned over Cecilia until he could touch his lips to hers. With his kiss, he promised her that, if she'd have him, she'd not have to face these partings on her own.

Her mouth clung to his, moving slightly. As their kiss continued, what had begun in innocence was quickly tainted with the embers of Christmas past. He breathed deeply in wonder at the sort of heat they could make between them.

"My pardon," the midwife said, speaking as if she viewed this sort of exchange between unmarried folk every day, "but we're not quite finished here. I'll be needing the afterbirth now, my lady. Give me the babe."

Elyssa gasped against his lips as she realized the midwife looked on. When she pulled away, her face was bright red. Embarrassed or not, when the midwife reached for the babe, she clutched her Simon to her. "Nay, I'll keep him."

"She's not one to easily let her sons escape her embrace," Geoffrey laughed, "so best you make do, Berta."

'Twas over in the next moments. While the midwife examined the afterbith, Geoffrey reached out to lift the babe's tiny hand with his finger. "It never ceases to amaze me that we were all once this small."

"Was I?" Cecilia asked, leaning down to look at the babe lying in her caretaker's arms.

"Aye, *cherie,* you were even smaller than he," Geoffrey told her with a smile.

" 'Lyssa, this is not my brother." Cecilia reached out to touch the babe's arm.

"True, poppet," Elyssa replied, " 'tis my son. Would you like to sit on the bed and see him better?"

Geoff's arms tightened around his daughter. He couldn't bear to think of releasing her. Mother of God, but he was as bad as Elyssa in this. "She wants to stay with her Papa," he said.

"Aye," Cecilia agreed, resettling herself into his lap so she sat more than was held. She looked up at him, tilting her head to one side. "Does it hurt you?" she asked, using her finger to follow the longer of his scars.

Her blunt question surprised him, but Geoffrey answered it nonetheless. "Nay, I am healed now, and there's no pain in it."

"You cannot see here." She touched the patch. " 'Tis like this, no?" Cecilia put a hand over her own eye.

Again, the openness of her question surprised him. "True, indeed."

"But, when I take my hand away, I can see again. You cannot." There was sadness in her voice. "I do not like that."

Astonished that Cecilia would worry over his lost sight against the greater scope of their tragedy, Geoffrey glanced at Elyssa. His ward watched them, her eyes brimming. When she caught his glance, she managed an encouraging smile.

Geoffrey touched his lips to Cecilia's brow. "Do not

cry for me, *cherie*," he said. "I still have sight enough to be your papa."

Cecilia nodded as if content, then sleepily lay her head on his shoulder. "Will Jocelyn die?"

Again, he glanced at Elyssa. New worries touched her face. "Nay, he is hale and well at Ashby, although his shoulder is injured. He, too, has a scar now, not like mine. His is on the top of his head. When last I saw him, he was crowing because 'twas longer than what lay on one of his friends. His bet over it had won him five shining stones." He smiled at Elyssa.

She rolled her eyes against such idiocy, but there was an easiness in her face that said she accepted his words. Cecilia shifted to look at the babe in Elyssa's arms once more.

"This is not my brother," she repeated, but this time her voice was thick with hurt. "My brother died, didn't he, Papa."

Geoffrey cringed against her words. The desire to refuse what she wanted from him was strong. Suddenly, Elyssa's hand lay upon his arm. He glanced at her. How could she be so certain that speaking of that day would aid Cecilia? But then, how could he know it wouldn't? He sighed and gave way.

"Aye, he did."

"Maman died, too." However quiet her voice, there was no mistaking her pain; it matched his own.

He drew his daughter closer to him, until she was cradled in his arms. "She did. I am sorry for that, *cherie*."

A lifetime of begging her forgiveness wouldn't be enough to replace what his enraged and instinctive reaction had stolen from her. For months at a time, Maud held tight to her sanity. During those periods, she had been a caring mother to Cecilia.

His child raised her head from his shoulder, then leaned back to look at him. Her hand came to stroke his scarred cheek. "Maman was going to hurt me, but you didn't let her." 'Twas but a whisper. "She hurt you, instead of me."

He rocked her in his arms. "Are you not my little love? How could I let anyone do you harm? I am only sorry I wasn't fast enough to keep her from hurting your brother."

"That shouldn't have happened," Cecilia said with more strength in her voice. The hurt in her had ebbed.

"Aye, that shouldn't have happened," he replied, agreeing wholeheartedly with his daughter, "but I'm sorry that it did."

"I love you, Papa," Cecilia offered as if to ease his pain. 'Twas a lesson she'd learned from Elyssa.

"And, I, you," he replied, his happiness so great he was beyond feeling.

Chapter 18

Someone shook her by the shoulder, and Elyssa groaned, not wanting to awaken. The sheets were fresh and she had bathed. Moreover, every muscle in her body ached. "Leave me sleep," she muttered.

"Lord Coudray wishes to know about the christening," Clare whispered. "He would send for those you'll name as godparents."

"Godparents?" Elyssa rolled onto her back, shoving still damp strands of hair from her face. *Jesu,* what man did she trust enough to tie to her sweet babe? Yawning, she glanced down into the cradle standing beside the bed. Her son.

She smiled, watching the rise and fall of his chest beneath his swaddling. Simon was not only beautiful, but healthy and strong as well. Once again, she sent thanks to the Virgin for giving him to her. She turned her gaze to Clare.

Her cousin's face was ragged, her brow creased as if she ached. Elyssa raised a hand to smooth the marks from Clare's forehead. "What is it that troubles you?" she asked.

Her cousin tried to smile. " 'Tis the midwife from Freyne. Lord Coudray has sent her back without prejudice. But 'Lyssa, she nearly killed you, whilst I helped."

"Now, Clare," Elyssa sighed, "we've been over this once already. Berta says the woman meant no harm, only used a backward method. How can you blame yourself when 'twas the same method used on Jocelyn and my Kate? If either of us should grieve, it should be me, for my ignorance and hers cheated me of my daughter."

Her cousin shook her head and never a more forlorn motion had Elyssa seen. "Would that I were as content with this explanation as you. . . ." Her voice trailed off into silence.

Elyssa eyed her for a long moment, then shook her head. Clare owned little in her life save her privacy. If her cousin didn't wish to speak of what truly troubled her, 'twasn't her place to take from her her one asset. Instead, she reached for Clare's hand in a declaration of appreciation and love.

Her cousin tried to smile, then said with a false cheerfulness, "Who will you ask to be his godmother?"

"His godmother?" Elyssa shot her an impatient look. "Goose, *you* shall be his godmother."

Clare stared at her in surprise. " 'Lyssa, you must choose a woman with good political connections, one with the substance to support your son in times of poverty. I am no one, not even able to bring yon babe a single gift upon his christening."

"Ah, but you have something more precious than a great name or gold cloth," Elyssa said, squeezing Clare's hand. " 'Tis your heart I want for my son. Promise him your devotion this day, and I'll be content."

'Twas the sun's dawning in Clare's face, melting away all trouble and worry. She leaned down to enfold her cousin in her embrace. " 'Lyssa, whatever should

I do without you to honor me? I vow to protect your son with mine own life." The intensity in her voice made the words more than just a proclamation of joy.

"Clare!" Elyssa protested, pushing free of her cousin's arms. "Now who's being morbid? Your life, indeed."

Clare only shrugged, yet the smile clung to her mouth, so great was the pleasure Elyssa's invitation gave her. "So, who will you have as his godfathers?"

Elyssa made a face at the question. "Must I put a man at his head?" She knew better; godfathers were an even stronger political bond in the eyes of the Church and state than that of godmother. The connection between boy and men was almost as close as that of blood.

"Aye, you must," Clare laughed. "No priest would ever accept only a woman as your Simon's guide. You know very well what the clergy thinks of we who are Eve's daughters."

"Let me ponder a moment."

Elyssa struggled to recall Aymer's friends other than Gradinton, who was totally unacceptable to her. Lavendon was out of the question, since he was already bound to Freyne through his daughter's betrothal contract. There was only one man Elyssa found she could tolerate in connection to Simon: Geoffrey.

As quickly as she thought it, a swift depression spiraled through her. Binding her son and her warden tied Geoffrey to her as if he were family. 'Twould be incest for her to kiss him again.

Kiss him again? Her breath caught in dismay. What in God's name made her think such a thing?

Only then did she see how Geoffrey's support during her delivery had harmed her. 'Twas the hours of him calling her his love that had done this. His touch, his words, his rejoicing when Simon breathed, all these things had worked their way into her soul until she desired him.

Oh, but this foolish wish to be precious to him was a terrible, dangerous thing. Geoffrey was a man like any other, not to be trusted and definitely not to be desired. Given a chance, he'd use her weakness against her, just as her husbands had. God be praised that she was leaving Crosswell in six weeks.

A hiccough of disappointment rose in her. What of Cecilia? Her poppet still needed her. Then, Cecilia must come with her—which meant Geoff would be a frequent visitor at Nalder. The thought of him sitting in her hall, conversing and laughing with her, brought with it another picture. In this one, he lay beside her within the privacy of her bed.

Elyssa stifled a groan at her idiocy. How could she think such a thing after the misery she'd suffered within the bonds of wedlock? She needed an insurmountable barrier between herself and her ridiculous dreaming.

"I'll have only Lord Coudray as his godfather," she said to Clare. The words fell, wooden and hard, from her reluctant tongue.

"Oh, 'Lyssa, I'm sure he'll be honored. He's quite taken with our Simon." Clare moved from the bedside to look down on her godson.

"Will you ask him for me?" Elyssa whispered. If she truly wanted nothing more to do with Geoffrey, why did her sense of loss hurt worse than the pains of last even'?

"Of course," Clare said with a smile, and turned toward the door.

Elyssa rolled onto her side and listened to the door close. She swallowed her tears, chiding herself once more for her foolishness. Once she was churched, 'twould be time to say farewell to Crosswell. When she rode from yon gateway, she'd be beholden to no man for the first time in her entire life. She drew a deep breath. Aye, once she regained her independence, surely this obsession with Geoffrey would disappear. Elyssa drifted back into sleep.

When she woke again, Simon was whimpering. Although she told Berta she'd needed a nurse for both Jocelyn and Kate, the midwife insisted she try feeding her son on her own. Berta claimed 'twould speed her healing.

Elyssa rolled toward the bed's edge with a sigh, only to catch back the sound in surprise. Geoffrey stood at her bedside, Simon cradled in his arms. He'd left the door partially opened behind him and sunlight streamed into the room. It gleamed on the strong line of his jaw and lay shadows against the perfect length of his nose. In the light's golden glow, she saw how his frequent journeys around the shire had set a browned tone to his fair skin.

As he watched her, his gaze slowly filled with that awesome intensity of his. Elyssa drew a swift breath. Once again, she came into the sudden and complete awareness of him as a desirable man. Ah, but look what hurt Ramshaw and Aymer had had done, and she'd not wanted to wed with them. In wanting Geoffrey, she made the hurt he could do her unimaginable.

Mary save her, but she didn't care; she wanted Geoffrey to lay claim to her. Thank God she'd sense enough to make him Simon's godfather. Now, no matter how foolish her desire, she couldn't have him.

Only as she tasted disappointment's dregs did it occur to her that Geoffrey wore his usual blue gown and brown chausses. She stared at him in confusion.

Godparents always dressed in their finest to bring the babe to church. Perhaps the christening was already done.

She looked at Simon. The swaddling he wore was the same he'd worn earlier. His christening gown yet hung from the cradle's edge.

"What are you doing here?" she asked.

"Bringing your son to your bedside," Geoffrey replied with a quiet lift of his lips.

"My lord," Elyssa protested, "have some respect for tradition and my privacy. You know as well as I that I must reside in seclusion for the next six weeks until I am churched." She glanced around the room. "Where is Clare?"

"Guarding the door to protect your reputation." He came to sit on the mattress beside her. Simon squirmed in his arms, then vented a wail, complaining of an aching emptiness in him.

'Twas her son's need that set Elyssa struggling into a sitting position, all the while keeping the bedclothes caught tightly to her chest. When she crooked her arm, Geoffrey set the babe in place. Simon immediately turned his face toward her, seeking to satisfy his hunger. "Does the priest refuse to christen him?" she asked. 'Twas unusual to have but one godfather.

"Nay, 'tis not that which brings me here," Geoff said, running a finger along the soft bindings covering Simon's shoulder.

"My lord, if there is no dire reason for you to be here, you must go," Elyssa said, her voice firm. She'd not set Simon to her breast while he watched.

"Ah, but my reason is dire, indeed." Geoffrey's expression was properly solemn. "There remains the matter of naming his godfather."

"I have asked *you*," Elyssa said in confusion. "Did Clare not carry my message to you?"

Her warden raised a single, scornful brow. "She did, and I could not believe my ears. What are you thinking, naming the devil's own as your son's godfather? I am disappointed in you, my love."

My love? Elyssa nearly groaned as his endearment set her heart to jumping with fear and something else within the confines of her ribs. Mary save her, he was going to pursue her.

"Disappointed?" she asked, proud that her voice gave no hint to the worry now living in her. " 'Tis family I would make of you. Think on it, my lord," she gave the honorific special emphasis. "Once our families are bound, I can be as a maman to Cecilia."

He reached out to lay his palm against her cheek. " 'Tis not the sort of family I wish us to be. I would wed with you, Elyssa of Freyne, and give all our children two parents."

"Are you mad?" she whispered. Mother of God, but his hand felt wondrous against her skin. It took all her effort not to lean her face into the cup of his palm. "We cannot go five minutes without arguing. What sort of marriage will that make?"

"One of great passion." Geoffrey moved his thumb until he stroked her lips. "So was it between my sire and dam. They fought as hard as they loved." He smiled at her.

Once again, Elyssa caught her breath at how his smile altered his face, setting strong lines in his cheeks and waking the small dip near the corner of his mouth. Oh, but even scarred, with his eye patched, he was a beautiful man. His simple amusement deepened into the beginnings of desire, and his face softened.

He combed his fingers through her hair, then let his

hand come to rest on her bare shoulder. When his fingertips drew soft lines down the curve of her upper arm, Elyssa shivered. If she wasn't careful, he would seduce her. And, if that happened, no amount of will would save her from the trap of marriage.

"What you want cannot be." She tried for a strong voice, but failed. The child in her arms squirmed, his complaints rising in intensity until he freed a high-pitched wail. "You are a wealthy man. I am no suitable match for you, not even when you include the income from my dower properties."

Geoffrey set his hand atop her blanket-covered knee, his fingers massaging gently. She shifted her leg. His smile broadened as he shook his head against her retreat.

"I married once for property. 'Tis a mistake I'll not make again. I say you are the woman I want as my wife. So would I say, if you had not a pence to your name," he replied. "Besides, who is there to tell me I cannot wed you?"

"Your elder brothers?" she asked, praying he would come to his senses.

"I think not." A new scorn touched his expression. "My father is dead. No man rules me, save my regent, and not even he can reject this petition, not when you already own the right to marry where you will. Come now, 'Lyssa. 'Tis a practical solution I offer you. Our joining will not only make me stepfather to Jocelyn and wee Simon, but 'twill make you Cecilia's stepmother."

"Practical, but out of the question," Elyssa retorted. "We'd soon come to hate each other, and I'll not do it."

"How can you be so sure?" He gave a quick lift of his brows. "Have we both not worked hard to hate each other throughout the past seven months, only to fail miserably?"

"We weren't wed to each other."

"Marriage vows will alter us so?" he scoffed gently.

Elyssa laid her hand on his arm in all earnestness. "My lord, all I know is that I have been bound twice in wedlock and both were miserable experiences. Yours, as well. Truly, I cannot comprehend why you'd wish to ruin what friendship now exists between us by proposing marriage. Nay, my lord." She shook her head in refusal as punctuation to her words. "Nay, I am flattered that one such as you would offer, but nay."

Geoffrey laughed as Simon howled against his plight. " 'Lyssa, your son cares even less for your answer than I do. He would have me as his father. Come now, Elyssa of Freyne, wed with me and bear my children. I vow to help each one enter the world."

Even so soon after her difficult labor, the very thought of making a child with Geoffrey was tempting, indeed. Those brief moments in the garden promised much of the pleasure their bodies could make. In pleasure's wake came the memory of how Aymer had used her body to sate them both, only to dishonor her passion by his perverse needs. Nay, 'twasn't in a man's nature to be either constant or kind to the woman who was his wife.

"My answer stays as I gave it. Besides, I am too old to carry another child, and you need heirs. Find yourself a bride of an appropriate age."

" 'Tis a poor excuse you cite me here, 'Lyssa," Geoffrey replied with surprising good humor. "Did not our old king wed his Eleanor when she was your age? She went on to bear him three daughters and far more sons than is good for this kingdom."

"I'll not do it, Geoff," she retorted, panicking at his persistence. "In six weeks' time, I will belong to myself for the first time in my life. I'll not let you push me where I refuse to go. Be my son's godfather."

"Nay."

" 'Tis a great honor," Elyssa started in an effort to convince him, but Geoffrey lay a finger across her lips.

"No more. This is not what I will have between us, and you cannot change my mind. Be you warned. When I set myself to a task, there's none who can stop me. In time, you will be mine."

Panic grew. "I like you too much to become your wife," she cried.

He only shook his head. The calmness of his expression was daunting. Mary save her, he was bent on this.

"Go away," she begged. "Go away from me. I tell you I'm no fit woman to be a wife. I am obstinate, contrary, and get more pleasure from a comfortable chair than I've ever had from a man."

Once again, Geoffrey laughed. "Do you know, I've even become fond of your ability to insult me? A chair, 'Lyssa?" His brows rose as his smile widened. "Then again, the thought of you sitting atop me brings with it haunting images."

"Geoffrey!" she cried in shock as he turned her protest into a lewd picture. Suddenly, she could see herself lying atop him, moving in passion's rhythm. His mouth would take hers, his hands would stroke and caress. She felt the heat of her blush creep up her neck to stain her cheeks.

" 'Tis even better now that I see it haunts you, too." His voice was warm, deepening with desire.

"Go away, Geoffrey," she said, mortified. Simon's cries were growing frantic.

She turned on the mattress until her back was to

him, then lowered the blankets. Simon caught back
his cry, then snuffled in relief as he found her breast.
From behind her, Geoffrey traced the bare length of
her spine with a fingertip.

"Who will you name as his godfather, for it won't
be me."

"What do I care?" she snapped, trying to snatch
the bedclothes up over her shoulder to hide her bare-
ness from him. To her surprise, he took the blankets
and settled them around her until she was covered.
"One man is the same as another to me. Let Sir Martin stand for Simon in your stead, then. It cannot hurt
to tie Freyne's child to him. The de la Bois's are a
respectable family."

Geoffrey lifted her hair free of the bedclothes, letting the stuff slide through his hands. Elyssa shuddered in reaction. "Please, Geoff, go away," she
begged softly. "You must leave me be."

"I will grant you the six weeks tradition requires,
after that, consider yourself besieged. Be warned, I'll
not cease until I have you, heart and body." He touched his lips to the spot where her neck joined her
shoulder.

Elyssa gasped against his caress. The mattress
shifted as he rose, then, a moment later, the cottage
door closed. When he was gone, she leaned her head
against the headboard, not certain whether she should
laugh or cry.

Damn him, but he'd use her desire for him against
her until she hadn't the will to resist him. When he
owned her will, he'd steal from her the independence
she'd always craved. Damn her, but she wanted him
to do so.

Chapter 19

Reginald stood atop one of Freyne's gate towers watching the troop of soldiers descend over the distant hills. Crosswell's men came steadily on toward him, riding single file along the road that passed through his outer fields and pastures. They thought they could retake his home, all because Aymer's wife had borne a healthy son, did they?

His gaze moved possessively across what he now named his. Freyne's orchards, having shed their spring finery in the past month, wore cloaks of green, while the newly shorn sheep were white specks against the lushness of June's grass. Haying had begun; from his vantage point the scythes gleamed in the sun, rising and falling in unison to the tune of a reaping song. The fragrant breeze brought him the rhythmic tones, more chant than lilt.

At the tangled border of the king's forest grew thick stands of wild rose, pinkish blossoms strewn along thorny branches. Oaks thrust their dark green heads high above the more delicate birch and hazel. Then, Reginald realized he gazed at the same section of woodland in which he and the commoner had laid Theobald to rest. A useless death, now that his brother's widow had borne Aymer another heir.

Freyne's midwife brought this news upon her return,

along with curses against Reginald for involving her in his plotting. Although he'd pointed out no harm was done, the bitch went on and on, moaning over her treatment whilst trapped in the sheriff's prison. It was obvious that, in time, her complaints would become extortion.

Foolish woman. At the first hint she needed coins to ease her suffering, she'd drunk one of her own nasty potions. Died, she had. Of course, 'twas he who'd made certain the foul stuff slid down her throat.

Reginald waited for revulsion to rise at the memory of doing murder. There was nothing, not even remorse in him. How had he come to this, when he'd so agonized over doing murder in autumn past?

His conscience had turned its back on him, and sneered over its shoulder. 'Twas his continual plotting that changed him. So long had he planned to do the foul deed that, when the need arose, murder seemed a natural and appropriate solution to his dilemma.

Reginald closed his eyes as he realized honor and self-respect had long since shattered in him, leaving naught but an empty shell. Just as well. His new nephew had to die. At least a babe couldn't fight the way the midwife had.

A touch of caution woke in him. Why did his brother's widow choose to bring her son here, when she liked Freyne naught at all? Was it a trap? Perhaps what he'd plotted for Lady Freyne hadn't gone undiscovered, as the midwife insisted. Ah, well, he was a patient man, and the babe need not die suspiciously on his first week home.

All at once a new excitement filled him. Where his brother's widow went, there went Clare. His conscience didn't even bother to protest he was no longer the sort of man Clare could admire. 'Twas far more convenient to excuse himself, saying once more that what he did guaranteed their future happiness. He almost, but not quite, convinced himself.

Reginald turned, descending the gatehouse tower's spiraling stairs. Past the machinery that worked the drawbridge he went, then exited at the tower's thick base. Standing in the arched gateway of Freyne's entrance, he prepared to welcome these unwelcome visitors.

Crosswell's undersheriff was first to ride beneath the stony arch. "Well come to Freyne, Sir Martin," Reginald called in false greeting.

"Glad to be here, Sir Reginald," the young knight responded with a broad smile. The spawn of Adam de la Bois had removed his helmet and shucked his metal hood. Traveling had stained his swarthy face to an even darker hue, making his eyes all the blacker. The boy grinned at him. " 'Tis nigh on parched, I am. I find myself praying you've got a vat of good wine hiding in this place."

Reginald forced his mouth to lift into a smile. Arrogant brat. What right had he to treat a man almost three times his age as an equal? Worse than that, that boy could and would claim Reginald's bedchamber for as long as he stayed. 'Twas his right as Crosswell's undersheriff. *Jesu*, but it galled Reginald to cede what was his.

"Why, then you must take your ease in the hall. I'll see the butler serves you the best we have in store." His words were honey sweet.

As de la Bois passed him, Reginald turned to watch the others arrive. He caught his breath in surprise. A woman rode in their midst. Lady Freyne's missive stated clearly she and her household were to follow

by cart and weren't expected to breach this gate until
June's end. 'Twas only just past the ides now.

He stared at her. With the day so warm, she wore
a straw hat to keep the sun from her face. Her tawny
gowns were dust-covered, dulling the fine orange color
until 'twas nigh on the same shade as the honey brown
plaits reaching past her slender waist.

"Clare?" The word was a strangled cry of need. He
caught back his surge of joy in an effort to offer her a
greeting appropriate to their situation. "Lady Clare,
well come home to Freyne," he called to her as she entered the dim coolness of the entryway. "I vow I cannot
believe my eyes. Freyne did not expect your arrival until
June's end when your lady cousin arrives."

Clare's shoulders seemed to tense at the sound of
his voice. When she raised her head to look upon him,
there was such sadness in her face, his heart sank to
his boots. Then new hope flared in him. Mayhap the
boy had died, and she grieved for him. Threading his
way through the walking horses, he took her palfrey's
reins to lead the creature across the bailey. "How is
it with you, my lady? You look as one aggrieved."

"That I am," she breathed, then continued in a
louder voice. "You mistake exhaustion for something
else, Sir Reginald. I am as well as can be expected
after a long and dusty trip. How is it with you?" Her
tone was blank, as if she exchanged words with a casual acquaintance, not her love.

Confusion reigned. Why did she whisper one message, then speak aloud a denial of what she'd said?
Damn this idiot world, anyway. What he wanted to
do was take her into his arms and kiss her until what
ached in her eased. Instead, the bonds of propriety
kept him trapped in a dance of inane formality. "I am
well as always, my lady. How surprised I was when

your lady cousin wrote to say she will return to
Freyne. She's made no secret of how deeply she dislikes this place."

"Let the others pass us," Clare whispered to him.

He brought her palfrey to a standstill, pretending
to examine its shoe for a stone. As the common soldiers passed them on their way to the stables, he
looked up at Clare. Some of the sorrow had left her
face, and her mouth lifted in a wry smile.

"She doesn't come by her own choice," Clare said,
using her casual voice. "She brings with her one who's
sire insists on the protection of strong walls and many
men. Since my cousin cannot bear to be separated
from this guest of hers, she relented and agreed to
live at Freyne. I come ahead of them to make this
place ready against their arrival."

When she was done speaking, she glanced around
her. The others were yards ahead of them. Clare
turned her gaze on him. The sorrow returned. "I come
to make Freyne safe for them."

"You are to make Freyne safe?" Reginald scoffed
gently. "I think me 'tis my duty to do so."

"Aye, so it should be," she responded, pushing off
her straw hat until it dangled by its ribbons down her
back. "I find myself in a very strange place, good sir,
my heart torn by two loves."

Reginald stared up at her. What he read in her
pretty eyes set a new nervousness in him. "What is it
you are saying?"

"I am saying we must speak and privately so." Her
voice was so low he strained to hear her. "Is there
such a place within Freyne where 'tis certain we cannot be overheard?"

In that moment he was certain she knew of his attempt to kill the babe. Panic woke in him. She, of all

folk, had to understand what he'd done and why.
"There is the garden," he offered, pointing to the
curve of the wall where that meager place lay.

"Nay, there can be no possibility of intrusion," she
said, her voice soft and sad. "What I must say will
forever remain between us."

Reginald's panic lessened. What she knew she had
not shared, nor would she ever do so. Unlike him,
Clare owned both honor and loyalty. But surely he'd
killed her love for him.

The woman who held his heart moved as if to dismount. Reginald dropped the palfrey's reins to take
her by the waist and assist. When she stood beside
the beast, he kept his hands atop her hips, glorying at
the feel of her slender waist beneath his fingers.

Clare caught him by the wrists, but didn't pull his
hands away, as if she, too, ached to prolong this moment. The love that touched her face was the same
now as it had been on that cold October day. How
could it be that what she knew had not changed what
she felt for him?

"The upper chamber of the keep tower. Will you
come there alone and in night's embrace?" 'Twas a
whisper that not even her steed overheard.

"I will come." She caught his hands, twining her
fingers between his for a brief instant before releasing him.

He nodded. "Matins. 'Twill be full dark by then."

Taking her palfrey's reins, she started toward the
stables. Reginald stood where he'd stopped, his hands
empty and his head bowed against the man that he
had lost.

From just inside the keep's upper chamber with the
door open, Reginald could look into the starlit sky

above him. The night was clear, the moon nigh on full. It swam high overhead, a pale disk marking the place where today became yesterday. Borne on a fresh, warm breeze, bats darted and swooped in their quest for their meal. All in all, 'twas a glorious night to be abroad.

A bit dizzy in his thoughts, Reginald moved until he nearly stood upon the landing. Sir Martin and he had shared more than a few cups of wine this even, but all he'd discovered was that the lad had honest respect for him and his stewardship of Freyne. Nay, he'd learned more than that. The guest Lady Freyne brought with her was the sheriff's daughter, but that information had been given freely, as if 'tweren't the secret Clare had made it seem.

Below and to his left lay the hall. Reginald scanned the darkened landscape for some sign of Clare. When she appeared around the hall's edge, the moonlight shimmered silver on her skirts. She came boldly toward the keep's mound, then climbed the pathway. Reginald moved outside the door, but was careful to keep to the shadows so he wouldn't be discerned.

Clare wore the same brief head scarf she'd donned this afternoon as she worked to arrange the women's quarters and solar to suit her. Between that and her hair caught behind her in a single braid, her face and throat were completely exposed. When she set her foot on the lowest wooden stair, she paused and lifted her head.

Reginald caught his breath. The silvery light gentled all sign of time's passage from her face. For this instant, she looked to be a girl of ten and eight. Dear God, why had no man ever offered for her? She was a beauty, worth owning even if she claimed not a furlong to her name.

A touch of concern marked her features, then Clare threw aside worry to climb the steps. Reginald awaited desire's rush within him as she drew near. Instead, there was only confusion and pain. She knew what he was, yet seemed to love him still. Why?

As she halted atop the landing, Reginald reached from the darkened doorway to take her hand. She neither gasped nor started as he appeared. He drew her into the tiny chamber behind him, their footsteps echoing hollowly on the wooden floor. Below them, the storage cellars were empty, awaiting autumn's bounty.

Wan light shot through the unshuttered arrow slits to mark his path to the two massive treasure chests set against the far wall. When Clare was seated on one, Reginald found his place atop the other. She leaned her head against the wall, and the moon's glow caught on her tears.

"You mourn us," he said, knowing he had slaughtered the one bit of goodness life could have offered him.

She sighed. "I ache in self-pity because I still believe in your love for me. If I grieve, 'tis because you have made what we wanted impossible."

Reginald closed his eyes as what might have been slipped forever from his grasp. "There is no more between us?" he breathed as his own ache grew to match what she said lived within her. "Your love is finished?"

"Nay, God forgive me, 'tis not." 'Twas a soft, sad breath. "My heart is fixed and will not be moved, not even when my head tells it how horrible what you've done is.

"How, Reginald," she cried, "how could you use me the way you did? I took that potion you gave me in autumn past to Crosswell's midwife. She told me 'twas an abortive brew."

As the full extent of what he'd done hit him, Reginald struggled to breathe. How could he have believed he'd not be found out? Worse, what he'd done wasn't only her betrayal, but his own.

"I did it for us," he tried, desperate to excuse himself. "All I wanted was a life worthy of you. I'd not have made you a simple steward's wife, barely better than a peasant. You deserved to be Freyne's lady."

"Avarice is a terrible taskmaster, Reginald," Clare replied in quiet bitterness. "The Church will not let us marry and handfasting to Freyne's lord would make me a whore. Your peers would have scorned you. Before long, you'd have turned your back on me, wanting a rich, young bride."

"Nay, not true," he protested, but deep within him, he knew she was right. Gone was his ability to tolerate a position of subservience. Banished was all patience with those he'd once considered his betters.

"Did you kill Theobald?" If her question was emotionless, there was something about the way she held her body that said she needed to know the whole truth.

Reginald turned on the chest until he stared out into the darkened tower chamber. "Nay, although I did participate in disguising what happened to him. 'Twas the father of the girl Theobald raped who killed him. The man was out gathering dried wood for his hearth when Theobald rode by. He knocked the lad from his horse with his pruning hook and was beating him as I rode up. When I realized Theobald was injured past recovery, I panicked." He shot Clare a quick, apologetic look.

"In all truth, I'd been contemplating murder as I

chased after my nephew. In that moment, the only thing I could think was that Gradinton and Lavendon would never believe I'd no hand in it. Together, his murderer and I moved his body, taking his horse with us to make it seem he'd gone astray in his grief. Since neither of us can afford to reveal the other, we continue on as if nothing occurred."

"I see," Clare said as if she truly did understand. "What of Jocelyn? What did you plan for my cousin's eldest son?" She made it sound as if 'twere as a casual question as "how grows your wheat this year?"

Reginald freed a scornful breath. "That weakling? Why bother with murder, when squiring will be his end. Don't you see? There'd have been no blood on my hands, save that my brother set a babe into your cousin's womb. I never meant to hurt her, I only wanted what is mine."

He braced his arms on his legs and fisted his hands against the frustration and greed that lived in him. "Clare, you cannot know what 'tis to work nigh on two score years making this place grow and prosper. Why should I be expected to give up the fruits of my efforts because I am second born, instead of first?"

"For the same reason I must live a barren life, without hope of my own home and happiness." If her bitterness was equal to his, she tempered it with a sigh. "Such is the world in which we live. I cannot even afford a place in a convent."

She looked at him. "Reginald, without my cousin's generosity, there'd be no joy at all in my life. Your greed nearly took from me what I most value, all because you cannot bear the thought of being steward to your nephew."

Reginald stiffened in sudden anger at her accusation, then sagged as the truth of her words stabbed through him. "Aye, you are right."

In admitting this, the darkness on his soul lifted. This brief respite from greed left him feeling wondrously free. Hope filled him. For this moment, he found again the contentment of being Freyne's steward. Aye, things would return to what they'd been. If he could but convince her to trust him once more, they would handfast and spend their remaining years in quiet comfort.

"Clare," he begged, "is there no way to win back your affection for me? No true harm has been done."

A lie. He'd done murder to the midwife. Her voice seemed to echo within him, crying out for vengeance. Once again, a shadow set on his heart. No matter how he wished it, he'd never again be the man he'd once respected and admired.

"There is one thing," Clare said softly, "but I think me you'll not happily take so heavy a penance."

"Nay, there can be no deed too onerous for me," he said, speaking swiftly, as if doing so might help him escape what clung to him. "Tell me and I vow I will do it. 'Tis your love I want, more than anything else."

"I would have you leave Freyne while my cousin and her son reside here."

Reginald threw himself to his feet, shocked at her impossible request. "Leave Freyne! How can you ask me to go from the only home I've ever known?"

She watched him in a sad calm. "How can I let you stay, knowing what I know of you?"

"I will give you my word," he started, only to fall silent as she shook her head in slow negation.

" 'Tis my godson's life you'd have me set into your hands, and that I cannot do, even as I cannot expose what you've done to my cousin or Lord Coudray. If you leave, I will know your love for me is stronger than your need to own Freyne."

"This is idiocy," he nearly shouted. "The only thing my leaving proves is that I fear exposure."

"Nay," she said softly, her gaze unflinching as it met his. "The fact that I live after confronting you with this in private is proof you do not fear I will expose you. If I cannot trust my Simon to you just now, you trust me with your life."

Reginald stared at her in surprise. Clare's death might well have bought him Freyne. He came to kneel before her. "I never thought," he whispered, begging her to believe where he doubted himself.

She smiled, her love for him clinging to the movement of her mouth. "I know." She raised her hands to comb her fingers through his hair in a gentle caress. "Beneath what has corrupted you, goodness resides. That do I believe with all my heart, thus do I love you still. Now, I would have from you proof of your intent toward me and mine. Leave Freyne. When you are certain the avarice has departed you, come for me. It matters naught to me if we live in a hovel for what remains of our lives. I want only your love to bear me company."

Reginald came to his feet, then took her hands to make her rise as well. Catching her in his embrace, he drew her close. Clare rested her head against his shoulder, sighing in a tangle of pleasure and longing. "What is your answer?" she murmured.

"I want your love. The morn will find me gone."

Even as he spoke the words, the greed that had plagued him these past months cried out in frustration and denial. What right had she to cheat him of his home, the only place he'd ever lived?

By force of will alone did he turn away from this

thought. Reginald closed his eyes and leaned his head against hers. God forgive him, but he'd not care to wager on how long even her love could serve as a barrier to his ambition.

Chapter 20

Elyssa fanned herself with her hand as she and Freyne's new castellan strode back toward their gate. Even shaded by a broad-brimmed straw hat, there was no relief from the heat. This day seemed one better fit to August rather than early September, and after a week without rain, her every step woke a fine cloud of pallid brown dirt. The stuff clung to the hems of her now-altered yellow gown and her ivory linen overgown.

Elyssa glanced at the man whose bigger feet were causing the greatest damage. "God be praised, there's now only the harvest home feast to provide before the season closes."

Long, lank, and half again her age, Sir Gilbert only nodded shyly. 'Twas a quiet knight Geoffrey'd sent to head the army that now occupied Freyne. Aye, and the longer Gradinton held his hand, making no move to capture Cecilia or her properties, the more men Geoffrey sent to guard them.

Elyssa sighed. Although Gilbert managed Reginald's military duties, he was no steward; those duties had fallen to her. Reginald's abrupt departure still galled her. It was as if he couldn't abide living in the same place as she. Yet, a deeper mystery nagged at her. Why had one so dedicated to Freyne left without a backward glance?

Reginald's account book told the tale. In the margins around his careful tallies were meticulous notes on everything from grain yields to the bloodlines of their bulls and rams. 'Twas that book which told Elyssa the traditional payment for the villeins who harvested Freyne's grain was a boon day feast. His notes told her how many oxen, sheep, and chickens were needed, including a cartload of bread and ale— enough for two cups per laborer.

"My lady." Sir Gilbert's quiet voice startled her from her thoughts, "Lord Coudray is come."

Elyssa stared through the gate ahead of her. Geoffrey's gray steed, stripped of saddle and bridle, but still wearing the marks of a long ride, grazed in a paddock. This glimpse of Passavant made her heart do the most amazing feat: it leapt, fell, then simmered in anger.

"So he is." The words barely managed to escape her tense jaw.

'Twas the pattern of his visits for Geoffrey to give no warning of his arrival, only appear, one or two men at his back. He'd bide a few days at Freyne, claiming her bedchamber for the duration of his visit, then depart. If the majority of his time was spent with Cecilia, summer evenings were long. Once his daughter was abed, Geoffrey joined Elyssa and Clare in Freyne's paltry garden. Their conversations often lasted until 'twas full dark, with Clare being the one to call the evening to its end.

If those quiet talks were originally centered on issues they shared in common, such as the houses offering to foster Cecilia and Jocelyn's continuing success at Ashby, they'd soon expanded to far more individual interests. Although this had taught her much about Geoffrey, the man, talking was all she'd had of him throughout the summer.

Elyssa glared at her dusty skirts. He seemed to have changed his mind about marriage. Not once in all these conversations had the subject been broached between them. Nor had he intentionally touched her, not since the morning of Simon's christening.

At first, she'd been grateful for his new indifference as it put their previous intimacy at a distance. But, as she came to know Geoffrey better, her affection for him had grown until desire plagued her. His last stay had left her wanting him more than she'd believed it possible for her to want a man. Mary save her, but each time he departed Freyne the image of Geoffrey sleeping in her bed haunted her dreams for days.

Damn him anyway. Elyssa scuffed her shoe against the path. If he'd withdrawn the offer, he ought to at least say so to her face. 'Twas only common courtesy. Damn her as well. If she had no desire to wed with him, why did she care what he felt for her?

As she and Sir Gilbert entered the brief dimness of Freyne's gateway, the knight turned to those who guarded their door. "Where is Lord Coudray?"

"He and Lady Clare left for the river taking Lady Cecilia to swim, sir," one man replied with a bob of his head.

"Good." Elyssa spewed the harsh word without thought, so great was her relief. The farther away Geoffrey was, the less she was tormented.

The soldiers looked at her, and the one who'd spoken raised a brow. "My lady, if you like, I'll send Robin here"—he jerked his thumb toward his underling—"to fetch Lord Simon and his nurse."

Elyssa blinked, her tangled emotions eclipsed by

surprise. She hadn't realized her daily habits were so deeply entrenched. 'Twas indeed her garden hour with Simon.

"Aye, if you please," she said to the man, "and my thanks for offering."

The soldier smiled, and his Robin raced for the hall. Sir Gilbert followed the man at a slower pace, while Elyssa crossed the bailey to the garden's gate. When she entered, she glanced around her in disgust.

It was no better in here now than it had been when she'd first returned to Freyne a year ago. In the main, this was due to Reginald's departure and Clare's lack of interest in gardening. Elyssa hadn't had time to do anything to the place. At least the pear tree offered a spot of shade, and the air was fresh. She'd barely reached the pear tree before Simon's nurse was opening the gate.

It had been the fourth day of Simon's life before Berta had conceded that Elyssa truly was starving her son. The girl she provided was dark of hair and eye, and very upright. Johanna's husband had died just before their first child's birth and, only weeks after his death, her babe had followed his sire. In Simon, the young woman found a child to adore.

Dressed in a plain red gown, Johanna came toward her lady, a worried frown on her broad brow. If Elyssa gloried in this hour out of doors with her son, Simon's nurse barely endured it. She'd shielded Simon's face from the sun with a thin cloth and bore over her shoulder a thick blanket to cushion him from the ground's rough surface.

As Elyssa claimed her son from his nurse, she swept the cloth from his face. Simon squinted as he peered up at her. Then, his chubby face widened into a grin of recognition. His arms and legs strained against his swaddling in excited reaction.

"Oh, how you long for your freedom." Elyssa laughed as she settled herself on the blanket Johanna spread. "Well then, my little lad, you shall have your heart's desire." She set to unwrapping her son.

"My lady, are you certain you should do that? He's not yet six months. What if he grows all crooked?" Johanna clasped anxious hands, repeating the complaint she voiced each time Elyssa freed Simon of his swaddling.

"What can it hurt him to have his will for just a little while?" Elyssa replied.

Once freed, Simon grunted in excitement, his arms and legs moving even before she laid him, belly down, on the blanket. Sunlight shot through the branches to dapple his bared skin with golden light as he worked to lift himself. Elyssa ran a finger along the soft curve of her son's skull. Fine golden red hair floated up at her touch.

Simon grinned, turning his head toward her. Much to his surprise, this motion resulted in him rolling onto his back. No matter. He happily squinted into the light, cooing at the ripening pears hanging above him. His hands raised, working in joyful expectation of reaching the impossible. Elyssa laughed at his optimism.

"His eyes!" Johanna cried out in a new fear, wringing the cloth she'd used to shield his face. "Oh, my lady, he'll be blinded."

A wry smile twisted Elyssa's mouth. She had no need to worry over Simon; Johanna did it for her. Taking her hat from her wimpled head, she held it between Simon and what he wanted, letting its embroidered ribbons dangle into his face.

He blinked, his round face alive with surprise at this change. Then he set to bubbling and burbling at the ribbons, his hands opening and closing in even greater expectations. Love washed over her, so deep, Elyssa thought she could die with it.

There was a sudden burst of noise from the nearby gate. Cecilia's piping tones were unmistakable against the deeper voices of the men who guarded her every move. Johanna's expression eased at the sound.

"Lady Cecilia'll be wanting to bathe Lord Simon. It has become her pet chore." Johanna well knew that, where her lady heeded her not, once Cecilia began to beg the deed was done. Simon would be swiftly returned to the safety of her arms and the darkness of the hall.

The garden gate flew wide. Johanna scooped up Simon as Cecilia raced toward them. Elyssa came more slowly to her feet, her emotions once again shifting beyond her control.

" 'Lyssa, we are home!"

Summer had bronzed her poppet's skin, making Cecilia's pale gray eyes all the more startling. Her blue gown clung damply to her body, while wet strands of dark hair streamed behind her. Cecilia wrapped her arms around Elyssa's waist and set her chin on her borrowed maman's belly to grin up at her.

Elyssa caught her closer still as her heart set to aching. There'd not be another summer with Cecilia at her side. Eventually Geoffrey would decide on a house in which to foster her. "You have been swimming, no?"

"Aye, because Papa is here." Cecilia's grin widened into the ultimate display of happiness.

Elyssa raised her gaze to look at Geoffrey. Frustration and hurt roiled in her. Dear God, but he was a beautiful man. His dark patch now lay against summer bronzed skin that made his scars naught but white lines. His eye color was a bright blue while, even damp, his hair gleamed like the finest gold.

Elyssa's gaze descended from his face to the broad line of his shoulders. He'd left off his tunic after their swim, donning only his shirt, chausses, and shoes. His shirt was made of a linen so fine it clung like a second skin to his damp shoulders and upper arms. His shirt strings were undone, and the garment gaped from throat to mid-chest.

As she stared at the exposed contours of his chest, the need to touch him, to run her fingers over every inch of him, was so strong she shuddered inwardly with it. But Geoffrey wanted her naught at all. Elyssa forced her gaze back onto Cecilia.

What a fool she was, letting her desires become fixed on him. Did not Geoffrey's casual indifference prove he was a man like any other? She'd been but a momentary amusement, something to divert him from Crosswell's boredom. His interest had died with her departure from his sphere.

"Did you enjoy yourself?" she asked her poppet, no sign of her new aching in her voice.

"Aye, I like swimming," Cecilia replied.

"She does more drowning than swimming," her father scoffed.

He lay his hand atop his child's head, his knuckles brushing Elyssa's restored waistline in an innocent caress. As he stroked Cecilia's damp hair, his fingers moved along the slight curve of Elyssa's abdomen. The thin gowns she wore were no barrier to sensation, and she swore she could feel his skin against hers.

"She does not," Clare retorted, stoutly defending the lass. Elyssa's cousin was yet dry, having been only their observer. "She swims very well, indeed. Her head rarely lowers beneath the water's surface."

Elyssa glanced to Geoffrey, expecting his reply, then was sorry she did. He smiled that wonderful smile of his, his teeth white against his sun-darkened skin, then leaned close. 'Twas pure lust that woke in her when he nigh on touched his lips to her ear and whispered, "What your lady cousin doesn't know is that 'tis my hand keeping my lass afloat."

As swiftly as he'd bent toward her, he was gone, turning to look at Simon. Elyssa freed a disappointed breath, then chided herself for hurting over his lack of care for her. This was foolish thinking.

Geoffrey lifted her naked son from Johanna's arms. "What ho? Someone has stolen your clothes, my lad," he told the chortling boy. When Geoffrey raised him high overhead, Simon squealed in enjoyment.

Cecilia released Elyssa and went to wrap an arm around her father's leg. "Make him laugh again, Papa," she begged. Geoffrey smiled at her request and joggled Simon. The little lad did as Cecilia wished, laughing as he kicked his feet in exhilaration.

Johanna squeaked in fear. "Have a care, my lord."

In deference to the nurse's wishes, Geoffrey instantly lowered Simon until they were eye to eye. Hurt spiked through Elyssa. Look how concern over a servant's feelings moved him, while he paid hers no heed at all.

Simon dug his toes into the man's chest, his wee red brows rising as he considered the face in front of him. With unexpected swiftness, the lad caught the black strap crossing from the patch into Geoffrey's hair. As he dragged it toward his mouth, he brought Geoffrey's face with it.

"Here now, leave that be," Geoff told him, gently trapping Simon's tiny fist to pry open his fingers.

Once again, Elyssa's hurt surged. Aye, Geoffrey was caring and loving toward Simon now, but what would happen once Cecilia left them to be fostered? He'd come no more to Freyne to visit Simon, that's what. Or, her.

Elyssa caught her arms around her middle. Mary save her, but Geoffrey's departure from her life would leave a terrible, aching emptiness, worse even than what Cecilia's loss would cost her. Didn't he realize how much she needed him?

Shocked, Elyssa stood stock-still. Mother of God, was this how she chose to squander her hard-won freedom? What was wrong with her?

Now cradled in Geoffrey's arms, Simon was happily sucking on a shirt string. Cecilia grabbed her father's sleeve, forcing him to lower the lad until she could tickle the babe. 'Twas Geoffrey's laugh, joined to Simon's delighted response, that sent love rushing through Elyssa again. This time, her heart wrapped itself around both boy and man. And would not be moved.

May God damn her soul, she loved him. Elyssa's jaw clenched in fear. Oh, but this was terrible. He needed to leave, before she did something she would regret.

Pushing past Clare, she grabbed Geoffrey by the sleeve and turned him toward her. "No more. Give my son to his nurse and leave my home," she told him, tugging at his arm with all the panic that now raced through her. "Go now," she insisted. "Mount your horse and leave."

Geoffrey stared at the woman he would make his wife, once again confounded by her. Now what had set her off? There was deep fear lurking in the shadows of her coppery eyes. The urgency in her voice had a strange tone to it.

As he recognized it, a subtle sense of triumph rose in him. 'Twas desperation, the sound of a woman who knew she'd lost the battle and sought to make a final stand against overwhelming odds. The corner of his mouth lifted. He'd breached her defenses, and she sought to drive him from her before he noticed. 'Twas with pleasure that he handed Simon to his nurse.

" 'Lyssa," her cousin cried out, "what is wrong?"

Elyssa crossed her arms in defiance, backing away from Clare. "Nothing is wrong, save that he must leave."

"Papa, do you have to go?" Cecilia's eyes were wide with sudden sadness as she looked up at him.

Geoffrey reached for her, and Cecilia eagerly latched her hands around his neck. The thrill of holding her hadn't yet left him, and he cradled her against his chest. " 'Lyssa and I need to talk. Can we do that alone?"

"We do not need to talk," Elyssa protested loudly. "You need to leave Freyne. I will call your men for you." She turned as if to be about this task.

Geoff grabbed her arm. "I think not."

"Leave go!" 'Twas a cry of pure panic. Elyssa struggled, but he left her no opportunity to break free of his hold.

" 'Lyssa!" Cecilia cried, sharp fear in her voice. She buried her head against her father's shoulder.

"Elyssa, cease!" Clare snapped. "You are frightening Cecilia."

Elyssa pressed a fist to her forehead in frustration, then relaxed in defeat. She took a step toward him, coming just close enough to lay her hand against Ce-

cilia's back. "I am sorry, poppet," she said softly.
"Your father is right, he and I must talk. 'Tis time
for Simon's bath, and you know how Johanna needs
your help."

Each time Elyssa set aside her own needs to care
for his daughter, the love Geoffrey knew for her grew.
'Twas this that he wanted from her. He'd not be content until she added his name to those she held dear.

His daughter relaxed in his arms, then raised her
head to look at him. "I must help Johanna," she told
him. The seriousness with which she took this responsibility made him smile.

"Then, you must go forthwith," he replied, setting
her on the ground.

Cecilia caught Clare's hand, and Elyssa's cousin hurried her from the garden, barely keeping pace with
Simon's nurse. "Will you come and watch me, Papa?"
his lass called over her shoulder as Clare was shutting
the gate. There wasn't time to answer before he and
Elyssa were alone.

"You will let me go," Elyssa hissed in that moment.
"I am a free woman now, and you have no right to
hold me against my will."

"True enough," he replied with a shrug, "but I do
not wish to let you go."

As she yanked on her trapped arm, he smiled, overwhelmed by the pleasure her face and form gave him.
Her embroidered belt encircled her waist, revealing
she'd regained every bit of her slender form over the
past months. 'Twas truly a shame she was wimpled.
The material clung to her face, disguising the gentle
curve of her cheeks and the slim line of her neck.

Despite her glare, he let his gaze trace the full outline of her lips. His attention set warm color in her
cheeks, and her face softened from anger to something

far more heated. 'Twas desire's glint that woke in her eyes.

Geoffrey swallowed. *Jesu*, but she wanted him with the same depth that he desired her. He could feel the power of her need leap across the space between them. Then her face flamed in embarrassment.

"How dare you look at me that way. Cease this instant, for I'll have no more of it, I tell you." 'Twas outrage, nothing less.

"I was but returning your interest," Geoffrey replied, his brows lifting against his amusement.

"I have no interest in you." Her arm still caught in his hand, she turned her back on him to shield her face from his view.

"Nay?" He fought his need to laugh. "If that is true, it shouldn't bother you if I stay and visit my daughter. Since 'tis my army that guards your gate, I think me you'll be hard-pressed to throw me out."

She glanced over her shoulder at him. Her mouth was tight and her eyes, narrowed. As he had done to her on the road to Crosswell, he once more left her without an answer. Then her mouth took a bitter twist. "If you will not go, I'll take my household and leave in your stead."

"I think not." He made it a soft comment as he pulled her back toward him. Although she dug her heels into the sod, the grass was dry and slick. She slid ever nearer.

"Cease, my lord." 'Twas a loud demand, as if she thought a hard voice would bring his compliance. "You've no right. I am not your ward anymore, but a free woman."

"So you keep saying."

Geoffrey wrapped his arm around her, until her back rested against his chest. He leaned his head

against hers and heard her sigh. When she realized
she'd relaxed against his embrace, she stiffened, as if
fighting off her reaction to him.

"Humor me," he said. "Tell me what troubles you
so deeply that you must command me from your hall."

"You trouble me!" she cried. "I cannot bear how
you appear without warning. You take my bed, sit in
my garden, intrude in my life, until—" She bowed her
head. When she continued, 'twas a hurt whisper, "May
God curse me, I want you there."

His triumph grew. All those evenings he'd spent
dying for a single touch had been worth it. "And wanting me in your life troubles you?"

"But of course it does," she snapped, peering over
her shoulder at him. "You want me no more. How
long, Geoffrey? How long was it before you wiped
your brow in relief, thankful that I'd refused your
offer?"

At the hurt in her voice, Geoff turned her in his
arms, then splayed a hand at her mid-back. Only the
slightest pressure, brought her against him. His shirt
was fine, her gowns, thin. The touch of her breasts
against his chest sent a bolt of wondrous feeling
through him.

"What makes you think I've rescinded my offer?"
He kept his voice low as he moved his other hand
down her back to her hip. *Jesu,* but touching her
brought a wild and fiery life to his body.

Elyssa's lips parted once more as a rosy flush crept
over her cheeks, the color having more to do with
inner heat than the day's warmth. "You do," she said.
Her hurt had eased some. "You have not pursued
me."

Geoffrey fought his smile with the same diligence

he used to tame the lust that lived in him. "Is that what you wanted from me? Pursuit?"

"Wanted?" she repeated in a breathless voice. "Nay, of course not." She gasped, then caught her lower lip in her teeth as even brighter color stained her cheeks. "Well, aye, mayhap. Mary save me, but I do not know what I want." She buried her head against his shoulder.

In the silence that followed her words, he released her from his embrace and stepped back from her. Elyssa made no protest when he lifted her head and found the pin that held her wimple in place. He tossed the bit aside, then ran his finger between her cheek and the modest head covering. It slipped from her head, drifting down to her shoulders, then onto the grassy turf.

Soft curls of hair had escaped her plaits to rest lightly against her newly bared throat. Geoffrey's pulse lifted to a new beat. He set his lips to the spot just beneath her ear. "I never said I would pursue you," he told her softly.

She shuddered against what he did, her breath escaping in a quick gasp. Laying her hands against his chest, she drew her palms downward in a slow caress. Beneath her touch his skin burned.

His mouth moved to her ear. "That would have been far too dangerous."

"Dangerous?" she murmured, her fingers lifting the hem of his shirt so she could lay her hands against his bare skin. As she did so, she also shifted slightly, until she stood between his thighs. It was his turn to shudder.

"You might have run to ground, and I'd never have pried you from your hiding place. Nay, 'twas a siege

I planned, willing to sit patiently outside your defenses waiting for you to starve."

Cupping her face in his palms, he let his thumbs follow the sharp peak of her brows, then lowered his mouth to hers. He brushed his lips against hers in a light caress, but she caught his mouth with hers. Her lips clung to his, begging him for more than this.

Heat exploded in him, and his kiss grew in passion, until they were both gasping. His mouth left hers to press a kiss to her cheek, her jaw, her brow. Then he stepped back from her. "Are you starving yet, my love?"

He caught his breath. Dear God, but she was. Her desire for him made her all the more lovely. Her lips were soft, her eyes sultry with her hunger. When she drew a deep breath, the rise and fall of her breasts made his knees weak.

"You are a devious man, Geoffrey FitzHenry," she told him. "All those evenings we spent together, while I thought you wanted me naught, you were seducing me into needing you."

"I nigh on drowned whilst I did it," he murmured, drawing her close once more. He'd hardly touched his mouth to hers before she was pushing him back again.

"Damn you, but you made me love you!" She sounded chagrined by this.

"Did I?" Geoffrey laughed. "Since I have achieved my objective, will you concede defeat and give me what I came to win?"

There was a sudden wariness in her eyes. "What is that?"

"Wed with me, Elyssa of Freyne."

Panic washed over her face. "You cannot ask that of me, Geoffrey."

"I can and have." He drew her back into his embrace. If she gave up trying to free herself from his physical embrace, she'd not yet conceded to the hold he had on her heart.

"You cannot wed with me. Have I not listened to you these past months telling me how Gradinton can take Cecilia should you wed again?"

He shifted easily past her first barricade. "Thus do I seek to foster her. When she is safely in some other house, I will cede her properties to her grandsire. Our wedding day will wait for that."

'Twas a relieved sigh that left her. "Then, we will never wed. You are unwilling to release Cecilia, refusing every offer, even if you must find some absurd reason to do so."

"I have not. Every reason I give is valid," he protested, then paused. He did resent having to give Cecilia up to reclaim his own life, the same life that Gradinton's daughter Maud had stolen from him.

Then Geoffrey shook his head. "You are right, I have stalled and that is a dangerous thing, when Gradinton has been quiet so long." Sybil had entered a convent. Somehow, Geoffrey doubted Baldwin would leave Cecilia alone through the seven years Baldwin must wait before he was free of his marriage to Sybil.

" 'Lyssa, however loathe I am to give up Cecilia, I must for her own safety. I am taking a lesson from you. See how you have survived releasing Jocelyn, while your son thrives in his new environment? So will Cecilia do. I have two fine houses offering for her right now. She'll be fostered within the month. Wed with me."

Elyssa's eyes widened in fright. "Nay."

"Wed with me." He touched his mouth to the curve of her throat.

"Nay," she breathed, and leaned against him. At

his continuing caress, she tilted her head to one side and freed a quiet sound of pleasure. Rising on her toes, she pressed herself against the part of him least likely to refuse her. Her hands slid down his chest until her fingers found a home between the drawstring of his chausses and his skin. It took every bit of strength he owned to catch her hands in his.

"You may not," he chided, his voice husky with longing. "Until you've given me your vow, I'll have none of you."

Elyssa struggled to free her hands from his, groaning softly in frustration. At her show of passion for him, Geoffrey almost gave way. But to do so would dishonor them both. "Wed with me," he demanded softly.

"Will you not take me without vows?" Elyssa's face was filled with longing and grief, as if their marriage were truly impossible.

A touch of anger filled him and was gone. "You and your insults," he murmured. "I want you as my wife, not my whore."

"I would rather be your whore," she cried, then what terrified her broke past her lips. "If I were but your whore, I would still own my freedom. I can leave you once you hurt me."

Geoffrey relaxed in relief. "Ah, so here at last is what troubles you. 'Lyssa, there are many ways I can hurt you, but I vow to you now, none of them will be intentional."

"True enough," she scoffed. "You are a man, you cannot help yourself. The day will surely come when I open our bedchamber door and find you in another woman's arms." Her voice faltered suddenly, and she looked up at him. 'Twas as if she already experienced the pain of his future betrayal. "I couldn't bear it,

Geoff, not from you," she whispered. " 'Twould be my death."

The corner of his mouth lifted as she revealed her soul to him. He twined their fingers. "Give to me that freedom you so prize and, along with my heart, I will give to you ownership of my body. But know you, this is an easy vow for me to make."

When Elyssa sent him a confused look, he only quirked his brows. "I've no taste for whores or a quick tumble under a blanket with someone else's wife. I never have. Say your vow to me, and 'twill be only you in my bed for your life's time."

Every bit of logic in Elyssa warred with her heart's need and her body's desire. She stared at him as if his face might tell her whether he spoke true or lied. Even if she knew, what he meant today would be different on the morrow. He was still a man like any other.

She caught herself mid-thought. But he wasn't. Never had she known a man like Geoffrey. Yet she still persisted in judging him by others' standards. 'Twas not much different from what she'd done to Jocelyn by clinging to fears long after they'd ceased to be valid.

The memory of Geoffrey holding Simon high above him returned. Although Johanna had cried in fright, Elyssa hadn't known a moment's worry. If she trusted Geoffrey with her son, whom she loved more than her own life, then she could trust him with herself.

As if he sensed her change, Geoffrey reached for her. Elyssa came gratefully into his arms. Geoffrey would not betray her. She lay her head against his shoulder.

" 'Lyssa, I love you. Wed with me," he repeated.

"Aye, I will wed you," she replied, then wrapped her arms around him. "But only on one condition."

Laughter rumbled quietly in his chest. "You'll not give her up." 'Twas an amused breath.

"Nay. She's mine. Find another way to satisfy Gradinton."

Geoffrey eased back from her, then crooked a finger beneath her chin to lift her face to his. His smile was glorious, his love for her radiating from him. It took her breath away. He ran a finger down the curve of her cheek. "I knew you would say that. As soon as Michaelmas court is done, we'll set our heads together and see what we can devise."

Chapter 21

Jesu, but 'twas hot for early September. Reginald, his tunic off and his head bared to the sun, let his steed plod along the narrow trail leading from the village behind him to the main highway.

With more luck than he was due, he'd found himself a temporary position as steward for Durham Abbey. The man who'd served that wealthy house yet languished in an illness contracted not too long after Durham lost its bishop. While the holy brothers prayed for the steward's recovery, Reginald offered somewhat hesitant pleas that the man would give way to what consumed him.

His reluctance sprang from a sort of general dislike for the position. Although the recompense was adequate and the monks congenial for their sort, the abbey's properties were far-flung. All this traveling left him saddle sore and irritable. On top of that, the villages he managed were a disappointment. Taken altogether, their yields did not meet that which grew in Freyne's rich soil. But the greatest part of his dislike rose from Durham itself.

The landscape here was nothing like Freyne's, which lay in England's far more civilized south. Homesickness ached in him, the need to return to the place of his birth twisting in his belly. He'd been wrong to do

Clare's will. A man who let a woman rule him was no man at all.

The distant beat of hooves against the hard-packed earth woke him from his thoughts. 'Twas a goodly number of men who came toward them, moving at a canter. He peered ahead, but the oncoming party was yet hidden in the valley below them. Behind him, his four stirred from their lethargy. Common soldiers all, they reached for their leather vests and loosened their bows.

"We'll not hurry to meet them," he said, snatching on his sweat-stained tunic. His hauberk, resting on the saddle behind him, was the same boiled leather his common companions wore; he'd been unwilling to fry in his mail this day. He yanked it on over his shoulders, leaving it untied as he thrust his hands into his gloves. While he loosened his sword, he also damned himself for storing his helmet in his saddle pack. An hour ago, it had seemed an intolerable nuisance, rattling on his saddle as he rode.

With a steady jangling of harnesses and squeak of leather, the first man, a knight in full mail, crested the hill. Reginald caught his breath in surprise when he recognized him. Baldwin de Gradinton, his head bared and his face red against the heat, rode toward him at the head of his troop. Reginald's stomach gave a bounce at the impossibility of coming across the nobleman at this far-flung corner of the world. "Well met, my lord Gradinton."

The baron called his troop to a halt, then let his mount walk forward as he greeted the brother of his dead friend. "Well now, Reginald of Freyne. How is it I find you here in the hinterlands of England?" 'Twas exaggerated surprise that filled the man's voice.

"I might ask the same of you, my lord," Reginald replied. Gradinton had no properties this far north.

"You might at that," the baron said with a lift of his brows and a smile. The movement of his mouth clearly said this meeting was at his design. "My men and horses crave a rest. Bide a bit with me, and we'll share our tales, my friend."

Caution woke in Reginald, and the urge to refuse the man was strong. Ah, but 'twouldn't do to insult one as powerful as Gradinton. "We'll rest with them," he told his small party, and dismounted.

His men gratefully left their steeds, drifting toward the others of their kind. Skins appeared, and men quenched their thirsts and those of their steeds. Gradinton dismounted and led his mount up the road with Reginald following quietly.

When they were far from earshot of their English servants, the Norman baron stopped. Reginald stripped off his hastily donned bits of armor as the nobleman offered his steed water. A new confidence grew in him. Gradinton had sought him out; the baron's need made them equals.

Reginald broke the silence between them. "I find it marvelous that our paths should cross so, my lord."

Gradinton's mouth twisted into a harsh smile as he wiped his hands on his surcoat. "Aye, 'tis a righteous miracle, of that there's no doubt. Shall I rush us through your news? Imagine my surprise at discovering you are the temporary steward for Durham Abbey. My outrage is surely great as I listen to your tale of woe, hearing how that devious bastard, Coudray, threw you from your rightful place at Freyne. Yet seething at the hurt done to your pride, I announce that I am presently in need of a commander at Gradinton. 'Tis a special position that one, incredibly well suited to your talents." He fell silent, waiting for Reginald's reaction.

The confidence in Reginald lifted another step. Gradinton needed his intimate knowledge of Freyne to retrieve what had been stolen from him. "Ah, but you have missed a bit of news. Your granddaughter now resides at Freyne."

Gradinton donned a shocked expression. "You do not say! That is news, indeed."

Now the bartering began. "Although I find myself less than satisfied with this position, the monks pay me well." Reginald dared not smile, but the new power in him was a heady thing.

Gradinton nodded, then stared out into the distance. "I understand that bitch of Aymer's gave him another son."

"She did." 'Twas a cold comment.

" 'Tis a sad thing."

"What is, my lord?"

"How easily children die in this world of ours." Gradinton shot him a sidelong glance. "Even boys nigh on into manhood can fall from their horses."

Reginald drew a deep breath. Gradinton believed him guilty of Theobald's murder and was offering to conceal another death if he but delivered to him Coudray's daughter. Caution rose a notch. He had something Gradinton wanted, but he'd not give it up for a useless promise.

"Aye, I suppose 'tis true. In that case, 'tis a good thing my brother has two surviving sons."

Gradinton freed a low, harsh laugh. "In September past, I found myself thinking how sickly that boy of Aymer's is. Aye, squiring him seemed like sending him to his death."

"So we all might have thought a year ago," Reginald replied slowly, "but here 'tis September once more and Aymer's son lives still."

Gradinton's brow creased as Reginald pushed him for aid in yet another life's ending. "Damn, damn, damn," the baron muttered to himself, again staring into the distance. At last, he threw aside all pretense and faced Reginald.

"You ask for what I cannot guarantee, at least not at this moment. Give to me my granddaughter, and I promise you, you'll be well compensated in my employ. If the time comes that you find the avenue leading to what you want, I will give to you the same support I gave Aymer."

Reginald grew drunk with longing. Gradinton would help make him Freyne's lord. Until this moment, avarice had been carefully banked within him. Now it woke from its uneasy rest to roar through him. Let Clare and love be damned to hell; Freyne would be his.

"My lord, I find your offer irresistible. I am certain the monks can find a replacement for me."

Elyssa climbed the stairs in Freyne's gatehouse behind Sir Gilbert with Clare on her heels. The spiraling stairwell was dark and narrow. Surrounded by thick walls, there was nothing to be heard save the hollow ring of their footsteps on the stone steps. In that moment, she could imagine they were the only three beings left in this quiet world.

As Sir Gilbert stepped out onto the wall, Elyssa looked above her. A thick blanket of gray concealed the sky. Mist entered the stairwell to settle gently on her face. This precious moment of peace was shattered when she stepped onto the wall top.

In the bailey behind her, chaos reigned. Folk ran at

their chores, moving supplies from hall to keep. The smith's hammer rang in double time, while the carpenters' efforts echoed his as nails entered wood. Men shouted and called as they rolled out the catapult, along with its stones, and barrels of quarrels from their sheds. The bleat of panicked sheep were silenced, one after another, as Freyne's flock gave its life in defense; their fresh skins laid atop wood would keep fire at bay.

When Elyssa turned, her vision was blocked by the hastily installed hoarding. This wooden defense clung to the exterior of their wall, overhanging the moat like some long corridor. Through holes in its floor, Freyne's defenders could pour all sorts of deterrents on their attackers; through its shutters, they could send bolts and stones down upon the army that surrounded them. The hoarding yet lacked its roof. Once those final panels bore the flayed remains of their flock, this defense would be complete.

Throwing back her cloak hood, she nodded to Sir Gilbert. The knight lifted out a panel that had yet to be nailed in place. Her heart pounding in her throat, Elyssa stepped into the opening as Clare came to stand behind her in support.

Never had she seen so many soldiers in one place. They swarmed as tents were raised and campfires came to life. Dray animals bellowed and brayed in complaint, while wooden cart wheels groaned under the weight of disassembled siege engines.

She scanned their ranks, looking for knights. Near the place where Freyne's drawbridge usually touched down were a clutch of mailed men. One pointed, and the others raised their gazes to her.

'Twas Baldwin de Gradinton who stepped forward, his dark hair exposed to the day's mist. "Lady Freyne, 'tis good to see you once again." The snide and superior tone of his voice woke her ire and gave spine to her back.

"How kind of you to say so, my lord," she retorted, her voice without a quiver of fear. "What brings you and your many friends atapping on my door this year?"

"Why, I would but visit my granddaughter."

" 'Struth, my lord?" She strained her voice seeking just the right tone of incredulity. "You should have written ahead. I fear I have no tolerance for those who come uninvited. 'Tis a shame you've come so far only to be turned back."

He laughed. "God's teeth, but you are a brave bitch."

"That you already knew, my lord," she stated. "There was no need to bring an army just to prove the point. Come now, be reasonable. What you want I'll not give you, and Lord Coudray will soon come to drive you from my gate."

Gradinton only shook his head as if dismayed with her. "How you delude yourself, my lady. Lord Coudray will not come. 'Tis but a daughter he has here. When I have her, he will remarry as he should and make himself better heirs."

Elyssa drew a sharp breath, realizing that Gradinton did not know she was the one with whom Geoff wished to make his heirs. It set a grain of hope in her.

"You are wrong. He values his daughter highly indeed," she said, the power of her confidence making her opponent frown. "Now we both know you haven't time to take down our walls before he returns from court."

"Think you so?" Gradinton was toying with her, enjoying this interchange. "I set my men to watching him on his journey, out of simple curiosity, shall we say? What with being laden with his witnesses and his wains, it took Coudray a full three weeks to reach his destination. 'Twill be October's end before you see him once more, my lady."

"What makes you believe 'twill be he who escorts his party home? Do you think we've not sent him warning?" She let scorn lay deep in her voice, all the while praying that their messengers had won free of the ring Gradinton had closed 'round them.

"Why, of course not." He signaled, and some of the knights with him turned. From a nearby tent, they drew forth two bodies, pulling Freyne's dead messengers by their heels.

"Two," Elyssa breathed to Clare. "They took but two of them." But which two? Although Sir Gilbert had instructed her to send two missives to Crosswell and to Geoffrey at the Michaelmas court, she'd added a third. This one went to Jocelyn at Ashby.

A relieved sigh escaped her in understanding. If Gradinton continued in ignorance of Geoffrey's affection toward her, 'twas the messenger to Ashby he'd missed. For Jocelyn's sake and in the hopes of teasing Lord Ashby into aid, Elyssa had scribed her intention to wed Geoffrey into that missive. Surely, Geoffrey's brother would fly to the aid of his future sister-by-marriage.

Confidence holding, if not growing, Elyssa lifted her voice once more. "Your timing is all awry, my lord. My cellars are full and my walls strong. We can last until October's end."

"You seem to be suffering from an excess of hope," the man laughed. "Might I introduce my siege captain?"

He waved forward a helmed knight. When the man stood beside him, he wrenched off his helmet. Behind

Elyssa, Clare gasped in shock as Reginald of Freyne looked up at them.

"Mary save us," Elyssa whispered. In Reginald's account book were many notes as to the strength of Freyne's walls, what needed repair and where the dry moat was vulnerable.

"Do you see now how your overconfidence can only hurt you? Give me what I came for, and I will be gone."

"My lord, I am astonished at your concern for me," she called back. "Set your heart at rest, realizing I am well nigh indestructible. Have I not already outlived two men? I think me I am about to outlive another."

Gradinton stiffened at her taunt, then let his shoulders relax. "Bold words when my ram will soon be pointed at your door. Now, there is a lewd image, indeed. Aye, I think me I shall breach your gate with ease. As you say, you are no virgin."

The men behind him laughed at his quip. One leaned forward to speak privately to his lord. Gradinton grinned at whatever 'twas the man said. "Hew, here, has just admitted he finds himself smitten by your beauty. Be warned, Lady Freyne, if I must break down your door by force, you'll be naught but a spoil of war. Be sensible, if not reasonable. Spare yourself rape."

"You are a most persistent man, my lord," Elyssa sang back, "but my answer can be but nay. As for Sir Hew, bid him my thanks. A woman my age takes her compliments where she can find them." 'Twas a saucy remark, belying Elyssa's growing fear.

Gradinton's men shouted in amusement, and Baldwin offered a salute to her courage, then raised his voice once more. "My lady, there will be no rescue for you. Give me what I want."

"I humbly beg your pardon, my lord, but that I cannot do."

She stepped back from the opening as two men set the panel back in place. When she turned on the lank knight, her confidence was gone, her poise shattered. Her knees trembling, she leaned against the tall knight's arm.

"Pray, Sir Gilbert," she told him, "pray you hard and deep. 'Tis Reginald of Freyne who directs this siege. He has lived here all his life and knows this place like his own skin, while we may have no hope of early relief. Mother of God, but Gradinton has planned this attack with care." Her fists closed in frustration.

"Aye, and I like naught the odds against us," the man told her, his voice harsh with worry. He let her lean a moment longer, then steadied her and stepped back. "We can but be strong and continue as long as possible, in the hopes that someone in the neighborhood sends word to Lord Coudray."

Elyssa glanced up at him. "Sir Gilbert, I sent a third messenger, and I think me that Gradinton has missed this man. What possibility is there we might have aid from Ashby?"

Sir Gilbert's eyes flew wide in shock. "You sent a man to Ashby?"

His wild words sent her heart tumbling to her toes. "Did I do wrong? I thought perhaps, Ashby being my lord's brother and my son being Ashby's squire, he might come."

The man startled her as his somber expression cracked into a broad grin. "I never thought! Aye, if Ashby knows, he'll send word not only to Lord Geoffrey, offering his aid, but I wager he sends to Graistan as well. If Graistan comes ..." his words died and when he looked back at his lady, his face was bright with hope.

" 'Tis your turn to pray, my lady. Beg God and all his saints that Gradinton doesn't toy with us, holding back news of the third messenger's demise to raise false confidence."

With that warning, Elyssa's spirits sank. If Gradinton had read what she's penned, he'd surely hold back what he knew until she was desperate, then use it to destroy her. "Prayer is all that is left to us," she murmured.

Beside her, Clare freed a quiet sob. Elyssa turned, thinking to comfort her cousin, but 'twas an ashen and trembling woman who pushed her away. "Touch me naught, 'Lyssa. Look what I have done." Clare stared at the hoarding's wall as if she could see through it. "Oh, Reginald, how could you do this," she cried softly, her voice fraught with pain.

"Clare, you cannot blame yourself for believing he was one sort of man, then discovering he is another," Elyssa said in gentle confusion.

"That is true enough, were it just this day I'd made such a discovery," Clare whispered.

"Be you clear, cousin," Elyssa insisted with a frown.

"Oh, 'Lyssa, I have known since June that he aided in Theobald's death, that he prays for Jocelyn's demise, and that he worked to kill Simon whilst that sweet babe yet resided within you. 'Twas why I sent him from Freyne, as he wants only to own this place." Clare caught a sharp breath, then grabbed Elyssa by the shoulders. "*Jesu Christus!* Gradinton has promised him Simon's life for his aid!"

Elyssa tore from Clare's grasp, fear for her son twisting through her. "How do you know this?" Her words begged Clare to tell her she was mistaken.

"It is the only thing that could set him to destroying his own walls." Clare's face fell into an expression of utter despair. She sagged between what weighed on her and sank to the floor of the walkway. With her head leaned against the hoarding, she closed her eyes. "Oh, Reginald, you've killed me, killed me," she whispered bitterly to her erstwhile love.

Despite how the words sounded, Elyssa's heart rejected the possibility of her cousin's betrayal. She knelt before her. "I think me if he attempted murder, 'twas without your knowledge."

When Clare opened her eyes, they were filled with tears. Her mouth trembled. "Aye, but he used me to reach you. First with the potion, then by Freyne's midwife. I should have told you, but I thought I would protect both Simon and Reginald, whose love I still cherish." She paused to free a hopeless sigh. " 'Lyssa, he loved me as none has ever before done, wanting marriage between us. I could not betray him."

Elyssa released a slow breath. 'Twas Clare's lifelong dream that now slipped from her cousin's fingers. Her heart ached for Clare, knowing well the pain of giving love only to have that love betrayed. "But, no more?"

" 'Tis Reginald I love and will forever more. The man beyond our wall is not he, but a new creature, all twisted and eaten by avarice." The tears in Clare's eyes spilled over to stain her cheeks. "Can you ever forgive me?"

"What is there to forgive?" Elyssa's mouth lifted in a small smile. " 'Tis that promise you made me at Simon's birth you have just fulfilled. Do you not give up the life that could be yours in order that Simon should continue in his?"

Clare paused in herself, then sighed. "Aye, I suppose I do, but for more than simply love of Simon, or even you. I could not aid Reginald in taking up such a life, not when it rests on the blood and bones of children."

"And that is why I love you so," Elyssa said, taking Clare's hands. "Come now, cousin. We have much to do if we're to keep Cecilia safe and guarantee our Simon a long and healthy life."

Chapter 22

"My lord sheriff, you have a visitor." The lilting voice of the wine merchant's young wife floated to Geoffrey from the chamber's door, just sweet enough to lift him from his sleep. Martin coughed as he woke in the other bed across the room.

'Twas the merchant's home and kitchen he'd rented for court's duration. If the cost was a might steeper than he thought to spend, it had been a profitable year for Crosswell. Bolstered by Martin's knowledge of the shire, the treasury not only received all it was due, Geoffrey had earned a goodly sum toward defraying what he'd paid for the sheriff's position. Secure in his profit, he'd dared to visit a jeweler, purchasing the bride's gift he would give to Elyssa on their wedding day.

He yawned, stretching as best he could in the short bed. Although the darkness around him said 'twas yet the depths of night, Geoffrey reached beneath the bolster seeking his eye covering. His fingers found both the patch and the fabric bag in which resided the necklet he'd bought his love, wrought with pearls and amber. Pressing the patch in place, he asked, "Who comes?"

"One calling himself Lord Meynell. He waits downstairs, in the hall, my lord."

He frowned, knowing no man by that name. "Tell him to return after dawn."

"Aye, and leave us to our rest," muttered Osbert, who lay among the many men stretched out on the bedchamber floor.

"My lord, he told me to say he comes on your daughter's behalf."

That brought Geoffrey upright in a hurry. 'Twas a fresh-faced lass the merchant had married, not a day over fifteen. She stood in the doorway with her lamp in hand, the yellowish glow gleaming off her rich silk bed robe. At three times her age, her husband kept his wife very well.

"Send him to me." Geoff found his sword as the girl turned to do as he bid. Its bared blade lay across his lap by the time footsteps marked his visitor's upward trek.

Lord Meynell entered, his mail jangling and his cloak swinging gently around his calves. The glow from the housewife's lamp showed Geoffrey the man's plain face, rawboned, with a bold jaw beneath his neatly trimmed dark beard. Anger roared through him.

"What sort of foul trickery is this?" 'Twas a vicious question he flung at his father's bastard. "Who the hell is Meynell? I'll kill him for lending you his name."

"I am Meynell now," Richard FitzHenry replied evenly.

"Temric!" Martin called from his bed in surprise.

Geoffrey's rage grew as Martin used the name his eldest brother adopted after tossing aside the one their father had so generously given him. "How dare you use my daughter to buy your way into my presence!"

Richard only raised his brows, untouched by this rude greeting. "Would you have seen me any other way? I bring you news, and I fear 'twill do you much hurt." It was his half brother's calmness, where Geoffrey's open dislike usually raised rage, that made Geoff heed him.

"Spew it, then."

"As of yestermorn, Gradinton has besieged Freyne."

"What?" Geoffrey cried in disbelief. "Nay, were that true, I'd have had word. Lady Freyne knows where I am."

"I have her message. It came to me by way of Ashby and Gilliam," his brother replied. "If you've not heard, it can only mean Gradinton took the man who carried news to you." Richard stepped to the bedside and offered Geoffrey the parchment along with the lamp.

Geoffrey opened the folded skin, recognizing Elyssa's strong, neat hand.

To my dearest son Jocelyn, squire to Lord Ashby.
I send you this missive only praying it may reach
you. This morn, Lord Coudray's enemy, Baldwin
de Gradinton, marched on Freyne with a vast army
and siege engines aplenty. He seeks to steal Cecilia
of Coudray, who is his granddaughter and now
his only heir. Although I have sent word to my
beloved Lord Coudray, the man I would make
your stepfather, he is presently at the Michaelmas
court. I can hold no great hope of his aid, knowing
he is duty-bound to remain there.

Geoffrey's breath hissed from him. *Jesu,* but the cocksucking son-of-a-sow had bided his time carefully, waiting until his foe was well and truly helpless against him. By law, 'twas the sheriff and only the sheriff who could report to the Exchequer on the shire's blanch and ferm. Geoff read on, his heart's ache growing with every word.

As I know Lord Ashby is brother to Coudray, 'tis my hopeful wish that you might ask Lord Ashby to send us what relief he can. If that cannot be done, we will attempt to hold Gradinton at bay until Lord Coudray can come. I sign this missive with all pride in my heart at your many and continuing successes, reminding you that I hold you first in my love for all time. Your dam, Elyssa, Lady Freyne.

He stared at what was a loving farewell to Jocelyn. She signed it as if she did not expect to survive and wished to assure her son of her care for the last time. Why? 'Twas only Cecilia Baldwin wanted.

The answer came from his innermost core. Elyssa loved Cecilia like her own blood; she'd die before she let Gradinton tear his daughter from her. Panic exploded in Geoff, and he dropped the parchment to grasp his sword hilt against the pain.

"Goddamn him!" he bellowed, coming to his feet. Gradinton would kill Elyssa. The lamp shattered against the wall as Geoffrey swung his sword with all his power into the bedpost.

Men shouted from a great distance. He tore his sword from the bed's support. Wood squealed and cracked. Acrid smoke filled his lungs. Dying in his helplessness, he swung again and again.

Someone had him by the shoulders, trying to wrestle him to the ground. Roaring against containment, Geoffrey tore free and turned on his attacker, sword already in motion. His blade clashed into another, the impact so ferocious it drove him back three steps.

"Geoffrey!"

'Twas his father's voice raised in command. In instinctive reaction, he lowered his blade. Even as he realized his mistake, his sword was wrenched from his grasp by his half brother.

With the loss of his weapon, rage died, leaving only impossible pain beneath it. Geoffrey stumbled back until he reached the wall behind him. The plastered surface was wet against his hands. Grief rolled over him.

"He'll take them while I am trapped here and cannot stop him," he sobbed.

The wine merchant's wife was shrieking in the doorway. Beside her her burly mate, his nightcap in his hands, puffed himself out in fury. "My bed! You've destroyed my bed and nigh on set the house afire," he shouted. "May God curse me for renting to you."

Richard turned on the couple, his sword yet in hand. "He'll replace what he's ruined," his brother shouted, "now, begone with you. This is a private matter." They nigh on ran down the stairs, their curses including all noblemen.

Geoffrey felt the cold emptiness he'd known after Cecilia's silent retreat reawaken within him. Even imagining Elyssa's loss made the emptiness grow until 'twas worse than the first time. He'd go with her if she died. His heart froze, his limbs chilled until they were stone.

Suddenly, Richard stood before him. The brother he despised set hands on his shoulders. There was unexpected comfort in his touch.

"So," Richard said, "you've found one on whom to

spend your heart, have you?" There was naught but kindness in Richard's brown eyes.

Beyond speech, Geoff only turned his head to the side as Osbert's voice rose behind Richard. "Bestir yourselves, you lazy slugs!" the knight shouted. "This is naught for the likes of your ears. Find the lamps and get to clearing the wreckage."

Martin came to stand beside Richard. "He fears Lady Freyne will die before she cedes Cecilia to Gradinton."

"Will she?" Richard asked them both in surprise.

"Aye," Martin replied.

Geoffrey's skin crawled at his undersheriff's reiteration of what he already knew. "May God damn that filthy bastard to hell." The quiet words barely escaped his frozen jaw.

"Mind your tongue," his bastard brother said with remarkable good humor, then he patted his taller and younger sibling's scarred cheek. "Geoff, take heart. All is not yet lost."

'Twas his brother's easy words and warm touch on him that drove back the coldness. Richard was right, all was not yet lost. Within Geoffrey flared the need to destroy Gradinton. May the kingdom be damned, he'd ride for Coudray and rouse his forces. Geoffrey groaned in dismay.

"Damn me," he hissed at himself. "All of Coudray is at Freyne, trapped behind those stinking walls. Crosswell's force isn't enough to finish Gradinton. What was I thinking?"

He pressed the heels of his hands against his forehead in frustration. 'Twas his need to keep Elyssa attached to Cecilia, and thus to him, that had caused this. At least, he had enough men to drive Gradinton from Freyne, if nothing more. He shoved Richard away from him.

"Leave the cursed bed," Geoffrey bellowed to his men, who were attempting to repair it. He grabbed his chausses from the clothes pole and jammed his feet into his undergarment. "Dress! Arm! We are for Freyne."

"Geoff, wait, you cannot leave court," Richard started to say.

"Why not? I am Freyne's warden by royal command, and Gradinton attacks what is under my control," Geoffrey interrupted, yanking the drawstring tight, while already clutching his shirt. He tugged his shirt down over his chest, then looked at his brother.

"You've delivered your news. For that you have my thanks. Now, leave me to do as I must to spare my family hurt. If you think to stop me, you do so at your own peril."

Richard's head jerked back as if struck. "Goddamn your arrogant hide!" he roared, and caught Geoffrey by his shirtfront, then slammed his younger half brother against the wall.

Growling in his own rage, Geoffrey shoved at his attacker, only to find Richard's sword at his throat. Although shorter and almost ten years his senior, they were evenly matched in strength. 'Twould be suicide to resist when Richard was armed and he was not.

There was complete silence in the room. Martin retreated to the corner, catching up his sword belt. Osbert stood near the door, his brows raised, as if he offered Geoffrey his aid in this battle.

"Listen or call your men to murder me," Richard growled, "for only murder will silence me. Which will it be?"

Rage simmered in Geoffrey, but blood was the

stronger. For all the times he'd sworn to kill Richard, he wasn't capable of ordering his men to harm his brother. "I will listen." 'Twas a harsh reply.

Richard kept his sword pressed across Geoff's chest to see he did. "Ever since our sire's death, you've set your course to proving you need your family naught at all. Now that you come to the one event where you do need us, you'd rather lose all you own than lower yourself to ask."

As the words left him, Richard's shoulders relaxed, then his sword dropped as rage departed. "Geoff, you are not alone. Ask, damn you," he almost pleaded. "Take what we long to give you. Ask Gilliam. Ask me, or, if you cannot bring yourself to take my aid, ask our brother Rannulf, and I will send my men to him. Even now, he waits for your word."

Richard's words brought more confusion than hope. "Rannulf? He called me fool for buying the shrievalty and disparaged my efforts to protect Cecilia. I cannot think he'd aid me now that I must pay the piper as he warned."

Richard only smiled. "You misjudge him. 'Tis his function as our father's surrogate to complain against our foolishness. Gilliam's messengers went not just to Meynell, but to Graistan as well. Rannulf calls every man he owns to meet him at Lavendon. There, like me, will he wait for you to command us against Gradinton."

A new peace crept over Geoff. Rannulf would come, as would Gilliam. Richard had offered as well. Together, the four of them would end Gradinton's threat against those he loved.

All four? He studied his eldest brother. Gone from Richard's face was the harsh dislike they'd shared since their sire's death. "You would aid me?"

"Am I not your brother, the son of my father, just as you are?" Richard raised a brow in a gentle chide.

Geoff freed a scornful breath. " 'Twas not what you said at our last meeting. Then did you call yourself Alwynason, severing your connection to the FitzHenrys." Two years ago, they'd retreated to the field and met sword to sword over how Richard rejected the father who'd loved him. 'Twas only Rannulf's intervention that kept them from killing each other.

"True enough, but much has happened between now and then," Richard replied softly. "I came not only to bring you this word, but to beg your forgiveness. I did our sire a terrible disservice when I rejected him, and you were right to despise me for it. I've since decided 'tis better to be the illegitimate son of my father, than any other man's legitimate child. Will you accept my aid?"

Geoffrey stared at Richard for a long moment. In the harsh outline of his brother's face and the set of his shoulders, Geoff saw their sire's reflection. This was his blood, no more or less so than were Gilliam or Rannulf. And equally as willing to lay down his life for his sibling's cause.

"Aye, with gratitude and love in my heart," he said with a surprised laugh.

"My thanks," Richard replied, his smile growing. "Now, go make your apologies to your host, and I will be on the road to Lavendon. We'll meet again at Freyne, once you've discharged your duties here."

Geoffrey shook his head. "I'll not stay while my enemy threatens the woman who holds my life in her hands."

"But, my lord, you cannot leave when 'tis only you who can make the report," Martin protested.

"He's right, Geoff, you cannot leave," Richard said.

After Geoffrey pulled on his tunic, he said, "How can the court complain? 'Tisn't as if I sought to cheat them. The taxes, the witnesses, Crosswell's men and undersheriff are here. If I do not appear, what can Hubert Walter do, but ask me to resign?"

The words fell unheeded from his lips, but when he heard them, exhilaration spiraled through him. "I *will* resign," he shouted to the ceiling. To be free of Crosswell was a wondrous thought.

Only then did the whole of Gradinton's intent come clear, and he laughed in soaring hopes. "And here lies Gradinton's flaw, Richard. Baldwin sees nothing but properties and coins. Since he would never turn his back on profit to save a woman or a daughter, he does not expect me to do so, either."

How careful Gradinton had been with his plot. Believing Geoffrey would not dare leave court, Baldwin insured himself there was no chance of Cecilia becoming an orphan, thus giving the royal court control of his granddaughter. 'Twas also a way of protecting himself. In case an army did appear, without Geoffrey at its head there was little chance the attackers would do more than seek to drive Gradinton away from Freyne.

In that moment, Geoffrey knew Baldwin's life was his. With her grandsire dead, Cecilia would be free from threat. Then Geoffrey and Elyssa could wed, keeping his and her children as their own and making life worth living once more.

"It could take you as long to resign as it would to wait for your appointed time," his brother warned. "You know how the clerks who control the schedule savor their power. I suppose with enough silver you might win yourself a day or two, but I wager you wait a week. Either way, you'll not have a hint as to when you might be departing court until after morning's

come. Bid me good journey, and I will see you at
Freyne."

"Richard," Geoffrey replied, yet buoyed by rising
excitement as he belted his tunic and tossed his mantle
on over his shoulders, "we sit in a town full of the
king's justiciars. William of Hereford is in his house
just down the street, soundly sleeping in his own bed.
Not a single petitioner awaits him in all his household.
Come with me and watch how, with our cousin's aid,
the bishop takes my resignation. Oswald has no choice
but to help me, when 'twas in part my recommenda-
tion that gained him his auspicious position."

He leaned over the wreckage of the bed and found
the necklet in its bag. His hand closed around it, taking its undamaged state as a sign. From under his bed
came his saddle pack. He tucked the piece into the
pack, then straightened and looked back to Richard.

His brother shook his head. "Best leave me behind
if you want Oswald's help. I'm not certain he's forgiven me for last autumn."

When Geoffrey raised a brow in question, Richard
only waved away his interest. " 'Tis a long story. Suf-
fice it to say 'tis by Oswald's influence that I now have
a wife and daughter of my own."

"You are wed?" Geoffrey replied in surprise.
"When?"

"In autumn past."

Disappointment and regret woke in Geoff. This
meant all three of his brothers had wed in the previous
year, and he'd not attended one ceremony. Of their
wives, he knew only Gilliam's wild woman, Nicola. It
had been wrong of him to so cut himself from his
family.

"Well then, if you'll not come, wait here for me and
we'll ride as one," Geoffrey said, and turned on Mar-

tin. "Do you still stand here in your altogether? Don your clothing and come witness my term's ending."

Martin grimaced against his own regrets at losing his employer, but did as he was bid. 'Twas Osbert who caught up Geoffrey's cross-garters and came to do this menial task for his departing master.

"My lord," the knight said to him as he wound the long strips around Geoffrey's stockinged calves, "I find myself in a dilemma. It seems my time at Crosswell has come to an end. I'm wondering if you might have a place at Coudray for one such as I?"

Geoffrey smiled at how great the changes in him had been. Until Elyssa's advent, this man had given him naught but dislike; now he offered his heart and loyalty. "We have come a long way, my friend. Do you know, Sir Osbert, I believe I do. I'll warn you that, should we fail in our endeavor, it might well be the pay is less than what you've known in the past. But, the food is good and the hall, well, the hall is superb."

"I thought as much." The knight came to his feet. " 'Tis just the sort of place I wanted, thinking to pass my later years in comfort."

Geoffrey's smile grew as he accepted the man's hand in his. He was not alone.

Candles, caught in brackets around the bishop's bedchamber, brought something near to day's light in the big room. Like the rest of Hereford's large town house, the walls were draped with panels made rich by the handiwork of whole nunneries. Where the gentle light touched, these elaborate embroideries showed their rich colors and detail.

If William of Hereford's massive bed had curtains of functional wool for heat's sake, he'd laid shimmering silk over them, then trimmed the whole with cloth of gold. Atop a nearby perch sat the bishop's hawk. Stirred from its nightly roost by the noise of visitors, it turned its hooded head from side to side in an effort to see what it could not. The tiny bells on the bird's head covering tinkled prettily in the room's quiet.

At the room's far table, Geoffrey's cousin, Oswald, poured wine into a bejeweled cup. At six years younger than Geoff, the slim, dark man was doing well for himself. Oswald's bed robe only marginally undershone the trappings on the bishop's bed.

Oswald turned to the servant who stood silently in the corner. The man sipped, then took the cup to the bed and offered it to his master. Rubies flashed as they caught the flame from a thick night candle, burning at William's bedside.

From the deep shadows, the prelate leaned out to accept the cup. Silver gleamed in his dark hair and beard, even sprinkled on his bared chest. He receded into shadows once more. 'Twas in the same silence he'd maintained since Geoffrey had finished his tale and presented his resignation, that William of Hereford turned the cup between his hands. At long last, he shifted into the light and raised his dark gaze to Geoffrey's face.

" 'Tis good to see them healing so well," he said, keeping his deep voice low and private.

"Aye, 'tis, my lord." Geoffrey freed a quick laugh, surprised to find himself at ease with the scars that lay upon his face. Elyssa had done this for him. Her acceptance made his own possible. "Even better, I have become accustomed to my one-sided sight. No longer do I spill cups in my lap by overreaching and my ability with the sword returns."

"If I refuse your resignation, then what?" William asked.

Although startled by this swift change of subject, Geoff's spine stiffened. "You'll need to imprison me, elsewise I will leave."

"Not a pleasant thought," the prelate murmured, then tried a personal tack. "You cannot afford to go, Geoff."

Geoffrey slipped easily into his other role as the same friend and hunting companion to this man that his father had been. "If I choose to beggar myself, William, 'tis my business, not yours."

" 'Tis a siege, not a battlefield," the bishop offered on another front. "I'll see your meeting held earlier. Surely, it will wait a week."

"Gradinton does not assault merely the keep where my daughter and the woman I take to wife reside, he attacks me," Geoffrey retorted, his voice rising in outrage with each word. "See how he plots to use the law against me so I cannot meet him as honest men do? Moreover, 'tis the harvest season. Have not all civilized men agreed that this is a time for peace? There is no honor in him."

William of Hereford raised his brows in reproach. " 'Tis a poor effort on your part, trying to bend me to your will by speaking of law and society."

"My lord," Oswald said, his tone fraught with impatience, " 'tis no good arguing with him. Once these FitzHenrys get their blood to boiling, they cannot see anything but what they want. If he says he must go, then go he must."

"I want you as sheriff, Geoff," William tried, ignoring his administrator's warning. "You've done a fine job creating order where there'd been but chaos before."

Geoffrey saw his escape and took it. "That rests more on this man's efforts, than mine, my lord." He set his arm across Martin's shoulders and brought him forward. "The de la Bois's are centered in the shire. Sir Martin, here, knows the place and its folk like none other. At every turn, it has been his suggestions improving our collections and straightening the accounts."

William's dark eyes shifted as he glanced from one man to the other. "Is this true, Sir Martin?"

"That my family is centered in the shire, aye," Martin said. "As for the success we've had, Lord Coudray is the cause—" Geoffrey's sudden fist in Martin's back made the young knight stutter. "I suppose I have been a greater help to him than another might have been," he managed.

"Hubert Walter is set on consistency of management for the shires. If you're convinced Sir Martin can reproduce this year's profits, I'll sell him the position," William said swiftly to Geoff.

"You'd sell it to me, my lord?" Martin's dark brows shot up. "I cannot afford it. I've not a shilling to my name, save for the value of my horse and armor."

"Ah, but you do," the bishop replied. "There's what you earned in profit this year. Give me that, and you'll own the position until Easter court. If the collection remains at its present level, we'll settle on a price. If not, then I'll have Geoff as sheriff, once more."

"My lord, 'tis your profit, not mine," Martin said to Geoffrey.

" 'Tis William's now, while you own all my best wishes. My lord sheriff, may you be blissfully happy at Crosswell." Geoffrey shook Martin's hand with fervor.

With that, Geoffrey went to William and knelt, kissing the proffered ring. As he rose, the bishop said,

"Coudray, you continue as Freyne's warden. Take with you those men Crosswell can spare to see the king's peace restored to that place."

Geoffrey smiled. "My lord, you have my deepest gratitude."

The prelate only snorted. "So I should. When you see Rannulf, tell him I think you as mad as your father's bastard. Now begone and let me sleep."

Chapter 23

Reginald listened as the battering ram impacted with Freyne's gate. The thunderous retort said the beam had finally smashed through the thick, straw-filled pad the defenders had laid over their door. Spotters called a warning, but Reginald was beyond the range of the stones and arrows that rained down from the walls. A few of their men cried out in pain, but most of Freyne's projectiles clattered uselessly off shields and the ram's wooden, skin-clad roof.

In the short moment of silence that followed this attack, mist drifted down onto Reginald's mantle. Its steady descent washed the scent of death from the air. Hidden from him by the thick gray layer of clouds overhead, he heard the call of geese on the wing.

Then the thick chains supporting the ram on its brace groaned as it was drawn back for its next blow. Stones clattered, crossbows were winched. Men shouted commands as the attempt at breaking through the door continued.

The trebucket beside which Reginald stood, groaned as its thick, upright pole was drawn downward. Once a great stone was fitted into the giant sling, the engineer gave his call. The locking mechanism clicked back. The pole sprang upward and crashed against its stop. The boulder soared free from the sling at the pole's top. There was barely more than a thud as it fell to the ground within Freyne's bailey.

"Another miss, sir," the trebucket's engineer told him, his explanation unnecessary.

"Let me think a moment," Reginald replied.

"Take your time, my lord. We have all day." The man grinned, his big teeth and long face giving him the look of a horse.

As Reginald paused in thought, a stab of resentment hit in him. Gradinton's plan had been impressive, even down to awakening the right tone of outrage in his vassals, when he'd recounted the many wrongs done him by Coudray. However, success grew from action as much as the plan. Gradinton lacked the patience to achieve his aim.

Resentment grew, and in frustration, he stared at Freyne's left gatetower. Over the last three days, his assault left the wall top broken. The hoarding lay in the ditch below, naught but splintered bits of wood and bone. All Reginald would have needed was one more day and the whole gate would have dropped.

Instead, Gradinton intervened, saying that if the towers could withstand this much, they'd not soon fall. He'd ordered the trebuchet turned onto Freyne's hall. 'Twas but a whim. Gradinton wanted to frighten the women, even when all his men protested that his effort was but a waste of stone and time.

The thought of destroying the place of his birth sent resentment flaring into anger, and Reginald freed a hot breath. He'd come to Freyne prepared to lose what he wanted due to fate, not to petty mismanagement. Ach, but what choice had he now?

In irritable acquiescence, he shut his eyes and in his memory counted the distance between himself and the wall, then from wall to hall. When he had the number, he related it to Gradinton's trebuchet engineer, along with a new guess on the exact direction.

Men sweated and shoved to the tune of the engineer's calls. Once again the post descended, and a stone was fitted into its sling. This time, when the boulder flew, there was a thundering, splintering explosion beyond the walls.

"We've got it," the engineer cried in excitement.

"So it seems," Reginald said sourly, and watched the men drag down the trebuchet arm for the next blow against his home.

"Sir Reginald?"

"Aye?" He looked around.

A slinger stood behind him. The man's stone-filled pouch hanging at his waist. His weapon, a miniature version of the trebuchet's sling, was draped over his shoulders. Struggling against the man's grip was a thin boy, no more than fourteen. The boy glanced up at him, then froze as if terror-striken at facing a mailed knight.

"We found this bit of offal creeping through our ranks. What should I do with him?" The man's French was so thick, his words were barely comprehensible.

Reginald opened his mouth to suggest a swift death, then caught back his words at the boy's strange appearance. The lad's pale brown hair had been shorn so closely to his head it barely covered his skull. He looked closer and found the cause. A jagged scar, a recent wound by the pink look of it, crossed his crown. The lad lost his hair so the healer could close his skin.

Still trapped in consideration, Reginald's gaze dropped to the boy's face. Beneath sharply peaked brows, his brown eyes were wide with pleading, his full lips caught in a fearful grimace. There was something familiar about him.

Frowning, he looked closer still, searching his memory for some reason he might know the lad. The boy had reached the age where the man he would become mingled with the child he'd been. Although yet beardless, his shoulders broadened. His build suggested he'd eventually own the same powerful chest and narrow hips that Reginald claimed.

With that thought came recognition. 'Twas Aymer's face he saw lurking here. Before him stood one of his brother's bastards from the village. Teased into curiosity by a sudden sense of kinship, Reginald said, "Ask him to explain his presence."

English words flowed around him as he waited. At last, the commoner turned on him. "He says his mother is very worried about his younger brother and his stepsister. I think his mother believes they've wandered into our camp, so she sent this lad asearching for him. He begs you to let him go, saying that he must return before his stepfather comes.

Reginald smiled thinly, the boy's words only confirming his guess; here was one of his brother's byblows. Enjoying the power of life and death over Aymer's get, Reginald chose to bestow life today. "We do not slaughter children in this camp. Nay, there's but one child to murder and that babe lies within Freyne's wall." 'Twas a wry aside, aimed more at himself than 'twas meant for the ears of those around him. To the slinger, he said, "Send him back to the village with a warning to keep his distance. His brother and stepsister will come home or naught on their own."

He gave a dismissing wave of his hand and returned to the task at hand, pleased at his generosity. Then his pleasure dimmed. What would he have to show for murder but a broken manor and years of debt to

rebuild it? Ah well, 'twas too late for doubts now.
He listened without emotion as another stone found
Freyne's hall.

"I am struck blind and deaf," Henry, Lord Lavendon told his darkened hall, his voice sour. The draft
from the door whispered through the room, as if in
gentle commisseration. Its chill breath lifted the few
panels covering Henry's wooden walls, then set the
torches high above to sizzling. With a final soft sigh,
it lifted the smoke from the hearthstone, sending it
swirling upward toward the hole cut in the roof.

Standing before that same stone, the plump nobleman crossed his arms and tried not to look around
him. His floor was laid deep with pallets on which the
armies from Ashby, Meynell, Graistan, and Crosswell
settled to their rest. Instead, he kept his gaze focused
on all four of Graistan's sons.

"Should anyone ever suggest that the FitzHenrys
came here to wage war against Baldwin de Gradinton,
I and all my servants will swear that such a thing never
occurred. Now I and they are leaving this room, wanting to hear nothing we must needs forget."

Geoffrey leaned back on the bench he'd claimed
from atop the stack at the wall. "Henry, although I
am sheriff no longer, 'tis Hereford who sends me to
keep the peace." His voice was hoarse in exhaustion.
After a day and a'half in the saddle, stopping only to
feed and rest the horses, every inch of him cried out
to shuck his mail and sleep. But rest would be impossible until he knew Freyne's status and had set himself
on some course of action. "As Freyne is the court's
property, Baldwin breaks the law here."

"Wondrous," Lavendon said with a frown. "I'll tell
him you said so when he comes to wreak his ven-

geance on me. My borders are far too vulnerable to him."

Richard cleared his throat. "When this is done, Henry, you must come and visit me at Meynell. I would be honored to show you my new home and my wife." Geoffrey glanced at his eldest brother. Also armed and haggard in exhaustion, Richard strove to smile at their host. "I am forest warden there."

"A sop, Richard," Henry said. Nonetheless, he relaxed against it. "I will consider your invitation. Now, if any of you want aught to eat or drink, best you say so before I take my folk all away with me."

Dressed in a chestnut-colored tunic, Geoffrey's youngest and full brother, leaned back against the wall behind him, then stretched out his long, booted legs. "Nothing for me, thank you, Henry." Tall and massive, Gilliam FitzHenry's voice was deep beyond his two and twenty years. 'Twas in Gilliam's face that Geoffrey found his closest kinship. Beneath curling golden hair, his younger brother owned the same length of nose and breadth of brow and jaw, his eye color a lighter blue.

"Nor I," said Rannulf, Lord Graistan, wearing a simple tawny tunic. "Take heart, Henry. Think what friends you make of we FitzHenrys by this boon." Only four months younger than Richard, Henry of Graistan's elder heir shared both height and build with Geoffrey, but he was dark where Geoff was fair. His features were long, his eye color the same transluscent gray Cecilia owned.

"You were friends to me already," Lavendon replied, a new caution in his tone as if he feared he might no longer be.

Rannulf smiled. 'Twas this smile that named him Geoffrey's brother. "Henry, you are an old woman, nattering on without cause. Go you to your rest and cease your worries. Are we not foster brothers?"

Henry gave a pleased huff, then turned and left the room. His servants trooped behind him. The logs on the hearth snarled and shifted as Geoffrey waited for the upper chamber door to close. When it had, he smiled at the circle of his family, including Elyssa's son Jocelyn, who sat at Gilliam's feet. "I would thank you all," he said to his brothers.

Rannulf glanced at Richard, then to Gilliam. "For being your family, I hope. Anything else would be an insult."

"Aye, so I am at long last remembering," Geoffrey replied. "How stands it with Freyne?"

"For that you must ask my squire," said Gilliam.

"Your squire?" Geoffrey looked at Jocelyn, who, God willing, would soon be his stepson.

Gone was the babe of last autumn, with his whining and his tears. Jocelyn, his pale brown hair still short after April's injuries, now sat among his betters wearing a quiet confidence that spoke well of the man he would become. "My lord, each day I enter Gradinton's camp to view how their siege progresses."

Geoffrey raised his brows in surprise and looked to Gilliam. "You send the one who is Freyne's heir into the hands of a man bent on destroying that house?"

If Gilliam laughed softly, Jocelyn's grin was cheeky. "I was never known at Freyne and what soldier looks askance upon a ragged village lad?" the boy asked him in fluent English.

While Rannulf and Richard laughed, Geoffrey turned to Gilliam, the only one of them unfamiliar with the commoner's tongue, to translate. Gilliam cocked a brow. "I know what he said." If his accent was heavy, 'twas still passable English.

"Good lad, 'twas past time you learned," Rannulf said, the "lad" he complimented bigger and heavier than he, then turned his attention back on Jocelyn. "Tell Coudray what you saw, child."

"Lord Gradinton has felled wood enough to fill the dry moat, making a bridge. He sets his ram against Freyne's gate, working it without pause the day long."

"What sort of defense does Freyne use against this attack?" Geoffrey asked.

Jocelyn gave a sorry shake to his head. "They padded the underside of the drawbridge, but the pad gave way before noon. Beyond that, they've sent down only stones and bolts, but far too few of those to have an effect. They've not much chance against the ram as the trebuchet has cleared the hoarding. But, 'tisn't this that most concerns me." The lad glanced at the men around him. " 'Tis my uncle, Reginald of Freyne, who leads Lord Gradinton's men in their efforts to destroy what is mine."

Geoffrey drew a sharp breath. He saw again the man's detailed account book. Without doubt, Gradinton knew every item Freyne had in store and would have prepared against those attacks. "No doubt Gradinton pays him well to betray his home. You are certain 'tis he?"

The corners of the squire's mouth lifted in a smile reminiscent of his foster father's. "We came eye to eye. I think he did not remember me as I have changed a mite."

"Just a wee bit, Jos," Gilliam laughed, dropping a huge hand onto the lad's yet thin shoulder. Jocelyn almost crumpled beneath its weight. When he straightened, his face was alive with a pleased grin.

Geoffrey nodded as he digested what he'd heard. The need to be done with Gradinton and his threats grew. If he couldn't succeed without his brothers' help, neither would he involve them in what could hurt them.

"Hear me out and decide for yourselves. I have had enough of Gradinton's harassment. When we attack him, 'twill not be my intention to drive him off, but to end this, here and now. If he attempts to retreat, I will not let him go. 'Tis his death I now seek." Such a thing was surely dishonorable, if not tantamount to murder.

There was a moment's silence between these men. 'Twas the youngest of them who spoke first. "If one man attacks another, he does so in full knowledge of what it might cost him," Gilliam said. "Who will fault you for seeking to keep your family from further harm? I, for one, am content to aid you in this aim."

Geoffrey's gaze slipped to his elder brothers. "And, you?"

"In a battle, the outcome is always in God's hands, not ours," Rannulf said. "If the boy counts as well as he creeps, our numbers are evenly matched, making the fight fair. Thus, 'twill only be murder if Gradinton kneels before you, pleading for peace as you cut him down. Should such a thing occur, I must step between you and he. Other than that, I can imagine no other need to interfere. Richard?"

"Nor can I," the eldest of them agreed.

"Aye then," Geoffrey said in relief, "we must be quick about what we do. Gradinton concentrates on the gateway because there is no portcullis, only a set of wooden doors and the drawbridge. If the defenders cannot harass the ram, as Jocelyn suggests, I cannot believe the doors will long stand. 'Tis paramount that we stop Gradinton before he breaches the walls."

"Why?" asked Richard.

Geoffrey's smile was grim. "Remember, Gradinton seeks not to own Freyne, but Cecilia. Should he gain the interior under our attack, he'll set his men to holding us at bay while he pries open the keep. Once he has her, our hands will be tied. I must let him retreat with impunity, fearing that Cecilia might be hurt if I attack him."

"Against the possibility that he takes the bailey while we are after him, what sort of defense stands between him and the keep?" Rannulf asked.

Geoffrey leaned forward and braced his forearms on his knees to ease his back's ache. "Freyne is made in the old style, with the keep set high upon a motte. Between the keep's hill and the bailey there lies a secondary dry moat, fully ringing the tower's mound. The motte's sides are mined with wooden stakes, and it wears a wooden pallisade around its crest, with the access from bailey to motte by drawbridge. While this sounds efficient enough, you must remember who 'tis that leads this siege. Reginald will know every step to opening that second gate."

"Then there's naught left to us but an open assault as soon as possible," Gilliam said with a certain morbid glee.

" 'Tis my thinking exactly," Geoffrey replied. "Tired as I am, I'd not wait past tomorrow's dawn to be finished with this."

"I see no other choice," Rannulf agreed.

"Dawn suits me very well," Gilliam said as he rose and stretched. "Aye, 'twill be a joy to fight this battle with my brothers at my side and Jos at my knee."

"You'll not take the lad to battle. He's too young," Rannulf protested.

Jos rose swiftly to his feet. "Lord Graistan, 'tis my home that Lord Gradinton destroys with my uncle's aid. 'Tis my mother and my brother he threatens. Thus is it my right to fight in their defense."

"Well-spoken, lad," Rannulf said, his voice warm with admiration, "but what can you do against men twice your age and three times your bulk?"

The frown on Jos's brow came and went quickly. "Give me the archers. 'Tis my strength, and I can lead them in our defense."

Gilliam laughed. "His aim is something to be reckoned with. My wife Nicola vows he left a burn across the back of her neck in April when he shot across her nape."

Geoffrey drew the boy to his side, laying his arm over Jos's shoulders. "Think he is too young, Rannulf? See the scars he wears? These he took in a battle to save his lord and lady. Although small in size, this lad owns a lion's heart."

"Thank you, my lord," Jos said, his face suddenly pink.

Against such a barrage, Rannulf gave way. "Gilliam, he is yours to do with as you see fit, and I was wrong to interfere."

" 'Tis time you learned that, old man," Gilliam retorted, grinning at the only father he'd ever known. "Rest well, we've God's work to do on the morrow." He waved the boy to his side and crossed the hall to the place where Ashby's men slept.

"I am getting too old for this," Richard complained quietly. "Where Gilliam finds his joy in battle, I see only a hard day's work and the possibility of injury, which pleases me naught at all. Of late, I find my life a very precious commodity." He rose, then set his hand on Geoff's shoulder. "What of you, brother? Is your heart at ease with all this?"

"At ease?" Geoffrey looked up at him, then smiled.

For the first time in his life, he allowed himself to savor the value of owning brothers such as these. "Ease will I have when my daughter and my wife are once again safe within my grasp. 'Tis confidence I've gained, because of you and your aid. Like Gilliam, I find myself looking forward to the morrow. Dawn brings me to the day I anticipated from Gradinton's first attempt at stealing Cecilia."

"Aye, but then I think me you wished only for your own death," Rannulf said, his voice low and soft. "Do you still see death in your future?"

Geoffrey stared at him in astonishment, then surprise gave way to understanding. How could he have believed he hid his thoughts from those who knew him best? "On the morrow, I fight for a long and full life, Rannulf."

"You have changed so?"

The man who had stepped into Henry of Graistan's shoes craved greater assurance than mere words. Geoffrey sought for, then found, the way to give him what he needed. "It has been a long while since we were all beneath one roof," he said, a slow smile spreading across his face. "Come to Coudray for Christmas."

Rannulf freed a quick laugh. "Will that be to keep Christmas or celebrate a wedding—the one you seem to have forgotten to mention to me?"

Geoffrey raised his brows. " 'Tis the pot calling the kettle black here. I seem to have been excluded from your most recent joining as well."

" 'Twasn't my fault," Rannulf protested, his mouth lifting into a smile. "Her father forced me to it."

Richard gave a scornful snort. "Do not believe it. Lust got the better of him, and he let a puny old man twist his arm."

"Nay, if Elyssa and I live past the morrow, I'll not wait until Christmas to wed her. As for Christmas, I know Gilliam will come," Geoff said. "Keep Christmas with me, Rannulf. You, too, Richard." He glanced up at his eldest brother. "I find myself even more curious as to what sort of woman you now own."

"Wait until you see," Rannulf laughed, and Richard cuffed him on the shoulder.

"Will it be only we four and our families?" Richard asked. "My wife is very shy and cannot abide those outside the family."

"It will be only family," Geoffrey replied, surprised at how deeply this event now appealed to him.

Pleasure colored his eldest brother's face. "Then, Philippa and I will come, bringing our daughter with us," Richard replied, and left them for his own men.

Geoffrey rose to follow. Rannulf looked up at him, his elbows set on his knees. " 'Tis good to have you back. I have missed you."

"And I, you. 'Tis good to be home," Geoff replied, then sought out Osbert and Crosswell's men.

Chapter 24

Although the grayness that had plagued them these past days lightened only a little, Elyssa sensed dawn's coming and roused herself from a fitful slumber. Over the past week, she'd managed only to grab an hour or two of nightly rest. Rain pattered against the keep tower's roof. Gentle and steady, it continued uninterrupted as night gave way to day. She breathed deeply. The air was cold, but fresh, washed clean by the moisture.

The woman on the pallet next to her turned, dropping her arm onto her lady as she did so. Elyssa pushed her aside. If 'twas crowded with only her women folk in this wee room, what would it be like once the gate fell and the few who survived to defend Freyne joined them?

From behind her, Clare sighed as she woke. "How fare you this morn?" Elyssa asked. For yet another night, her cousin had sobbed in her sleep.

Clare drew a shaking breath as tears once again overtook her. "I never knew I could ache so," she said quietly. " 'Lyssa, in all my life, he is the only one I have wanted, and I cannot disregard my caring for him."

"But he takes Freyne down around our ears,"

Elyssa protested, rolling onto her stomach to see her
cousin. "You yourself say he comes for Simon."

Clare's face was ragged with grief. "I know that in
my head, but my heart is fixed and cannot be moved.
Knowing he loves me no more is more than I can
bear. I cannot understand it, I can only feel it."

Elyssa shook her head and lay her hands atop
Clare's. " 'Tis a strange and mysterious thing, love,
no?"

Clare tried to smile, then sat up. Their quiet conversation had set more women to stirring. Johanna
prayed the singsong words like a lullaby as she cradled
Simon in her arms. Elyssa's usually happy son had
fussed the night long. She didn't doubt he was affected
by the tension of the women around him.

There was no need to dress; all of them had slept
in their clothing. Elyssa now wore the same rough
homespun attire Freyne's maidservants owned. Her
finer things, gowns and furniture, were stored in a
shed along with her steadily diminishing hopes for
the future.

Wetting the hem of her overgown in their bucket,
she wiped away what grime she could, then straightened and plaited her hair into a single braid. There
was no wimple to cover her head. Propriety had long
since given way to need, and head coverings had become bandages for injured men. A rustling woke in
the keep's darkest corner, and Elyssa's heart broke
for her poppet.

Easing her way over women and behind Johanna,
she crouched beside Cecilia. The child clung tightly to
her plaything, her sad face pressed against the hard
stone walls. "Will my grandsire throw stones at us
today?" she asked in a tiny voice.

"Come, poppet," Elyssa said, bringing the child into

her arms. " 'Tisn't right that Gradinton should make you a pawn to his greed. Let him throw what stones he wants. I'll not give you to him."

"I want Papa," Cecilia cried softly, her tears warm as they soaked through Elyssa's gowns.

"So do I," she agreed wholeheartedly, even while she fought back her own certainty that Geoffrey knew nothing of their plight. "I must rise now, poppet. There's more work to be done, but I'll soon be returning to you."

Aye, 'twould be soon, indeed. Sir Gilbert said the gate would not withstand another day's punishment. When it gave way, they'd all be trapped into this chamber, waiting for a rescue that didn't seem to be coming. If they couldn't starve, not with all the food stored below them, Reginald would surely take down their door, or so she hoped. Such a death would be far swifter than one brought on by disease. With so many in such close quarters, illness was more than a possibility, and her infant son its surest victim.

Elyssa reached out to where her son's head curved beyond Johanna's arm to run a finger along the thickening thatch of Simon's bright hair. Only Cecilia would survive. But what sort of life might she own after watching yet another mother and brother die? Elyssa sighed, fearing only her mother's madness for Cecilia should the girl be witness to more violence.

Despair, born from days of falling stones, splintering wood, and injured men, washed over her. She pressed a kiss to Cecilia's head, then rose and picked her way over women to the doorway with Clare on her heels. When she drew open the door, they stood together at the floor's end, nothing but open air beyond their toes. The stairway was already gone. In its place hung a net of hemp, easy to climb and easily lifted up after their last retreat.

"Will you descend first, 'Lyssa?" her cousin asked, her voice yet hollow.

"Look at what he's done," Elyssa said in sorrow, overwhelmed by the enormity of it all.

Directly below them, bits of greased cloth clung to the motte's wooden palisade, shielding the men too injured to battle on in Freyne's behalf. The dead lay near the gate, stiff and still. 'Twas well over half their defenders who awaited eventual burial. Campfires dotted the hill's flattened top, men lying as close as they dared while rolled in blankets against the October's damp chill.

In the bailey, the hall was no more. Walls were bent at sharp angles over the raised, stone cellar, the roof in pieces on the torn floor. Near the gatehouse, only rubble adorned the top of their wall. The damage was so extensive none could walk safely upon its broad width. Their catapult was shattered, Gradinton's stone yet standing at its center.

Looking beyond the wall, Elyssa studied Gradinton's army. Nothing her men had thrown at them seemed to decrease their numbers. So many were their fires, the smoke hung like a cloud near the ditch. She could barely see the ram where it crouched on its bridge of felled trees.

'Twas a trick of the stone wall that let her hear the echoes of the besiegers when she couldn't hear those directly below her. In yon camp, soldiers coughed and cleared their throats as they rose. Spoons scraped at iron pots. Someone began to whistle. 'Twas a lilting tune, the high-pitched piping eerie against dawn's quiet.

Beyond Gradinton's lines, the village stirred warily,

yet unconvinced of the army's disinterest in them. Framed by a forest alive with autumn's color, thatched roofs gleamed brown over white walls. Plows had turned fallow fields until only dark, rich earth showed, apples lay in bright piles near presses, sheep and gray geese grazed on golden stubble.

"How can so beautiful a world contain such violence?" Elyssa murmured sadly as she watched doves rise from their cotes to circle in placid appreciation of a new day.

In her grief she turned her gaze on the remains of Freyne's garden. Gone were the peas and beans that had once garnered her scorn. Where the pear tree had stood, there was now only a tangled pile of branches. Tears filled her throat.

"I think me, this will be the day I must let both Cecilia and Simon go." She freed a harsh laugh. "Is this not an irony? My life's ending will be but a reflection of my worst years. Here, again, do I face a man who, by might alone, steals my happiness and my will from me."

"You are doing all you can," Clare said, trying comfort when she had none to give.

" 'Tis not enough," Elyssa said softly, then turned to climb down the ladder.

Her foot had barely settled into the netting when chaos erupted from across the wall. Men screamed commands. Shields rattled as soldiers ran. Ladders appeared from beneath cloths. The ram's chains shrieked in complaint.

Watchers on Freyne's walls shouted, begging for aid against attack. Elyssa fairly flew to earth as the motte's drawbridge thudded down against its stop. Their own soldiers sprinted into the bailey, grabbing up crossbows and long poles to dislodge ladders as they went.

Sir Gilbert was at their head, wearing only his gambeson and chausses.

The ram crashed against their gate, the sound echoing throughout the bailey. By the time she'd reached the motte's gateway, Gilbert had scaled the ladder that had taken the place of the gate's crumbling stairwell. Gradinton's slingers sent a volley winging over the ditch while Freyne's men ducked behind merlons or shields. Pebbles and stones hit the wall like a hailstorm, pinging where they struck metal.

Again, the ram groaned as it was drawn back from its brace. On Freyne's wall top, men fanned flames from the coals beneath the scattered cauldrons. Left to simmer last night, the oil and sand remained at a skin-searing temperature. Bags of quick lime were sent, hand to hand, to those places left without another defense. Elyssa hied herself to the wall's base.

"What goes forth?" she called frantically to Sir Gilbert.

As the ram again thundered against their door, he leaned over the edge of the wall, his thin face bright with a broad grin. "Gradinton thinks to scale the walls."

"And this makes you smile?" she cried.

"Nay," he whooped, then slid down the ladder to stand before her. "His men are crying that a force comes to relieve us, my lady. Do you not see?" he shouted. "He is trying to break in, thinking to protect himself from attack while he uses us as hostages."

Sir Gilbert grabbed her by the shoulders, his face suddenly intent. "We must throw everything we have at them, seeking to thwart them or, failing at that, to deplete our stores so there will be naught left for them to use against our saviors. Know that as we do this, we'll make ourselves defenseless. When 'tis gone, we can but retreat into the tower and hope. Here's the rub. Gradinton'll spread his men along our wall's base, more concerned in gaining a foothold atop the wall than how many he slaughters while he does so. I have too few to do what must be done. Will your women help us?"

"Aye," Elyssa answered without hesitation.

"Run, then. Have them take shields from the injured. His slingers and archers will not be idle."

As the ram again tapped on her gate none too gently, Elyssa turned and ran.

Elyssa freed a frightened breath, then glanced again into the distance. There was no sign of horsemen. She turned her attention back to the task at hand.

It had taken but a few moments to learn she must wait until men were on the ladder before she tilted it off the wall with her pole. If it was empty, the men only caught it and set it right once more. Once climbers were upon it, 'twas possible to cause them injury when she toppled it.

It took her but a few more moments to realize she would soon be exhausted. A strand of hair fell forward as she strained against the weight of three men now racing upward toward her. They shouted in dismay as the ladder shifted. Although the lower two leapt free, the third fell back into the dry moat where he lay still among the growing number of men that filled that ditch.

Good. She leapt from her stance to Clare's aid against two ladders. While Clare shoved at one, Elyssa tore open the stitching on the quick lime's bag. On the second ladder, the men neared the top. She leaned into the crenel and emptied the contents onto those below her. The caustic stuff took the first man's eyes as it ate his skin. As he fell, it left the others vulnerable. Screaming men dropped until the ladder was empty. Taking up her pole, she shoved viciously. The ladder tumbled into the ditch, broken beyond use.

The ram again struck the door, while the trebuchet groaned in warning of attack. "Down," Elyssa shouted in general warning.

She and Clare ducked behind a merlon. The boulder roared as it flew. With an echoing retort, it hit the wall top, then bounced down the outer wall.

Although one of Freyne's few screamed and another fell silently to his death, the stone crushed a ladder full of Gradinton's men as it dropped. A cry of triumph rose from Freyne's defenders, while their enemies moaned in protest against this turn. Again, the ram knocked.

Elyssa leapt up, her eyes again at the horizon. "Where are you?" she hissed to these rescuers who had yet to appear. Surely, it must have been hours since the assault began. Down the wall from her a man was reaching for the crest, four more hot on his heels.

" 'Ware!" she cried out to the two maids guarding that section. The women rolled a cauldron toward the rising man. As he lifted his head, they tipped their kettle. Boiling water poured over him and down to the climbers below. The first screamed in agony, others yelping as scalding liquid reached them.

Men fell. Balance lost, the ladder dropped. The two women rolled the empty iron pot toward another ladder and threw it at the climbing men. It took five with it.

Sir Gilbert stood farther down the wall from these maids. Dressed in his mail, his helmet was in place, his sword in hand. Its blade was rusty as he yet again separated a hand from its owner. "They call back the trebuchet!" he shouted in relief, then pointed to the crushed remains of the merlon. "Can you take their place, my lady?"

Ducking behind her shield as the slingers and archers fired, Elyssa ran from Clare toward the empty spot. Pain tore through her, so stunning she stumbled and fell behind the merlon. Her pole dropped unheeded from her fingers, and she grabbed her thigh. Where she was sure there was a bolt, there was nothing.

Her eyes watering against the pain, she drew up her skirts. So hard had the stone hit her, it left an indentation and broken skin. Blood trickled down her leg.

"They come!" Sir Gilbert roared in triumph.

Blood oozing between her fingers, Elyssa lifted herself to see. Even this small motion made her leg scream in agony. Horsemen broke from the woodlands. The gray day couldn't disguise the flashing silver of mailed men.

"Rid yourselves of what's left now," Freyne's castellan shouted, the message carried, voice to voice, from either side of him.

The ram struck their door one more time. There was a terrible splintering as the great bar broke. Hinges squealed in defeat. Gradinton's forces raised their voices in a ferocious battle cry as the ram swung again.

"To the keep!"

Gilbert's cry echoed in Elyssa'a brain. She tried to rise, but her leg refused to hold her. Tears filled her eyes. How was she to reach the keep and protect her babes? Catching back her despair, she started toward the inward ladder, trying to drag her leg behind her. Stars woke before her eyes. The door below moaned as it gave way.

" 'Lyssa!" Clare shrieked, racing across the wall to her.

"Down, Clare," she gasped. "I'll follow as best I can."

"You'll follow or I'll carry you," her cousin retorted. She started down the inner ladder, then held out her arms to brace Elyssa.

Biting her lip, she eased over the edge. When her feet met a rung, Clare fixed her hand into the back of her gown. Down they went, each step agony. And down was easier than up.

"Lean on me," her cousin commanded as Elyssa almost fell into her arms.

Behind them, the doors rumbled as the men outside them forced the thick panels apart. On one side what was left of the bar tilted, its end jamming into the ground like a stop. On the other, the thick wood tumbled from its bracket, hitting the earth with a deep, hollow thud. It rolled far enough aside to allow one man to slip between the panels. Another followed him and, together, they pushed at the broken bar. One arched, a bolt in his neck.

"Go, my lady," Sir Gilbert shouted as he and those few he yet commanded raced toward the invaders. "Have them close the gate after you."

Braced on Clare's shoulder, Elyssa hobbled as swiftly as she could toward the inner drawbridge, behind the flow of women seeking safety. 'Twas with a disbelieving breath that Elyssa crossed the final barrier between Gradinton and Reginald, and Cecilia and Simon, with her life yet in her hands. Once they were within the gateway, she cried to Clare, "Stop, we must bring up the bridge."

She and Clare turned. Near the door, three men surrounded Gilbert, who was all that remained of their defense. "Nay," she breathed, then determination firmed. "You take that rope, while I take this one." As Clare leapt to the opposite side of the bridge, two women returned to lend their aid.

The bridge raised, the machinery caught, but none of them knew how to lock the winch. Through the arrow loop in front of her, Elyssa could see the bailey. Gradinton's men swarmed near the gate, shouting as they tried to close what had just been pried open. A small group raced for the motte's gate, grappling hooks and a ladder in hand. 'Twas Reginald who led them.

"Knot them!" Panting against what her efforts cost her, Elyssa finished her task and grabbed for Clare's arm. "The keep. We haven't long, and I'll be slow to climb."

Before they'd reached the netting's end, they heard the first hook catch on the drawbridge's tongue. Women, dirty and bloodstained, called down for them to hurry. The ram creaked as it was drawn back once again.

"Go you first," Elyssa shoved one of the maids toward the ladder, "and hie you after," she told the other.

" 'Lyssa," Clare gasped.

"All of you together might be able to pull me up if I cannot climb," she insisted, shoving Clare toward the netting.

Clare did as she was told, then Elyssa set her foot to the hemp mesh. As the stuff sagged beneath her weight, her leg screamed in protest. She dragged herself up, her head swimming against the pain. The ram hit the door once more, and there was a terrible shriek as the hinges gave way.

"They're pulling down the inner gate," Clare cried,

her voice barely audible over the shouting men and dying door. Elyssa caught hold of the ladder sides. Rough hemp burned her palms as she hauled herself another step. Freyne's outer door thundered to the ground.

"Pull up the netting," Clare shouted.

Women heaved the stuff upward, dragging it into the keep. Elyssa's stomach lurched, then the netting swung, slamming her into the keep's side. Something struck her shoulder as it fell past her. Stars again popped into being before her eyes, and she wound her arms into the rope work, with only prayers to keep her from falling.

Just as she thought she'd lose consciousness, her body jolted as Clare and Johanna grabbed her, dragging her into the chamber. Another woman reeled the remainder of the ladder into the room. The door slammed. The darkness was instantaneous, sliced through by vague gray shadows from the arrow loops. Elyssa lay breathless on the floor, beyond movement.

"Bar the door," she gasped.

There was a rustling near the doorway that quickly became frantic. "My lady, the bar is gone," a woman shrieked in rising hysteria. Sobs broke out all around.

"Mary save us," Elyssa muttered, understanding what had hit her as she was being raised. "Are there any men in here?" she managed after a moment.

"Nay, my lady," Johanna answered, a quiver in her voice.

"Well then, did anyone think to bring a sword?" she asked, her voice harsh as deep worry filled her.

There was a moment's silence. Then, one of the older women freed a nervous titter, her voice echoing around the room. Another, this one but a girl, released a high-pitched giggle, but it sounded more like a sob than a laugh.

"I think not, 'Lyssa," Clare replied in despair.

" 'Tis quite a flock of ewes we are," she said bitterly, then rolled onto her back. She lifted her voice and called to the wooden ceiling above her. "Mother of God, we are trapped, defenseless, in the keep. 'Tis long past time you repaid my devotion with action. I mean it. If I die because you failed me, 'tis quite a discussion we shall have upon my arrival at your kingdom. Open the gates to our rescuers and spare these helpless children."

Chapter 25

Gilliam's black brute easily kept pace with Passavant, a steed lighter than he. Crosswell and Ashby's men followed Geoffrey and his younger brother, some mounted, some of them racing on foot toward Gradinton's camp. 'Twas Graistan and Meynell who brought up the rear. Cradled between one set of brothers and the next, rode Jocelyn and his chosen archers.

"They've cracked the gate," Gilliam bellowed, peering through the rain as they headed along the dry moat's edge for Gradinton's encampment.

Little could be seen of his brother, what with his chain-mail hood wrapped around chin and brow. The helmet with its protective nosepiece hid the remainder of his face. Gilliam shouldered his great kite-shaped shield and bared his sword as they passed the outer tents.

No less covered than his brother, Geoffrey drew his sword and lifted his own long shield onto his left arm. 'Twas good to have it, but it did little to protect his vulnerable right side. Ignoring this warning thought, he shouted back to Osbert, "We'll fight on through to the gate. Leave these men to Ashby."

Gradinton's men leapt at them from behind carts, tents, and barrels, seeking to drop as many riders as they could from their saddles. Thrusting out with his shield, Geoffrey knocked one man off his feet. Passavant screamed in rage, his massive hooves flying as he sought to vent his vicious nature.

"Drive them away from Crosswell," Gilliam commanded his own men, dropping back to aid them as they spread around Geoffrey's troop and attacked those trying to stop them. The foot soldiers raced to surround them. Swords clashed as the battle was joined.

His sword swinging, Geoffrey used knees and heels to urge his big gray onward when Passavant would have stayed and fought. Lifting himself, the massive horse brought all his weight crashing down on those in front of him. Men féll, and he trampled them before leaping beyond their broken bones.

"Shields!" Osbert shouted.

Geoffrey raised his left arm until he was hidden by it. A bolt clanked against the piece, its trajectory saying it came from Freyne's walls. Jos freed a piercing whistle twice the size of him, and the archers he'd picked closed around him and cut their way toward the dry moat's edge. By the time the next volley flew, more than a few men atop the wall cried out as Jocelyn's men sent them a deadly retort.

Gradinton was closing the doors on them. "To Crosswell!" Geoff roared, glancing left, then turning his head right to see. There was no one with him. Hinges popped as the doors moved. Iron shrieked, rising above the clash of swords and screams of men. Then one side caught.

Osbert joined him at the edge of the temporary bridge, made of logs roughly wedged together. Across from Geoff, Freyne's doorway was filled with men desperate for refuge, while those already within were trying to drive them back from the doors and into battle. A moan of defeat woke from the bridge top. Rather than fight, all but one leapt into the ditch. That panicked soul tried to run toward them. He slipped, then fell screaming to the moat's littered floor.

Quarrels hissed as bowstrings sang. Flames took light beneath the ram, fed by the oil Gradinton had spread. The fire did not take at first, struggling against the rain and sodden green wood.

Above Geoff, three archers clung to what remained of the gatehouse wall, their bows aimed at the ram, the tips of their quarrels aflame. Jos's troop sent two screaming off the uncertain stones, their bows tumbling with them. The last freed his shot, only to pay with his life.

Geoff threw himself from his saddle, picking his way as fast as he dared to the ram. Behind him, Passavant turned and began to charge any who came near him, not caring if they were friend or foe. Only after Geoff ducked beneath the peaked roof protecting the ram did he look to see who followed. 'Twas nigh on his whole troop.

"Do what you can to douse it," he commanded three of them. "The rest of you help me draw back the ram."

Gradinton had done his work too well; there was no way to prevent Geoffrey from using Baldwin's own machine against him. Those firing at them from atop Freyne's walls turned their bolts on Graistan and Meynell as they flowed over what remained of Gradinton's camp. When Jos's archers again made themselves felt, even these men retreated.

Geoffrey heaved along with the rest, then released the heavy pole. Iron rings grated on each other as it swung toward the already injured door. 'Twas a death blow.

Iron squealed as the great hinges gave. One door broke free and dropped. The ground shook as it struck, the logs beneath Geoff shifting. Two of Crosswell's men lost their footing on the rain and oil slick logs. Where one man caught the ram's brace to hold himself in place, the other slid over the edge and was gone.

The fallen door balanced upright for the briefest of moments, then listed. It crashed against the opposite side of the portal. Again, the logs shook, but held.

Geoff grimaced at the partially blocked entryway. If there was no way to keep anyone out now, Gradinton's men would be concealed at the opposite end. He waved Osbert and his men to the doorway, then turned to warn the others.

Gilliam and his men loped toward the gate, leaving the trebuchet toppled in their wake. Jos leapt up from his hiding place to follow his lord, his force at his heels. Only Graistan and Meynell, who yet chased down the last of those outside the walls, had not seen the smoldering entryway.

"To Coudray!" Geoffrey bellowed.

Atop his chestnut mount, Rannulf raised his sword in acknowledgment as Richard's brown gelding circled so his rider could see the brother who called. "The bridge is oiled and is afire," he shouted as smoke swirled around his feet, then followed Osbert into Freyne's doorway.

"With your shield and mine, we can make our own concealment and protection. The others can pass between us, one by one, each adding their shield to ours," he told the knight.

Osbert grinned. "A corridor of sorts."

"Aye, but I'd keep you to my right if you will." 'Twas a wry remark.

"My pleasure," the knight retorted.

Extending shields, they ducked beneath the door's confining overhang and worked their way through it. At the end, swords crashed against Geoff's metal panel, the impact nigh on knocking him to his knees. Keeping his shield tight against Osbert's despite the pounding, he waved another man forward. One after another added their shield to the new wall, until there were enough of them to explode into the bailey.

Men fell on them driving Crosswell's force into a tight circle. Geoffrey landed a blow against some knight's shield, then retreated behind his own for the man's answer. As he did so, he glanced toward the motte where Elyssa must surely be.

The upper chamber's door was shut tight, without ladder or stair leading to the door. Around the motte, the wooden palisade stood, whole and unblemished, its drawbridge under attack. 'Twas but a small group of men and one knight trying to bring it down. Triumph rose in Geoff; there'd be no hostages for Gradinton.

"Look how few they are!" Baldwin's call was a scornful bellow, his own sword working against one of Crosswell's commoners. The man fell beneath the nobleman's assault. "The bridge is afire, and they'll have no help from those they brought with them. Finish them, but for God's sake and mine do no damage to Coudray in the yellow!"

Geoffrey's heart clenched at this. If his brothers had not managed to cross the bridge, his few would most likely die trying to keep Gradinton from capturing him. This meant that Gradinton not only cheated him of one family and threatened another by foisting his

mad daughter onto him, he now sought to take his
honor as well. Geoffrey had a right to die in defense
of those he loved.

Rage so deep 'twas more ice than inferno that
roared through him. His need to destroy Baldwin grew
beyond all bounds. "I'm for Gradinton," he told Osbert in astonishing calm, "and only death will stop
me."

"I'm at your side," the knight assured him, even if
Geoffrey couldn't see him on his blind side.

Together, they forced their way through the surrounding men. Their shields became battering rams,
used to send men flying, the rain of their blows ferocious. Seeing the one they were ordered to preserve,
Gradinton's men reluctantly fell back and let Geoffrey pass.

"Hie you all, come swiftly!" Gilliam's deep voice
rang against the wall. "Set on them!"

Geoffrey breathed in relief. 'Twas now Crosswell
and Ashby against Gradinton. Those around him had
no choice but to turn and face the new men.

As quickly as the threat had come, 'twas gone.
Geoff wrenched his blade from the final man in front
of him and swung around, seeking Gradinton. Baldwin
and a group of twenty were backing toward the now-
lowered inner drawbridge, fighting off any who
followed.

"Gradinton, I come for you," Geoffrey roared,
starting forward. He forgot even Osbert in his need
to meet Baldwin, blade to blade.

"Keep him here, but don't hurt him." With a jerk
of his helmed head, Baldwin set half of those around
him on Geoffrey.

"Coward!" Geoffrey shouted, his rage growing.
Gradinton only hied himself toward the gateway that

led him to the motte and the hostages who would save him.

Forced to a standstill by those around him, Geoff lifted his shield. 'Twas meager protection against so many swords. As he drove his blade into one, from deep within him came the feeling that someone raced toward his right. He swung his head to the side, lifting his sword in defense as he did so.

" 'Tis Meynell and Graistan, Geoff," said Richard, calling back his brother's blow.

Never had his brother's voice been more welcome. "I'll have Gradinton," Geoffrey shouted to them as swords clashed in earnest.

"Take him," Rannulf commanded as he and Richard opened a corridor to the gate for him.

Geoffrey started for the inner drawbridge as Gradinton and his ten crossed it. There was now a ladder against the keep's side, the climber fastening it to the stair supports. If Baldwin raised that inner bridge, he'd buy himself time Geoff couldn't afford to lose.

"To Crosswell," he called out in new panic, loping after him.

Too late! The men were across, two reaching for the ropes. One stumbled back—bow shot. The other hauled on his rope, from inside the gate's protective walls. Another bolt flew to pierce the rope, pinning the twisted hemp to the gate's side.

As he reached the bridge's foot, Geoffrey turned to see who followed. The fire in the ditch had taken life. Stinking smoke poured through the broken doors to fill the bailey, cloaking groups of men in its sooty clouds. Only the steady clash of iron to iron and cries of the wounded spoke of the continuing battle.

Crosswell's men came, but they were yet a distance behind Geoffrey. There was no time to waste. Those at the other side threw themselves into the gate's opening to discourage Geoff from passing. Shoulder braced against his shield, he ducked behind it and ran toward them. He could only pray the others arrived swiftly enough to prevent his death.

Sword moving even as he burst through them, he felled one, then kicked him off his blade. Footsteps thundered over the bridge, following him, and his attack was quickly echoed by others. Ahead of him, Gradinton and his few protectors had set their backs to the ladder's foot. Their shields were down, their swords at the ready.

Satisfaction roared through Geoffrey. Baldwin would stand and fight, not beg for mercy. Aye, he'd fight as long as he believed he might yet pry Cecilia from her hidey-hole. If he yet dreamed of success, it must be Reginald on that ladder.

Geoff ran up out of the gateway and onto the motte's flattened top. Behind him, his men raised their voices in triumphant cry. They'd claimed the inner gateway as their own.

"Hold him," Baldwin shouted. "We've almost got her."

There wasn't a knight among the men that Gradinton set on him. "What sort of coward are you?" Geoffrey cried in outrage as he knocked the third man aside. "Meet me as you must!"

"What? And have you die on my blade?" Baldwin glanced upward, backing toward the keep. He sidled away from Geoffrey's first blow. "Nay, I'm not so great a fool as that. All I want is my granddaughter as custom dictates," he panted. "You've no right to keep my only heir from me."

"If I give her to you, you'll but make her as mad as you made her mother." Geoffrey swung wildly in his rage. Baldwin easily dodged the blow. "Take her from me, Baldwin. Kill me! Only in death will I give you my daughter."

Geoffrey reined in what boiled in him and dropped a blow onto Baldwin's shield. Filled with all the hate he carried for Maud's father, Geoff's blow drove Baldwin to one knee. Geoffrey rained blow after blow onto his raised shield.

"Rise," he shouted, "rise and meet me, you coward! You knew Maud was mad when you gave her to me! You foul son of a bitch, you knew! You used me."

At last the insults did what open attack could not; Baldwin roared to his feet, his sword swinging. "You blame *me*?" 'Twas an enraged bellow.

Their swords met, Geoffrey's shivering against the power of Baldwin's attack. He took the next two strikes on his shield. Their swords clashed once more, driving both apart.

From high above, women screamed. Baldwin glanced upward, then grinned. "And now that I have what I came for, I'll be going."

Geoffrey looked up. The keep door was open, and Reginald forced himself between women seeking to push him back. He caught one and sent her flying from the doorway. Her cry was abruptly silenced. She lay upon the motte's grassy surface, a broken tangle of skirts. Reginald disappeared into the chamber.

"Nay," Geoffrey breathed. Now Elyssa would die and Baldwin would take Cecilia.

"Damn you," he bellowed in agony far greater than his rage. Careless in triumph, Baldwin had dropped his shield a fraction. Geoffrey drove his sword into his former relative with all the power of what ached in him. The bloody blade cut through mail and gambeson to bury into the man's ribs. Bones cracked.

Baldwin choked in surprise and pain, then his eyes narrowed. "Kill the girl," he shouted upward, then slid down to sit. "Make yourself another heir," he gasped to Geoffrey. "You'll hold none of what was mine."

Geoffrey drew back his sword. It hissed through the air, then crashed through Gradinton's midsection, spilling entrails. "Damn you," he whispered again, then whirled, meaning to scale the ladder.

"Nay, Geoff." Gilliam grabbed him around the waist. There was no escaping his younger brother's powerful hold. "If you go, he'll but throw Cecilia from the room. Stay and we'll tease him down from there before he does any harm."

Johanna's shriek echoed against the thick clouds. "Nay, do not hurt my son," Elyssa begged. Geoffrey looked up in helplessness at the door as the sky cried for the babes.

"Come down, you," Gilliam bellowed, his voice carrying easily over the ever-decreasing sounds of fighting men. "The battle is done, and you've lost. Do them no harm, and you'll still hold your life."

Reginald lifted his sword's tip to place it against his sister-by-marriage's throat. "Grab for him again, I'll kill him for certain. You, as well."

Lady Freyne's face, already ashen, went whiter still. If she said nothing, her eyes continued to plead for her son. He glanced at the wee babe he cradled against his chest.

His new nephew wailed as the beringed, metal shirt Reginald wore tore through the lad's swaddling. He studied his tiny kin. Here was one child where Aymer had left no trace of his heritage, not in nose or mouth, especially not in his coppery hair.

Earlier, a poorly thrown and too quickly retrieved grappling hook had torn a great rent in his mail. A flap of metal fabric hung down from his breast, exposing a section of his padded gambeson. For no reason he could fathom, Reginald lifted the babe until the wee thing rested against that garment's softer, woolen surface.

"Reginald, what will you do?" 'Twas Clare who spoke, her voice soft and utterly without fear of him or his intentions.

Scorn woke in his heart. Did she yet believe she had some hold over him? Until this moment, he'd avoided looking at her. Now, his heart hard, he met her gaze.

The delicate lines of her face teased up the memory of his mouth against hers. If her touch had made such a heat in him, her love had turned heat into something far more pure. In her eyes lingered the same remembrances. Her mouth lifted as she acknowledged he yet held her heart. Scorn and anger died in the face of her enduring love. How could this be, when she knew what he'd done?

"There can be no gain in harming him now." Her voice was sweet.

Reginald stiffened, trying to convince himself what he saw was a lie. Aye, 'twas but a pretense, meant to tease him into freeing the babe.

He turned from her, scanning the room for the other child. "Stand aside," he told the women in the corner.

They parted, revealing Coudray's daughter. He let his sword clatter to the wooden floor. As long as he held this babe, no one here would do him harm. Reaching into the darkened corner, he caught the back of the lass's gown and drew her forth. She fought a little, but he gave her a swift shake and she hung, limp and placid from his grip. Turning, he went to stand in the keep's open door.

The battle was done. The quiet that had fallen over Freyne was punctuated only by the cries of the wounded. The ditch was full of oily smoke. It snaked through the broken gate, tendrils lifting over bodies and winding around fallen stones. His gaze flickered to the hall.

A terrible aching woke in his heart at the twisted remains of his home. 'Twas destroyed, and he'd done it. Of a sudden, the thought of living on past his home's demise was inconceivable. Yet to go into death without striking a blow against those who denied him what was rightfully his seemed equally as empty and pointless.

"I am Reginald of Freyne," he called down to the knights and soldiers gathering in the motte, then stepped even closer to the chamber's edge. The babe in his arms began to complain again as Reginald lowered the arm in which he cradled his nephew so that he might balance both lass and lad. He held Coudray's daughter out over the drop. "Look upon what I hold here."

"Drop my daughter and you die for certain," shouted Lord Coudray. "Spare her and you'll live."

"For what?" Reginald laughed bitterly. "Mine has been an empty life. I think me, 'tis better to go into death accompanied rather than to continue here on earth."

"Nay, Reginald, do not take them," Clare called to him.

"Uncle!"

The soprano call came from the palisade. Reginald scanned its length until he found the boy. Dressed in

a metal-studded leather hauberk with mail coif and
conical helm to protect his head, the lad had a loaded
crossbow in his arms.

"Do you remember me, Uncle?" Jocelyn reached
up and shucked both helm and coif, letting them fall
to the motte's floor. The lad's pale brown hair was cut
close to his skull. 'Twas the same boy he'd freed the
previous day. "I am Jocelyn of Freyne."

"You are Jocelyn?" Reginald called back, stunned.
Nay, this couldn't be the frail and whining lad of last
autumn. There was power and confidence in this
boy's voice.

"Indeed," his nephew retorted. "How disappointed
I was when it seemed you'd forgotten me. Just in case
your memory continues to fail you, best I remind you
'tis my brother you hold there. I'll not be letting you
do him any harm." Jocelyn of Freyne lifted his loaded
bow to his eye.

Reginald freed a scornful laugh. "What an arrogant
brat you've become, worse even than Theobald was.
You delude yourself if you think you can reach me
from there." Even if there was a possibility Jocelyn
could hit him, the children he held were both targets
and shields.

"My limit is two hundred yards," the boy called, his
eye sited and the sound of steel in his voice. "I guess
you at one seventy-five."

"Coudray!" Geoffrey shouted in protest.

Elyssa watched, beyond hope or prayer, when suddenly Reginald jerked, then stumbled backward with
the bolt's impact. Cecilia fell from his grip, hands and
feet landing solidly on the floor. "Come, poppet," she
cried, her voice hoarse with tears. When the lass flew
into her arms, Elyssa clutched her close. In her heart,
she knew Simon was dead.

Reginald turned, her son yet cradled in his arm. Elyssa gasped. The bolt had pierced only him, missing Simon. Her brother by marriage wore an expression of complete surprise, as if he did not realize 'twas his life's blood now pumping from him. It stained Simon's swaddling, and her son wailed in complaint.

Clare rose and went to Reginald. Her cousin took the man she loved by the arm. "Reginald," Clare said gently, "give me Simon."

He released the babe without protest. Clare cradled the lad close, pressing a kiss upon his forehead, her face bright with love. "Grow you well, my little love. Thrive and prosper."

Elyssa caught her breath against what sounded like words of farewell. "Clare?"

As her cousin came to crouch before her, Cecilia freed a terrified sob. "Papa," she managed in a wispy voice.

"We have heard him, no?" Clare said. "Your papa is coming soon. Now put out your arms for Simon. You are so very good at holding him, and our Simon will need you more than ever now."

"Clare," Elyssa said, the fear in her growing at her dearest friend's strange manner.

"Nay, 'Lyssa," Cecilia assured her, her face alight with pride. " 'Tis mine to do." She settled onto the floor, her arms extended. "Now Tante Clare."

Clare set the crying child into the lass's arms, then touched her lips to Cecilia's crown. "See that she is not injured by what I do, 'Lyssa. See that they both remember me."

Elyssa grabbed for her cousin's arms. "Clare, what is it you plan," she asked, knowing exactly what it was her cousin meant to do.

Her cousin broke free of her grasp, then stood and

backed out of reach. "You have given me much, making me special where others saw only a useless mouth to feed. May you find the happiness you deserve in your Geoffrey's arms." Clare turned to the man she loved.

Reginald now leaned against the door's frame. Elyssa watched as Reginald lifted his hand to trace the delicate rise of Clare's cheekbone, then the fine hollow beneath it. He instilled great love in that simple touch.

Elyssa's eyes filled. He would seduce Clare into going with him. She couldn't allow that. "Clare," she cried out, "he has ruined Freyne and tried to kill Simon."

"So I have," Reginald agreed, his voice harsh with pain. "Clare, I know you cannot now credit me, but I love you still. Why couldn't I have been content with stewardship and you?" His sigh was ragged with what he'd cost himself.

Clare lay her hand against his wound as if her touch would keep life from leaving him. "Would that I knew the answer, my love."

"My love? Despite what I have done?" He begged her to say 'twas true.

"What goes forward up there?" 'Twas Geoffrey's worried shout.

"All is well, my lord. Give us another moment," Clare called back, then touched her lips to Reginald's jaw. "I have told you before, my heart is given and there it stays. You were a good man before ambition came to eat at you."

Reginald drew Clare close. "I fear my afterlife will be but an eternity of missing you."

"As might my life here be, without you," Clare said. "Thus do I think I shall come with you."

"I would like that," he breathed.

"Nay," Elyssa sobbed. She struggled to rise, but her damaged leg would not support her. With a cry, she fell back to the floor. "Clare, do not leave me. Not for him. He's naught but tried to kill us," she pleaded, the pain in her heart so great her words could barely escape around it.

As Reginald put his arm around Clare's waist, Clare turned to face her. " 'Lyssa, you have your love. Do not be selfish and deny me mine." Her cousin wound her arms around his neck.

When Reginald kissed her, their mouths met only briefly. "Think again. We may see each other no more as I am hell-bound for what I've done," he told her.

"As will I be by choosing to take my own life," she replied calmly. "Set your dagger between us and hold me close so we fall as one."

He drew the blade and held it between them. Clare leaned her forehead against his cheek, and drew a final breath. With Clare in his arms, Reginald stepped from the floor into empty air.

"Clare, nay," Elyssa whispered, Cecilia's head caught against her breast to prevent the lass from seeing Clare's demise. 'Twas too much to bear. In her grief, the blackness crept up on her once more. She fought it, but exhaustion of both body and soul left her helpless against its oncome. In its grip she was reminded that Simon was safe, Cecilia was safe, as was Jocelyn and Geoffrey, whose voices she'd heard. Nor had she any right to deny Clare her heart's desire. Now, sensing peace waiting for her in its velvet depths, Elyssa sighed and sank into the quiet.

Chapter 26

There was a gentle touch against her face. Elyssa sighed, coming slowly from her unnatural sleep. With alertness came pain's return. The bruise on her shoulder throbbed, but her leg ached with a vengeance.

How could a single pebble have made her leg so incredibly sore? Then, again, over the past week she'd seen men with broken bones, even death, wreaked by the slingers' stones. 'Twas fortunate she was only bruised.

Aye, but it hurt so. 'Twasn't fair that healing should hurt worse than the taking of injury. Amusement rose in her at so petulant a thought. Did she not live still? As her smile grew, she offered the Virgin both thanks and an apology for being so demanding a servant.

"What makes you smile?" As always Geoffrey's voice was like music. He drew a finger down the curve of her cheek.

"Pain," she said, her smile dying as she opened her eyes. The ceiling above her was tent silk. Gradinton's. She'd never forget this shade of red, not for her life's time. 'Twas no doubt Gradinton's cot on which she lay. Thick with furs and linens, the mattress was soft. He'd spared himself no comfort.

Her gaze moved to Geoffrey, who sat on a stool beside the cot's edge. He yet wore his mail, but had freed his head of helm and coif. Love washed over her. Even stained with the gore of battle, he retained his beauty.

She let her gaze flow from his wide brow to his high cheekbones and strong jaw. Then, she lifted her hand to trace the line of his longest scar until it disappeared beneath his eye's shield. He turned his head and pressed a kiss into the cup of her palm.

"And, why should pain make you smile?" he murmured against her wrist as he touched his lips there.

A shiver wracked her at this caress. Oh, but lust was a lovely thing to know for him. "In feeling pain, I know I live still, when dawn saw me thinking I would not. You came." This last, 'twas nearly a sob.

He drew back to look at her, a slight frown on his brow. "Did you think I would not?"

"Nay," she replied in quiet confidence. "I only feared you did not know to do so."

The corner of his mouth lifted in a gesture that was now achingly familiar and wondrously precious. "'Twas your message to Ashby that reached me. And for that will I ever thank you. Only with my brothers' aid could I have freed you, my love."

"I am no less thankful," she replied, then sadness washed over her. "What of Sir Gilbert? I saw him fall."

Geoffrey's smile grew. "He lives still, his injuries dear but survivable. He looks forward to returning to Coudray for his recovery."

Elyssa sighed in relief. "Praise God, I am grateful. He worked so hard to save us." Her next question trembled a long moment on her tongue before she dared release it. "What of Clare?"

Geoffrey only shook his head, then his brow creased

in confusion. "Why did she go with him? The maidservants all say 'twas by her own choice."

"For love's sake," Elyssa breathed, yet working to understand. Then again, even to imagine Geoffrey's passing left in her a terrible emptiness. 'Twould be difficult to continue in life with such a burden on her heart.

Geoffrey enfolded her hand with his. "Think not of that, love, but of our many triumphs. Our children are alive and whole, as are we."

"Is the threat to Cecilia done or will he be back again?" 'Twas a hopeful question.

"She is ours now, and Gradinton is dead." His smile transformed his face. The dip in his cheek appeared, then the creases that marked his lean cheeks. 'Twas a victorious grin, this one.

"Thank God," Elyssa said, then sent additional thanks wending their way to God's Mother, who had this once made her Husband and Son listen.

Geoffrey's smile dimmed and he leaned down, catching her mouth with his. There was much of love in his kiss. She gloried in his caring for her, then returned his heart's affection with her own. After a moment, love was not enough. As if he, too, felt the lack, his kiss deepened, speaking of the fire she woke in him.

Elyssa gasped as her own passionate nature came to brilliant life. Her wanting for him made her forget pain. She raised her arms, catching him around the neck. With her fingers locked at his nape, she trapped his mouth against hers and told him of her need.

He groaned, the sound deep and low. Her pulse leapt to the tune of it, naught but a goad to her own desire. He'd tell her nay no longer; she'd have him, will he, nill he.

His hands came to cup her breasts, then his thumbs brushed against their sensitive peaks. 'Twas her turn to cry out, the sound broken by a gasp. Geoffrey shuddered at her reaction, then eased away from her. She caught his hands in her, not willing to be free of his touch.

"*Jesu*, 'Lyssa, but I want you. 'Tis time to keep that vow you made. Cecilia is ours, wed with me."

Elyssa feigned a disgusted look. "More fool I, for vowing it to you. Now you've left me no choice."

"None whatsoever," he said, turning his hands in her grip until he could twine their fingers. "As the victor, 'tis my perogative to name the date."

She lifted her brows. "Aye, and when will that be?"

"In two weeks. 'Twill give time to make some sort of ceremony and call the banns."

Disappointment washed through her. In two weeks her woman's flow would be here. "Nay, I'll not wait so long."

"What choice have you?" he asked with a quirk of his brows. "I've won the right to set the date."

"I'd wed with you now," she insisted.

"Would that we could do so," he said with a negative shake of his head, "but folk will think something amiss if we join in so hasty a manner."

"What care I for other folks' thoughts?" She tugged on his hands, pulling him from his stool, until he knelt beside the cot. Drawing one of his hands to her breast, she again caught her arms around his neck. She could play the game of siege as well as he.

"If they question, let them count the months. Two weeks is too long," she murmured, pressing a kiss at either corner of his mouth. As she took his mouth with hers, she arched beneath his touch on her breast in a fair approximation of how she could move be-

neath him in love play. Her fingers danced lightly
across his sensitive nape.

Growling softly against her maddening tricks, his
hand slid down past her waist to her hip. The force
of his need for her made him set the heel of his hand
against what now cried out for his touch. She moaned
and lifted her hips into his caress as she suckled at his
neck. When she nuzzled his ear, 'twas to murmur,
" 'Tis too long, Geoff. I would have you abed with
me, touching me. Loving me."

He drew a shaking breath at her words. "I yield,"
he said with a short laugh. When he straightened, his
face flushed with the same heat she knew. "On the
morrow, then."

"Wise decision," she murmured.

"You do not mind a simple, private ceremony?" he
asked, restoring the stool to its upright position and
receding from her bedside.

"Mind?" She freed a scornful breath. "Hardly. In
my past marriages, I met the man only just before our
grand and glorious ceremonies, and the marriages
went on to be disasters. You and I have done it backward, coming to know each other before wedding and
bedding. A private ceremony but means we'll begin
our life together carrying none of my past into our
future."

Again, his wondrous smile awoke, his eye color
darkening to nigh on violet with his pleasure. "Now
that Cecilia's borders abut his, I suspect Lavendon
might see fit to let us use his chapel, serve us a decent
meal, then borrow a chamber."

"Perfect," Elyssa said, lifting her hand to trace the
outline of his smile.

Chapter 27

The noise in Lavendon's hall was deafening, what with so many men all seeking to outshout each other. From her place at the high table's center, as befitted a bride, Elyssa smiled as she watched Geoffrey. He'd gone to join his brothers and Lord Lavendon at the hall's corner, supposedly to share some private conversation. Instead, they were toasting each other, celebrating both wedding and victory.

Geoffrey wore his court attire, which had come with him in his saddlepacks: a fine yellow gown trimmed with cloth of gold, a brown mantle lined with mink and held in place by a massive gold chain. 'Twas quite a pair they made, for she matched him well, her own clothing having been rescued from that undamaged shed. Atop her gold colored gown she wore her best overgown, a tawny thing with trailing sleeves. The fabric was only wool, but she'd embroidered it from neckline to hem with an intricate pattern wrought in shimmering threads. Over her hair she wore her finest wimple, a headcovering so sheer 'twas hardly visible, held in place by a single hair comb at her crown. The wimple was caught around her neck with the necklet Geoffrey had given her as a bride gift.

When Geoff raised his gaze, 'twas to seek her out. Elyssa's only reaction was to lift her brows, letting their movement tell him how lonely she was for him. He smiled and bid the others adieu. As he started toward her, happiness glowed in Elyssa. Geoffrey put her first, even above his own kin. 'Twas but a reminder of how rare this man was.

"My husband returns," Elyssa told Lady Lavendon, who'd come to bear her company in Geoffrey's absence.

Henry of Lavendon's wife was as plain as he, but despite her mousy manner, Lady Adelicia was friendly and a veritable miracle worker. In one day's time Adelicia had turned what could have been a barren day into a joyous celebration.

Sprays of autumn blossoms and foliage were pinned to the tablecloths. Their recently finished meal had included four fine dishes in each of the three courses. Even cold, the rich smell of cloves still rose from the fowl on the platter before Elyssa. There were musicians, or so they called themselves; they poured more heart than talent into their tunes. Lady Adelicia had even cleared her own bedchamber, setting Elyssa's undamaged bed into that room in order to honor the new couple.

Now, Lady Lavendon shot Elyssa a wry look. "So would my husband come running to me, tongue lolling like one of his dogs, were I to look at him the way you look at yours. Before I leave you to him, tell me what think you of our lass and your lad?"

Elyssa's gaze slipped to the great ring of folk circling the hearthstone. At that moment, the musicians increased their tempo as the tune required, demanding even swifter steps from the dancers. Jocelyn nearly stumbled into the petite girl next to him.

Although Avice of Lavendon was sweet-faced at eight, there was no hope of her ever owning much in the way of beauty. Her hair was a nondescript brown, her eyes that same gentle shade. Nonetheless, the child owned a gay smile and a charming laugh. On her part, Avice was much taken with Jocelyn; her eyes came to life each time she looked on the one who would someday be her husband. And, each time she looked, Jocelyn blushed a deep red, just as he was doing this very moment.

Elyssa laughed. "I think they are well suited, or will be once Jocelyn outgrows a boy's disdain for lasses." Her happiness grew until 'twas like a great bubble within her. Aye, she was content with all the world just now.

"Well then, I shall leave you to your man. Let me know when you are ready to retire," Adelicia said, as a silvery giggle escaped her. She turned to join the dancers.

Geoffrey came to stand behind her. "What was that about?" he asked as he sat beside his new wife on the bench they had shared during the meal. He put his arm around her back and drew her close against him.

"Naught," Elyssa replied, trying not to smile. Leaning her head against her husband's shoulder, she lay her arm around his waist. The fine fabric of his yellow gown was soft against her hand.

It took only this mere touch to make Elyssa's contentment explode into longing, fed by Lady Adelicia's offer of the bedchamber. Her pulse leapt at the thought of shutting their bedcurtains on the world. Turning slightly in his embrace, she pressed her breast against Geoffrey's chest, then touched her lips to his throat.

His arm tightened around her, but it had too much of a fond embrace in it and not enough of a lover's clutch. She lifted her mouth to his ear, nuzzling. "Geoffrey, I would retire now," she breathed.

He laughed quietly. "So would I, but we must not insult our host." Still, her request teased his hand into sliding from her waist to her hip. Heat washed over her, promising much pleasure. To even contemplate waiting the usual hours before bedding was sheer torture.

"I'm told the chamber's ready now," she murmured against his jaw.

" 'Twouldn't be right. We should at least pretend we have some awareness of custom, love."

Elyssa frowned. Did he think to set convention against her, when there was naught in their relationship that was conventional? Then, the corners of her mouth lifted. Did he think he could resist her will?

Inspired by her need for him, Elyssa recalled that day a month past, when Geoffrey's shirt had clung to his wet torso. Her free hand rose, gliding up the soft surface of his gown to trace the hard contour of his chest. Beneath her palm, she felt his heart's beat quicken. Her hand slipped downward.

His gaze met hers, at first startled, then his eye color deepened as he understood she meant to toy with him. He tugged his mantle around him to hide her play from any onlookers. When her hand rested against his shaft, a slight, dusky color stained his yet-sundarkened skin, creeping along his fine cheekbones. His lips parted slightly as, with the tips of her fingers, she explored what could not be hers soon enough.

Leaning down to press his mouth to her ear, he breathed, "Dear God in heaven, I have given ownership of my body to a terrible tease."

She turned her face to brush his mouth with hers. He tasted of the fine wine they'd shared. His skin was smooth, newly shaved, and smelled clean. "So you have," she agreed, dropping her words softly against his lips. " 'Til death us depart, Geoffrey. Can you bear it?"

Her palm replaced her fingertips, stroking gently. The strength of what lay beneath her hand made her gasp and her womb to melt. His lips closed over hers, his kiss burning. Every inch of her came to roaring life and she trembled against his need.

She let him take her mouth just as he would soon take her body, then gave him as good as he offered her, her fingers still teasing him. He eased one hand beneath her loose wimple to bury his fingers into her hair. His kiss deepened until it was nigh on bruising in its intensity.

Their bench grated against the wooden flooring as he moved it back from the table. His arm across her back tightened, until he lifted her. With a sharp cry of surprise, Elyssa laced her hands behind his neck against her fear of falling.

Geoffrey sat her across his lap. "Cease, 'tis all of that I can stand," he laughed.

His aching need now rested against her hip. Elyssa made a tiny, feral sound; so near, yet so unattainable. Desire raged beyond any caring for propriety. She moved against him, her mouth finding his, her kiss begging him to touch her, to take her.

With a deep gasp, he tore free, then leaned his brow on hers. "Cease," he pleaded softly, his word breaking as she moved again. His arms encircled her, forcing her to remain still. Elyssa plagued him with tiny, tormenting kisses.

His breath shivered from him. "Jesu, stop, 'Lyssa, else I vow I'll embarrass us both before all these witnesses."

"Is that a promise?" she breathed against his lips.

"What has happened to the prim and proper woman I wed?" he managed, as she kissed her way along his cheek to his ear. "Are you not the same Elyssa who raged when I looked upon your unbound hair?"

"Ah, but that was then. Now, I am your wife. There is no shame in showing my husband all the passion and love I bear in my heart for him." Her words fell softly into the cup of his ear, making them more caress than statement. Beneath her hip she felt his shaft strain.

Elyssa straightened, her fingers combing through the soft fair hair that lay against his nape. "Come now, you gave me ownership of your body, Geoffrey. I am but claiming what is mine. Take me to bed," she commanded him.

"We must wait," he said.

"Take me to bed, Geoff." She touched her lips to his throat, just beneath his jaw.

"We shouldn't," he murmured against her caress.

Her fingers moved on his nape, making him shudder, as she nipped at his lower lip. "Take me to bed, Geoff. My need to touch you is terrible, indeed."

He released her to catch her face between his hands. His eye was bright with wanting. "Where?" he asked. "Where will you touch me?"

Elyssa's smile was slow as she recognized his resistance to her need was crumbling. She slid her hands forward until they rested against his shoulders. "From here," she flattened her palms and drew her hands downward until they'd move no farther, "to your hips. But not your shaft."

His brows raised and the corner of his mouth lifted. "No?" 'Twas an aching plea that she shouldn't deny him such a caress.

Her smile grew. "No, that I will save for later, when I touch you again with my mouth."

"Oh, my God," he breathed and his brow furrowed. His walls fell beneath her assault. She need only claim what she'd come to fetch. Catching one of his hands in hers, she drew his palm to her mouth. With her gaze yet fastened on his face, she kissed each of his fingertips, then rested her lips against the sensitive skin at the cup of his palm. Using her tongue's tip, she drew draw a circle there. He shuddered. She kissed his inner wrist, then, again, tasted his skin.

When she was done, she lay his hand against her breast and once more laced her fingers behind his nape. His hand fitted itself around the roundness of her breast and he did not resist as the pressure of her hands on his nape drew his face toward hers.

She spoke between small kisses. "Come now, let me show you what I know of making pleasure in a bed. I vow I'll leave you screaming, even before you spill your seed."

Geoffrey groaned and snatched her close. Cradling her in his arms, he rose so quickly the bench crashed against the floor. Elyssa laughed softly and buried her face against his neck.

"Quiet!" he bellowed at the musicians. "Quiet!"

The hall fell still, every eye was fastened on them. Adelicia called her maids and moved toward the bridal couple, already knowing what would be said.

"I beg your pardon, Henry, but 'tis time for the bedding," Geoffrey called to his host, "and, if any damn one of you complains, I'll slay you right now." The room exploded into laughter.

"Put me down, Geoffrey," Elyssa said. "I must go upstairs first."

"Not if my life depended on it," Geoffrey returned.

"Should my brothers get hold of me, they'll keep me from you for hours. They are ruthless men." He looked down at Lady Lavendon. "We will disrobe together, my lady."

"If you say so, my lord," she replied, her face alive with amusement. "Come you upstairs."

The commoners hooted and howled. The drummer pounded on his drum. Shields were brought forth from hiding and fists banged against them, properly heralding the bridal couple toward the stairs. The pipers followed them up, making no attempt to even find a tune. In this instance, 'twas sheer volume that counted, the purpose being to distract the newlyweds until they couldn't complete their first joining.

Lavendon's chaplain led the way up the stairs and into the bedchamber. 'Twas a heartless and windowless room with but a single linen panel on its wooden walls, but, here, too, Lady Adelicia had been busy. Sprays of foliage and blooms hung on each corner of the bed, while a ewer of watered wine and two cups sat on a small table near the bed. The floor had been strewn with fresh rushes mingled with mint, leaving the air spicy. Beeswax candles stood in sconces around the room, bringing a gleaming, sparkling life to an otherwise dim atmosphere.

The priest went to bless the bed as Geoffrey set Elyssa's feet on the floor. With a final, brief kiss, they separated, going to opposite sides of the chamber. Adelicia, her maids, and even little Avice followed Elyssa, while Geoffrey's brothers, Jocelyn, and Lord Lavendon closed around him. Elyssa peered over heads to watch her beloved.

Lord Ashby was tearing at his belt. "Have you a care with my gown, Gilliam," Geoffrey warned. "If you ruin it, I'll make you buy me a new one."

"I am only trying to aid you, Geoff," the big man retorted, throwing the belt aside as the others behind him removed Geoff's thick chain and mantle. "Was I wrong in thinking you couldn't wait to be free of these garments?"

Elyssa laughed as her own, far gentler attendants stripped away her wimple and mantle, then set to loosening her belt and laces. She pulled her plaits over her shoulders and freed them as her witnesses worked. All the while, Elyssa watched her husband.

He lost his gown, then his shirt, leaving him dressed only in his chausses. By the time she was in her undergown, Lords Meynell and Lavendon were unwinding Geoffrey's crossgarters. Heat washed over Elyssa as she watched Graistan's lord help him step from his chausses. The men moved back and her husband stood before her, unclothed.

Elyssa sighed. Her imagination hadn't done him justice. Candlelight glowed against Geoffrey's skin, gleaming against his broad shoulders and tracing the masculine swell and fall of his chest. Shadows outlined the muscular curves of his arms. He stepped forward, his legs long, his thighs powerful. Elyssa let her gaze follow the flat stretch of his belly to his narrow hips. His shaft's earlier reaction to her had died. Then, the women were pulling off her undergown.

As Avice freed her of the last stocking and shoe, handing the items to her mother as she backed away, Elyssa shrugged off her sleeveless chemise. Having once been as thin as Jocelyn, each successive babe had added to her bulk until she finally claimed a woman's natural roundness. Unclothed, she tossed her hair back behind her shoulders, then stepped forward, awaiting Geoffrey's inspection.

Her husband's gaze flowed over her, from the gentle

curve of her breasts to her waist, past the flare of her hips. "You are perfect," he murmured, his shaft taking notice of the ruddy curls covering her woman's flesh.

Lord Gilliam roared in appreciation of his brother's masculine reaction to his wife. "And we thought you dead, Geoff!"

Rannulf of Graistan cuffed his youngest brother. "He wasn't dead, only sleeping. Look on in jealousy at how she's awakened him." Then, Graistan's lord looked at her, a teasing expression in his gray eyes. "Come now, Lady Coudray, let us hear your judgment. Does our brother pass as unblemished save for what lays upon his face?" 'Twas less a warning over speaking of Geoffrey's scars than a goad to see if she'd rise to his bait.

Elyssa's mouth curved. "My eyesight fails me at this distance," she replied. "I think I must come closer."

The movement of her hips was sultry as she strolled toward Geoffrey. With each step, proof of his need for her grew. Even the chaplain laughed at Geoffrey's bold display.

"Aye," Lady Lavendon called after Elyssa, supporting the wife in her torture of her husband, "the light in here is dim, indeed. She is wise to make certain there's naught hidden. Who's to know if that upthrust of flesh is truly what it portends to be." She once again added her silvery giggle.

"Turn about is fair play," Lord Meynell retorted in defense of his brother. "Geoffrey, take you a closer look, as well." Geoffrey's eldest brother shoved him toward his bride until they were less than arm's length apart.

"One thing's for certain, he sleeps no longer, at least not this night," Lord Ashby called.

"You are a terrible tease," Geoffrey whispered as

Elyssa set her fingertip to the dull white shape of an old scar on his chest.

"Oh look, he's marked here," Elyssa called to the men behind him, fighting with her smile. Her fingertip flowed down his chest to the next scar. Geoffrey drew a deep breath, his reaction to her growing even stronger.

"Best you check that thing there between his legs, my lady," a maid called. "It has the look of an infection, all swollen and angry."

"Geoff," Lord Rannulf called, "it seems to me she's doing all the looking. What sort of inspection is this? Come now, have you no defense against her?"

Elyssa put her hands on her husband's shoulders, then raised herself on her toes to look behind him at his brothers. Her breasts brushed his chest. "I've found me another scar," she complained. "I fear I cannot accept him. Damaged goods, you know."

Much to the amusement of the women behind her, Geoffrey caught her by the buttocks and lifted her until her woman's curls touched his shaft. "Are you certain, 'Lyssa?" he breathed into her ear.

Elyssa sighed and caught her arms around his neck. Dear God, but his skin felt good against hers. "I have changed my mind," she managed in a husky voice. "There is no defect." With that, she took his mouth with hers, sliding upward on his body to make accessible the entry he craved.

"Jesu Christus," Lord Gilliam shouted in a truly awestruck voice, "she'll have her way with him in front of us. Best we leave them be. Geoff, I shall return in an hour to see if you yet live."

Geoffrey laughed against Elyssa's mouth, then straightened to look over his shoulder at his younger brother. "Do it and you'll not live to see the morrow's dawn." To the women, he said, "Have pity on us and drive them from the room, else they'll stay, wishing to witness all of it."

If the men shouted and cried out in protest, the women were the victors in the brief battle. A moment later the door closed. As soon as the nobles were gone, the commoners took up their posts. The drum's tenor beat threaded into the deeper rumbling of fist beating on shields. Elyssa did not move nor did Geoff release her. To do so would destroy the incredible sensations flowing between them.

"One of us must bar the door, else they'll be back," he murmured, his mouth brushing her cheek, then her ear.

"In a moment," Elyssa said with a sigh. Every inch of her was alive with him. She felt his heart beating against hers and her breasts flattened so nicely against his chest. And, Mary save her, his shaft was hot against her belly.

That was not where she wanted it. Elyssa stretched, rising to her tallest. Her whole body shuddered as the head of his shaft slid between her thighs to tease her woman's flesh.

To feel what she desired so near to where she needed it sent waves of wanting through her. Desperate to hold him within her, Elyssa struggled to make herself just a little taller. Geoffrey drew a shaking breath, understanding what she wanted. His fingers dug into the soft flesh of her buttocks, lifting her higher still. The tip of his shaft found the entrance to her womb.

Elyssa caught his mouth with hers and ever so slowly eased herself down upon him. Her legs came to rest around his hips as he held her aloft. When he filled her, she gasped in surprise at the power of the pleasure washing over her. She let her love for him feed her enjoyment, making the sensation sweet and wicked at the same time. The next wave came, making her shudder. Oh, already 'twas better than anything she'd ever known. The thought of how wondrous the coming hours, months, years would be brought yet another wave.

As she moved against him, his heat grew to sear her. Then, he was gasping against her mouth. " 'Lyssa," he groaned softly, "Cease, else I will disappoint you."

She leaned back in his embrace. His gaze was soft with desire, his face ruddy with need. "That is not possible," she whispered, teasing him as she moved in tiny, subtle motions.

His eyes widened and he forced her down upon him. "My God," he said, his voice ragged. "Stop, or I will spill my seed this moment."

"I cannot wait," Elyssa pleaded, kissing his jaw. "Lay me down, Geoffrey. I would have you atop me." She caught his mouth with hers, sucking and nibbling at his lips.

'Twas no less than two steps to the bed, but Elyssa did not feel him move. She gasped as they dropped, still connected, onto the mattress. He held himself above her for a moment, then tried to ease from her.

Arching beneath him, Elyssa gripped him tightly with her legs, her arms coming around him to clasp him to her. "Do not leave me," she murmured.

Geoffrey's face was taut as he fought to control what raged in him. After a long, tense moment, he sighed, then settled atop her. Bracing himself on an elbow, he combed his fingers through her hair. When he touched his mouth to hers, his kiss was gentle. " 'Lyssa, I'll not use you to pleasure only myself. I would take time to make you feel the passion you raise in me."

His words shattered her, setting a wave of joy just outside her reach. "My God, Geoffrey, you have," she panted. "Can you not feel I am on fire for you? Love me, Geoff," she pleaded. "Let me love you, making all of you, mine own."

Her words destroyed his hard-won control and he thrust into her. "Oh, my God," he whispered as he moved.

Elyssa lifted her hips to meet him with her own desire. When he thrust again, she cried out as mere joy exploded into something even better. Her fingers dug into his back and she arched, goading him on in his efforts. Heat devoured her, her heart sang. She cried out as his need for her pushed her into a sensation so deep she thought it would devour her. When he filled her with his passion, what grew in her burst, flooding them both with her joy.

Panting, he caught her in his arms and rolled to the side, his mouth claiming hers. His kiss was but a reflection of his physical love for her. When she pulled away from him, she was still gasping at the power of his caring.

The candles' light spilled into the bed's enclosure to lay gentle shadows on Geoffrey's face. 'Twas a tangle of passion and love that set Elyssa's finger to tracing the fine line of her husband's brow and nose, the lift of his cheek, then the outline of his lips. To own such a man was beyond belief.

He smiled against her touch, his eye color impossibly blue. "You are beyond marvelous," he whispered, then kissed her fingertip.

"Nay, 'tis you who is marvelous," she replied in a

soft breath, yet stunned by their loving. "Never have I felt so. 'Tis all you, Geoffrey."

She let her finger follow the scar at his mouth's corner upward to where it disappeared beneath his damaged eye's shield. The patch was damp with his exertion. She caught her finger in its thong, meaning to remove it.

Geoffrey stiffened and caught her hand. "Nay."

"Why not?" she asked, startled by his reaction, until she realized he feared her reaction to his disfigurement. "You are my husband, the man I love. Nothing can change that."

"I would not ..." his words died and his hand dropped from her wrist.

Elyssa removed his patch, tossing it aside, then touched her lips to the lid of his damaged eye. " 'Tis all of you I love, Geoffrey, not just the beautiful parts."

He made the smallest of sounds, then caught her close. When his mouth took hers, 'twas with such love that her heart broke and was healed all in the same instant. Then, he drew away.

"You own me, 'Lyssa, body and soul," he murmured.

"For all time?" she begged.

"Aye," he breathed, "and after that as well."

She smiled, then eased down to put her mouth against his chest and kissed a line to his nipple. He moaned when her tongue teased that sensitive spot. The sound sent new and stronger need careening through Elyssa.

"Geoffrey," she breathed against his skin, "I think we have made a good start in consummating our marriage, but there is so much left to do."

He shuddered. Against her thigh, she felt his shaft

stir. "I can only hope I do not disappoint. I have been celibate for far too long."

Elyssa gazed up at him, her mouth yet exploring his chest. "You'll have no trouble once I've finished with you." 'Twas a sultry promise. "I've a mind to sit astride, this time."

"Oh, my God," he whispered.

Epilogue

Coudray's keep tower guarded the king's highway where it traversed a long, fertile valley. The bottomland was threaded by streams, its expanse given over to fields and orchards, while the rolling hills made perfect grazing for the estate's ever-growing flocks. Their forest cover had been cleared long ago to meet the needs of hearth and homes. What remained of that thick expanse was a bluish line in the distance, a contrast to the soft white blanket left by last night's snowfall.

Winter was far colder here in England's inland north and the snows had begun after December's ides. This day's gentle gray sky suggested more of the same awaited them in the coming days. Despite the chill air, Elyssa stood in her solar window, her mantle clutched tight, watching the quiet world spread out beyond Coudray's walls.

Smoke drifted lazily above the many houses and cottages making up the large village; nay, 'twas almost a town that found its home here. Folk hied themselves to and fro along the narrow lanes as they worked on this Christmas Eve day to prepare for the morrow's celebration. Their garments, all in shades of red, blues, and greens were bright spots against the prevailing tones of white and brown.

A goodly sized group of children skated on the millpond just outside the town's walls. While the lads shoved and pushed, their laughter boisterous, the lasses caught hands to form a long string of flying skirts. Then someone threw a snowball from the bank and war was engaged, and the sexes joined ranks to do battle against their attackers.

The bedchamber door behind her opened and closed. Elyssa's mouth lifted as she listened to Geoffrey cross the solar toward her. Even before he'd put his arms around her, she'd leaned back against his chest, tilting her head to the side to look up at him.

His hair was newly washed and shone like bright gold, his jaw freshly shaved. As always, his fine features made her pulse leap to a new beat. She studied him, yet awestruck at the happiness and love she'd discovered with him. A year ago, had anyone suggested that such a thing was possible within a marriage, she would have called them a liar.

"Watching won't make their arrival happen any sooner," he murmured, rubbing his smooth jaw against her cheek. His brothers, their wives and families were expected to arrive this day. Geoffrey's relatives came as one, choosing to travel the distance as a group.

"I've nothing left to do in preparation, save watch," she replied. "Besides, 'tis beautiful this day."

They made quite a pair, once more dressed in their wedding finery. Geoffrey's yellow gown gleamed in the solar's dim light, the same golden color as the massive gold chain that lay atop his mink-lined mantle.

She smoothed her tawny embroidered gown over her torso in nervous anticipation, then straightened her wisp of a wimple. Her fingers rested briefly on the necklet Geoff had given her. The smooth pearls and amber beads reminded her of how dearly he held her.

As if he knew her thoughts, Geoff turned her in his arms, then touched his mouth to hers. It never mattered how he sated her, his simplest touch woke the craving for him anew. Elyssa caught her arms around his neck and returned his kiss with her own.

The door to the women's quarters flew open and struck the wall with a bang. " 'Lyssa," Cecilia wailed as she flew across the room to bury her face into her stepmother's skirts. Clutching Elyssa's leg, the lass sobbed as if heartbroken.

Geoffrey laughed against his wife's mouth. Elyssa pressed her lips to his scarred cheek, then turned to console his daughter. "What plagues you, poppet?"

Cecilia, wearing her green gown with its fox-lined mantle, the hem extended to accommodate a year's growth, looked up, her beautiful face twisted in sorrow. "Johanna says that Jocelyn is to wed Avice and I cannot have him. Make her stop saying that."

"Johanna is right, lass," Geoffrey replied. "You cannot have him."

His daughter stared at him as if shocked at such a refusal. After an instant's stillness, she dropped to the thick mats covering the solar's wooden floor. Her sobs would have been more believable had they been just a little less dramatic.

Elyssa cleared her throat at this performance, then looked away, not wishing to encourage its continuation. Her gaze wandered around the chamber. From the moment of her arrival, it had become the heart of her new family.

With four true windows, not merely arrow slits, cut from the thickness of the south wall, 'twas a bright and cheery place. The stone wall had been faced with

brick, while the inner, wooden walls had been plastered, then painted. 'Twas a crisscrossed pattern of
yellow atop a background of rich green that decorated
the chamber. Only one embroidered panel hung in the
room, this in the place of honor above the hearth.
'Twas Clare's final piece, left uncompleted, just as her
life had been.

Elyssa's furniture from Nalder mingled well with
what Geoffrey's dam had left behind her. One large,
high-backed chair, its tall back meant for catching the
fire's heat, stood near the hearth for Geoffrey's use.
There were two smaller chairs, with wider and shorter
backs; Elyssa's basket of threads set between them.
Cecilia's first attempt at needlework was strewn over
the arm of one, while Elyssa's own framed work sat
before the other. Two small tables stood at the wall,
offering a spot to rest lamps or candles and an evening's meal tray.

Yet sprawled on the floor, Cecilia peered up at her
parents from the concealment of her crossed arms.
When she realized they weren't listening, she redou-
bled her efforts. So great was her noise, she didn't
notice either Johanna or Simon's arrival in the solar.

Elyssa's son came chugging across the mats on his
hands and knees. The skirt of his gown flew, so quickly
did he close the distance between himself and Cecilia.
Grinning in happiness, he clambered onto his stepsister's back, patting and yelling his approval of her ability to make noise.

"Stop, Simon," Cecilia told him over her shoulder.
"I am too sad for you."

Geoffrey leaned down to claim the lad. Simon
laughed, displaying a good number of teeth, reaching
as always for Geoff's eye shield. When Geoffrey denied him the strap, Simon uttered a string of nonsense

sounds to chide him, then claimed the gold chain in its stead.

"He'll make a mess of you," Elyssa warned with a smile.

"Better that he does it, than I," Geoffrey retorted, tucking the lad into the crook of his arm. "I shall let you be my excuse, eh, my lad?"

Elyssa turned to close the shutter, then caught her breath. Along the road, half the distance from the valley's far entrance to the town walls came a grand troop of mounted men, surrounding a traveling cart. Racing ahead of this troop came three steeds, a massive black and two fine brown palfreys. There was no mistaking Geoffrey's youngest brother on that black beast of his. Although dressed only in leather armor, Lord Ashby was a giant. Elyssa's heart leapt. If that was Ashby, then the smaller figure, cloak streaming in the wind, was Jocelyn. The third rider was a woman.

"They come," she cried in excitement. She shut the panel, then caught Geoffrey's arm. " 'Tis Ashby first. Give Simon to Johanna and come greet them with me," she begged. Even after their wedding his brothers and their easy acceptance of her awed her. It remained purely a miracle that his powerful elder brother had made no complaint against her.

"As you will, love," Geoffrey replied, giving the boy to his nurse.

Cecilia's wails stopped abruptly. "I would come, too. Will we have gifts before or after we eat?"

"Neither, as gifts are for the morrow," Elyssa said, then shot her an arch look. "You've mussed the front of your gown and made your mantle askew. Johanna will have to straighten you before you can come down."

" 'Tis Christmas, 'Lyssa," Geoffrey said, lifting his

precious child. "Let her come. You can blame me for
her mantle," he said. "Besides, if I know my brother,
she'll be hanging upside down between her uncle's
hands before a few more minutes, her skirts indecently
in her face."

"Uncle Gilliam is here!" Cecilia shouted.

With a shrug, Elyssa gave in. "Come, then." She
led the way to the stairwell in the room's corner, then
descended the spiraling stairs as swiftly as she dared.

She stepped from the opening at the hall level and
started into the big room, once again savoring Coudray's special beauty. Although this room spanned the
entire length and width of the keep's tower, save for
the areas at the back set aside for the pantlery and
butlery, the atmosphere was miraculously smoke free.
This was because their main hearth was set into a
niche carved into the thickness of the wall, with an
odd channel leading out of the keep. The door needed
to be only slightly ajar to draw air through the hall,
letting all the smoke flow up that channel and out
from the room.

Elyssa gave a final look at the hall and was pleased
with what she saw. The tables were ready for their
feast, the high table set nearest to the hearth to enjoy
the greatest warmth. Their finest cloths lay atop the
long planks of wood, their best cups set for their
guests' usage. Garlands of fir, yew, and ivy clung to
the tables' edges, great clutches of bright holly berries
added for color's sake.

In any other hall, the garlands would have hung
along the walls, but not here. 'Twas the fruit of Geoffrey's dam's needle that had softened the martial purpose of the hall and made this room a place of beauty.
Not a single stone showed around them. Disliking the
damage torches had already done to these hangings,

Elyssa had asked Coudray's smith to create extended scones, setting these essential lighting sources away from the fragile linen.

"It glows in here," Geoffrey said, setting Cecilia down. He took Elyssa's hand as they crossed the hall together. "You've done a fine job preparing, 'Lyssa."

She shot him a grateful look. He knew how much she wished this event to be perfect. Her fingers laced between his as the dogs preceded them out of the hall, the kennets and greyhounds yipping and baying their way down the inner courtyard floor.

They had only started down the steps when Jocelyn's palfrey careened through Coudray's inner gate. With a cry at his sharp rein, the creature lifted itself. Elyssa froze in an instant's terror, then released her fear. Jocelyn held firm in his saddle, his face alive with a broad grin.

"I've won, again," he shouted to the sky, then threw himself out of the saddle.

"Jocelyn!" Cecilia screamed in happy greeting, struggling past her father in an attempt to embrace the one she deemed her beloved.

"Nay, you'll wait here, while his maman bids him welcome," Geoffrey said, grabbing her by the mantle's collar. He freed Elyssa's hand. "Go," he urged.

Elyssa skipped down the steps as her son came toward her, then caught her breath, once more stunned by the changes in her boy. The child was almost gone now; in his place stood a young man. Jocelyn was nigh on as tall as she and, dressed in his steel-sewn hauberk, he owned a far greater bulk.

"Maman!" her son called, spreading his arms in invitaton.

She accepted. His arms closed around her, his embrace strong. Elyssa let him hold her for a moment, then retreated just far enough to lay her palms against his cheeks. His hair had grown back to a more usual length, disguising his scars. The line of his jaw had firmed, while the hair on his face coarsened. Pressing a kiss to his brow, she stepped back. "Who are you? Mary save me, I hardly know you."

The child who yet resided in this new body had the grace to blush at her compliment. " 'Tis just your Jos, Maman."

Then, Lord Ashby and the woman who rode with him entered the inner yard. "Geoff! Call your bravest grooms to come fetch my pet," Gilliam bellowed to Geoffrey, his deep voice echoing off the stone walls.

Elyssa's son turned, his arms raised in triumph. "I've beaten you again. You'll soon have to honor your vow and sell me your steed's colt, my lord."

As Geoffrey came to stand beside Elyssa, Cecilia nearly leapt into her stepbrother's arms. "Jocelyn," she said.

Elyssa's eldest son gave a pleased smile and lifted the lass. "Poppet! 'Tis good to see you again."

Cecilia wrapped her arms around his neck. "You must tell them we will wed," she said with a resentful look at her parents. "And I am too old to be your poppet. Take me inside. I am cold," she commanded.

Jocelyn looked over Cecilia's shoulder at his mother and stepfather. "I would hate to be her husband. She's such a demanding little thing. As you will, Cecilia," he said to his charge, then started up the steps.

Lady Ashby, or so Elyssa assumed of the female rider, waited to dismount until Lord Ashby's vicious mount was led away. When she finally came to earth, Elyssa gawked. Mary save her, this woman was as much a giant as her lord. Lord and Lady Ashby turned as one and started toward their host and hostess.

As Gilliam threw back his cloak hood, Elyssa was once again startled by his resemblance to Geoffrey, but her husband's younger brother wore a boyish grin and a wicked sparkle in his eyes. When he was in arm's reach of his brother, he swept Geoffrey into a bone-crushing embrace. "Well met, my mother's oldest son!" he cried out, lifting Geoffrey off his feet.

"Put me down, you great oaf," Geoff gasped, then slammed his fists down onto his brother's shoulders. When Gilliam had once more set him on the ground, Geoffrey cuffed him more gently. "Good Christmas to you, my mother's youngest son. And, to you, Lady Nicola," he said, turning on the tall woman. "What, no sword at your side, my lady?" he said, a teasing tone in his voice.

"Not this day, Lord Coudray," Lady Ashby laughed, throwing back her hood to greet them. Curling dark hair tumbled forth, free and uncovered, but reaching only to her shoulders. Lady Nicola was no great beauty; only her fine hazel eyes saved her from plainness.

"A sword?" The question fell unconsidered from Elyssa's tongue. "Why would you wear a sword?"

'Twas the lady's husband who answered. " 'Tis her greatest talent," Gilliam said, then paused as if truly considering what he said. "Nay, 'tis her second greatest talent, her first one being—"

His wife gave a quick shriek and caught her hand over his mouth. "Gilliam!" She blushed a fiery red.

Above her restraining fingers, Gilliam's eyes sparkled, and he quirked his brows. " 'Tis true," he muttered against her palm, then caught her hand with his, keeping it as if he could not bear to let her go.

Geoffrey laughed. "True that you lust for your wife or that she's gifted with a sword?" He glanced at

Elyssa. "While they are here, we should make them spar. 'Tis awesome to see this frail flower beat my brother senseless. I missed you at Freyne's siege, Lady Nicola," he said.

Nicola gave a shy lift of her shoulders. "Gilliam would not let me come." She opened her cloak to show the way her green traveling gowns clung to the roundness of her abdomen. "He tried to make me ride in the cart with Lady Rowena and Lady Philippa, but I'd have none of it. Sometimes, he confuses me for a weak woman." 'Twas a sly aside, directed toward her hostess.

"I would never insult you in such a way, Colette," Gilliam protested, drawing her close. Nicola briefly lay her head on his shoulder, her plain face made lovely with what her heart knew for this man.

Elyssa smiled at their affection, liking the bold couple. "When does the babe come?"

"April, I think late in the month."

From the bailey, outside the inner wall, came the jingling of harnesses and the creak of the traveling cart. The dogs went streaming out the gate to greet the new set of visitors.

"Gilliam, I would go upstairs," Nichola said, a sudden urgency in her voice. "My lady, if you do not mind?"

Elyssa glanced at Geoffrey, then to Lord Ashby. Gilliam's mouth struggled not to lift. Elyssa looked back to her guest. "But, of course. There is wine waiting, spiced and warmed. If you're not feeling well, you may retire to my solar and there take your ease."

"My thanks, Lady Elyssa," she said in deep relief, then hied herself up the stairs.

"What plagues her?" Geoffrey asked his brother when she was gone.

"Rannulf," Gilliam replied. "Although he's long since forgiven her, she doesn't believe it and seeks to avoid him at every turn."

"What did she do?" Elyssa asked, wondering what it took to raise the ire of her husband's most powerful but levelheaded brother.

"My lady, Colette was Rannulf's prisoner for months before she and I wed. He didn't like the way she kept battering his men in escape attempts," Gilliam said in an inordinately casual voice. "The final insult came on our wedding day when she kicked him in the stomach just before she stabbed me with her pin." Gilliam's words were filled with laughter.

"Nearly ran me down escaping, she did," Geoffrey added.

Elyssa looked up the stairs after her sister-by-marriage, torn between disgust at so violent a woman and satisfaction that one of her own sex had fought for control of herself. Satisfaction won. "I think I am glad this woman is my son's foster mother."

"How so?" Geoffrey asked, startled by her approval of the highly unfeminine Lady Nicola.

"Such a woman will never allow Jocelyn to treat her with disrespect. In demanding it from him, she also teaches him to behave so toward other women, especially his future wife." Elyssa lifted her chin a notch.

Both Geoffrey and Gilliam laughed. "Of that there is no doubt," Gilliam assured her. " 'Tis a dangerous woman I married, and I am respectful, indeed."

Men on horseback now filled the courtyard, surrounding the cumbersome cart. The wains curtains were lowered to protect its occupants. Coudray's servants rushed to throw back the greased panels. Lord Graistan dismounted, recognizable by his height alone

as he was as tall as Geoffrey. Smaller than his younger
brothers, Lord Meynell joined Graistan in aiding two
women from the cart. Like Gilliam, they wore leather
armor over dark tunics and thick, woolen chausses,
boots cross-gartered to their legs.

The two women who emerged were petite and concealed in dark cloaks, one of them bearing a limp babe
over her shoulder. Following them came a boy around
Cecilia's age. As this troupe started toward their hosts,
the lad trailed after Lord Graistan, hopping and singing to himself.

The group halted before the stairs, Lord Rannulf's
wife's cloak parting to reveal her gown and overgown
were both dyed a rich scarlet. Her overgown's raised
hem wore a thick band of silver and gold. Lord
Meynell's wife handed her child to her husband, the
movement exposing a bluish green gown beneath a
darker blue overgown. Sparkling stones trimmed the
collar of the topmost garment.

"Rannulf, Richard, well come to my home," Geoffrey called out.

"Good Christmas, Geoff," Lord Graistan replied,
his hard features softening as he smiled. He turned
his pale gray gaze on Elyssa. "You, too, Lady Elyssa."

"Uncle Geoffrey," cried the lad behind him. The
child darted past his sire to throw himself at his uncle's
knees. "Is Cecilia here?" The child claimed a strong
resemblance to Lord Rannulf, owning the same brown
hair color and gray eyes.

"Elyssa," Geoffrey said by way of introduction as
he set his hand atop the lad's head to hold him still a
moment, "this is Rannulf's natural son, Jordan. And,
aye, Jordan, Cecilia is here. Jocelyn took her upstairs
only a moment ago."

"Come with me, Jordan," Gilliam offered, thrusting out a hand. "I'll take you into the hall."

"Not yet." 'Twas a gentle reprimand from Lady Graistan. "What must you do first?"

The boy made a face. "Good Christmas," he said dutifully to his uncle, "and thank you for inviting me." His words trailed off as he raced up the stairs. "Cecilia, I am here!" he announced at the doorway.

"Rowena, 'tis hopeless." Gilliam laughed, then turned to follow his nephew. When he reached the landing, he leaned into the hall and roared, "I am going to catch you!" Several children screamed in delight.

"I agree with Gilliam, Wren," Lord Rannulf said to his wife as he drew her forward. Offering her hand to Geoffrey, he said to his brother, "Geoffrey, Lord Coudray, and Elyssa, Lady Coudray, I proudly present to you my wife, Lady Rowena of Graistan, otherwise known as Wren."

Lady Rowena threw back her hood. This woman was no drab wren, but as glorious in color as a peacock. Eyes so blue they were nearly violet shone beneath gently curving ebony brows. Her nose was short and straight, her jaw soft. Ebony plaits reached to her waist.

Lord Graistan's wife bobbed to Geoffrey, then set her hand upon his arm. "Lord Geoffrey, I would have known you anywhere, having made Gilliam's acquaintance whilst he yet dwelt at Graistan." She turned to Elyssa and smiled. " 'Tis good to meet you, my lady. My lord has told me your tale. Glad I am he could aid his brother in your rescue."

" 'Twas not what she said at the time," Rannulf remarked. "She moaned and cried over my leaving, begging me not to go, convinced I would never return."

"Hush, Rannulf," she chided, turning on him. Her crown barely reached her husband's jaw. When she looked up into her husband's face, the love that flowed between them was nigh on visible. "I am being polite."

"So you are," he replied, "but why waste such an amenity on family? Come now, upstairs. That child in you demands you rest."

"How far gone?" Elyssa asked with the familiarity granted to women when they shared their female experiences.

"Only two months." Lady Rowena's smile was brilliant. "I'd begun to fear 'twould never again happen after I lost my first."

"Come then," her husband insisted, "else I bear you upstairs in my arms."

His worried tone made Meynell's lady laugh, the sound of her amusement sweet. "Rowena, he treats you as if you might break in the next instant." Elyssa turned toward the wife of Geoffrey's eldest brother Richard, as, beside her, she heard Geoffrey's gasp.

The similarity between Lady Meynell and Lady Graistan could not be coincidence. 'Twas the same face, the same lift of cheekbone, short jaw and short, straight nose. The only difference was that Lady Meynell's brows showed a color as golden as Geoffrey's, while her eye color was an odd mix of blue and green.

"Geoffrey," said Lord Meynell, "close your mouth and do not stare so at my wife, else she will think you rude." Richard of Meynell grabbed his brother's hand, then placed his wife's into it.

"Geoffrey, Lord Coudray, this is my wife, Philippa,

orphan of Stanrudde, now Lady Meynell." Laughter touched the man's roughhewn face and glowed golden in his brown eyes. "This," he said, lifting the limp and sleeping babe from his wife's arm, "is my daughter, Alwyna."

Lady Philippa offered Geoffrey a swift show of respect, then looked shyly, almost fearfully, up at her host. "Temric is teasing you, my lord. I am Rowena's half sister, our mother's bastard. 'Twas for this reason that you were asked to keep the event private as our relationship cannot bear much scrutiny."

Indeed, it could not. No less than incest had happened when they wed. Elyssa glanced at Geoffrey. The corner of his mouth lifted.

" 'Twas Oswald who did this?" he asked his eldest half brother. "This was why you would not face him?"

"Rannulf twisted his arm tightly indeed," Richard agreed with a smile. "But I was determined my daughter would not be bastard, as we are." The child on his shoulder stirred, crying out against the change of warm cloak into chilly leather.

Lady Philippa turned to claim her babe. Elyssa craned her neck to see. "How old is she?"

"Nine months now." Philippa cradled her daughter close, making soothing sounds to ease the babe.

"You named her for your mother?" Geoffrey asked of Richard.

"Nay, I did," Philippa replied quietly. "His mother wagered me her name that Lord Rannulf would see us wed, when I had no faith that my husband's brother would even accept me."

Elyssa felt an instant liking for this woman, then her heart expanded to include the man who loved her so, he fought the Church to make her his wife. She glanced to Lord and Lady Graistan, again aware of how deeply they loved. Lord Graistan laid a possessive arm around his wife, his worry for her no less than his caring. 'Twas no different than the emotions shared by Ashby's lord and lady.

She turned on Geoffrey. "They are all like you, every one of your brothers. They cherish their wives." 'Twas a disbelieving cry. "How can there be four such men in the same family?"

Geoffrey's face softened as he drew her closer to him. "For that, you must blame my parents. I think none of us were willing to settle for less than the happiness my father found in my mother." He touched his lips to her brow, then looked at his elder brothers.

"Good Christmas to you both and well come to my home," he said. "Will you come upstairs and keep the day with us?"

"Aye," Elyssa added, "come and make merry with us as family should." She went to Philippa offering her arm. "Come, sister, bring that babe of yours to my solar so she might rest in a decent bed. You, too," she said to Rowena. "The solar here is comfortable indeed. 'Twill ease your husband to know you rest."

"She is such a maman, always fussing over folk." Geoffrey laughed and started up the stairs.